The Testament of Gideon Mack

By the same author

Close & Other Stories

The Ragged Man's Complaint

Sound Shadow (*poetry*)

Scottish Ghost Stories

Voyage of Intent: Sonnets and Essays from the Scottish Parliament

The Fanatic

Joseph Knight

The Testament of Gideon Mack

JAMES ROBERTSON

HAMISH HAMILTON
an imprint of
PENGUIN BOOKS

Thanks to Natasha Fairweather and Judy Moir for their support and advice

The poem 'Black Rock of Kiltearn' by Andrew Young is reproduced from his *Selected Poems* (1998) by kind permission of Carcanet Ltd

HAMISH HAMILTON

Published by the Penguin Group
Penguin Books Ltd, 80 Strand, London WC2R ORL, England
Penguin Group (USA) Inc., 375 Hudson Street, New York, New York 10014, USA
Penguin Group (Canada), 90 Eglinton Avenue East, Suite 700, Toronto, Ontario, Canada M4P 2Y3
(a division of Pearson Penguin Canada Inc.)
Penguin Ireland, 25 St Stephen's Green, Dublin 2, Ireland
(a division of Penguin Books Ltd)
Penguin Group (Australia), 250 Camberwell Road,
Camberwell, Victoria 3124, Australia (a division of Pearson Australia Group Pty Ltd)
Penguin Books India Pvt Ltd, 11 Community Centre,
Panchsheel Park, New Delhi – 110 017, India
Penguin Group (NZ), cnr Airborne and Rosedale Roads, Albany,
Auckland 1310, New Zealand (a division of Pearson New Zealand Ltd)
Penguin Books (South Africa) (Pty) Ltd, 24 Sturdee Avenue,
Rosebank 2196, Johannesburg, South Africa

Penguin Books Ltd, Registered Offices: 80 Strand, London WC2R ORL, England

www.penguin.com

First published 2006
1

Set in 12/14.75pt Monotype Dante
Typeset by Rowland Phototypesetting Ltd, Bury St Edmunds, Suffolk
Printed in Great Britain by Clays Ltd, St Ives plc

A CIP catalogue record for this book is available from the British Library

ISBN-13: 978-0-241-14325-4
ISBN-10: 0-241-14325-X

For Marianne, with love and thanks

BLACK ROCK OF KILTEARN

They named it Aultgraat – Ugly Burn,
This water through the crevice hurled
Scouring the entrails of the world –
Not ugly in the rising smoke
That clothes it with a rainbow cloak.
But slip a foot on frost-spiked stone
Above this rock-lipped Phlegethon
And you shall have
The Black Rock of Kiltearn
For tombstone, grave
And trumpet of your resurrection.

Andrew Young

Prologue

In presenting to the world the following strange narrative, I find it necessary to offer a word of explanation as to its provenance. Being a firm believer in the principle of the division of labour, I do not usually divert myself from the business of publishing books in order to write prologues to them. However, Mr Harry Caithness having declined to provide an introduction – on the grounds, he says, that he has more than cancelled any debt he owed me by (a) sending me a copy of the original manuscript in the first place and (b) submitting the report which forms the bulk of the epilogue – I am left with no option but to write this myself.

Sir Walter Scott, with whose work, as you will read, the Reverend Gideon Mack was intimately familiar, once described publishing as 'the most ticklish and unsafe and hazardous of all professions scarcely with the exception of horse-jockeyship'. I have this salutary warning typed up on a three-by-five-inch card taped to the wall beside my desk. Whenever I fall to wondering why I persist in trying to make a living in this profession, and whether some other form of gambling might not offer a greater return for less effort, I read those words of Sir Walter – penned long before he himself fell so heavily at the high fence of publishing – to remind myself that it was ever thus. Then I take a deep breath and carry on.

So it is with this book. One voice in my head tells me that it is a mere passing curiosity in which few will have any interest; a waste of my time, the printer's ink and the forests of Finland. Another whispers that it is outlandish enough to attract a cult readership, if only that readership can be identified. A third – the voice, perhaps, of my conscience – deplores the exploitation, for commercial gain, of the outpourings of a ruined man. A fourth loudly protests at this: the man is dead and therefore cannot be exploited, and the book, though some may dismiss it as a tissue of lies or the fantasy of a damaged mind, is a genuine document with its own relevance for our times. All these and other arguments have jostled in my brain when I have pondered Gideon Mack's story. In the end, what has persuaded me to publish it is its very peculiarity: in twenty years, I have come across nothing like it. It is not a fiction, for Gideon Mack undoubtedly existed; yet nor, surely, can it be treated as fact. What, then, is it? It is because I am unable to answer this question that I consider it worthy of the public's attention, so that others can make up their own minds. But first I must recount how it came into my hands.

One Monday morning at the start of October 2004, I received a phone call out of the blue from my old friend Harry Caithness. I was sitting at my desk sipping my third coffee of the day, turning the pages of the latest edition of our Scotch whisky guide, *A Dram in Your Pocket*, newly back from the printers. It looked very handsome, all the more so for being a reliable mover, and I anticipated some healthy sales in the run-up to Christmas.

I had not heard from Harry for a while, but I recognised his gravelly voice at once. He is a freelance journalist, based in Inverness but roaming from there east along the Moray Firth, and to Fort William and all points north and west. He picks up stories of every kind and sells them to the highest bidder. He is what one might call – and I hope he will take this as a compliment – one of the old school. He smokes, drinks too much, eats unhealthy food at unhealthy hours and doesn't respond well to sunlight. But he is a first-class reporter, hard-headed enough not to let go of a good story yet sensitive enough to deal with people in such a way as to secure it. He has also written a book, *Crimes and Mysteries of the Scottish Highlands*, which I published. It has done very well over the years. I paid Harry a decent advance for it, and twice a year he still receives a royalty cheque, which, as he says, would pay for a week's holiday if he ever took one. To me it is business, but Harry used to say, when we spoke on the phone, that he owed me something. He doesn't say this any longer.

I asked him how he was, and he said he was fine. We might at this juncture have exchanged further pleasantries along these lines, but Harry doesn't do pleasantries. Instead, he came straight to the point. He had something for me, he said. It was somewhat sensitive, but he thought it would be of interest. Had I ever come across a character called Gideon Mack?

The name rang a bell, but I couldn't place it, and I said so.

'He was a minister,' Harry said. 'Church, not state. He went missing earlier this year.'

He reminded me of what had happened. There had been quite a bit in the papers at the time, and as Harry talked I recalled some of it. The Reverend Gideon Mack had vanished from his Church of Scotland manse one day in January, and nothing had been heard or seen of him since. Before his disappearance Mack had gone spectacularly off the rails, causing something of a stir in Church circles and in Monimaskit, the small town on the east coast which was his charge. I suspected that Harry was going to tell me that he had turned up and wanted to sell me his life-story – a prospect, I confess, that did not fill me with eager anticipation – but I was wrong. Mack was still missing, but something of his *had* turned up, and Harry said he thought it had my name on it. When I asked him what he meant, he said, 'Well, it's something he's written. A kind of memoir, or a confession, I suppose you'd call it. I think you should take a look. I read it over the weekend. I'm going to stick it in the post to you.'

I asked him how he had got hold of it, and what exactly Mack had confessed to. 'Quite a lot, for a minister,' Harry said. 'Adultery, for example, and meeting the Devil.' This second item also rang a bell. I asked Harry again how he had come by the thing.

'One of my contacts in the Northern Constabulary photocopied it for me,' he said.

'That was decent of them,' I said drily. 'Why did they do that?'

'Never you mind,' Harry said. 'I'm a journalist. I have to protect my sources.'

I remonstrated at this, and he relented and told me that he happened to have been at police headquarters in Inverness, chatting to some of his acquaintances there, and the Mack missing person case had come up in the conversation. 'Your man's memoir, autobiography, confession, whatever you want to call it, was sitting on a desk,' Harry said. 'There was a photo of him too. Now I'd actually seen him once before, in the flesh, years ago. He ran a marathon up here, in Elgin, back in about 1990, and raised a lot of money for charity. I saw him crossing the finishing-line. So we were talking about all that and they let me have a look at the manuscript, and I hinted I'd like to read it at my leisure. They'd made several photocopies, so it was almost in the public domain anyway. I took it home to read, and it was so strange I thought of you straight away.'

'Thanks, Harry,' I said.

'No problem,' he replied. And then he told me the rest of the story.

A few days earlier, a Mrs Nora MacLean, who took in guests for bed and breakfast at her cottage in the village of Dalwhinnie, some fifty miles south of Inverness, had appeared at the local police station in a state of agitation, and had handed in a hold-all containing a man's clothing and a heavy padded envelope. No identifying marks were on the clothes, which consisted of a pair of carpet slippers, some socks and underwear, a tee-shirt and a handkerchief. The envelope contained a bulky manuscript. The bag had been left by a gentleman who had stayed with Mrs MacLean back in January. She described him as quite tall, very thin and slightly stooped, aged about fifty, with long, unruly hair in need of a good trim, and a pronounced limp in his right leg. He had stayed for two nights, the 15th and 16th to be precise. He had given his name as Mr Robert Kirk.

Mrs MacLean was a simple soul, it seems. She feared some official or officious connection between the Northern Constabulary and the Inland Revenue and was therefore embarrassed to admit that, although she had written Mr Kirk's name on the calendar when he had phoned about the room, she had not asked him to fill in her visitors' book and thus had no record of his address. He had not booked in advance, but, on the afternoon of the 15th, had phoned from the shop in the village where she kept a card in the window. He said he had come by train from Perth. He was wearing stout boots in good condition and outdoor clothing suitable for walking in the hills. His weatherproof jacket was light blue in colour. Mrs MacLean frequently had walkers and climbers to stay, so none of this was remarkable, although that week the weather was wet and misty, far from ideal for those activities. She did wonder how able a walker Mr Kirk could be, considering the limp, but felt it was not her business to inquire on this subject.

The conversation they had on his arrival, as far as she could recall, and which she related to the police officer who took her statement, went like this:

MRS MACLEAN: 'You'll be here for the hills, I suppose.'

MR KIRK: 'Yes, I hope to do some walking in the hills.'

MRS MACLEAN: 'It's not really the weather for it, but it can change so quickly.'

MR KIRK: 'Yes. I'll just hope for the best.'

MRS MACLEAN: 'There's an electric fire in your bedroom and a chair and table. You're welcome to stay in the house if the weather doesn't improve. There are some books in the sitting room if you want something to read. There isn't a television in your room but there's one in the sitting room, and you can use that if you want; the reception isn't always that good, though.'

MR KIRK: 'Thank you, but I won't bother. I have some work to do if I can't go out.'

MRS MACLEAN: 'Oh, well, make yourself at home, and just ask if you want anything. What time would you like your breakfast?'

MR KIRK: 'About eight o'clock or half-past?'

MRS MACLEAN: 'Half-past eight is fine. Do you like porridge and a cooked breakfast?'

MR KIRK: 'Porridge would be fine, but no cooked breakfast, thank you.'

MRS MACLEAN: 'Oh, but if you're going hill-walking you'll want a good breakfast to keep you going.'

MR KIRK: 'No, thank you, just some porridge.'

MRS MACLEAN: 'I can make you up some sandwiches if you go out. And a flask of hot soup.'

MR KIRK: 'That won't be necessary. I may not go out at all.'

MRS MACLEAN: 'Well, I see you don't have a rucksack. You would need a rucksack if you were taking sandwiches with you.'

MR KIRK: 'I don't think I'll need a rucksack.'

MRS MACLEAN: 'I don't do an evening meal, but you can get something to eat at the hotel or the café along the road.'

MR KIRK: 'Yes, thank you.'

MRS MACLEAN: 'If there's anything else you want, just you ask.'

MR KIRK: 'I will. I really don't want anything except a bed for two nights. I have some work to complete. If you don't mind, I'll just go to my room now and have a rest. I'm a wee bit tired.'

According to Harry, the policeman must have thought this was all potentially useful information, because he had written it down verbatim – it was in the report that Harry had also managed to get a copy of, which he was reading to me down the phone (and which he later sent to me).

I couldn't see the point of all this, and I said so, but Harry told me to be patient, so I was.

That exchange was the longest that took place between Mrs MacLean and her guest during the two days of his stay. She served him black coffee and porridge for breakfast on both mornings, and tried to engage him in further conversation, but while perfectly polite he made it clear that he preferred to communicate only as far as was required for the transaction of business between them. This, Mrs MacLean said, 'put her neither up nor down'. She was quite used to some people being less friendly than others, and he was probably shy.

Mrs MacLean had no other guests staying at this time and, being a widow, as she told the police, lived alone. Although Mr Kirk was rather withdrawn, there did not appear to her anything especially strange or unusual about him, apart perhaps from the limp and his unkempt hair. She was not in any way afraid or distrustful of him. Indeed, on the second night of his stay she went out to visit a friend, leaving him alone in the house. Apart from going out for a newspaper on the morning of the 16th, and for a short walk that afternoon, he never left his room except for breakfast and to use the bathroom. Once, when she took him a cup of tea – which he accepted, she thought, more to make her go away than because he really wanted it – she found him reading from a large pile of handwritten sheets of paper, apparently making additions and corrections to them. She thought at the time that he might be a writer working on a book, a deduction which, as it turned out, was not so very wide of the mark.

On the day of his departure Kirk paid for his accommodation in cash. The bill was thirty-six pounds. He produced two twenty-pound notes and refused the change. When Mrs MacLean tried to insist, he suggested she give the four pounds' difference to her favourite charity. He then returned to his room in order, she assumed, to pack his belongings.

Mrs MacLean was busy in the kitchen, and it was some time, perhaps half an hour, before it occurred to her that he must still be in his room. She wanted to change the sheets on his bed, so went and knocked on the door. There being no reply, she knocked louder and called out, 'Are you all right, Mr Kirk?' After a further silence, she opened the door. The room was empty. She went to the front door of the cottage and opened it. It was brighter that morning, with patches of blue sky among the clouds, and she could see the whole length of the road, but there was no sign of her guest. It seems that he must have slipped out while she was in the kitchen. She never set eyes on him again.

Once again I interrupted Harry to ask why he was telling me all this, and once again he told me to have patience. 'I'm just giving you the background,' he said. 'You need it, believe me.'

At the time Mrs MacLean assumed that Robert Kirk had taken his hold-all and its contents with him. Mrs MacLean 'kept herself to herself', as she put it, and, while she was well acquainted with events in the village, did not take a great interest in the wider affairs of the world. The disappearance of a minister of the Church of Scotland, around the time that Mr Kirk stayed at her cottage, was widely reported in the press and on radio and television, but Mrs MacLean paid little attention to this news, and did not make any connection between her guest and the missing minister. It was only in September, when she was preparing to redecorate the room he had used, that she discovered the hold-all placed on an upper shelf in the built-in cupboard. Subsequent guests, presumably thinking it belonged there, had not interfered with it. She took it down, opened it, and found the padded envelope containing a quantity of loose A4 sheets of close-written handwriting. This recalled to Mrs MacLean her guest of the previous January. She began to read the document. A neighbour arrived at the door just then, and Mrs MacLean showed it to her. Coming across the phrase 'To the world at large I was just Gideon Mack' on the first page, the neighbour remembered the story that had been in the news nine months before, and advised Mrs MacLean to go straight to the police.

'That's the reason,' Harry said, 'why the local bobby made his report in so much detail. As soon as he saw the name he knew he was on to something. There'd been a notice sent round all the local stations back in the winter, when they were looking for Mack. HQ here in Inverness took it up and they've reinstated the search. I reckon it's only a matter of time now before they find him.'

'Presumably,' I said, 'Mr Kirk was Mr Mack.'

'Of course,' Harry said. 'They showed her a photo, and she said it was him. It's pretty likely that when he checked out of Mrs MacLean's he set off into the hills. He was dressed for it anyway.'

Armed with this new information, and having read through the manuscript for clues, the police were carrying out a detailed search of the hills around Dalwhinnie, and in particular – for reasons that will become clear to the reader in due course – the massive and remote Ben Alder. There was a strong indication, Harry told me, that that was where Mack had been heading.

I made the obvious observation that he wouldn't still be there after all these months, not unless he were dead, and Harry said that it wouldn't be the first time a corpse had been found on Ben Alder. He reminded me of a chapter we'd inserted into the most recent edition of *Crimes and Mysteries of the Scottish Highlands*. Back in the mid-1990s a body had been found there with a bullet wound to the chest, and an old-fashioned gun lying near by. The body had lain for months, buried under the snow. On that occasion the police had taken more than a year to establish that the dead man was a young Frenchman who had disappeared from his home near Paris and chosen that remote spot to end his life.

Harry thought it highly likely that Gideon Mack would also be found there. When I read what Mack had written, he said, I would see why he was so sure. He would post the document to me first-class, so that I'd get it in the morning.

'You think I might want to publish it?' I asked.

'It has possibilities,' he replied, and rang off.

The photocopied manuscript duly arrived the next day, Tuesday 5th October, 2004. It consisted – consists, in fact, for I have it before me as I compose this – of 310 pages of A4 paper, numbered, very neatly written for the most part, in black ink, with deletions and additions clearly marked, extra passages inserted at the margins and on the reverse of many sheets, and the whole thing divided into sections headed by Roman numerals. Only towards the end of the document does the handwriting deteriorate, although it is never illegible. (Of late, looking at it again, I have mused if some of the corrections and deletions might not be the work of another hand, but the style is so closely matched that I am inclined to ascribe these variations to tiredness or stress on the part of the author.)* I started to read. After twenty minutes I went out into the main office and told my assistant to hold all my calls. I sat and read that manuscript for the rest of the day.

The next morning, with impeccable timing, the newspapers reported that human remains had been found on Ben Alder. By that time I had done some research on the internet. There was quite a lot about Gideon Mack. I have since acquired a good deal more information, so that the following gives a pretty fair summary of the background to his disappearance.

The Reverend Gideon Mack, minister of Monimaskit, a small

* I should point out that three independent witnesses, identified in the epilogue, have verified that the manuscript is indeed in the handwriting of Gideon Mack.

town on the east coast of Scotland between Dundee and Aberdeen, seems to have left his manse on the weekend of 10th–11th January 2004. He had not been performing his official duties for some months, otherwise his absence would have been noticed immediately at the Sunday service. As it was, it was not until Wednesday 14th January that the alarm was raised. Police in Perth, checking up on a red Renault that had been collecting parking tickets for several days in a street close to the railway station, found that it was registered in Mr Mack's name. Inquiries were made, and when a colleague, the Reverend Lorna Sprott, expressed concerns for his safety and wellbeing, a nationwide search was instigated. No trace of him was found. The fact that he had abandoned his car in Perth, perhaps in favour of public transport, suggested that he did not want to be located. After a while he became just another missing persons statistic.

Before that happened, however, the Scottish media got hold of the story, but the diverting embellishments of the tabloid press need not concern us here. The facts concerning Gideon Mack were these: in September of 2003, he had been involved in an accident a few miles from Monimaskit, at a river gorge known as the Black Jaws. Attempting to save a dog (belonging to the Reverend Lorna Sprott, as it happened) which had got into difficulty, he had slipped and plunged more than a hundred feet into the water below. A rescue was attempted, but it proved impossible to lower anybody to the bottom of the gorge, and the river, the Keldo Water, was too dangerous to be entered from downstream. It was assumed that the minister must have perished, either killed by the fall or drowned. Given that the gorge is nearly half a mile long, and so narrow and impenetrable that the river is believed at one point to go completely underground before re-emerging and continuing on its way to the coast, there was little prospect of his body ever being recovered.

However, three days after this incident, while the community was still coming to terms with its loss, the body of Mr Mack was found washed up on the bank of the Keldo a short distance downstream of the Black Jaws. Not only had the water apparently carried him through its unknown course, but, even more amazingly, he was alive, and without a broken bone in his body. True, he was badly battered, he had a large bruise on the side of his head, and his right leg had sustained some kind of internal damage which left him with a severe limp, but he had somehow survived three nights outdoors and a subterranean journey that no creature, except a fish, could have been expected to survive. He was taken to hospital in Dundee, where he remained unconscious but stable for a day and a half. When he came round he astonished medical staff by making such a speedy recovery that less than a week after the accident he was discharged and sent home.

Back in Monimaskit, Mr Mack convalesced at his manse and seemed in no great hurry to resume his pastoral duties. It was at this time that he began to talk to some people of his experience. He claimed that he had been rescued from the river by a stranger, a man inhabiting the caverns through which he said it passed, and that he had been looked after by this individual. This seemed improbable enough, but Mr Mack went on to assert that this person was none other than the Devil, and that they had had several long conversations in the course of the three days. These remarks were taken by the minister's friends as indication of a severe shock to his system, and possibly of damage to the brain sustained during his ordeal. Others, however, were less concerned with his health than with the injury his words might do to the good name of the Church of Scotland.

A few days later, Mr Mack, despite his seeming physical and mental frailty, insisted on taking the funeral service of an old friend, an inhabitant of Monimaskit, conducting the event in a way which some considered not just unorthodox and irreverent, but incompatible with the role of a Church of Scotland minister. After the interment he publicly repeated his story that he had met and conversed with the Devil. Finally, at the gathering in the church hall which followed, he made declarations of such a scandalous nature that the Monimaskit Kirk Session had no option but to refer the matter to the local Presbytery.

The procedures of the Presbyterian court system are complex, but need not long detain us. Presbytery, having heard the evidence, invited Mr Mack to defend himself. He admitted the truth of the allegations made against him, but denied that he had committed any offence. Presbytery decided to suspend him forthwith pending further investigation and consultation with the Church's legal advisers, until such time as Mr Mack could be brought before a committee of Presbytery for trial. A libel was drawn up and served on him, but no date had been set for the case to be heard when Mr Mack's disappearance brought all proceedings to a halt.

This is the text of the relevant part of the libel served on Gideon Mack:

Gideon Mack, minister of the Old Kirk of Monimaskit, in the parish of Monimaskit, you are indicted at the instance of John Gless, Session Clerk at the same Old Kirk of Monimaskit, Peter Macmurray, Elder of the same, and of [various other names] that on divers dates in September 2003 you uttered wild, incredible and false statements concerning an alleged meeting and conversation between yourself and another person, supposedly the Devil or Satan; and that in reporting this alleged conversation you made remarks contrary to the fundamental doctrines of the Christian faith and the Confession of Faith of the Church of Scotland, which as an ordained minister of this Church you have sworn to uphold; and that on 22nd September 2003, while conducting a funeral service at the Old Kirk of Monimaskit before a large congregation, which included young children, you introduced unchristian rituals into the proceedings; and that you condoned the use of an illegal drug and were in possession of a quantity of the same; and that you later used profane, blasphemous and scandalous language in the Old Kirk hall, making reference among other things to having had carnal relations with a married woman of the parish; and that you allowed alcohol to be supplied on Church property on this occasion in contravention of the General Assembly's ruling on this matter; and that your whole conduct was an abrogation of your responsibility as a minister of the Church to perform such duties with dignity and sobriety; all this as detailed in the appendix to this libel, and as attested by the witnesses named and listed hereinafter . . .

In due course, through dental records and other evidence, the remains found on Ben Alder were identified as those of the Reverend Gideon Mack. A forensic investigation was carried out and a report made to the Procurator Fiscal. It seemed likely that the body had lain undiscovered for several months, and this suggested that death had occurred not long after Mr Mack's stay at Dalwhinnie. Due to the body's advanced state of decay, it was not possible to establish the precise cause of death, but there were no signs of the involvement of a third party. The Procurator Fiscal ruled that there were no suspicious circumstances, and the remains were buried without any kind of ceremony in a cemetery in Inverness. Apart from his elderly mother, who suffered from senile dementia and was quite unaware of these events, Gideon Mack had no relatives, but it was notable that neither any of his friends nor any representatives of the Church attended the interment.

Harry and I talked on the phone a few more times during October 2004. There was another flurry of interest in the press, and much speculation as to why Gideon Mack had taken himself off to Ben Alder. Some said that he must have made a deliberate choice to end his life, others that he had been mentally unstable and hadn't known what he was doing. People in Monimaskit were interviewed, and a few offered their opinions, none of which was particularly illuminating. Meanwhile, I was reading and rereading the manuscript Harry had sent me. I felt I had access to information that nobody else had. The police had their copies, of course, and the original, but, having established the identity of the corpse, their professional interest in the case was over. Mine, on the other hand, was only just beginning.

Harry had, however, picked up another couple of stories from the police, which he passed on to me. I include these here less in expectation of their being taken seriously by any rational reader than because they are typical of the kind of stories that spring up around almost any unusual death. When it was announced at the end of September that a fresh search for the missing man was to be undertaken, and that this search would concentrate on the Ben Alder area, three new witnesses contacted the police. The first two of these were a Mr Sean Dobie and a Miss Rachel Annand. They had been walking, in mid-August 2004, from the train station at Corrour, via Loch Ossian and Loch Pattack, to Dalwhinnie, a long west–east journey through some of Scotland's wildest terrain. They had stayed a night at the youth hostel at Loch Ossian and set off early to make the journey of some twenty miles to their destination. It was a fine day, and they could see their route stretching out through the mountains far in front of them. Around midday, as they skirted the north-western flank of Ben Alder, they saw a man walking on the track about a mile ahead. He appeared to be moving quite slowly, and they began to close the distance. They could see that he was a tall, thin man with long, straggly hair, that he was wearing a light blue jacket and that he was limping. They wondered if he was in difficulty. There came a slight rise in the path, followed by a dip and another rise. As Mr Dobie and Miss Annand came over the first rise they saw, very distinctly, the man labouring up the second one. They assumed that they would overtake him in the next two or three minutes. They descended into the dip, climbed up the second rise and – nothing! He had vanished. There was an expanse of moor to their left, and to their right were the slopes of Ben Alder, but in all that vast landscape not a solitary being was to be seen. Mr Dobie and Miss Annand continued on their way, but though they met several other walkers that afternoon, none of them was the man they had seen; nor, when they asked, had anybody else seen him. They puzzled over this incident until they read about the search for Mr Mack, whereupon they reported it to the police.

The other new witness was a Dr Roland Tanner, who was hiking alone from Dalwhinnie to Loch Rannoch via the northern shore of Loch Ericht, a route which again goes through the heart of the country around Ben Alder. This Dr Tanner keeps a journal of his trips. The relevant part of the entry for Sunday 1st August, as transcribed by the police when he contacted them, reads as follows:

Camped beside Benalder cottage. Bothy empty but full of midges so pitched tent. Up at seven having slept well, despite midge bites. Quick breakfast while warding off hundreds of the little bastards. Threatening rain so struck tent and set off. Within quarter mile came upon man sitting on rock. Assumed must have camped near by but no sign of tent, rucksack or other equipment. Passed time of day. No reply, but smiled and raised hand. Something odd about him. Not sure what. Walked on. Had misgivings, wondered if he was all right. Had only gone fifty yards so turned back. He was gone. Retraced steps almost to cottage. No sign, not a trace. Begin to wonder if I should do these walks alone any more. Very peculiar.

Dr Tanner confirmed that the man was wearing a light blue jacket. He could not say whether he limped, as he had not seen him walking. When shown a photograph of Mr Mack, Mr Dobie and Miss Annand had been unable to say with any certainty whether he was the man they had seen: his back had been to them and they had never got right up close to him. Dr Tanner, on the other hand, stated that the man he saw sitting on a rock was an exact likeness of Mr Mack. On both occasions, the police asked, was Mack alone? Yes, said Mr Dobie and Miss Annand, the man they saw was quite alone. Dr Tanner said that had there been anyone else with him he would not have been concerned.

These separate experiences were reported to the police *before* the discovery of Mr Mack's remains on 6th October, but had taken place seven months *after* the likely time, according to the forensic report, of his demise. This had stirred up Harry Caithness's curiosity. 'I phoned this guy Tanner,' he told me. 'My police friends gave me his details. He's a medieval historian. He didn't want to talk to me at first, but I buttered him up, mentioned a few of my favourite climbs. These hill-walking types just can't resist when you start name-dropping mountains. I said I'd done the Aonach Eagach ridge in Glencoe and he was impressed – he'd done it a couple of years ago. It kind of melted the ice.'

I'd always assumed that the only form of exercise Harry took was lifting pint-glasses from table to mouth. 'I didn't know you climbed mountains,' I said.

'I don't,' he said. 'At least not in reality. But people have devoted entire websites to their Munro-bagging* experiences. I've *virtually* climbed most of the hard ones. When I was in my prime, you understand. It's amazing what doors a bit of hill talk can open up. Somebody tells you how they were nearly blown off Ben MacDui, and you tell them about the time you got lost in a blizzard there, and it creates a bond, a buddy thing, you know, and they start spilling all kinds of information. Anyway, after a while I brought up the subject of Gideon Mack and asked Tanner what he thought about the fact that he'd seen a ghost. He wanted to know what I was talking about. I said, "When you saw the man sitting on the stone near the bothy, the man you identified as Gideon Mack, Mack must have been dead for more than six months. So either you made a mistake or you've seen a ghost. What do you think of that?"'

'And what did he say?' I asked.

'"I didn't make a mistake. It was definitely him." So I said, "Then you saw a ghost."'

'And he said?'

'He didn't say anything for a while. I said, "Dr Tanner, are you still there?" "Yes," he says, "I am. I'm thinking." "What are you thinking?" I asked. "I'm thinking I'm going to go and pour myself a large whisky," he says. And then he hung up. So much for breaking the ice. He wouldn't pick the phone up again. I just got his answer-machine after that.'

'You spooked him,' I said.

'I don't know,' Harry said. 'Aye, maybe. Something did anyway. He had no reason to lie. I think he saw *somebody*. He sounded pretty shaken. I don't blame him for heading for the whisky.'

Dr Tanner might have been a brilliant historian, but he didn't sound to me like a very reliable witness. In fact, I said, the whole thing seemed a bit far-fetched. That, Harry said, was why he had contacted me. 'You're into ghosts and mysteries and all that stuff.'

* For those unfamiliar with the term, it is perhaps necessary to explain that a Munro is a mountain in Scotland over 3,000 feet in height. There are 284 of them, and the activity of climbing or 'bagging' them all has become hugely popular in recent years. They were first listed by Sir Hugh Munro in 1891. – P.W.

I felt obliged to correct him. 'I publish books on "all that stuff",' I said. 'That doesn't mean I believe in it.'

'Neither did Gideon Mack,' Harry said, 'until the stone appeared in the woods.'

'Ah, yes,' I said. 'The stone in the woods is where it all starts, and from there we move on to the Devil in the cave. Far-fetched, you see. Maybe Mack was just mad and that's all there is to it.'

'Maybe,' Harry said, 'but that's no argument against publishing his memoir. There are lots of crazy people out there who'll love it.'

I asked Harry why he had sent the document to me. He said he owed me a favour, and I said he didn't, and he said all right, but now that I had it, what was I going to do with it? I said I would think about it.

I heard his smoker's laugh down the line, and he proceeded to give me several reasons why I should publish Gideon Mack's work. None of them, I should say, reflected well on his understanding of the higher motives of a reputable publisher such as myself. He jocularly suggested that I was imagining a full-page review in *Life and Work*, the magazine of the Church of Scotland. When I denied this he said that he thought it might become a 'cult best-seller', and when I again expressed doubts he said that at least it would be guaranteed lots of sales in and around Monimaskit. 'It's probably the biggest thing that's happened there for a hundred years,' he said. 'Their minister wandering off to die in the frozen wastes after chatting with Auld Nick? Plus all the other stuff he was up to? It'll go like snow off a dyke. Everybody loves a scandal.'

He had a point: everybody, including any publisher worth his salt, does love a scandal. But that same thought prompted another concern.

'What if someone sues me?' I said. 'There's some fairly hot stuff in there if it's not true.'

'True?' Harry said. 'Are you kidding me? Do you think the Devil's going to set his lawyers on to you? The Devil's advocates,' he laughed.

'Very good, Harry,' I said. 'I mean what he says about real people. Real people still living in Monimaskit.'

'Oh, come on,' Harry said, 'you live with the threat of being sued every day. You put information out there, knowing that some of it might come back and bite you. Can they sue you for printing the words of a dead man?'

'I don't know,' I said. 'I'll need to ask my lawyer.'

'You've got the manuscript, or a copy of it: there's no doubt that Mack wrote it. My understanding is that you can't libel the dead.'

'It's not the dead that bother me,' I said. 'Sure, you can't libel the dead, and you might not be able to sue them for libel, but I bet you can sue their publisher.'

Harry said, 'Who are you thinking about?'

'The Moffats,' I said. 'Elsie Moffat, specifically.'

'There's been plenty about her in the papers already. I haven't seen her sue anybody. I wouldn't worry about it.'

But I did worry. Those words of old Sir Walter were up on the wall just a few feet from me. And then there was Gideon Mack's estate. Although I didn't then know if his mother was still alive, there would surely be an estate, with all the possible complications that entailed.

'Harry,' I said, 'if I go ahead with this, will you do something for me? I'll pay you, of course. Cover all your costs.'

'What is it?' he said.

'Will you go to Monimaskit and talk to people? Talk to John and Elsie Moffat. Ask them if they thought he was insane. He was their friend, after all. Talk to other people. Talk to Lorna Sprott. Find out what's true and what isn't.'

Now it was Harry who hesitated. 'It's a bit out of my territory,' he said. 'My geographical territory, I mean.'

'It needs to be done if I'm to publish,' I said.

'Why don't you do it?' he asked.

'You're the journalist,' I said. 'That's your job. You'll ask the right questions.'

'The Moffats won't like it,' he said. 'I might get something out of some of the others, but they're the ones who really *won't* like it.'

'That's why it needs to be done,' I said. 'They're the crucial ones.'

We knocked this back and forth a bit, and eventually Harry agreed to go to Monimaskit. His findings are recorded in the epilogue at the end of this book, which is the right place for them. All that is left for me to do here is to present this strange and original document, which I have taken the liberty of entitling *The Testament of Gideon Mack*. This is – almost – my only interference with the actual text. Except for one or two explanatory footnotes I offer no remarks on its contents, and in nearly every other way it remains exactly as it was written by its author. I make no additions, alterations or deletions other than those insisted upon by my legal advisers, and leave every reader to judge it for him or herself.

Patrick Walker
Edinburgh, June 2005

The Testament of Gideon Mack

'And they were offended in him. But Jesus said unto them, A prophet is not without honour, save in his own country, and in his own house.'

Matthew 13:57

'The waters compassed me about, even to the soul: the depth closed me round about, the weeds were wrapped about my head.'

Jonah 2:5

'I say, we good Presbyterian Christians should be charitable in these things, and not fancy ourselves so vastly superior to other mortals, pagans and what not, because of their half-crazy notions on these subjects . . . Heaven have Mercy on us all – Presbyterians and Pagans alike – for we are all somehow dreadfully cracked about the head, and sadly need mending.'

Herman Melville, *Moby Dick*

I

When I was a child I spoke as a child, I understood as a child, I thought as a child: yet I was already, in so many ways, the man I would become. I think back on how cold I was, even then. It is hard to recall, now that I burn with this dry, feverish fire, but cold I certainly was. There was ice built around my heart, years of it. How could it have been otherwise? The manse at Ochtermill saw to that.

I have walked and run through this world pretending emotions rather than feeling them. Oh, I could feel pain, physical pain, but I had to imagine joy, sorrow, anger. As for love, I didn't know what it meant. But I learned early to keep myself well disguised. To the world at large I was just Gideon Mack, a dutiful wee boy growing in the shadow of his father and of the Kirk.

As that wee boy I was taught that, solitary though I might be, I was never alone. Always there was one who walked beside me. I could not see him, but he was there, constant at my side. I wanted to know him, to love and be loved by him, but he did not reveal himself. He frightened me. I had neither the courage to reject him nor the capacity to embrace him.

This is the hard lesson of my life: love is not in us from the beginning, like an instinct; love is no more original to human beings than sin. Like sin, it has to be learned.

Then I put away childish things, and for years I thought I saw with the clarity of reason. I did not believe in anything I could not see. I mocked at shadows and sprites. That constant companion was not there at all: I did not believe in him, and he did not reveal himself to me. Yet, through circumstances and through choice, I was to become his servant, a minister of religion. How ironic this is, and yet how natural, as if the path were laid out for me from birth, and though I wandered a little from it, distracted or deluded here and there, yet I was always bound to return to it again.

And all the while this fire was burning deep inside me. I kept it battened down, the door of the furnace tightly shut, because that seemed necessary in order to get through life. I never savoured life for what it was: I only wanted to get to the next stage of it. I wish now I'd taken a little more time, but it is too late for such regrets. I was like the child in the cinema whose chief anticipation lies not in the film but in wondering what he will do after it is over; I was the reader who hurries through a 500-page novel not to see what will happen but simply to get to the end. And now, despite everything, I am there, and for this I must thank that other companion, in whom also I did not believe, but who has shown me a way through the shadows and beyond the shadows.

I have not preached for weeks, yet I am full of texts. If I am a prophet then I have yet to be heard. If I am Jonah, then the fish has vomited me out but nobody believes where I have been: nobody except the one who saved me from the belly of hell. Who am I? I am Gideon Mack, time-server, charlatan, hypocrite, God's grovelling apologist; the man who saw the Stone, the man that was drowned and that the waters gave back, the mad minister who met with the Devil and lived to tell the tale. And hence my third, non-Scriptural text, for what is religion if not a kind of madness, and what is madness without a touch of religion? And yet there is peace and sanctuary in religion too – it is the asylum to which all poor crazed sinners may come at last, the door which will always open to us if we can only find the courage to knock.

Few suspected it, but all my life was a lie from the age of nine (when, through deceit, I almost succeeded in killing my father); all my words were spoken with the tongue of a serpent, and what love I gave or felt came from a dissembling heart. Then I saw the Stone, and nothing was the same again. This is my testimony. Read it and believe it, or believe it not. You may judge me a liar, a cheat, a madman, I do not care. I am beyond questions of probity or sanity now. I am at the gates of the realm of knowledge, and one day soon I will pass through them.

II

A misty Saturday afternoon in early January, cold heart of the winter, the start of this year of revelation. I am running through Keldo Woods on the forestry workers' track, my mind tuned to the clean sound of my breathing and the slap of my trainers' soles as they crack frost-veined dubs and spatter icy mud up my shins. I turn off the track and on to a narrow footpath that climbs slightly as it winds through the trees. After a few hundred yards it levels out, then divides in two. I go left, then at another fork left again. (I remember all this as clearly as if I had it on film. In fact, sitting by the fire, remembering, is a little like watching a film.) By now I am deep in the woods, where few people venture, but there comes an open area where the tall pines give way to tummocks of coarse grass and thick, springy moss-cushions that turn green in summer but are frosted and brown on this wintry day. And there it is. To the right of the path, in the middle of this space, a stone, looming in the mist like a great tooth in a mouth full of smoke. It brings me to a sudden and astonished halt.

I remember my breath coming in hard puffs punched into the darkening air. The sweat began to run off my brow, stinging my eyes, obscuring my vision. I lifted the front of my sweatshirt and wiped my face and head on it, closed my eyes and pictured what I imagined I'd seen. Then I looked again. Twenty yards away, it was still there.

I stared at it intensely. (Did I have some subconscious notion that this might make it vanish, or move, or speak, or make me come to my senses? I have no idea. Perhaps I just didn't know what else to do.) Anyway, I stared for a long time, and the stone, not surprisingly, was quite impassive to my stare.

I stepped off the path and crunched over the spongy, ice-laced ground to where the stone stood. It rose three feet taller than me, a lichen-blotched molar, a giant's blunt pencil, a solitary petrified stob. I know very little about rocks; I knew even less then. I couldn't have said with any confidence what it was, except that it wasn't sandstone, the predominant rock of this area. (Later, I identified it from a geology text book as being, probably, metamorphic gneiss.) It was grey, mostly, but with streaks of other shades, and spotted with dots of dull glassiness. Centuries of rain and wind, it seemed, had in some places smoothed and in others wrinkled the surfaces. It looked as if it were made up of layers of stone melted and fused one on top of another, a fossilised ice-lolly with its stick long since rotted away. It looked as if it had been there for ever.

But it hadn't been there two days earlier, when I'd come that way for the first run of the year. I was sure of it. The first day and the first run. For fourteen years I'd been running the byways of the countryside around Monimaskit; I reckoned I knew them as well as anyone. It wasn't one of my regular routes – in fact, when I'd run it on the Thursday, for the first time in months, it was like renewing a forgotten acquaintance, which was why I'd come again so soon – but I'd done it often enough to know that there'd not been a stone there before. There had never been a stone there. I *was* sure of it.

I put out my hand and, tentatively, as if expecting an electric shock, let the backs of my fingers brush over the cold surface. Then I pressed my palm against it, leaning into it the way I did against the door-jamb when warming up, to stretch the muscles in the backs of my legs. What was I expecting? That it would shift a little, maybe even topple or crumble to dust?

It didn't even flinch.

III

I went running every second or third day. I ran not as a member of a club, not in training for competitions (although I have run marathons for charity), not even to keep fit (although it had that effect), but because I enjoyed it. Yes, running filled me with joy, contentment, as nothing else did. It took me out of myself. Also, it was how I released the energy inside me: as if the fire blazing away in there was my fuel. If I went four days without a run, I grew hot and tense and felt as if my chest was about to explode. I *needed* to run. It was how I got the heat out of my system.

Running made me aware both of the countryside in which I lived and of my physical self. When I set off through the streets of Monimaskit, I could feel the disapproval of some of my parishioners boring into the back of my neck – there was something just *no richt* about a minister in shorts, and sweating. But once out of the town I left all that behind me. I avoided traffic-heavy main roads and ran on narrow, deserted unclassifieds, farm tracks, paths that led me through woods and alongside fields and over burns. I ran along the shore, I ran up into the low hills, I ran beside the crashing of the sea on sand and shingle and I ran above the roaring of the Keldo Water as it fought through the Black Jaws on its way to that sea. I loved the idea of myself – was this vanity? – running among the shadows of trees, against the backdrop of hills, in the echo of birdsong and bellowing cows. I could run for a couple of hours at a time if I chose, barely pausing at gates or stiles, sensitive to the different noises my trainers made when I went up or down a hill, or when I moved from hard road to soft path or grass. Usually I ran in the late afternoon, the dead time between daytime appointments and evening visits and meetings, and I seldom met anybody else. A woman walking her dog, perhaps, or a couple of lads on their bikes. Sometimes the woman would recognise me and say hello. Sometimes she'd recognise me but pretend not to, embarrassed by the ministerial knees. If the boys had a clue who I was, they never let on.

I loved that time of day in all seasons and all weathers, the bright hot stillness of summer and the dark moody dampness of winter. I loved it for itself, but running made it more special still. Running emptied my head of work, the Kirk, the world. Difficult issues and awkward individuals were repelled by the force of my energy, and their ghosts faded into the trees. In Israel young fanatics with explosives strapped to their bodies were wiping themselves and busloads of hated strangers off the planet; insect species were being extinguished every five minutes in the Amazon forest; military coups were being bloodily launched in Africa; dams were being built in China, making tens of thousands homeless; but in Keldo Woods, alone and immune and having slipped his clerical collar, Gideon Mack was running. Sometimes a line from a song or a hymn got trapped in my head and I ran to its rhythm, half-enjoying it and half-annoyed by it. Phrases from the Scriptures that became strange and mantra-like in the repetition: *Nec tamen consumebatur*; 'The Lord is with thee, thou mighty man of valour'; MENE, MENE, TEKEL UPHARSIN. Sometimes I heard my own voice in there, bits of poems I'd read, things I wished I'd said at the right moment, heroic and true things I might say in the future – nothing, as it's turned out, remotely connected with what I would actually say. Sometimes I saw myself as I do now – as if in a film, splashing through puddles to a soundtrack by Vangelis: *when I run I feel God's pleasure*. But that was somebody else: Eric Liddell, the Flying Scotsman, a missionary, a kind of saint. *The loneliness of the long-distance runner*: phrases like that would enter my head and bounce around in there as I ran; but that was someone else again, a Borstal boy, a figure of fiction. I was somewhere in between – an escapee from my professional hypocrisy, a minister off the leash, a creature, neither wholly real nor wholly imagined, hurrying through an ancient landscape. Yes, even then I suspected what I now know to be true: that life itself is not wholly real. Existence is one thing, life quite another: it is the ghost that haunts existence, the spirit that animates it. Running, whether in the rain or sun, felt like life.

Keldo Woods lie between the new or high road that runs into Monimaskit from the west, off the Dundee to Aberdeen dual carriageway, and the old or low road that ambles into town along the coast. On the other side of the dual carriageway the land rises steeply to form a rocky rampart, where the Keldo Water is forced through the ravine of the Black Jaws, and far in the distance beyond this rampart are the dark outlines of the Grampians. By the time the Keldo comes out of the Black Jaws and under the dual carriageway it has had all the excitement squeezed out of it: its banks widen and it flows calmly and decently beside the high road on its last few miles to the sea. On the edge of town there is an old footbridge across the river. If you cross it you find a path that curls through a scattering of ash trees, then descends into the pine woods of Keldo. It joins the forestry workers' track that eventually brings you out on a narrow road with only a few houses dotted along it. This is the low road into Monimaskit, and one of the houses is the home of John and Elsie Moffat and their two young daughters, Katie and Claire. Sometimes they'd be out in the garden, and I'd wave and shout hello to them as I ran past on my way back to town.

I am writing of less than a year past, but it seems decades ago since I stood in those woods, staring at a stone that shouldn't have been there. The only word that came to me that expressed what I was feeling was *fuck*. I started saying it between breaths as they slowed down a little. 'Fuck. Fuck. Fuck.' The breaths were mine but then they were outside and away into the atmosphere. I was in front of a standing stone that didn't exist. 'What the fuck is going on?' I said loudly. A minister using that word might be thought daring or dangerous, but my voice sounded wee and lonely in the silence, a voice bleating in the wilderness. If God was out there he was either deaf or didn't care; he didn't, at any rate, strike me down. I thought of Peter Macmurray, one of my elders: had he chanced to overhear my expletives, he would certainly have expected God to take a pot-shot. But nothing happened.

The stone, certainly, was not offended. It continued to be there, continued not to disappear. It didn't give a damn about me, or even a fuck. I started to shiver. Don't get cold, I told myself, but I wasn't cold. I backed away. The stone remained. It looked disapproving, as if it knew who I was. I didn't like it, felt a strange panic rising in me. I returned to the path and started running again.

All the way back to town I could not get the thought of the stone out of my head. There was something cruel and alien about it. I even glanced over my shoulder a few times to see if it was pursuing me. I remembered one of the few children's books my parents had had in their house – our house – one from which my mother used to read to me before, learning to read myself, I relieved her of that tiresome task: it was about a little Dutch girl who didn't want to go to church, and who was chased by the huge church bell until she changed her mind. A fascinating, scary bedtime story: I both loved and hated it. The stone was like that bell in some way. It was fixed, upright, embedded in the ground – yet perhaps it was able to move as well.

After all, how else had it got there? Maybe my mind was playing tricks on me, and it hadn't been there at all. If the light had not been almost gone I would have turned around and run back, to see if I'd been mistaken. I found myself saying 'Stone, stone, stone,' in time with my out-breaths. My god-daughter Katie, John and Elsie's four-year-old, had a bear called Bear and an imaginary friend called Friend. The stone acquired a capital S in my mind. The stone became the Stone.

IV

It is the start of December as I write this. Autumn has been long and soft, but now come the first barbs of winter. There was a flurry of snow this afternoon, whisking through Monimaskit as if it didn't think much of the place and was in a hurry to get away again. I had stepped out for some air and I met the snow, or it blew into me, halfway down Baxter Loan. In a few seconds it infested my upturned collar and every opening of my coat, like a swarm of ice-cold midges. It was a curious thing, however, that the sun continued to shine for the entire ten minutes that this little blizzard lasted. Sunshine slanting through snowflakes is a rare delight: you feel as if the seasons are playing tig, or showing off how clever and contrary they can be. I went home through the kirkyard wishing I still had one of Catherine Craigie's kites to send up amidst the sun and snow. So when two boys leapt from behind a gravestone, shouting, 'Mad Mack the minister!' I was more inclined to laugh than be angry, and when they launched two hopeless attempts at snowballs, scraped from the top of the stone, and showered themselves with powder, I did indeed laugh – loud and long enough perhaps to sound slightly unhinged – and the boys fled like rabbits. The wind carrying the snow was sharp, but I limped back to the manse feeling better than I had done for weeks.

And I still feel it. I am active again, my mind is buzzing, excited, and a great burden of doom and duty has been lifted from me. This task of ordering my thoughts and writing them down is doing me good. It brings me ever closer to a conclusion.

I have been called many things over the years – Dirty Mack, Marathon Mack, Mystic Mack – and to be called mad by two young laddies, who at least had the grace not to snigger it behind my back, is no great injury. I can hardly blame them, anyway, since the general view of the town seems to be that the Reverend Gideon Mack has lost his marbles.

Am I mad? Well, I talk out loud when alone, but then what minister of religion doesn't? Some talk to God whether or not God is listening, or there at all. Others rehearse their sermons, or practise the kind words they will offer bereaved families or the advice they will give to couples about to marry. I acknowledge the possibility of my insanity – nobody can have pondered this longer and more deeply than I – but at the same time, as I have already said, there is at least a little madness in us all. And since I hear myself speak, am aware of my state of uncertainty, can I really be mad? Does this read like madness? It doesn't *feel* mad. But then, what does madness feel like?

If I could simply be classified as eccentric, then Presbytery – which is even now contemplating putting me on trial for my failings – might find a way to explain me. There is plenty of eccentricity in the Kirk, indeed it is encouraged – up to a point. To be eccentric is to be a 'character', and every institution needs characters. If the pulpits are full of characters there is a better chance that people will come to church, for the entertainment if nothing else, than if they are full of nondescript pedants and bores. I know of one minister who spends his days trying to convince people that a youthful Jesus, as in Blake's hymn, came to Britain with Joseph of Arimathea to learn the secret wisdom of the Druids. Another plays the bagpipes at the weddings he conducts. Another plays saxophone in a jazz combo in a Glasgow club every Friday night. Then there is Lorna Sprott, who brings her Labrador into church, as the shepherds used to bring their collies, and lets the beast sleep on a cushion by the pulpit. Nobody seriously objects to this kind of thing: on the contrary, it adds a little local colour, which may in turn encourage a few more folk through the doors on a Sunday. But there comes a point where eccentricity tips into madness, and there the Kirk draws a line.

In a way, though, it would suit everyone best if I *were* mad. The talking to oneself, ultimately, is unimportant. So, at a stretch, is whether or not the Stone in Keldo Woods exists. Likewise, the last funeral service I conducted might have been passed over as eccentricity: there is no sacrament attached to death in our Church, and no requirement for a funeral to follow any set pattern. Even some of the things I said on that occasion could be ascribed to my recent ordeal by water. But what makes life difficult for everybody is my having met with the Devil.

O tempora! O mores! Oh holy shit! In the seventeenth century a minister who claimed to have seen and spoken with Satan in the flesh would have been not only believed but, assuming he had given a good account of himself, hailed a hero. In the twenty-first century such a minister is simply an embarrassment. I am not the face the Kirk wishes to show to the modern world. The most plausible way of dealing with me, then, is to find me insane.

Letters have been flying between Monimaskit, the Presbytery and 121 George Street;* the phone lines have been buzzing with conversations, faxes, e-mails, all with the problem of Gideon Mack as their theme. I imagine a file somewhere in the depths of 121, that palace of paperwork; I imagine the file becoming a drawer in a cabinet, the cabinet being moved to a bigger room deep in the labyrinth, the Kirk's officials droning like worker bees as they construct a model of my madness from the reports of Presbytery. But can a whole Church find a single man insane in this day and age? Can a man meet the Devil in this day and age? The answer to both questions, be assured, is yes.

* 121 George Street, Edinburgh: the administrative headquarters of the Church of Scotland, 'the repository of a byzantine bureaucracy' according to one commentator. – P.W.

Because the Kirk prides itself on its democracy I would have the right, if found insane by Presbytery, to appeal to the General Assembly, to drag things out by enlisting the expert evidence of doctors, psychologists and theologians. But what would be the point? What good would it do? The happy resolution I have come to is not to engage with the process at all. I will not be there, here, or anywhere. Then they can find me neither bad nor mad but absent, permanently absent – absconded, demitted, disappeared, kidnapped! – and the case will be closed. But not quite, for I will have my say – and hence this pen and this paper.

It is nonsense, of course, to think myself unique, as if doubts and fears and loss of faith were never visited on a Scottish clergyman before. What is the history of Christianity in this dark wee country but a history of doubts and fears, graspings at metaphysics from hard stone and wet bog? True, some came up bloody and triumphant with their fists full of certainties, but it is a delusion to look into our past and see only grim ranks of Covenanters and John Knoxes scowling back. Even then there were plenty of holy wobblers and switherers making up the numbers. Had I lived in those fierce times, would I have been one of them or one of the zealots? I do not know. I only know that in this life I have lived behind a mask, adapting my disguise as circumstances required. For nearly forty years I have let the world assume that I believed in God when I did not.

I sit in my study with the curtains open and the night crowding at the window to watch me at work. Somewhere out there the foxes have holes, and the birds their nests, but the son of the manse hath nowhere to lay his head. A joke. Of course I do. There is a double-bed up the stairs, more beds in the three spare rooms that might have been children's bedrooms, and here in the study the armchair is high-backed and comfortable, very good for writing and dozing, dozing and writing. This is where I spend nearly all my time now. The fire, which I lit after my walk, is settled and cosy. But I am restless. There is someone out there with the foxes and birds, and I am waiting for him. I am anxious to see him but I know he will not come till I have finished writing this. And so I write. It is the prelude to our final, silent journey into knowledge. I long for that: utter silence.

I felt a twinge in my left arm just now. Barely even that. A tiny submerged ripple running down it like an echo, an old memory. That arm has been quiet for weeks, hasn't bothered me since my fall. But the twinge reminded me – as if I need reminding – of a hand reaching to me, pulling me from freezing water. Oh, that hand! But it was as if the arm, not I, remembered. I waited for more ripples, but they did not come. The arm is like some sleeping animal, separate and distinct from the rest of me. My right leg too: it doesn't quite belong to me any more. I do not altogether trust either of these limbs, but I have picked up my pen with the hand of my left arm, and it is writing again.

For several evenings in a row I sat at the blinking screen of the manse computer, trying to find a place to start. But the computer was unfriendly, and I realised that since I'd be leaving this place I would have to leave it as well. A floppy disc is too frail a thing on which to store everything I have to say: I prefer the pen. There is something elemental about the glide and flow of nib and ink on paper. Also, there can be no dispute, later, that this testament, written in my hand, is mine. So here I am now, finally, with a board across the arms of the chair, my good fountain pen, a sheaf of blank paper, and at my side a bottle of Dalwhinnie and a small glass. Here I am, in other words, for the duration. As long as it takes to tell my story.

There was only one place to start, and that was with the Stone. But my head has been full of my father and my mother, my childhood and student days, my eleven-year marriage and my nearly fifteen years as minister here. So now I must go back: back to that other manse at Ochtermill, where I first became conscious of the world, and of that empty vessel in which my spirit, like the genie in the lamp, was condemned to dwell, and which went by the name of Gideon Mack.

V

I was born on 17th March, St Patrick's Day, 1958, so when I first came upon the Stone I was forty-four, approaching forty-five. My father, the Reverend James Mack, was that age, forty-five, when I was born. My mother, Agnes Campbell, was six years younger – an age when many mothers are seeing their offspring leaving home for good – when she produced me, her only child. I was therefore brought up by parents who were old enough to be my grandparents.

Of my actual grandparents, by the time I was born three were dead: my father's father killed in the First World War; my mother's felled by the influenza that swept the world in its aftermath; my father's mother a victim of pneumonia in the harsh winter of 1947. The fourth, my maternal grandmother, died when I was three, leaving me with only the vaguest memory of a small, silent figure dressed in black from head to toe. I don't recall that she was ever unkind to me, but somehow that figure infiltrated my early dreams, taking on an aspect of menace, and for a period I would wake screaming as she approached from the shadows of my mind. My mother, wearing a fawn dressing-gown, would enter the room and calm me. She was not a natural comforter: she was herself too nervous and timid a character to banish bad dreams for ever, but she did her best. One of my earliest memories: my mother holding me to her bony breast, the thin heat of her through the fawn wool. 'Try to sleep now, Gideon,' she would say. 'We must not wake your father, must we?' She was from Argyll originally and spoke impeccable English in a soft West Highland accent. We'd stay there for long minutes in the dark, clutched together in a kind of conspiracy against him, until sleep overtook me again.

Later, when I was seven or eight, I went through a phase of sleepwalking. I would wake and find myself on the stairs, or in the kitchen, my bare feet cold on the linoleum. I did not panic on these occasions. Perhaps I only half woke up, although I remember the sensation even now. I simply turned around and went back to bed. But whenever it happened, my mother would be near by, standing like a ghost, watching me. This did not frighten me either: it was as if I expected to see her. That, at least, is my memory, but was she always there, or did this happen only once? I will never know now whether some instinct made her wake and follow me, to make sure I came to no harm, or whether she also wandered the house at night, and our meetings were chance occurrences. Whichever it was, in this too we were conspirators against the sleeping minister.

James Mack, my father, was the son of a baker from Lanarkshire. He was five when his father was killed at Passchendaele. His mother removed to Glasgow, where she met and married another baker, an elderly man who died almost immediately, leaving her twice-widowed but reasonably comfortably off. There was enough money for my father, a good scholar, to go to the University. He'd always been serious, sombre and religious: it was natural, and highly satisfactory to his mother, that he should study for the Kirk. First as a probationer, then as a minister, he worked in some of the poorest parts of the city in the 1930s, a time of terrible hardship for many. This, he once told me, prepared him for what came next. When war broke out in 1939, he demitted his charge and became an army chaplain. He said he owed it to his father, even if he wasn't going to fight, at least to get an idea of what being a soldier was like. He took part in the landings in Normandy in 1944 and advanced with the Allied forces all the way to Germany. One might have expected this experience to have generated a dislike of Germans, but it didn't. He was suspicious of them, but he was suspicious of everybody. 'We,' he said (meaning, I think, the Scots of the Lowlands in particular and the people of Britain in general) 'are all Germans under the skin.' The people he really disliked, because of their brashness, which he saw as arrogance, and their drawling carelessness, which he saw as ignorance, were the Americans. I think he found the sheer might of the US armed forces repulsive. He knew that they were necessary to defeat Hitler, but something about them deeply offended him.

He didn't talk much about the war, but it must have affected him. How could it not have? He had, I presume, held the heads and hands of scores of wounded and dying men, said prayers over hundreds of bloody, dismembered and barbecued corpses, seen thousands of destroyed homes, starved bodies, ruined faces. I imagine him striding eastward through the shattered countryside and villages, gazing in awe at endless miles of man-made destruction and wondering what it all meant. What purpose was served by such bloody chaos, what plan or grand design could require such devastation? Nothing kills people's belief in God more surely than war. But my father raised his eyes above the carnage, and God was there, stronger than ever.

I have always envied him this single-minded devotion. How clear the view must be from that vantage point! For him, without God there was nothing *but* carnage. It wasn't that God had absented himself, or was responsible for the mess human beings had made: for my father, God was the only redemption from the mess.

In 1946 he returned to Glasgow, and in 1947, the year his mother died, he was called to the charge of the Stirlingshire parish of Ochtermill. It was there that he met Agnes Campbell.

Agnes's grandparents had spoken nothing but Gaelic, and she still had that otherness of the Gael that has always tried the patience of Lowlanders, even those attracted by it. She was the only child of a widow in his congregation – the woman in black of my infant dreams. It seems that Mrs Campbell brought her daughter out with the tea service whenever James Mack called at the house, and presented her at the door of the kirk every Sunday, and on every other possible church or social occasion, with something like pleading in her eyes. In 1957, having known Agnes for ten years and never spoken alone with her for more than three minutes, my father proposed to her. Far from succumbing to Mrs Campbell's constant pressure I believe he probably wasn't even aware of it, although something must have kept making him visit. He asked Agnes one evening at the garden gate, and, according to my mother, seemed more surprised than she was that he'd finally got around to it; almost as if he'd remembered that marriage was something he was supposed to do, he was getting on in life, and it might as well be Agnes as anyone else who replaced the housekeeper. Mrs Campbell was delighted, and showed it by breaking out of her habitual black to don something garish and flowery for the wedding. Apart from her outfit it was a very quiet occasion, conducted by an aged minister from a neighbouring parish, attended by twelve guests and followed by high tea at the Ochtermill Hotel and a weekend honeymoon at Crieff. The following year I was born, to the further delight of Mrs Campbell: her grandson, a son of the manse! Having achieved all she could have hoped for, she went into a three-year decline, at the end of which she expired.

Son of the manse. The phrase conjures up a whole set of stereotypes, all as close to and as far from the truth as stereotypes always are. You could draw up a battalion of sons of the manse and it would strike something, though maybe not terror, into the heart of anybody with an imagination: among its members would be Gordon Brown, David Steel, John Reith, John Buchan, John Logie Baird and William Kidd. I wonder what elements of such an upbringing conspired to produce a Lord Reith or a Captain Kidd, a Chancellor Brown or a Governor-General Buchan. Well, anyway, stereotypical or not, these were some of the features of the manse at Ochtermill that informed my early years:

The house: large, solid, stone-built, cold, its eyes heavy-lidded with brocade curtains, its mouth always decently, firmly shut; windows that rattled in their frames in spring breezes and were thick with frost etchings on the inside on winter mornings; walls devoid of pictures, prints or any other decorative addition; woodwork clogged with dark paint, green outside and brown within; linoleum in the hallway, flags in the back lobby; thin carpets that ended two feet short of the skirtings in the reception rooms; worn rugs in the bedrooms, islands of relative warmth on the lino; a house in need of rewiring, at an estimated cost that so frightened the Kirk Session that we were still using brown bakelite round-pin plugs and adaptors, and lights with plaited cord flexes, long after they had disappeared from other homes; a house devoid of central heating or any other fripperies, and equipped only with essentials; its atmosphere quiet, stern and restrained, as of a household setting an example to others – but, as visitors were few and infrequent, failing.

The minister's study: a room with a coal fire never lit before November or after March, and between these months only *in extremis*; its walls lined with books – Hebrew, Greek and Latin texts, theological tomes of great worth and tedium, dictionaries, encyclopedias, histories, tracts, biographies of long-dead heroes of the Kirk. Not a sniff of a work of fiction except a set of the Waverley Novels, and even these (until I discovered them when I was nine or ten) with their pages uncut; a huge desk of dark, stained oak, with drawers stuffed with letters and Church business, and a leather-backed chair on a swivel; another leather armchair near the window where my father would sit when he was thinking, looking out on the vegetable plot in which my mother cultivated, not very successfully, soft fruit, potatoes, cabbages, carrots and onions; a room in which, over a period of twenty-odd years, nothing changed and nothing moved except the books as they were taken out and replaced on the shelves.

(Those Waverley Novels were a wedding present from my mother's mother, who had herself received them when she was married in 1914, an era when the novels of Sir Walter Scott were considered a safe, sensible gift, the kind of thing any respectable couple could happily display in their drawing room, whether they read them or not. That was the point about Scott: one didn't have to read him, only to have him in the background along with – an option eschewed by my parents – a tasteful print or two of Highland scenery; and nothing perhaps demonstrates better the antique character of the manse at Ochtermill than the fact that the only novels my parents possessed were ones that they had never opened, and that most of the rest of the world had closed for a good three decades before.)

The minister: grave, forbidding, slow to anger but fearsome when roused, emotion displayed by a slight reddening of the usually grey upper cheeks; sense of humour not entirely absent but so dry you could have used it for kindling; the lawmaker, the sayer of grace before and after meals, the inculcator of good manners, the overseer of cleanliness and industry; a man, to my childish eyes, so fashioned in what I presumed was the image of God that God, looking at him, might have momentarily thought himself in front of a mirror.

The minister's wife: dutiful, timid, destined always to wear beige and browns, or unshocking blues, unremarkable blouses, shapeless skirts with hems well below the knee, and no make-up; a worrier, thin and birdlike, habitually apologetic and creeping for cover; sense of humour crushed like chalk beneath a schoolmaster's heel.

And the son: gangly, nervous, good at schoolwork, fumbling and awkward at all games except cross-country running; well practised too at running away from trouble in the playground or the street; having few friends, and those few kept at bay by the fact of his being 'of the manse'; sense of humour present but suppressed, biding its time; a lonely boy politely storing up rebellion until it would least inconvenience his parents, probably after they were dead.

I was so alone that I wonder I never had an imaginary friend, like Katie's Friend, but I have no recollection of one. I did, of course, have Jesus at my side, but I never thought of him as a friend. 'What a Friend we have in Jesus,' the hymn says, but I found the tune too sugary and the words slightly menacing.

Love and fear: they are not so far apart. Once, when I was about nine, my father was giving his usual short address to the younger children in the congregation before they left for Sunday School. Other nine-year-olds still slipped out at this juncture, but I was expected to stay. He was talking about God's infinite wisdom, how he knew what was best for us all. 'He is our father,' my father said, 'and because he is our father he cares for us, even if sometimes we make him angry because of the foolish things we do. Doesn't your own father ever get angry, and isn't it often for your own good?' I heard a dispersed squeaking sound – small backsides squirming on the pews – and imagined small faces looking up at parents to check what they were thinking. 'It's no bad thing to be afraid of God. It doesn't mean he doesn't love you. Aren't you all just a little afraid of your own fathers? Hands up if you are.' There was a pause. I risked a backward glance. Small hands were raised like flags of surrender throughout the kirk. Titters of quiet, approving laughter ran round the adults. Some of them even had their hands in the air. I too had my arm half-lifted, and my father gave me a tiny smile as he surveyed his flock. Then his gaze alighted on something that displeased him: his eyes went cold and his nostrils flared. I half-turned my head again and saw, three pews back across the aisle, a boy of about my age sitting alone on his hands, boldly staring back at the pulpit. I turned back. All my father's concentration now focused on that boy. 'Really?' he said. 'Not – even – the tiniest – bit – afraid?' The words came out like hard little pebbles. There was a long silence: a contest of wills between the minister and the errant boy. I knew that my father would keep it up indefinitely. Fifteen, twenty seconds passed – an eternity. I could not see, but could feel, the boy wilting. Then his hand must have gone up, for the smile returned to my father's face. 'Yes,' he went on, 'it is right to fear God. He is mighty and he loves us with a mighty love. Very good, you may all put your hands down. Away you go now, and enjoy your Sunday School.' There was a rush of movement as children fled. When I next looked back, the wilful boy was gone.

It was my father's decision to name me Gideon – I doubt if my mother had any say in the matter – and, perhaps to close off any softer options in later life, he gave me no other names. Although his faith was Christianity, he preferred the Old Testament to the New: its theology was simpler and its stories better. He liked the Book of Judges and the story of God working through Gideon. He liked the way Gideon, an ordinary man, did extraordinary deeds because God was on his side; and therefore he called me after him. He must have told or read me that tale dozens of times: how God called Gideon when he was threshing wheat by the wine-press, to keep it hidden from the Midianites, and made him the leader of Israel; and how he instructed him to reduce the Israelite army from 32,000 to a mere 300, first by sending the fearful home, then by separating the men who took water to their mouths by hand from the majority who lapped it like dogs on their knees; and all this so it would be clear, when victory came, by whose arm the Midianite host was felled. And when I stumbled as a bairn, or was too small to reach something on a shelf, it was my father's habit to help me, but only just enough to enable me to help myself; and it was a joke of his (almost his only one) to say as I clambered to my feet, or grasped the desired item, 'The Lord is with thee, thou mighty man of valour'; and, on occasions of supreme achievement, such as when I learned to ride a bicycle, to applaud thunderously with the words, 'The sword of the Lord, and of Gideon!' So that I, who felt duty-bound to live up to his expectations but often failed, thought of myself, aged six or thereabouts, as some kind of pale imitation of an Old Testament hero.

Did my father love me? Was he capable of love at all? I think he loved the idea of a son more than he loved the actuality. He wanted a Gideon, but what he got was a Gideon Mack. Thus, when he saw his progeny for the first time in the hospital, the girning, black-haired beast with elfin-like lugs and a screech in its mouth, perhaps his heart jumped with some spontaneous feeling he could not identify. (This is conjecture, from a distance of forty-six years, based on my mother's unreliable memories and a single, small, black and white photograph of me in my pram that must have been taken by someone else, for my parents never possessed a camera.) He may even have felt warm and grateful towards my mother; perhaps at that moment he held her hand and thanked her, and together they thanked God, and he imagined the great things his son might do, and the pride he would have in seeing him do them. But as I grew to a boy and then to a young man, he must have seen my failings increase with every inch of growth. He must have understood that in the biblical tale *this* Gideon would have been one of the thousands who went home fearful, or one of those who lapped like a dog. And he must have recognised that, apart from my height, I was more like Agnes than him, and this would have depressed him, that the blood of a feeble body like hers should have overmastered his in the one product of their union.

For whether or not my father ever loved me, I am certain he never loved Agnes Campbell. He tolerated her, in the way somebody not keen on dogs will thole a dog so long as it doesn't lick or bark or seek attention. My mother learned not to seek my father's attention during the ten years preceding their marriage, and practised the lesson for the twenty-three years it lasted. I don't think he was being deliberately cruel, but that sort of neglect drives a person back on their own resources, and my mother didn't have many of those.

And yet I didn't grow up loathing my father, as a better son might have, for treating her in this way. I imitated him. I inherited from him an indifference to my mother's views and opinions, and she in turn distanced herself from me just as she'd learned to distance herself from him, as if it were indecent to display her feelings in that hushed house. We were not strangers to one another but we kept ourselves apart. The three of us were really a good match for one another; and I took my lessons from them accordingly.

From my mother I learned how to function in a reasonably practical everyday way: how to wash and dress myself, how to eat and drink, how to go shopping, when to speak, and when to keep silent. I followed her around the house and garden, and through the village, observing and copying. It was the natural thing to do.

From my father I learned many things, but two in particular stand out. The first was the beauty of austerity. As a child I didn't like the sterile, unadorned barrenness of the manse, but now I have greater respect for his dedicated rejection of possessions. Austerity is not highly regarded these days: not to have *things* is considered a mark of poverty. But there is more than one kind of poverty, and I have not seen more wretchedly impoverished people than the desperate crowds shopping for the sake of shopping in the post-Christmas sales.

The second thing I learned from him was how to think, how to argue, how to hold my own in a conversation. The evening meal, which the three of us ate together promptly at six, was an important time, when he would quiz me about my day, and I, in turn, would quiz him about his. He wanted detail from me, accuracy, precision – facts rather than impressions – and I would demand the same of him. He liked debate and controversy, in the way that some people like crosswords. Debate sharpened his tongue, made him re-examine his beliefs and confirm their correctness, but all the pleasure was in the arguing, not in the conclusion: like a completed crossword, the outcome was meaningless. His mind wasn't closed, but it shut out the trivial and the unnecessary. I think the world for him was often a theoretical place, not a real one. Thus in our theoretical way we communicated for several years, filling the air with information that was about the world but emotionally detached from it, competing with each other, although at the time I didn't know it was a competition.

We were also competing with the rest of the human race. 'There are many, many stupid people on this earth,' my father said. 'They are not born stupid, they are made so through their enslavement to material things, to the petty concerns of the world. The brain is one of God's greatest gifts to us, and to abuse it is an act of gross ingratitude. Yet most people are stupefied by the world. I hope, Gideon, that you will not be one of them.'

My mother said virtually nothing at meal-times: apart from her role as cook and server she was a spectator, and even had she wanted to participate she was not invited to do so. My father regarded her as stupid, although he could hardly have argued that an excess of possessions had made her so. If she and I had once been conspirators against my father in the night, he and I conspired against her at meal-times. And yet, in some unspoken, grey alliance of age against youth, at other times they conspired against me.

I think my father saw me as wavering between the grace of intelligence and the damnation of stupidity. He wanted me to be saved, but there was only so much he could do – the rest was up to God and me. He would look for symptoms of my condition – glimmers of intelligence, dark clouds of stupidity – but sometimes he saw negative signs in other things – in my awkward thinness, for example, or my aversion to cabbage, or my left-handedness.

By the time I was three it must have been obvious that I was what elsewhere in the village they called 'corrie-fistit', and within a few years we were having battles over my use of cutlery at table, as my natural preference for applying my left hand to spoon and knife asserted itself. Left-handedness used to be seen as a mark of the Devil. I wonder if that old superstition occurred to him and disturbed him. It occurs to me now, obviously, but it does not disturb me.

The manse was a place, overwhelmingly, of silence. If I stood on the stairs and held my breath, often the only sound was the ticking of the grandfather clock in the hall. What scant noise the three of us made, while outside the world's volume was getting constantly louder! In the kitchen, where my mother toiled, even the pots and pans and plates seemed muted: if she had to perform a particularly clattering task, she would wait till my father was out. We hardly ever had guests, and all parish business was conducted behind the closed door of the study. The only voices heard in the manse other than our own came from the radio, which was located in the back parlour on the mantelpiece. It was switched on for the news, the football results on a Saturday (football was my father's one earthly weakness) and not much else. I was forbidden to turn the dial or change the wavelength so I had no notion of the world of music that could have been accessed through that squat brown box. I had very few toys – some bricks, an assortment of plastic soldiers, some Dinky cars – and when I played with them I suppressed the sounds of my play to a low murmur. This reticence was much approved, so I continued to be quiet. I had no reason to suppose that other children's lives were any different.

As soon as I was at school and could half-read, my mother took me to the library and selected three picture books, each with a few easy words in them, and let me carry them home. I thought this was an act of great generosity on her part: it was a while before I realised that she chose only books I could manage by myself, and that they were intended to keep me occupied and silent. Still, I was grateful. The trip to the library became the weekly highlight of my home life.

My father had learned to drive in the army and owned a grey Morris Minor, bought second-hand, which was used for occasional long journeys. He also had an old black bicycle on which he sometimes wobbled round the village, making his pastoral calls. When I was seven he bought me my first bicycle and taught me to ride it. Again I was deeply moved by this bounty, and again it was only later that I understood the motivation: the bike would take me away from the house – first on to the manse driveway, then into the streets of Ochtermill and the surrounding country roads – and allow me to burn off my energies elsewhere. Between the weekly supply of library books and the bike, which was replaced a few years later by a larger model with three gears, I believed I had all the good things I could ever deserve. I experienced a kind of dull, warmish ache in the company of my father and mother, which I took to be the manifestation of that honour mentioned in the fifth commandment.

The first ten years of my life in Ochtermill passed in this dreary atmosphere. I had had no conception of how dreary it was until I went to school and saw how other children interacted with teachers and with their parents. School was an explosion of colour, from the posters and pictures on the walls to the different chalks used on the blackboard and even to the clothes the teachers wore. I began to see us, the Macks, in a different light, and it was not a comfortable view. My father should have been one of the most influential figures in a place the size of Ochtermill, but, with each passing year, his influence was dwindling. In the early 1960s he could walk down the main street and bickering groups of boys in shorts would look guilty and fall silent while he passed; some men touched their bonnets; others crossed the street to avoid him; women in head-scarves would smile nervously and then whisper behind his back. But by the middle of the decade there was change in the village: even at seven or eight I was conscious of it. The gangs of boys, now wearing jeans, ignored him or stared insolently; young men grew their hair till it covered their ears and collars; young women abandoned headscarves and wore skirts that barely covered their thighs. Meanwhile the grocer's turned itself into a new kind of shop where customers picked up wire baskets and helped themselves to things off the shelves; pop music, a complete mystery to me, played on a jukebox in the Italian café, and crashed tinnily from dozens of transistor radios carried by girls with long, pale legs and false eyelashes; rumours of students smoking hashish and women 'going on the pill' were confirmed as facts. Some people claim that the sixties never happened in Scotland, but they did; and in places like Ochtermill, where they ran headlong into the remnants of the 1930s, it was impossible to pretend otherwise. In 1960 the church's pews were all full; by 1970 they were more than half-empty. My father, the Reverend James Mack, stood like a breakwater in the ebb of the decade, while those for whom organised religion meant nothing any more went out with the tide and did not return.

But it was not just a clash of eras or generations, it was a clash of cultures too. The sixties was an American decade: the Americans might have gone home after the war but they were back in these years, influencing the form of music, books, art, fashion, social attitudes. British pop groups sang with American accents, teenagers dressed in denim, Marvel comics filled the racks in station newsagents, and American shows and the American war in Vietnam filled the staid black-and-white screens in homes which had television. My father hated all this: the triumph of stupidity. He saw it too as an invasion of privacy, which it was. The sixties demolished privacy, encouraging people to explore their inner selves and lay them out for all to see. To my father, this was like passing a law permitting indecent exposure in public places.

Looking back, I see that the decline of his influence was rapid, but at the time it seemed gradual, partly because he remained such a conspicuous figure. He stood over six feet tall, with a long, straight back and arms that reached almost to his knees. He had big, meaty hands that he would clasp behind him as he walked, so that his arms formed an inverted Gothic arch. He walked very stiffly, as if that arch outlined the end of an invisible ironing-board stuck down his back. He never had good colour, and his ashen complexion made him seem even more forbidding. His grey hair had receded far up his head when I was still a toddler: his brow was like an expanse of polished rock and his jaw like a jutting piece of granite. His bright blue eyes, set in deep sockets, shone like crystals in this bleak terrain.

He was not a talkative man, but when he spoke it was impossible to ignore him. Although he had banished Scotticisms almost entirely from his vocabulary, he had a strong west coast voice that accentuated every guttural and fricative, and made him use English as if it were a chisel or gouge that had to be gripped hard and applied with precision. This made him sound extraordinarily emphatic and combative even when saying something simple like 'Good morning' or 'Thank you' or 'Let us pray'. When he read from the Bible, the effect was very powerful, and when he prayed aloud in the kirk it sounded more as though he were challenging God than beseeching him. My mother and I sat in the front pew, beneath the pulpit, so I don't know if anybody was in the habit of nodding off during his sermons, but if they were I can't imagine that they slept easily. Sometimes, if he was particularly enthused, I would have to wipe his spittle from my hymn book.

He could be fierce, but it took extreme provocation to bring his awesome ferocity to the surface. I have mentioned the reddening of the cheeks which was the sign of an imminent explosion; I used to watch in cowering anticipation as people who didn't know him so well blundered on unaware of this warning signal and then received the full blast of his wrath. The things that set him off were all appropriate targets for a minister's anger – blasphemy, deceit, extravagance, waste, selfishness, greed – but he did not always keep a sense of proportion when he saw these sins manifested. He could with equal vehemence decry slum landlords, deplore the nuclear arms race (which he also saw as blasphemy, the ultimate setting-up of false gods) and castigate me for not eating my greens. In the pulpit his rage was mesmerising and inspiring; in the manse or street, it was sometimes irrational and, yes, even stupid.

I began to be conscious of this from about the age of seven or eight. His moods affected the entire house, making it feel like a place where all spontaneity was left, like outdoor shoes, in the lobby, where all pleasure was suspect, where all that was entertaining was measured and tested for impurities. In describing the manse, I seem to have paid most attention to the room my mother and I spent least time in: the minister's study. It was the nerve-centre of our existence. The gloom seeped out from there and filled our lives.

I also became conscious of something about myself. Like my

father, I was boiling away within, but I kept a lid on my passions. Somewhere in his *Journal* Walter Scott says something about this, I forget the exact words: 'Our passions are wild beasts: God grant us the strength to muzzle them.' Unconsciously at first, and then deliberately, I learned how to do this. It was what enabled me to survive, but it is what prevented me, for so long, from really living.

It is midnight, but I am not sleepy. The fire bakes and breathes and I breathe with it. Another dram. Soon the night will be at its heaviest and darkest. I will sit for a while in its midst, then begin again.

VI

The importance of evidence, the necessity of facts. Like Mr Gradgrind in *Hard Times* I believed in facts. I believed in them that day I found the Stone, which was why it disturbed me so much. I remembered Thomas called Didymus, who would not accept that Jesus had risen from the dead unless he saw and felt for himself the print of the nails in his hands. I'd have been with Thomas on that. I'd read David Hume on miracles, his argument that although a miracle was possible you'd need so much evidence to persuade you it had happened that it wouldn't be a miracle any more – and my sympathies were with him. I used to discuss all this with John Moffat when we were students together at Edinburgh, and long after that too. Now John teaches history at Monimaskit Academy. He believed in facts then, and still does. We argued vociferously but in those days we were on the same side. Yet we also recognised that evidence could be misleading or wrong, could even be lies; that truth is a variable and slippery thing. One of the exercises John used to do with his pupils was read out extracts from the old burgh annals of Monimaskit – items presumably recorded in all sincerity and not by some sixteenth-century joker intent on pulling the leg of posterity – in order to demonstrate this point:

1567. In this yere in the moneth of Aprile, ane kow broucht furth eight dog whelps of monstrous size insteid of calfs. Nane could controul thame even in thair first houris, and thay killed and devoured thair mothir. The nixt day fiftene strang men cast thame in ane fischerman's net and thay war draggit yowland and teirand the net with thair teeth and war dround in the sea.

1570. In Julii, ane of the servand lassies at Keldo beand seik, a doctour of physick wes summond, that did give her an emetick; and she did vomit furth twa puddocks and a spider, and efterwards ane littil houss all compleat with lum, door and winnocks; but althogh ane watch wes keepit, the pepill that bade in that houss war nevir discoverit.

So where did that leave me, as far as the Stone was concerned? What would posterity make of me? I jogged in through the outskirts of town that January afternoon and imagined the item some future teacher might read out:

2003. In January of this year, the parish minister did claim that there appeared at a certain place in Keldo Woods a mysterious stone that was never seen on that spot before. And the townsfolk laughed at him, and when he persisted in his delusion they were enraged, and he was dismissed as a fabricator of tales not worthy to be a pastor to the people, and died in shame and poverty in Dundee.

I really did construct that text in my head as I ran, and though I may not die in shame, poverty or Dundee, how true the rest of it has turned out to be.

I stopped running at the manse gate and walked up the gravel driveway, limbering down. I went round to the back door, lifted the key from where I usually hid it under a broken slate, and unlocked the door. I took off my trainers, knocked the loose mud off them against the sandstone wall and put them on newspaper in the utility room. I thought of my father's gleaming black brogues, how he used to polish them till the sweat stood on his brow. In the kitchen, the time on the cooker changed soundlessly. I thought of

Jenny. In the hallway, the grandfather clock from Ochtermill ticked peevishly. On the stairs, silence. In the bedroom, silence. I thought of Jenny again. Whenever I came in from a run, she was there in the house. And then she wasn't.

In the shower the water poured over me and I imagined rain running down the many faces of the Stone. Something strange, unnerving and wonderful was happening. I was frightened, I was excited. I wondered who I would dare to tell about it.

I would, almost certainly, have told Jenny if she'd been there. She'd have been in the kitchen: baking, perhaps, or ironing, or at the table reading a book or doing the *Scotsman* crossword. The kitchen and bedroom were Jenny's rooms, they seemed permanently filled with her warmth, her smell, whether or not she was there. Even after all those absent years – eleven of them, blown away day by day like calendar leaves in an old movie – she lingered. The big pine kitchen table had six matching chairs, but Jenny had banished one of these to a corner of the room and put in its place an oak Windsor chair with a faded blue cushion tied to two of the spindle-shaped uprights. It never looked that comfortable – it never *was* for me, I'm too long and bony – but small, soft Jenny loved it, could sit in it for hours, one leg tucked under the other, read whole books, fall asleep and wake unstiff and without a crick in her neck. After the accident – not immediately but a few months after – I moved the Windsor into the corner, and the exiled pine chair came back to its rightful place. I never sat in Jenny's chair, but I couldn't sell it or give it away. Sometimes a wisp of her was there, curled up in its arms. More often than not it was empty.

'Hiya. How was it?'

'Fine. Cold, but good for running.'

'See anybody?'

'Not a soul. What are you up to?' Silly bloody question if she had a book in her hand.

'Page 467. *Bleak House*.'

'I thought you'd read that before.'

'I have. Twice. It gets better each time. Mr Krook is about to spontaneously combust.'

'Oh. Well, I'd better not hold him up. I'm going for a shower.'

'Good.' I can see her smile. 'You're far too sweaty for a minister.'

I smile back. 'Jenny?'

'What?'

'Something happened today. On the run. I don't really know what, though. It's hard to put into words.'

'Try. Words are what you do.'

'I was in the woods, and there was this stone. This standing stone. It's just appeared. It shouldn't be there at all. It *wasn't* there on Thursday.'

She tucks a strand of hair behind her right ear, raising her eyebrows at me. 'What are you talking about, Gideon?'

'I don't know. I saw this stone. It's just appeared, like Dr Who's Tardis.'

'Ri-ght. Um, hallucination, perhaps?'

'No, I touched it. It's real. But it can't have just materialised out of thin air. Can it?'

'Your department, not mine.' Her voice was always soft, but she could be firm too. 'Go and have your shower and tell me about it later. I want to find out what happens to Krook.'

'You know what happens to Krook. What about what's happened to me?'

Hopeless. She wasn't there. Anyway, she wouldn't have believed me. Maybe I wouldn't have mentioned it after all. The same way I'd never mentioned the arm. In the hope that it would come to – nothing.

Not long after we first arrived in Monimaskit I'd become aware of twitches and spasms down my left arm. The first few times, I didn't think anything of it. Then I began to notice a pattern: I'd feel the arm getting ready to shudder, and a fuzzy, numb sensation would come over my head and face. There would be a dim roaring in my ear, like waves breaking on a gravel beach, then the arm would start to shake from the biceps all the way down to the hand. It only lasted a few seconds – ten or fifteen at most – as if whatever was going on had been cleared out of my system, out through my fingertips maybe. I felt that it wasn't happening to *my* arm but to somebody else's. I observed it with a detached curiosity.

For a long time I explained this away as God telling me not to get above myself, God saying, 'Gideon, my man, you may be on my team but don't think I don't know your heart, don't think I can't see right through to the oily slick of your soul. I'm tolerating you, because the Kirk needs to keep all the ministers it has, and on the surface you put in a pretty good performance, but don't get above yourself, my friend, because if you do I can deliver a blow so stunning, so devastating, that you'll wish you'd been on the bench for Satan from the opening whistle. Remember what happened to your father? You think that was just chance? Think again, Gideon.' This was when I was in my early thirties, a newly called minister who, unknown to everybody except my wife, did not believe in God. I didn't believe in him and yet he was still there, a hovering doubt in the background of every move I made: *somebody out there may be watching you*. I thought I'd got it all out of my system as a boy, but I hadn't. You don't, not if it's in you in the first place. Anyway, the point was, he was there or he was not there, whether you believed in him or not. I happened not to believe in him, but he was still there. And that was the twist: even if he didn't exist, he would still get you, sooner or later. My left arm was a manifestation of that.

One autumn day, I came in from a meeting and went upstairs to change into my running gear. I'd taken off my shirt and was just reaching for the cupboard when I felt the arm sending out its preparatory signals. I'd found that the event passed more quickly and easily if I stood still and didn't try to control it. This time, though, it was different. The fuzziness that was usually outside my head seemed to have got inside; clouds closed in around me, reducing my vision; the noise in my ears wasn't the distant roar of the sea but the booming sound of being completely under water. I felt myself lift and tilt. The arm began to behave like a disembodied conductor's arm at the finale of some great orchestral concert, jumping and jerking in wild circular movements. I watched it, unable to interfere. I went down on my knees, then on to my right side, then on to my back. A stricken ship. I felt I might sink right through the carpet, the floorboards. Slowly I came to rest. The arm came down on top of me, heavy and triumphant, as if it had defeated me in a wrestling bout.

For a few minutes I didn't move. To begin with I wasn't that worried; I felt I'd witnessed something happening to someone else, to someone else's arm. I heard water running in a pipe behind the wall. Downstairs Jenny was banging pots in the kitchen. I didn't call out – it seemed pointless. You are your father, I thought, it's happened to you too. You've had a stroke. You're paralysed. You'll never walk again, let alone run. Wait here for a while and see what happens. Then I didn't call out because I was frightened. Would I even be able to speak? I wondered if I'd become incontinent.

That was what snapped me out of it. Don't be fucking ridiculous, a voice said, you're not wet down there. I reached out a hand – the left hand – and felt around my groin. Not even a damp sweat. The hand moved the way it was supposed to; so did the whole arm. A few seconds later I was on my feet. I felt normal, but I did not trust this feeling. I decided to skip the run that night.

When I appeared in the kitchen, Jenny glanced round from scrubbing carrots in the sink. I'd put on jeans and a jumper. 'I thought you were going out,' she said.

'Changed my mind,' I said. 'I'm a wee bit tired. Think I'll just do some reading instead. Unless there's anything you want me to do?'

'No,' she said. She carried on with the carrots. Evidently she didn't see any difference in me. 'Away and sit down. You must be tired if you're not going running.'

'I think I must be,' I said. I went into the study, sat behind the desk and pretended to be busy. You are your father, a voice said. Not my voice, someone else's. I went through what had happened. The arm had acted quite independently: either that or some other force, possibly God, had taken control of it. Certainly it had been nothing to do with me.

I didn't say anything to Jenny. I was afraid. If I didn't talk about it maybe it wouldn't happen again.

And it didn't, not as dramatically or intensely as that anyway, although the tremors seemed to come more often. Sometimes the arm would take me by surprise, jerking things from my hand or making me spill my coffee. Once every few days I got the fuzziness in my head, but it cleared if I didn't fight it. It was as if I had a smouldering Vesuvius buried inside me. It gave wee belches and boaks once in a while, but I felt it was only teasing me. Or God was – testing and teasing, building up for the big one. And there wasn't anything I could do about it. If I had another attack like that big one, I told myself, I would go and see Amelia, but I wasn't convinced she could help.

Amelia Wishaw was my GP. Jenny and I were on her list at the Monimaskit Health Centre. In fifteen years I've been to the surgery no more than three or four times, usually because of some virus picked up on my parish rounds. I saw Amelia socially more often than I ever did for health reasons. Her husband Gregor is head of John Moffat's History department at the Academy. I don't see them at all now.

Amelia can be quite intimidating, very bright, a little arrogant as doctors often are. Maybe that's why I never did tell her about the arm: a decade and a half of twitches and shudders and the knockout blow still never came, so why bother her? I did think about doing so, from time to time: after Jenny's accident, but I'd felt so knackered then that it seemed utterly unimportant, a mere fraction of the total pain; after the first of my marathons, when the arm quivered in bed all night, as if in protest; and that day I came in from the run in Keldo Woods, my mind still on the Stone, the arm giving little twinges as I dried myself after the shower. I imagined telling Amelia not just the physical symptoms, but about the sense I had that the arm didn't belong to me at all, that somebody else had a set of puppet-strings attached to it. 'Could it have anything to do with my being left-handed, Amelia? Sinister, you know? Could the arm be bewitched, have a mind of its own?' Oh yes, I could see myself coming out with that, and leading on neatly to my story about what I'd found in the woods. I could see the look of impatience and irritation on her face. 'Don't waste my time, Gideon.'

VII

My father, I've already said, had one indulgence, and that was an enthusiasm for football. He'd helped to organise competitions among unemployed men in Glasgow in the thirties, and had played a lot himself at that time. Although he did not admit to supporting any particular team, except the national one in its annual clash with England, he still liked to watch a good-going game, and occasionally would stride down to the park where an Ochtermill eleven took on other local teams in a junior league. More often on Saturday afternoons in winter he would break off from work in his study and come into the back parlour to listen to the commentary and results. At such times he would fix the radio with an intense stare, as if he could actually see the action being described, as if he could discern some meaning in the haphazard progress of the ball as it was dribbled and passed. If I spoke to him, he very often did not hear me.

At tea-time one evening in the spring of 1966, he made an announcement.

'I have ordered a television set,' he said.

We stared at him, my mother with incomprehension and I with a tiny, thrilling hope that this might not be a perverse attempt at a joke. Almost all my schoolmates had television, or their neighbours had, but there had never been any question of it being allowed in the manse. It was like alcohol in that respect. My father's opinion had always been that television was a distillation of all the vices he most detested. Furthermore, John Logie Baird notwithstanding, he associated it with America, in his mind the wellspring of those selfsame vices. And now here he was, telling us he intended to bring this monster into the manse.

'A television set,' was all my mother said. I, for fear of betraying secret desires, didn't dare speak.

'We must move with the times,' my father said implausibly. 'I would like to see the news rather than just listen to it. There are, I believe, some good educational programmes which you may enjoy,

Gideon. It will be useful for other things too, major sporting events and the like.'

'I see,' said my mother, although she didn't, having even less interest in football than I had. But this was the end of April. I knew the World Cup finals were to take place in England in July: clearly my father could not resist the thought of watching Pele and the other Brazilians, the Italians, the Russians and, most of all, the Portuguese, with their star player Eusebio. To do this, he required a television. It was despised and unwanted but necessary. A necessary evil, in fact.

'The licence fee and rental cost are not unreasonable,' he went on. 'We will take it on trial for three months, and if I see no harm in it, it can remain.'

Thus my father admitted a television – black and white, still, in 1966 – into the back parlour. It came with an internal aerial that you had to move around the room to get the best picture. Although the idea had been entirely his, my father treated the television from the day of its arrival with a kind of suppressed horror: it wasn't actually part of the contract with Radio Rentals that if its output proved corrosive to the morals of his wife and son it would be removed at once, but it might as well have been. He glowered at the box in the parlour as if it were a guest of extremely doubtful character and it was only a matter of time before it did something outrageously offensive. And on the second-last day of July it did: it showed England winning the World Cup. Still, it had also allowed him to watch international football at the highest level. Furthermore, he had let the beast in, and it would be an admission of error if he had to put it out again. The television remained, and gradually the rules that governed what was watched, and when, were relaxed.

Two things, however, were beyond the pale. One was watching 'American trash': shows like *The Munsters, Mr Ed* and *Bewitched*, none of which my father knew anything about, but all of which I homed in on rapidly, picking up information from school and then watching surreptitiously whenever I could. The other was switching on the set on a Sunday.

These were still the days – just – of old-fashioned Scottish

Sundays. On the Sabbath the swings in the park were chained up, and the newsagent's was the only shop which opened, for a couple of hours in the morning. Not that we patronised it: *The Scotsman* was delivered to our door through the week, but I was a university student before I was exposed to the wickedness of Sunday papers. The one place I went on a Sunday was to church. I was not allowed out on my bike, nor even for a walk beyond the manse gates, although if the weather was fine I could sit in the garden with a book. Despite my father's professed desire to move with the times, we were well behind them even then.

It was on some of these elongated afternoons in the late 1960s that I raced through Scott's best novels and ploughed through the less digestible ones like *Peveril of the Peak*. I was a precocious and voracious reader, but I'm not sure I would have persisted with Scott had I not felt duty-bound, once I had started a book, always to finish it. By extension, having begun the Waverley Novels, I was determined to work my way through the entire set. This was 1967, I think, when I was nine: I can't imagine anybody under sixty reading Scott nowadays. My schoolmates were listening agog to *Sergeant Pepper*: I was reading *The Antiquary*.

I was also acquiring a small stock of books of my own, mostly 'children's classics' deemed suitable because they were at least half a century old and their authors dead. I read R. M. Ballantyne and Rudyard Kipling, Jules Verne and Rider Haggard, with uncritical pleasure. To me, these writers were as new and exciting as the Beatles and the Rolling Stones, whose music I only heard in snatches outside the manse, were to my peers. My favourite was Robert Louis Stevenson. I must have read *Treasure Island* three times in the space of a year, and *The Strange Case of Dr Jekyll and Hyde*, which I didn't understand but was gripped by, I managed twice. Best of all was *Kidnapped*. Something in the friendship between David Balfour and Alan Breck, the strait-laced schoolmaster's son and the wild Highlander, dug deep into me as it has into thousands of would-be adventurers. For a day and a night I ran on hands and knees across Rannoch Moor with that pair, 'dragging myself in agony and eating the dust like a worm', till I reached the 'dismal mountain of Ben

Alder'. There was something both awful and fine about Ben Alder in Stevenson's book, and I have thought of it with two minds, as it were, ever since. A place of danger, a place of refuge. A destination where a man finds both the strength and the weakness that is in him. And now it looms again in my thoughts.

But other delights were vying for my attention around this time. A feverish excitement ran through Ochtermill Primary School: the television series of *Batman* had arrived on British television, and, uniquely at the time, each weekly adventure was served up in two half-hour parts, the first on Saturday afternoon, and the second on Sunday. Invariably the Saturday episode ended with Batman or Robin, or both, facing imminent death. How naive we were back then; how ridiculous and innocent that our nerves could be made to jangle for twenty-four hours because Batman was about to be made history by some character called the Joker, but that's how it was. We *believed* in the Joker, the Riddler and those other ridiculous, camp villains – or at least, I did. No wonder I thought holding back the second part till Sunday a mean trick and a massive provocation. How could I possibly watch the Saturday episode, knowing that the Sunday one was utterly out of bounds to me? Yet how could I *not* watch the Saturday programme? I did, dreading that my father, coming through for the football results, would find me there before I could switch channels; and knowing that I'd be unable to watch the next day. It was temptation of the worst kind. Every Monday morning the other boys at school dissected the way in which the Dynamic Duo had managed to escape, while I listened intently, ashamed to admit my feeble ignorance. And week by week the perception grew in me that my peers were not suffering for breaking the Sabbath. On the contrary, they appeared to be thriving on it, while I hung in the desperate limbo of a life filled with *Batman* half-stories.

One Sunday, after a year of this torture, I could bear it no more. My father seemed settled in his study, and my mother, who was feeling unwell, had gone upstairs for a nap. I sneaked into the back parlour, turned the television's volume control down and switched it on.

The set took its usual minute and a half to warm up. Then the dot in the screen expanded into a full picture. Batman and Robin were trapped in a chimney stack that was filling with deadly gas. It was up to their necks. The expressions with which they looked at each other said, this really is it this time, pal. Then, as if to get it over with quickly, they both lowered their heads into the fog of gas. That was where we'd got to on the Saturday. 'Is this the Joker's crowning jest?' the voice-over had said. What was to become of them? I waited, wide-eyed. A few seconds later they emerged, back to back, feet planted against the walls of the stack, and, like a human spider, began to work their way up, out of danger. It was so obvious, so impossibly simple, that it was almost disappointing. But I was not disappointed. They had escaped, and I had seen how they escaped! I would be able to talk about it with total authority the next day at school.

Another few minutes must have gone by. I forgot where I was and what day it was. The sound was louder than I'd intended. I was only a foot away from the screen, finger hovering near the off switch, and maybe that was why I failed to hear my father's footsteps in the hall. By the time the door opened and his voice filled the room – 'Agnes? I thought I heard somebody . . .' – there was no point in even bothering to switch the television off. I did, though, and jumped to my feet in a flush of shame and fury.

He closed the door behind him. I stood between him and the television set as if to protect it, as if to say it was not to blame. I could see the wee flames in his cheeks. I bowed my head, fixing my eye on a crack in the skirting-board. I heard him say, 'Put it back on.'

'No, no, it doesn't matter, I'm sorry,' I mumbled. Entirely the wrong thing. He cut me off, his voice shaking.

'It doesn't *matter*?' he said. 'Do you dare to disobey me? Put it back on.'

I turned and reached for the switch. The television, being warm, came on at once. If my father understood that, he made no allowance for it.

'I see you have become very skilled at operating that thing,' he said quietly, almost admiringly. 'How often have you done this?'

'Never,' I said. It was true that I'd not touched the set before on a Sunday. 'I promise, this is the first time.'

'It will be the last,' he said. 'Come here.'

He pointed beside him and I went and stood there. His huge right hand descended on my neck and the thumb and fingers gripped it so that I cried out. He increased the pressure. I thought my head would snap off. His breathing was like that of some monstrous creature in its den. The blood in his fingers pulsed furiously against my neck.

Thus we stood in front of the television together, father and son, for the remaining ten minutes of the programme. It felt like an hour. If I squirmed to try to ease the pain, his grip tightened. I hated him then, hated what he was doing to me and hated my own helplessness. *ZAP! BLAM! POW!* I hated the screen with its cartoon punches and I hated the way the parlour echoed with screeching tyres and wisecracks delivered in American accents. I saw it as if through his eyes – cheap, tawdry, meaningless rubbish – and I longed for it to end.

He pushed me from him as the credits rolled and the inane theme music played. 'Turn it off,' he said. I did as I was told, rubbing my neck and wiping away the tears that he had squeezed out of me.

'What . . . is . . . that?' he said, dropping the words methodically into the silence.

'*Batman*,' I said.

'Bat . . . man,' he said.

'Yes,' I said. And then again, 'I'm sorry.' But I don't think he heard that.

'It is not bat . . . man,' he said, and I could not stop myself, I was trying to explain, I said, 'It *is*.'

'Do not interrupt me,' he said. His voice grew louder and harder. 'Do not contradict me. It is not bat . . . man, whatever that means. I'll tell you what it is. It is drivel. It is the most unutterable garbage I have ever witnessed. Garbage from the land of garbage. I can hardly credit that you have opened your mind to such trash, that you have defiled the brain God gave you with it. But then . . .' – he was gathering himself, I could feel the storm coming – 'but then, to have played this game of deceit, to have lied to me . . .'

'I haven't lied,' I said, but the storm broke and I was muttering into a mighty wind.

'You have lied, Gideon,' he roared, 'and you know it full well. You have betrayed me and you have betrayed God with your creeping and your skulking, your wallowing in that filth. You have taken your sin into a corner to play with, guilt all over your face. You have disgraced this house and you have sullied this day, that is God's day and his alone. How can you have done this under my roof, Gideon? I can hardly bear to look at you. The very sight of you makes me sick.'

Even at this distance I remember all those words. He was so angry, so revolted, that he did indeed turn his head from me, keeping his eye fixed all the time on the television set. I wonder now what he was seeing: perhaps his own reflection in the dead screen, a parody of a ranting minister, or a man in a fable seeing his own son corrupted by the magical box he himself has brought home. To be told by your father that the sight of you offends him is a terrible thing. The contempt in his voice sounded as though it would last for ever. Which it has. Here I am, four decades on, and I can still hear it.

Tears streamed from my eyes, but I wasn't crying, I was too shocked for that. I stood as still as I could, waiting to be struck. He hardly ever hit me: his hands were so big and hard that I took great care to avoid giving him reason to do so. But if he did it was over in seconds, a few heavy, stinging blows on my backside with the flat of his hand or a stick. I could have taken a beating with a stick, but I feared what he might do if he attacked me again with his hands. I stood there on the edge of something unknown, waiting for him to act.

The door opened. My mother appeared, wrapped in her fawn dressing-gown. 'James,' she said. And then, 'Gideon.'

He turned on her furiously. 'What do you want?'

'Your voice woke me,' she said. 'What is going on?'

'Nothing,' he said, 'except that this boy, your son, has defiled this house, the Lord's day and himself. I am dealing with it. Go away!'

'I don't think . . .' she began.

'Get out!'

I expected her to scurry away, but she didn't. She had seen something that I had not, something peculiar perhaps in the blotches on his face or the tremor of his body. Then she did what I had never seen her do before: she reached out a hand to him.

'James,' she said. 'Please calm yourself. You will do yourself an injury.'

'I will do *you* . . . an injury,' he said, and his right arm came up as if to hit her. At that point I too realised that something was far wrong, for though he thought my mother stupid he had never raised a hand to her. His threat sounded empty, like a line in a play delivered by an actor who doesn't understand it. His voice went up at the end, more like a question, and his hand stayed high, quivering where he had raised it.

'Are you all right, James?' my mother said.

'Why?' he said. 'Don't I look all right?' And the next thing he crumpled in a heap on the floor, all six feet of him folding like a collapsible wooden ruler.

I stood there like a statue, or an imbecile, convinced that it was I who had delivered the blow that had felled him.

'Gideon,' my mother said, suddenly efficient as she knelt down beside him. 'Phone for an ambulance. Dial 999. Quickly now.'

My father convulsed and a little pile of yellow vomit appeared on the carpet by his mouth. That was the thing that unshocked me and set me free again. I ran to the telephone.

VIII

The day after I found the Stone was a Sunday. As I made my breakfast I ran over in my head the sermon I would deliver at that morning's service.

Some ministers slave the entire week at their sermons, turning them inside out and worrying over them sentence by sentence, and then deliver something bland and tedious to people who don't care what they say so long as they say it in less than a quarter of an hour. They write these homilies out in full, but until quite recently the written sermon was scorned in Scotland, seen as a kind of soft English aberration, a sign of feeble character and suspect faith. My father preferred to rely on divine inspiration: if God so willed it, holy words would pour from the mouth of his servant. Week after week as a boy I saw this happen – thunder and lightning, showers, gusts of wind and shafts of sunlight all rolled into one thirty-minute word-storm with my father at its centre. It was impressive, and thus I grew up sympathising with the old school. I could have half a dozen potential sermons gathering pace in my head, interweaving and overlapping as they grew; and as Sunday approached one of them would suddenly leap into focus and stand out from the rest. Yes, I would make notes and headings, but once in the pulpit I tended to abandon the prepared structure and let the words take me wherever they were going, and in this I was like my father, except that I put my trust in language rather than in God. Despite my professed preference for facts, evidence and logical argument, I have always found giant leaps of the imagination, which are akin to leaps of faith, exhilarating.

My theme, appropriate to the beginning of January, was to be newness, and my text was from the Book of Revelation, the second-last chapter of the New Testament: 'And I saw a new heaven and a new earth: for the first heaven and the first earth were passed away . . . And God shall wipe away all tears from their eyes; and there shall be no more death, neither sorrow, nor crying, neither shall there be any more pain: for the former things are passed away.' I always made a point of using the King James Bible. The New English Bible had been in use in Monimaskit before my arrival, but I reinstated the Authorised Version despite protests from Peter Macmurray and some of the other elders. They thought the King James too antique, beyond the comprehension of the general populace. I thought the New English unspeakably bland.

'I don't think people who come to church want the language of shopping lists and breakfast TV,' I said. 'They don't want the Word of God to be as mundane as the word of the weather forecaster. They want a Scripture that has poetry in it, and mystery and beauty and splendour.'

'*You* want that,' Macmurray said. 'I think they want the Word of God in a language they understand.'

We had repeated arguments about this in the Session, but I held my ground. My arrogance was astounding. What right had I, who did not believe it anyway, to champion the seventeenth-century version of Holy Scripture like some elitist literary critic? And yet I am proud that I did.

Now, as I stood over the cooker, stirring my porridge, I rehearsed what I would say. 'What is it we want at New Year?' I asked. 'We make resolutions, promise new starts to ourselves and to others. We'll stop smoking, exercise more, give up this bad habit or that, take up a new hobby. "This is the year I'll learn to swim." "This is the year I'll find a more fulfilling job." But what is it we really want? Perhaps the answer lies in that passage from Revelation . . .' I left the porridge to sputter, flicked the kettle switch again, and when it boiled poured water over the coffee granules in my mug. 'No more death, no more sorrow, no more pain! Don't we all long for that? Don't we watch the news every night and long for it? When we say, "This is the year I'll do this, or that," aren't we saying, "This is the year when I'll try to make things better"? Usually we mean for ourselves, but sometimes we mean for others, and in a way we believe that if everybody kept their New Year resolutions, the world would be a better place.'

I took the pan off the gas and transferred the porridge to a bowl. I poured on milk, added brown sugar, began to eat. I thought of my mother, whom I would see later. She'd always made porridge with cheap, tasteless oats and put too much salt in it. My father had covered his with *more* salt, and, until his stroke, had not allowed me to sprinkle mine with sugar. After the stroke, his rule was diminished, and I tipped it on. I went back to the sermon, thought about working in a reference to the Stone. 'As many of you know, I do a lot of running. I was out yesterday. It seemed a good way of getting the old year out of my system, a bit like that tradition of opening the doors and windows of the house, front and back. Blow out the old, let the new air in. Well, I was running in Keldo Woods. And I came across a standing stone. Yes, I did. I know what you're thinking, if you know those woods – there *is* no standing stone in Keldo Woods. But there is, I've seen it. How did it get there? What can it mean? You don't believe me? We live in unbelievable times, days of trials and wonders. Blessed are they that have not seen, and yet have believed. But never mind about that, I'll show you. Come on, let's go.'

Maybe not. I sipped my coffee. The porridge sat rich and warm in my belly. The sermon would look after itself. I cared, but not enough to let it worry me. Of course I would leave the Stone out of it. I'd have to go back and check that it really was there. I didn't want to blow my credibility: it was all I had. Still, I did want to tell someone. I thought again of my mother. I could tell her, without any risk to my credibility or hers.

She'd been in the care home for five years, and was so far gone in her mind that nothing would surprise her, and nothing she repeated would surprise anybody else. I could tell her that Martians had invaded and she'd just smile and nod her head acquiescently in the manner learned through the years of being married to my father. She seldom knew who I was when I visited. She would stare searchingly as if she'd just noticed me and was wondering how I'd got there. I could tell my mother about the Stone, and she wouldn't ridicule me, wouldn't accuse me of fabrication, would just accept, then forget. She might even, in a flash of lucidity, say, 'That kind of thing happens to me all the time,' but I doubted it.

The turn-out for the service was about what I expected for the first Sunday of the year. The church was a third full, a hundred folk or so, most sitting quietly, the usual unhealthy minority coughing or blowing their noses throughout. The sermon went off all right: I felt that surge of excitement about halfway through that told me I was on form, that I had their attention, that the words were firing out of me and hitting a few targets. Heads nodded; smiles, frowns and poker-faces greeted me; my sentences flew beneath the vaulted ceiling and drifted down on to people's ears and through the gratings in the aisles. Good ground and stony ground. Whether they had any effect on the listeners was another matter altogether.

Outside, I shook hands with them all, wishing them a good New Year, receiving their wishes in return. I reflected, as I did nearly every week, that not a single one of those I regarded as my friends – the ones who had me round for dinner, the ones in whose company I could relax, laugh or have serious conversations, the ones who treated me as a normal human being – none of them attended church, except a very few at Christmas. Why was *I* still there? Why was I not, like them, nursing a hangover, reading the fat newspapers, sleeping late, gardening, shopping, walking, watching TV?

Peter Macmurray was inside the doorway collecting hymn books. Our eyes met briefly. He'd had me rumbled for years, and was thinking the same thing: why didn't I just own up and go away? But I wouldn't, I had nowhere else to go. And anyway, with my doubts and my insincerity, wasn't I just the man for the job? Whatever else, I was a man of these times.

I went home and made myself a sandwich and another cup of coffee, then walked over to the Monimaskit Care Home, where I went every Sunday to conduct a short service – a hymn, the Lord's Prayer, a few prayers for anyone sick or dying or recently dead, another hymn, the benediction. The residents had had their lunch, and this was their entertainment before the telly came back on. Fifteen minutes was quite enough for me – though not for a few very devout old ladies who would happily have sung hymns all afternoon, and sometimes did. Then there were the ones who either slept through the proceedings or talked loudly during the prayers. The devout ones suffered in silence or shrilly told them to be quiet. Desiccated chaos; formal religion gone to pot. I almost enjoyed it, it made me feel at home.

I had a few minutes with my mother afterwards in the main dayroom. I saw her twice a week, on Sundays and Wednesdays. There didn't seem much point in going more often. She was well looked after, ate well, slept well, was still pretty mobile. 'She's no bother at all,' Mrs Hodge, the manager, told me. 'Really, she's a delight. She just ticks away like an old clock.' Clocks have no conception of their own mechanism, they do not know what makes them tick, so Mrs Hodge's analogy was a good one. 'Don't you worry,' she said, 'you're a busy man. We know where you are if she needs you.'

But she didn't need me at all. I could do nothing for her, physically, emotionally or spiritually. Whatever state she had reached was how it was going to be till she died. She ticked away and I sat beside her with her hand resting on mine like an artefact, a paper model of a hand. She was humming something to herself. I tried to make out if there was a tune. We had sung 'O God, our help in ages past' but it didn't appear to be that. I waited until she fell silent.

'What was that, Mum?'

'What?'

'What you were singing just then.'

'It's a bird.'

'Oh?'

'Yes, it's in the garden.'

'That's nice.'

'No, it's wet. We'll not go out today.'

'It's a lovely day, Mum. It's not raining.'

'It's in the garden.'

She hummed again. I wondered which garden she meant, the home's, or the manse's – she lived with me here for nine months before she became so confused that I could not leave her alone – or our old garden at Ochtermill. When she stopped humming, I said, 'I went for a long run in the woods yesterday.'

'Always running,' she said. 'Always running.'

'Yes,' I said, 'that's right, I am. Do you know what I found?'

She said nothing.

'I found a stone,' I said. 'A great big standing stone that wasn't there before.'

'Not much good in that,' she said. 'Leave it alone. Come away from that. It's dirty.'

'No,' I said, 'it's all right. It's strange, though, don't you think?'

'It's a bird,' she said. 'It's in the garden.' The humming started again.

Betty, one of the staff, was near by. 'You'll get a cup of tea soon, Agnes,' she said loudly. 'Would you like a cup, Mr Mack?'

'No, thanks,' I said. 'I'll need to get on. Why's she going on about a bird, I wonder?'

'Who knows?' Betty said. 'Better that than a moose, though, eh? Mrs Doig over there's aye seeing a moose, but there's nae mooses here. Sure you'll not have a cup?'

'Thanks, but no,' I said. 'I've things to attend to.'

This was a lie. All I wanted was to shut the manse door on the world. I walked home through the kirkyard, feeling the ice in the gravel of the path crunching under my feet. I felt the graves murmuring behind my back: *apostate, hypocrite, man of straw*. I silently berated them: *fuck off, you flinty old buggers, times have changed*. Stones everywhere: upright ones, leaning ones, flat ones, broken ones, ones you couldn't read the words on. I was getting hassled by stones, they were crowding in on me, and now there was one scowling at me in the woods. I needed some space. I needed some sleep. It was only the 5th of January and I was exhausted.

IX

My father was in hospital for three weeks, then convalesced at home for several more. The stroke was not a severe one, the doctors said, but it was a warning shot across the bows. He would have to take things more easily.

He came home greyer, more distant. Gentler too, in a way that was disturbing: the beast of that Sunday afternoon in the back parlour still prowled behind his eyes, ready to emerge at some unknown, unknowable future moment. Physically, he did make an almost complete recovery. Three months after the stroke he conducted his first service, and by the end of the year everything was, on the face of it, back to normal. But inside he was changed, there was no question. For a start, he did not order the removal of the television. *Batman* was never mentioned and, as for the actual set itself, from the day of his return from hospital he simply avoided it, even for football. In fact he could hardly look at the thing, on or off, without wincing.

Neither could I, while he was in hospital, but once he was home and I understood that it was going to stay, my guilt wore off, and I began to watch it more and more. He never objected, though he surely knew. He continued to pay the rental and the licence fee, but he stayed in the safety of his study, away from the television itself. Perhaps he was trying to appease the force that had leapt out and floored him.

He was wary of me too. In hospital he'd smiled at me and we shook hands, but if I sat too close to the bed he seemed to shrink away. My mother had told me that it was not my fault, that a stroke might afflict anyone at any time, but I knew he was thinking about it differently, just as I was. I'm sure that, like me, he was trying to work out whether God had struck him down, and if so why he had targeted him and not me. Neither of us could entertain the possibility of my mother being right. When he came home we re-engaged with each other at a polite, passionless distance. I would sometimes catch him looking at me as if he suspected me of being a spy, but he never raised what had happened. I never heard him absolve me from responsibility for his stroke and I never felt obliged to say sorry.

We lived like that for the next few years, as the sixties, which had infiltrated the manse via the TV set, drew to a close. The grown-up world was becoming more sordid just as I was reaching an age when I wanted to be part of it: rock stars died of drug overdoses in miserable motel rooms; their music was waylaid in acrimonious break-ups, traffic-jams, mud and murder. I acquired a transistor radio around 1970 or 1971, determined to catch up on the music I was missing. I heard the disbanded Beatles telling me to let it be and a dead Jim Morrison instructing me, when the music was over, to turn out the lights.

The old public library in Ochtermill had been replaced by a

bigger and better one, but I'd long outgrown the children's section. I persuaded the head librarian to let me have tickets for the adult department. How could she have suspected me of motives that were anything less than pure? I was a son of the manse.

Meanwhile, like some footsore moral policeman, my father continued to make his rounds, but he was increasingly powerless in the face of change. His old anger still boiled up once in a while, but the big things he wanted to oppose were too big, and he was left to rail against trivialities. My mother took some of the flak for his increasing sense of irrelevance; I took some too. We tiptoed around him until he tired even of being angry with us. The manse became a refuge for him from a world which no longer thought as he did; and within the house he had a further place of retreat, his study, where nothing he disapproved of need penetrate. My mother stole through the hall, knocking gently at his door to tell him dinner was served, or to bring him black tea and biscuits on a tray. Apart from going to the Ochtermill shops and to church, the journeys of her life lay almost entirely within the manse and its garden. The pair of them were like ghosts, haunting the present but not part of it; haunting each other too. But then, it wasn't so very different for me. The present was a mere waiting room for the future; *that* was where I would really begin to live.

I feel this now more than ever, though for different reasons. The present has narrowed to a mere sliver of time. All that rests between me and eternity is the sliding of this nib across the page.

X

By 1970 I was at secondary school in Tulloch, the nearest town of any size to Ochtermill. The world was coming to me, and nobody, least of all my damaged, unworldly father, could prevent it. While he was out, or ensconced in his study, I would sit on the floor in the back parlour and sample what the television had to offer. I stayed close to the screen with the sound down low, but not because I was afraid of being caught. It was simply easier, in those days of internal aerials and no remote control, to sit within arm's reach of the set. I saw programmes my parents didn't know existed: plays, sitcoms, game shows, cop shows, cartoons, soap operas, Hollywood movies. Even the news was exciting: watching film footage of the Vietnam War, I found myself silently cheering on the Vietcong. I didn't understand why – gut over reason, perhaps, jungle overthrowing order – but I wanted them to win.

Up until the time of my father's stroke, I'd never questioned his authority. Every week I attended church and heard him praying and singing, reading out lessons and intimations and delivering sermons. Every week my mother sat beside me, gazing up at him with an expression that seemed to betoken both wonder and acceptance. Every week I saw the other familiar faces of the congregation – people who afterwards would smile at me, ruffle my hair, shake my hand – and they too seemed to have no dispute with anything that my father said. How could I *not* have believed? It was all I knew. But after the stroke, all was changed. I could tell that even the older members of the congregation were dubious about this man and his great truths. Did he really *know*? He was less convincing, and they were less convinced. And so, too, was I.

God might move in mysterious ways but, until the stroke, and for a while after it, he was a definite fact of my life. He was watching me all the time. My innermost secrets were known to him. He knew, for example, about my television habit. But did he approve of it, or was it a trap, the open lid of a sewer of temptation? I worried about this, and the felling of my father made me worry about it more. Had God meant to strike me down, and missed? Or was he punishing me more subtly, with contempt rather than blows? I prayed earnestly at night, asking God to tell me what he was doing, and why. What did he want from me? My father had taught me that prayers were seldom answered directly, but by an indication: a pricking of the conscience or an uplifting of the soul – these were what assured you of the nature of God's response. I assumed, from the jaggy and guilt-ridden twinges I was getting, that God was telling me that watching television was bad for me. So before I went to sleep at night, having mulled all this over, I would apologise and promise not to do it again. The next day I would do it again. Even the recurring vision of my father lying crumpled on the floor did not stop me.

Then I wondered why God allowed me to go on sinning in this way if he so disapproved of it. I was twelve years old, having a religious crisis over whether or not I should be watching the Vietnam War and *I Dream of Jeannie* on television. Gradually it came to me that I was being toyed with. Did God set traps for children? I thought less of him for that. I watched the programmes because I found them interesting: I found the *world* interesting. And it dawned on me that it didn't actually matter whether God liked it or not: I was going to go on doing it. The television was a tunnel to the outside, and I was halfway along it already.

I was a Boy Scout at this time, and went to weekly meetings in the Legion Hall. My mother had suggested that I join the Scouts, my father had approved it, and every Wednesday evening I was sent out of the manse for a couple of hours to take my oath of duty to God and the Queen, to participate in so-called 'wide games' of a militaristic nature and to be tested on my proficiency in map-reading, knot-tying and the lighting of fires. I detested this enforced camaraderie and the fact that I was required to be a member of a patrol and engage in teamwork. I knew the other boys quite well, but at Scouts an unbridgeable void opened between us: they actually seemed to enjoy the activities and were better at them than I was. But something else entirely made me decide, after a year and a half of Scouts, that I'd had enough.

On the wall behind where the Scoutmaster usually stood there hung a painting called *The Pathfinder*. A Scout, wearing the pre-First World War uniform, including the broad-brimmed hat that had been dispensed with only a few years earlier, was standing beside a table on which a map was spread out. He had one hand on his hip and was half-turned, as if aware of a presence in the room behind him. The presence, resting a hand on his shoulder, was the ghostly figure of Jesus. Although I didn't know this at the time, copies of this painting hung in Scout halls up and down the country. It was supposed to fill boys with hope and courage. What it filled me with was fear and unease. Was Jesus *haunting* the old-fashioned-looking boy? At the opening and closing ceremonies of meetings, I found my eyes drawn back and back to the painting. It was nothing less than a visual representation of how I thought of the presence of Christ in my own life. Yet when I considered this, I became angry: I didn't *want* that spooky figure hovering behind me and touching me whenever I tried to make a decision. I wanted to be left alone. The following week I prepared myself for what I reckoned would be a difficult tussle with my parents.

'I don't want to go back to the Scouts,' I told my mother. We were in the kitchen, preparing the evening meal. I was trying to win her favour by peeling potatoes while she cooked the mince.

'Oh, why not?' she asked.

I couldn't explain the problem about the picture to her. 'All we do is play games,' I said. 'We don't learn anything, and anything we do learn is useless. Apart from knots, but I know all of those.'

'That's a shame, Gideon. Don't you like playing games?'

'I'm tired of them,' I said.

'You'd better see what your father thinks.'

I'd expected this. She still deferred to him on anything that was not purely household management. I let the silence hang there for a moment.

'Could you tell him? He'll not like it.'

'Now, Gideon, that's not fair.'

'I don't want to bother him. You know, upset him . . .'

'You won't upset him. Speak to him yourself.'

My father at that moment came into the kitchen, carrying an empty cup and saucer.

'Speak to me about what?' he said.

'Gideon wants to give up the Scouts.'

'Oh? Why's that?'

'He says all they do is play games.'

'The boy has a tongue, Agnes. Let him use it.' My father's speech, always clipped and deliberate, had slowed still further since the stroke. It was as if he had to inspect the words one by one before he allowed them out of his mouth.

My mother fell silent. I turned from the sink.

'Well?' he said.

'It's pointless,' I said. 'We just have games between the patrols. We don't achieve anything. I'd rather stay here and read.'

'The exercise is good for you,' my father said.

I'd thought of that. 'I'd rather spend more time cross-country running,' I said.

'Oh, you'd *rather*, would you?'

'Mr Henderson says I could be good,' I said. 'I want to run at least twice a week after school. That'd be more useful than going to Scouts.'

This argument sounded better out loud than I'd anticipated, and it was based, more or less, on truth. My running had attracted some attention from Mr Henderson, the Tulloch High School PE teacher. My father's blue eyes were still bright, and for a moment his gaze was so intense it was as if he was exploring the inside of my head. And then, without warning, the light flickered and dimmed and he breathed out with a sigh.

'Well, it's up to you, Gideon,' he said. 'You shouldn't have your head in a book all the time, and I'm not sure if running all over the countryside achieves very much, but if you think what you do at Scouts has become trivial . . .'

I leapt on the word.

'It has,' I said. 'It's become very trivial.'

Something approaching a smile played on my father's mouth. 'Then I've no objection. Just make sure you don't waste the time that's made available to you.'

'Thank you,' I said, amazed at the ease of it all.

'What are you reading these days anyway?' my father asked. 'You must have gone through all of Scott by now.'

'Dickens,' I said quickly. There was a copy of *Great Expectations* on my bedside table, with a bookmark stuck in the middle. Although I hadn't yet read any Dickens, I was on safe ground because I knew my father, who considered fiction beneath him, hadn't either. 'But also,' I went on, adding what I thought would be the *coup de grâce*, 'I've started reading the Bible – from the beginning.'

I was on safe ground here too, as I knew the first ten chapters of Genesis intimately, but my father wasn't impressed.

'I've never done that,' he said. My mother glanced round from the cooker in surprise. 'Of course,' he went on, 'I have read all the Bible, but not from start to finish. I always thought, if you did it that way, it would become a kind of chore. You'd feel you had to read a chapter every day, the *next* chapter, whether it was the right one to read or not. I'm not going to stop you – I'm pleased that you're not entirely neglecting the Scriptures in favour of Scott and Dickens' – he made them sound like a pair of beatnik poets – 'but don't persist in that scheme if it becomes a chore. Read widely throughout the Bible, but read it with care and reflection, not as if you were trying to complete a running race.'

'I'll bear that in mind,' I said, and my father's faint smile vanished. I had overreached myself, and sounded smug and patronising. Could I, at twelve, have patronised my father, nearly five times my age? Yes, I could. I did. It was easy. After all, I'd also just told him an outright lie.

I was learning fast: it was a very short step from knowing that I would go on doing things under the watchful eye of God, whether he liked them or not and awful though the consequences might be, to not caring what God thought. I had taken *Great Expectations* out of the library as a cover for some much more recent fiction, which I kept discreetly in the bedroom press behind my jumpers. There were some very interesting passages in these modern novels: descriptions that gave me a peculiar spiralling feeling in my stomach, which in turn made me read the words again, which gave me the feeling again. Men kissing women; women removing their clothes; men and women doing astonishing things together; even women doing things together without any men present at all. I read these pages and found that part of the male anatomy which was never mentioned in the manse standing to attention as if it had a mind of its own and wished to see the words too. I wanted to touch it. By some means of which I have no recollection it had been instilled in me that touching it for any reason other than to direct it while urinating was a wicked act. At school everybody called it your willie. In these books it had other names: cock, prick, dick, phallus. I wanted to touch my cock, prick, dick, phallus, but the ghostly Jesus was looking on, shaking his head. But if he knew what I was reading he must have been reading the same material over my shoulder.

I need hardly say that neither of my parents ever breathed a word to me about sex, the so-called 'facts of life'. Meanwhile in Biology at school we hadn't reached animal, let alone human, reproduction. The fiction section of the public library became the basis of my sex education.

Tulloch High School, which served Ochtermill and several other surrounding villages, was new. The town of Tulloch – or Tullie as the locals called it – was big and rough, and I'd already taken some abuse on account of my first name and my background. There were kids of all kinds at Tullie High: their fathers were shopkeepers, factory workers, farmers, salesmen, plumbers, engineers, car mechanics, miners. If there were any other sons of the manse in the school, they were keeping quiet about it. Other ministers sometimes sent their sons to private schools in Edinburgh, but even if my father could have afforded it, no son of his was going to be pampered and protected from the world, not in *that* way. Anyway, Tullie High was a new school, and the authorities were determined to make it shine and had transferred the best teachers from other schools in the area to be its staff. My father was probably right: I would get as good an education at Tullie, if I could survive outside the classroom, as I'd get anywhere.

I'd already grasped the rudiments of self-preservation at primary school by becoming something of a chameleon between classroom, playground and home. English was the only medium of communication permitted in the manse, but this monoglotism would not do further afield. I'd learned, from five to eleven, when to speak formal English, when to switch into a broader Scots, which was what most of the other children spoke, when to show intelligence and enthusiasm in lessons and when to stay quiet. It all depended on whom I needed to impress: my parents, my teachers or my peers. But Tullie High was a very different proposition to Ochtermill Primary, and I was having to adjust my survival skills.

There were boys at school, not much older than I, who professed, some more convincingly than others, to have already done the things my library books described, or at least to know how to do them. The air at break-time was thick with rumour, assertion, denial and curiosity. Meanwhile I was beginning to have confused dreams at night and would wake with the feeling that I'd done something exciting, like gone over a hump-backed bridge on my bike too fast – but better than that, more dangerous but more fun too. I read the library books again and realised that the feeling I got from them was almost the same. I shut the Jesus figure out of my head and read the books and rubbed my penis on the sheet and found I could make the feeling happen that way, my belly would suddenly flip and I'd get a sensation right deep in where my legs met, not in my penis but behind, under, in – a kind of unbearably pleasant ten-second tickle. I apologised to God. The next night I'd do it again. It was the business with the television all over again. Soon I was used to it. Then I stopped apologising.

One night I woke in the middle of one of the dreams and found I'd wet the bed. I thought, it's just a dream, I'm imagining it. But in the morning I was horrified to see that the dream had left a stiff stain on my pyjamas and on the bottom sheet. This happened two or three times. I didn't dare mention it to my mother, but she'd surely notice the sheet. I decided to make some cautious inquiries to see if anybody knew what was wrong with me.

At morning break I mentioned it to Danny Gilfillan. Danny was from Ochtermill too. We hadn't been that friendly at primary school, but we'd formed a temporary alliance: we would stick together at breaks until we felt more confident. Unfortunately another boy from Ochtermill, Michael Fyfe, overheard what I was saying and, howling with glee, made it public information.

'Dae ye no ken whit a wank is? Hey, Gideon Mack canna wank.'

'I can so.'

'He pees the bed.'

'I dinna.'

'Ye jist said ye did.'

'I said ye get this mess on the sheets.'

Others began to join in.

'Can ye no toss yersel aff, Gideon?'

'Use a toss-rag, ya spazmo. A hanky.'

'Is there nae toilet-roll in your hoose?'

'Yer big posh hoose.'

'Naw, they jist tear sheets oot the Bible,' said Michael Fyfe, attempting wit.

'Use yer da's dog-collar,' someone said, to top him.

'Use yer ma's knickers,' said someone else.

The other kids knew how to swear and talk dirty. I had to catch up. I'd had enough of running away or having to defend the purity of the Christian faith by taking blows from bigger boys who saw me as a soft target. I'd even once, on the advice of Jesus Christ, turned the other cheek after I'd been punched. After I was punched again I'd decided that that was the last time I was doing that. Now I thought hard and fast.

'Course I can wank. But I don't need tae. I can dae it jist by thinkin aboot it.'

This stopped them. *They* had to think about that.

'Nae hauns?' This was a boy called Alan Busby. Buzz for short. Buzz was big for his age. He came from a mining village. He said he saw the sixteen-year-old lassie next door taking her clothes off every night. He reckoned she knew he was watching. She paraded around with her tits to the moon and her finger up her fanny. Buzz sat at his bedroom window and pulled his whang till it spat on the glass. Just the way he said it made us fall about laughing. We were jealous, I suppose.

'Nae hauns?' said Buzz. 'That's no possible.'

'Aye it is,' I said. 'It's better actually, but ye've got tae get yer mind tuned intae it. For example, ye can imagine . . .' – I was digging deep into the stuff from the library books now – '. . . imagine a woman daein it tae ye. Suckin yer cock. Till ye go aff in her mooth.'

There was a chorus of horror and envy. For twelve-year-old Scottish boys in 1970, fellatio was about as far-fetched and filthy as you could get.

'Aw man, that's disgustin.'

'She might bite it.'

'Bite it aff!'

'Ye're a dirty bastard, Mack.'

'Dirty Mack!' Buzz shouted and everybody laughed.

'Ye'll go tae hell if yer dad finds oot ye're thinkin that kind o stuff,' said Danny Gilfillan, who seemed about to switch allegiances.

'How's my dad gonnae find oot? It's in my heid, in't it?'

'Well, God'll find oot. He probly kens awready. That's worse.'

'The thing is,' I said – and it was only later that I wondered, with awe at my invention, where all these ideas had come from – 'it's better fae God's point of view if ye dinna touch yersel. It disna count.'

'Disna count how?' somebody asked.

'As sin,' I said. 'It only counts as sin if ye touch yersel.'

I had them now. They thought I must be an authority on sin.

' 'Zat right?' one of them said. He sounded disappointed.

'Ye can rub yersel on the bedclothes, though,' I conceded. 'Jist so long as ye dinna use yer hauns.'

'And then when ye're aboot tae come,' somebody else asked, 'whit dae ye dae then?'

'That's the tricky bit,' I said. 'That's the bit I've no mastered yet. But I'm workin on it.'

I sounded like a technician. Some of them didn't believe me, but others were looking at me with new respect.

Then Buzz stepped forward. 'Ye're a gasbag, Gideon Mack,' he said. 'Ye're full o shite. Ye canna wank withoot yer haun. It's jist stupit. And onywey, there isna a fuckin God.'

A chorus of 'oohs' went round the crowd. That was a challenge I surely couldn't ignore, not with my father being a minister. They circled, expecting a fight, expecting Buzz to give me a hammering.

'How dae ye ken that?' I asked.

'Cause my da says so. My da's a Communist and he says there's nae God, religion's jist somethin the rich invented tae keep the poor fae startin the revolution.'

It's easy to say this more than thirty years later, but I know that I felt it at the time, right as Buzz was speaking: that I was above, outside what was going on, Gideon and Buzz were preparing to fight and I was their witness – but there was no second Buzz floating there with me, no spirit of Buzz anywhere in sight. It was just me outside of Gideon, and I suddenly knew where all this was leading, even if Gideon didn't. It was leading me to say something so outrageous, so far removed from everything I'd ever thought before, that if I was wrong God surely would strike me dead on the spot.

'Maybe yer da's right, Buzz,' I said. 'Maybe there isna a God. *I* dinna ken.'

'So why's yer faither a fuckin minister then?' Buzz said.

'Cause he is,' I said. 'Why's your faither a fuckin miner?'

'Whit's wrang wi being a miner?' Buzz roared.

'Whit's wrang wi being a minister?' I roared back. And I saw myself in my father's pulpit, roaring at my father's congregation: 'Whit's wrang wi being a *fuckin* minister?' The shock and horror on their faces. I knew I should have been concentrating on Buzz but I couldn't drag myself back. In that moment I stopped believing in God.

I was probably within a second of getting hammered when the bell rang for the end of break. The crowd dispersed and the argument went no further. And I was still standing. Buzz hadn't knocked me down because of the bell and God hadn't knocked me down because he wasn't there. I went back into school feeling pretty pleased with myself.

After that, Buzz and I became quite friendly for the next three years, till he left school to go down the pit. I don't know if he stuck with it but if he did he'd have got about twelve years' redundancy when they closed the pit after the miners' strike in the mid-eighties. I wonder where he is now. We learned something from each other that day, and it wasn't about masturbation.

XI

The academic education I received at Tullie High was as thorough as the social one. I excelled at English, was good at History, Geography, French, Latin – still quite a common subject in state schools in the 1970s – and nobody came close to me in Religious Education, but then nobody else cared a button for it. I ran cross-country for the school but had no interest and no skill in team sports. I found my days at school rewarding and refreshing; a welcome release from the tedium of life at home.

In the 1970s my parents retired still further from the world. My mother spent more and more time alone in the back parlour with the television for company; there were no longer any restrictions on what could be watched, and she watched anything and everything with the same apparent indifference. Was she, I wonder now, practising for her last years in the care home?

My father still carried out his duties around the parish, walking in the village (he'd given up the bicycle after the stroke) and, at great peril to himself and other road-users, driving the old Morris Minor when he had to go further afield. But it was obvious that he was presiding over decline. The church buildings were in disrepair; the congregation was, collectively and individually, shrinking and ageing. At home he stayed in his study, supposedly poring over Church papers or pursuing abstruse theological points in the ranks of commentaries and tracts he had accumulated over the years. But once or twice, passing the door and seeing it slightly ajar, I observed the Reverend James Mack apparently asleep in the leather chair by the window; a man in his sixties, tired of living. I was an adolescent, brimming with energy and opinions: I should have despised, deplored or raged at my parents, but I didn't. I simply didn't care about them.

Nevertheless I continued to lead a double or even triple life for most of my teens. It suited me to do so. The fewer people I crossed, the easier life was. At school – outside the classroom – I could be as coarse-mouthed and broad of accent and disrespectful of authority as any of my peers, although I always remained at the edge of the crowd, careful to avoid serious trouble. But in classes I kept my head down and worked. Others, who didn't have my knack of disguise, were mercilessly taunted and assaulted for being good at schoolwork. I studied hard enough to be successful, so that my teachers had no cause for complaint, but my talent for duplicity enabled me also to avoid being the victim of the bullies. Some of my more academically challenged fellow pupils even admired my fraudulence: it was the kind of thing they couldn't get away with, but I could make life easier for them too by helping out with their homework. I was sleekit and cowardly, even though my name was Gideon.

At home, I maintained an air of piety. Although within myself I had abandoned my faith, I continued to go to church and be the dutiful son of the manse. My hair may have grown longer, and I may have slouched in front of the TV watching *Monty Python* – in comparison with which, had he ever seen it, my father would have found *Batman* a beacon of lucidity and common sense – but that was about the extent of my revolutionary activity. I had hypocrisy down to a fine art.

And so, when my father in his systematic, post-stroke slowness began to instruct me for my first Communion, when I was thirteen, I did not refuse to participate, but went through with the whole business. This was a rigorous undertaking. One of my father's jobs was to prepare others for admission to the Kirk, and indeed throughout the year a trickle of young people came to the manse for this purpose. He didn't let them off easily, I am sure, but turned his fierce eyes on them in search of the light of conviction in theirs; and a few abandoned the process under his interrogation. This flushing out of the unworthy he would have reckoned almost as much of a victory as bringing the chosen few safely into the Kirk. But from his own son he required an even greater commitment.

Think of this: the 107 questions and answers of the Westminster Shorter Catechism, in all their Calvinist glory. You would have to go a long way west and north of Ochtermill in the 1970s to find Presbyterians who learned their Shorter Catechism by heart, but

I did. I was no Calvinist, the Church of Scotland had long since paid only lip-service to the tenets of the Westminster Confession of Faith, and even my father, old-fashioned in so many ways, had moved some distance from a rigid interpretation of such ideas as election and justification. Yet he used the Catechism to educate me in the Presbyterian faith; and we worked through the questions and answers much as we'd once worked through the detail of our days over the dinner table, as a kind of exercise in pigeon-holing holy information. We dissected and deciphered the nature of God, the nature of mankind, the nature of sin, the nature of faith, the requirements of the ten commandments, the form of the sacraments and the meaning of the Lord's Prayer. 'What is prayer?' he would ask me, and I, who had given it up months before, would say, 'Prayer is an offering up of our desires to God, for things agreeable to his will, in the name of Christ, with confession of our sins, and thankful acknowledgement of his mercies,' and then we would talk about what that meant, and look at the several texts from the Bible that proved the points. And all the while, the many, many hours that this took, the apostate in me was picking holes in the arguments, but saying nothing, and the voluble hypocrite was mending them. I'll say this: the grounding for the ministry I would later have at New College was less thorough than the one I had from my father in his stoury study. We understood each other better then than perhaps we ever did. I wouldn't say there was warmth between us, but there was something like mutual respect. And yet, though I was there with him, a part of me was keeping its distance.

At the end of that time, I made public profession of my faith, took Communion, and was received as a member into the Church of Scotland. In spite of that long and rigorous induction, I thought lightly of it. It seemed, considering under what roof I was raised, just a small step, almost an insignificant one, beyond where I already was. But I was wrong, for it took me further along the road to where I find myself now.

There is one incident that occurred at this time that I must record. For most of my childhood, I had been discouraged from disturbing the books on the shelves of my father's study – with the exception of the Waverley Novels. But while I was being catechised, we made use of Brown's *Self-Interpreting Bible*, Knox's *History of the Reformation in Scotland* and other great tomes (many of which are on my own shelves now). Inevitably, as I reached for this book or that, others would catch my eye. There were some very boring volumes there, and some very ancient ones, and some that were both boring and ancient. But I would have missed one particular book altogether had it not fallen from the shelf one evening when I pulled out the larger volume beside it. I would not say it had been deliberately hidden, but it was pushed far back on the shelf and its spine was not visible until I accidentally dislodged it. It landed on the desk between my father and me, a slim blue book in a grey dustjacket, about six inches by eight. I picked it up and read the title: *The Secret Commonwealth of Elves, Fauns and Fairies*.* I opened it and saw an inscription in blue ink: *To remind you of better days and other worlds. G.M.*

'What's this?' I asked.

I had never before seen my father with what I can only describe as a sheepish expression on his face.

'That?' he said. 'A piece of silliness from my youth. Put it back, Gideon.'

'Elves, fauns and fairies?' I said, still clutching it. 'What on earth is it?'

'A curiosity,' he said. 'A curious book, written by a curious man. I use the word curious in both its senses.'

He held out his hand and I passed him the volume. He turned it over, opened it and leafed through a few pages, as though he hadn't looked at them in a long time but hadn't forgotten them either. Then he closed it and put it on the desk between us.

'You'll not have heard of Mr Robert Kirk,' he said. 'We will have a diversion for five minutes. He was a man who should be

* Published at Stirling in 1933 by Eneas Mackay. Originally written around 1691 by Robert Kirk, it is doubtful if a printed version of this peculiar work existed before 1815, when an edition of 100 copies, based on a manuscript in the Advocates' Library in Edinburgh, apparently a transcription of the original by the author's son, was produced by Longman & Co. – P.W.

remembered for one thing, but because human beings are fickle and fanciful he is remembered for quite another. He was the minister at Aberfoyle, over in the Trossachs towards Loch Lomond, a very beautiful part of the country. I used to go there sometimes before the war, when I was in Glasgow. Robert Kirk was minister there in the 1680s, an era we have spoken about often, the time of the Covenanters and the persecutions. Kirk was an Episcopalian, though not a bad man for all that. He gathered the old classical Gaelic translations of the Scriptures, which were printed in Gaelic script and hard to read, and modernised them. Most of his parishioners were Gaelic-speaking. It was a skilful and scholarly undertaking, and his Bible was widely used for eighty years and more. It was a great thing he did for the Gaels, to give them the Word of God in a modern form, but it's because he was the author of *this* book that his name has come down to us.'

'I don't understand,' I said.

'He was interested in fairies, Gideon. In his day superstition and religion still walked side by side. People believed that there was a land under the earth, where the fairies lived. Not flittery things like Tinker Bell in *Peter Pan*,' he said, betraying a literary knowledge I hadn't suspected, 'but dwarfish, devilish, thieving folk who could do you great harm. This book is a study of those beings.'

'He believed in them too?' I said.

'Perhaps. As I said, he was a curious man. *We* know it was all nonsense, but things were different then.' He paused, staring at the ceiling, and I had to remind myself that he was speaking of the sixteenth century, not of his own youth. 'Well,' he said, snapping out of his reverie, 'that was Mr Robert Kirk, and that was our diversion. Now, where were we?'

I made a last effort to keep him on the subject. 'Did you buy it?' I asked.

'No,' he said. 'I had better things on which to spend what little money I had. It was sent to me during the war, when I was in France.'

I flipped open the front cover, pointed to the inscription. 'G.M.,' I said. 'My initials.'

'So they are,' he said. 'A coincidence. Somebody I met on one of those jaunts in the Trossachs sent it to me. He thought it would amuse me, bring some light relief. Hence his foolish note. He was a foolish man.'

And yet my father still possessed it. It was an incongruous item in his library – as incongruous as the idea of him going on a 'jaunt' – but then again he very seldom threw anything out.

'May I borrow it?' I asked.

'No,' he said, 'you may not. It is not suitable.' His big hand slid over the slender book and pulled it towards him. I could have kicked myself. The next day, when my father was out, I searched the study shelves for Kirk's book, but he had put it somewhere out of my reach, and I did not see it again for years.

XII

My teachers approached my Higher exams with more visible confidence than I did, but in my heart I knew I would easily pass them. There was no question of me not going to university, but what was I to study? My strongest subjects were English and History, so an arts degree was the obvious choice; but Law was a possibility, and so too was Divinity. Not that I had any intention of becoming a minister; but it would be a natural extension of the training my father had already given my mind, and would not inevitably lead me towards the Church. I didn't care much what I ended up studying. All I really wanted was to get away from Ochtermill and establish some independence. The idea of being a student was all that concerned me; but, knowing that this wouldn't satisfy my father, I decided that, some time in the distant future, I could possibly be a teacher.

The question of *where* to go also had to be addressed. He had studied at Glasgow, but I thought I'd prefer Edinburgh. It was bonnier, older, more compact. Also, it wasn't where my father had been.

He summoned me to his study one evening after we'd eaten.

'Come and see me,' he said, 'when you have finished helping your mother with the dishes.' He himself didn't indulge in that activity. I was almost done when my mother told me to go to him. 'He's been wanting to talk to you about university,' she said. I was surprised she had any idea what my father wanted, but, as I've said, there were evidently times when they conspired together.

He was sitting behind his desk, and as usual it was covered in papers and books. The room had that powdery smell you get in second-hand bookshops where the heating is inadequate and the books are slowly mouldering. I don't think he'd opened the window for years. He was wearing his habitual grey suit with the clerical grey shirt and white collar. His face, as ever, was also grey. If you'd stood him in a mist you would have taken him for a gatepost or the end of a dyke, or you would have missed him altogether.

'Well, Gideon,' he said, 'we must make some kind of decision about you. About what you wish to study, and where. What are your thoughts?'

'I'd like to go to Edinburgh,' I began, but immediately he waved a finger at me.

'Let us start with why you would *go* anywhere,' he said. 'What is it you hope to achieve?' It sounded like the Catechism all over again, though nearly four years had elapsed.

'To get a degree,' I said.

'And then what?'

'I'd like to teach.'

'What would you like to teach?'

'English,' I said. 'Literature.'

'Literature,' he repeated. 'I suppose it is necessary to teach it. You didn't have to be taught to read Walter Scott, but then his books aren't very literary, are they?' There was a twitch about the corners of his mouth which I failed to interpret.

'How do you know?' I said. 'You've never read any Scott.' I saw the twitch become a smile. 'Have you?'

'Enough. Whenever you returned one of those' – he pointed to the twenty-five black cloth spines on the shelf – 'with its pages newly cut, I turned them. Not unintelligent,' he said, 'but harmless.

Harmless now anyway. The damage was all done when he first wrote them.'

'What do you mean?'

'He gave a wrong view of history,' my father said. 'A learned and godly man called Thomas McCrie exposed him when he defamed the Covenanters in *Old Mortality*, but McCrie was a minister and people thought him a humourless spoilsport.' He sniffed, his equivalent of a dry laugh. 'Scott had already turned the heads of too many silly women and romantically minded boys with his kind of history, and the generations that followed believed in it. The Victorians then were like Americans now. They thought the story of the world was theirs, and that it had been written by authors like Scott. It is the great danger of romance: too many people succumb to it, and forget the one true Author. But, as I say, Scott is harmless now.'

This was infuriating. I had waded through millions of Scott's words and he, who had flicked through a few pages, was telling me that I had been taken for a ride. A *harmless* ride at that. It must have shown on my face, for he twisted the knife a little further.

'If it were not so, do you think I would have let you read them?'

'Then you were letting me waste my time,' I said.

'Not at all. You had set yourself a challenge, and I didn't want to interrupt that contest between you and Scott. It helped to make you a very good reader, which is to be commended.'

'But you didn't want me to read the Bible from start to finish.'

'Not if you were doing it as a chore or a contest, no. Scott is ideal for either, but there is no comparison between him and the Bible, Gideon.'

'Well, I've read a lot more than Walter Scott,' I said, thinking of my sex education courtesy of the local library.

'No doubt you have. You've had your head in books most of your life, as I have. Different books, and maybe some of those I have valued are harmless too. Wrong-headed, even. Maybe. In the end there is only the one that matters.' Before I could respond, he went on: 'However, I won't oppose you reading English. But do you really see yourself as a teacher?'

'I think so,' I said. 'I'd have some years to think about it, though, and make sure.'

'That's true,' he said. 'You would have to attain a degree first. Training to be a teacher would come later. As would any other training,' he added. 'Do you never think of following in your father's footsteps?'

It sounded almost as if he were speaking of someone else, not himself. He might have been some village worthy or my guardian – my real father having gone off on an expedition and got lost – telling me it was my duty to go and find him.

I dissembled, as ever.

'Yes, I do. But it's a calling. I don't think I have the commitment.'

'That's a good answer, Gideon. I am not discouraged by it. I thought that too, when I was your age. I doubted whether God really wanted me to do this. Doubt's a better place to start, you know, than certainty.'

'I think,' I said cautiously, 'I need more time. I'm still at the doubting stage. But if I studied English, it wouldn't rule out anything. Even that.'

'Even *this*,' he said, and turned his head slightly as if to remind me of who he was. I looked at him, this grey man in his cavern of slow decay, and it occurred to me that he might not have ended up there by choice, by a deliberate stratagem, but by a series of accidents. I vowed then that I would not do the same, that I would be different. And, if indeed he was there by accident, then different I have been. For I, in time, *chose* to enter the ministry. Though I did not believe, I *chose* to follow after him. Or did I? Perhaps I had no choice. I did it in part, as I thought, to spite him, and yet now, if he can see me, he is having the last laugh. Here I sit in the half-light, in a book-lined study in an empty manse, nearly thirty years on, and I have become him.

XIII

I didn't run on a Sunday. There are many things I've felt I had to apologise for on God's behalf, but Sunday as a day of rest isn't one of them. I wouldn't wish on anyone the Sundays of my childhood, and I have no objection to ferries or newspapers or play-park swings or television on the Sabbath, but I understand where the impulse to ban such things comes from. Sundays for too many people have become noisy, unrestful days. I like quiet Sundays, Sundays of thought and reflection, churchgoing, family lunches for those who have families, long walks, long naps in front of old movies on the box; Sundays without supermarkets and traffic, loud neighbours and trouble in the streets. Sundays without sirens. Even the wicked have to rest, in spite of the proverb, and if they do it gives everybody else a break too.

The Session would certainly have objected to my running on the Sabbath, but I too felt that somehow it wasn't acceptable, whereas walking was. So I couldn't go running in Keldo Woods, and the thought of the Stone up there lay on my mind like a dead weight. I tried to shrug it off but couldn't. Eventually I got in the car and drove down the coast road, parked where the forestry track comes out, and set off for a walk.

It was nearly four o'clock, the light was failing, and there was nobody else around. I found the woods different at walking pace: the paths seemed less well defined, less like passageways fashioned from the bend and surge of my running. Also, when I ran through the woods I usually came in the other direction, from the high road, and now I had to pause occasionally to check I was going the right way. Apart from the odd flaff of bird wings in the branches, everything was still and silent. The gloom crept in about me. I thought of all those ancient stories that had their dark souls located in woods, stories not just from Scotland but from across northern Europe. Once upon a time people had lived in settlements that were little more than clearings in the vast expanse of forest: now it was the forests that existed only in patches – scattered remnants of what they had been – and the old stories had declined too. But there in Keldo Woods on that January afternoon I could feel them stirring, shuffling over twigs and frosty leaves, whispering at me from the shadows.

I came to a fork, swithered for a moment, took the path to the right. After fifty yards it petered out. I retraced my steps, set off along the other path. It went down a slope quite steeply, and I remembered running up it coming the other way. I strode on. The trees thinned out. This was the clearing where I had seen the Stone. It would be over to the left, set back. I peered into the space and made out a dim shape rising from the ground. I moved towards it.

It was very real. I leaned against it, feeling its ponderous stability. The surface was dry and cold. I thought, there's been some kind of repeated error of omission, somehow all the historians and archaeologists have missed this. I thought of my friend Catherine Craigie, the font of all information about Monimaskit's past. She'd written a book about the standing stones of the district and I was pretty sure she didn't mention this one. I had the book in my study, I'd check later. But I knew I didn't need to check. I'd run on this path for years, and there was no stone beside it.

'What are you doing here?' I heard myself ask. 'Somebody put you here. What is it you want?'

I reached my arms around, hugging it, as if that would prompt an answer. I was embarrassed by my own behaviour, but fortunately there was nobody else to see me. An artist had recently arrived in town, an Englishman called William Winnyford, who had a commission from the local council to devise 'an audio-visual experience based on the area's natural and social heritage' and run it in the museum as an exhibition, to mark the 600th anniversary of the town's royal burgh status. I'd met him just once, thought him a young, earnest, pleasant idiot with absolutely no sense of his own idiocy. Stone-hugging was the kind of thing I imagined he did for a living. I stepped back, admonishing myself for my foolishness.

The daylight had all but gone. Stars were coming out, and I was getting very cold. I retreated to the path and hurried back to the car.

The Moffats' house was only half a mile back along the road.

Their gate was open so I swung in and parked by the back door. Light filled the steamed-up kitchen window. I knocked at the door.

I had known John and Elsie for more than a quarter of a century. They looked after me with a kindness that I didn't deserve, dropping in at the manse every few days – separately now, since their lives revolved around young children. John tended to catch me in on his way home, after staying late at the school to get paperwork done. We'd sit and chat over a beer before he went down the road. Elsie visited less often, because of the children, but before she'd had Katie she'd come by on her way to or from the library where she worked. I would sometimes go to theirs for a meal. We'd share a couple of bottles of wine and watch a video. Occasionally I ended up staying the night.

Five years before – nearly six now – when it seemed that they wouldn't have children, Elsie had fallen pregnant. After Katie was born, they'd asked me to be her godfather. It wasn't that they thought she needed God on her side: they wanted me to be part of the family. Baptism wasn't mentioned. This suited me fine. With the Moffats, I wanted to be myself, not the minister.

As I stood stamping my feet at the door, I thought of Katie, four and a half and bright as the stars overhead. Now, *there* was someone I could tell about the Stone! She'd enjoy it, a kind of fairy tale, but then again it would be like telling my mother, not much use to me.

The door opened. 'Gideon,' Elsie said. 'Happy New Year.'

She kissed me on both cheeks, her skin brushing me twice as her mouth retreated. I stored up the sensation.

'Happy New Year,' I said back. I hadn't seen them since I'd come for a meal on Boxing Day.

'Come in quick, it's freezing. John, it's Gideon!' she called, as I followed her through the back lobby into the kitchen.

That she could be so easy at my unexpected appearance was Elsie through and through. There was history between us, and it gnawed at me like a dog, but Elsie continued to be as she'd always been – affectionate, caring, relaxed. No one was ever so giving as Elsie: she gave herself unstintingly to her children, so that her good humour and kindness rubbed off on their own still-forming personalities; to John, who I thought didn't appreciate her as he should; to the snail-slow pensioners and lonely borrowers of romance and crime whom she served in the library; she never seemed to tire of giving. Even as I shrugged off my coat, she was putting the kettle on to boil and asking me if I'd stay to eat. Something that smelt good was simmering away in a pan.

'No, no,' I said, 'I'll not stay long. I was walking in the woods and thought I'd stop by. How's everybody?'

'Ask them yourself,' Elsie said, as the door from the hallway opened and John, carrying two-year-old Claire, came into the room. They were followed by Katie, wearing a purple cloak and waving a wand. 'That's the video over,' John said. 'Hello, Gideon. *The Lion King*,' he explained. 'Third time we've watched it since Christmas. Can't say we're not getting our money's worth.'

We shook hands and exchanged good wishes, and I kissed Claire on the forehead and went down in a crouch to give Katie a hug. 'Happy New Year, sweetheart. How are you doing?'

'I'm fine. I'm going to turn you into a frog,' Katie said. She muttered an incantation and I bounced around on my hunkers croaking until she turned me back into a minister. 'That's a good spell,' I said. 'Where did you learn that?'

'Friend taught me it,' Katie said. She trailed the wand across the back of a chair and looked slyly at me.

'Oh, is Friend a magician then?'

'Sometimes.'

'Could he make me disappear entirely?'

'No!' She frowned at me, giving a passable impression of a frog herself. 'Don't be silly!'

Elsie poured mugs of tea and set a plate loaded with sliced Christmas cake on the table, and told me to sit down. John put Claire on the floor, where she and her sister began to play together, and fetched some glasses and a bottle of Grouse. 'Want one?' he asked Elsie. 'Aye, all right, just a wee one,' she said, 'seeing as it's Gideon.' John joined me at the table.

'Tell Gideon what Friend did yesterday,' John said as he poured out the drams.

Katie glanced up at her father. 'I don't remember,' she said.

'Aye you do,' John said. 'What did Friend do to Bear?'

Katie looked into the distance and shook her head. 'Don't know.'

'Don't be mean,' Elsie said to John, but she was laughing.

'What did Friend do?' I asked Katie. 'I'd really like to know. You can whisper it if you want.'

She came over and craned towards my ear. 'He gave him a haircut,' she said.

'Really?' I said, adopting a low, conspiratorial voice, but the others could hear too. 'Was it a good haircut?'

'Quite good,' Katie said, forgetting to whisper.

'Not very,' John said. 'Bear's gone into hiding till it grows in again.'

'He looks like a prize-fighter,' Elsie said, sitting down. Katie went back to her sister on the floor, and they began taking turns at covering one another up with the purple cloak. 'It's a nightmare, this Friend business,' Elsie went on. 'It's like having another child in the house, but you can't speak to it. Him. I needed to give him a piece of my mind about the haircut, but I had to relay it through Katie. She absolutely insists it was Friend, not her.'

'She'll have taken the message on board too, though,' I said. 'It won't happen again. Will it?'

'No chance,' Elsie said. 'You'd have to take clippers to Bear to get his hair any shorter, at least on one side. I'll need to try and even him up at some point. Well, *slainte*. Here's to a good year.'

The three of us raised our glasses. '*Slainte*,' John and I responded, and we all drank. Elsie put a hand over my hand. 'All right?' For a moment it was as if she and I were alone in the room.

'I'm fine,' I said. She still thought it hurt me: this time of year, the absence of Jenny. Well, it did and it didn't. Sometimes I was amazed at how little it hurt. I looked at her hand on mine. She smiled, but it was a smile of kindness, nothing more. She took her hand away.

'So what else is new?' I asked. When she smiled it was sexy without her meaning it to be. If she had deliberately smiled sexily I'd have felt as gauche and hopeless and tongue-tied as a fourteen-year-old. I hated the way other men watched her in the street or at dinner parties, I hated the way John didn't watch her – as if he'd become bored, blind to her beauty. The way her hair lay in rings against her neck and clustered behind her ear thrilled me. I could have studied the jut of her collarbone under her cable-knit jumper for hours. But when we touched, only I was sick with desire. She cuddled and kissed me, as if trying to make up for Jenny after all that time, but that was all she was doing, making up for Jenny. She was a friend and my best friend's wife, and I was the minister, and these things made her unattainable.

'Not a lot,' John said. 'We had Elsie's mum here at New Year. Apart from that we've just been lazing about, entertaining the masses.' He nodded at the girls. 'And I've been doing a bit of work in between.'

'Not school work?'

'God, no. Writing.'

John wrote stories. He got them published too, in wee magazines and even in the odd anthology. He was trying to write a novel. It had been going on for years. I'd read the stories – they were competent, if a bit dull – but I'd never been invited to read any of the novel. He was pretty phlegmatic about how long it was taking, which made me think it might not be very good. If it was good, would he not feel more urgency to get it published? 'Ach, well,' John would say. 'It'll make someone rich when I'm dead.'

'The novel or a new story?' I asked.

'Novel,' John said.

'Are you making progress?'

'A bit.'

'I don't suppose you ever get to see this opus, do you?' I asked Elsie.

'What, me? No way. Not till it's finished, anyway. I will, one day,' she added, quickly, as if to banish the idea that it never would be.

'I know you authors don't like talking about work in progress,' I said, 'but can you not even tell us what it's about?'

He shook his head. 'Wouldn't know where to start.'

'In one sentence.'

He smiled. 'I can't.'

Elsie made a gesture of hopelessness with her hands. 'You see?' she said.

'How about you?' John asked. 'What have you been up to?'

'Oh, the usual,' I said. 'You know they used to call these holidays the Daft Days, but I think that was a reference to drink and debauchery, not running around daft. I don't have time for debauchery – too much social work to do. But I appreciate the drink,' I said, raising my glass again.

The holidays were a busy time for me. There was the watchnight service on Christmas Eve, then the morning service on Christmas Day itself. After that I always went to the care home and had a drink with the staff and dinner with the residents. Then there were visits to the elderly and poorer kirk members, the organisation of deliveries of extra food and presents to parishioners in need, and various other pastoral duties. Monimaskit is a douce, prosperous-looking place on the surface, but it contains a surprising number of people trying to cope with financial or personal disaster. And then, it being winter, there were usually deaths between Christmas and New Year. I had two funerals to conduct the following Tuesday.

'I always thought it was pretty damned inconsiderate, Jesus being born in the middle of the holidays,' John said. 'Just when a man like you should be putting your feet up.'

'Aye, well,' I said. He always liked to mock my trade. He considered it his duty as an atheist to challenge the absurdity of what I represented.

'Still,' I said, 'I did manage to get a run in on New Year's Day. And again yesterday.'

'Oh? Are you training for another marathon?'

'No, no more marathons. Just keeping the engine ticking over. I was running in the woods. I saw something very odd yesterday.'

'How do you mean, odd?' Elsie said.

'Well, what do you know about the standing stones around here? I mean, where they're located and so on.'

'I know there's twelve of them,' John said, 'but I couldn't tell you exactly where they all are. Miss Craigie's the expert on that kind of thing.'

'Aye, I know. But, for instance, do you know if there's one in the woods up there?'

John shrugged. 'Don't think so, but I could be wrong.'

'We've got her book somewhere, haven't we?' Elsie said. 'That would tell us.'

'I've a copy in the manse,' I said. 'I'm going to check it later. But I know for a fact there isn't one. A stone in Keldo Woods, I mean. But now there is.'

'Now there is what?' John said.

'A standing stone. It wasn't there on the first, but yesterday it was. I saw it when I was running. I've just been back to double-check. It's definitely there.'

'What, where it wasn't before?' Elsie said.

'Exactly.'

John shrugged again. 'How could it be?' he said. 'You must have made a mistake. It must have been there all along.'

'That's what I told myself,' I said. 'But it wasn't.'

'It must have been. You just never spotted it before.'

'That's the obvious solution, I know. And I admit I don't run that particular route all that often, but I'm absolutely positive about this stone. It *looks* like it's been there for ever, but it hasn't.'

John lifted the whisky bottle, tipped it significantly. 'A wee bit too much of this lately?' he asked with a grin.

'I'm not kidding you,' I said.

'Okay,' John said. 'So how did it get there? Somebody must have put it there.'

'Not possible. It's eight feet tall. There must be several more feet of it in the ground. It's stuck solid, and it must weigh at least a ton. You'd need a tractor or a forklift truck or something. There'd be tracks everywhere.'

'What's it like?' Elsie asked.

'He just told you,' John said. He made a little gesture of impatience with one hand. 'It's a standing stone.'

'No, I mean, what's it *like*?' Elsie repeated, and I felt a rush of gratitude towards her. She was trying to picture it. 'It must be, well, weird.'

'It *is* weird. It's spooky, actually. It was just standing there in this clearing in the mist and it felt like it was giving off some kind of power.'

'Bloody hell,' John said. 'You're not going all *Lord of the Rings* on us, are you?'

'No, I'm not,' I said. 'It was more like that big monolith thing at the start of *2001: A Space Odyssey*. If Neolithic apes had come out of the trees and started leaping about in a frenzy it wouldn't have altogether surprised me.'

'Hobbits more like,' John said.

'Bugger off,' I said.

'Language,' Elsie warned, indicating the girls giggling on the floor.

'Well,' said John, 'if nobody put it there, and it hasn't always been there, then the only possible explanation lies somewhere else.'

'Where?' Elsie asked.

'With him – Gideon.'

'In his head, you mean?'

'Aye. Clearly he's delusional.'

'But he says he's not, that it's real.'

'Well, he would, wouldn't he, if he's deluded.'

'Do you feel deluded, Gideon?'

'Nice of you to ask,' I said. 'Actually, I feel great. There's nothing wrong with me.'

'They always say that,' John said, shaking his head sadly. 'The job has finally got to you, Gideon.'

'Look,' I said, 'I'm not making this up. Would you come and have a look at it with me some time, just so you can see what I'm talking about?'

'Well, all right, if you insist,' John said. 'When?'

'Later in the week. I've got two funerals on Tuesday. I need to spend time with the families tomorrow.'

'From what you're saying,' John said, 'this stone's not going anywhere. Give me a call during the week and we'll go for a walk in the woods.' He slipped into a detective drawl for a few seconds. 'See if this preacher guy's story checks out. Meanwhile, how about another dram?'

'No,' I said, 'I'm going to head off. The road'll be getting icy.'

'Stay and eat with us,' Elsie said. 'Stay the night.'

'Thanks,' I said, trotting out the old lie, 'but I need to get back. I've got stuff to do.'

XIV

I went to Edinburgh and became a student in the last four years of the seventies, the fag-end of the post-war consensus, when Scotland was a land of unwashed jeans, rotten beer, heavy industry creaking at the joints and endless arguments about something called devolution, and the United Kingdom as a whole was stumbling towards the tender arms of Margaret Thatcher. In Edinburgh I became friendly with a History student, John Moffat, who came from Monimaskit, a small town on the east coast I knew nothing about; and with him and others I, who had never drunk alcohol, smoked a cigarette or eaten a meal in a restaurant, set about catching up with the life that had been waiting for me. I took to it with astonishing ease: it was like picking up a new mask and putting it on. We sampled the pubs and cafés of Rose Street and the Royal Mile, the student haunts of Greyfriars Market and Better Books, and the sardine-tight parties of Marchmont and the Southside. We arrived at these all-night affairs carrying as our passes bottles of 'vino collapso', the cheapest wine we could find, foul vinegar with which you could have cleaned drains. If we gained entry, the next task was to scrum our way into the heaving throng. The windows would be streaming with condensation, the air thick with tobacco and marijuana smoke, sweat, alcohol fumes and a mist of assorted cheap perfumes. I couldn't stand these parties now, but at the time I reckoned I'd passed on to a higher plane of being.

John, early on in our friendship, had adopted an avuncular concern for my wellbeing. He found it difficult to accept that someone of my background was not only able but happy to misbehave as he did.

'Doesn't it bother you?' he asked me on one of these nights. 'I mean, don't you have pangs of guilt or anything?'

We had teamed up with another History student called Colin, who had taken us to a party in a flat somewhere off Leith Walk, a part of town we didn't know. The atmosphere was wilder than we were used to. There'd already been a fight in the kitchen, a man in a frock was asleep in the bath, a drinking competition requiring participants to climb on each other's shoulders was in progress in the hall, and in the front room, where we were, half a dozen roaring men in beards were circling a very drunk woman and encouraging her to do a striptease. If I was going to have guilt pangs, this was probably the place to have them.

'Why, do you?' I shouted back at John over the racket.

'No,' he said, 'why should I? But you're different.'

'No I'm not, I'm the same,' I said. 'I stopped being guilty years ago. I don't believe the reward for enjoying yourself is eternal hellfire.'

'What?' he shouted.

'I don't believe in hell,' I screamed. 'And I don't believe the reward for not enjoying yourself is a place in a celestial choir. If I'm wrong, well, I'm wrong. I'll have a good-going argument with God about it, though, before he casts me into the pit.'

'Pascal said if the choice is heads God exists, tails he doesn't, you're as well to call heads,' John shouted back. 'If you're right, you hit the jackpot. If you're wrong, you lose nothing. But you're calling tails. That's a risky option for a son of the manse.'

'Same for me as anyone,' I yelled. 'Anyway, there's a flaw in Pascal's strategy. Do you think God would be fooled for a minute if you called heads but you didn't *really* believe in him?'

He shook his head and pointed at his ear to indicate that he couldn't hear properly. I called to Colin, who was standing in a bemused stupor on the other side of John.

'How do you know these guys anyway? Who are they?'

'I don't,' Colin shouted. 'I just met them in the pub. They're

Divinity students. Everybody says they're the worst. They've got to do *everything* they want to do before they graduate. After that they have to be good for the rest of their lives.'

I could see the logic of their position. I studied through the week, but the weekends were what being a student was for. That first term I only went home to Ochtermill once, and after that I didn't go at all. There, I would have been obliged to eat my mother's tedious meals and go to church to watch my father chiding his ever-diminishing flock. I wouldn't have had even a sniff at a drink. In Edinburgh, I could spend Sunday mornings in bed if I wanted, go to the pictures in the afternoon, go to the student union in the evening. Nobody – not my father, not ghostly Jesus, nobody – was looking over my shoulder.

I, who had never experienced a kiss that didn't take place on the page of a novel, lost my virginity in freshers' week, in a clumsy grapple with a girl whose name, I'm ashamed to say, I cannot now remember. I decided that this didn't count and set out to lose it several more times during the rest of that year. Each time the sense of disappointment grew. I suppose the girls I slept with woke up disappointed too, because any post-coital relationship always fizzled out after a week, or a day, or an hour. John Moffat's sex life was equally sporadic, but a desperate anxiety not to miss the next opportunity kept us turning up to every party we heard of. Sometimes we went to three or four in one night.

But we didn't meet Elsie and Jenny at any of those parties. We met them in a café on Forrest Road one Saturday at the start of our second year. It was one o'clock, the place was busy, and the only spare seats were at a table already occupied by a dark-haired girl, our sort of age, in a red polo-neck sweater, who was reading a book with an empty cup in front of her. A copy of the *Guardian* was folded on the table under her elbow.

'Anybody sitting here?' John asked.

She hardly glanced up. 'Go ahead,' she said.

The waitress came over and we ordered bacon-and-egg rolls and mugs of tea. The waitress looked about twenty too; she was tall and shapely with short blonde hair and an open, smiling face. When she'd written the order down on her note-pad she said, 'Do you want another coffee, Jenny?'

'That'd be great, thanks,' the girl in the red polo-neck said. This time she looked up properly to smile at the waitress, and I saw her big brown eyes beneath a mass of black curly hair. They were attractive, but so too were the retreating buttocks of the waitress. I turned back to the girl's eyes, and she caught me and held my stare for a second, then went back to her book. I clocked it: *The Big Sleep* by Raymond Chandler, not an item on any of my course reading lists.

'Sorry to bother you,' John said, 'but could I get a borrow of your paper? If you don't mind.'

'Go ahead,' she said again, in the same careless way. She had a very soft voice, an English accent.

'Thanks,' he said. He picked up the paper, turned to the sports pages and started reading the previews of that day's football. John was into football, knew infinitely more about it than me, but he later confessed that he only asked for the paper in order to speak to her. So there we were, me staring after the waitress's backside, John eyeing up the girl with the *Guardian*. Strange how things work out.

The hot drinks arrived first. John did a complicated set of signals with his finger, pointing at the newspaper and then the coffee, and said to the waitress, 'Just put it on our tab, will you?'

'No, no, it's all right,' the girl protested.

'Just the second one,' John said, making an attempt at an easy laugh which came out as a squeak. He was trying to be magnanimous and hold on to his pennies at the same time. 'Fair's fair,' he said. 'Jenny, is it?'

The girl nodded, embarrassed. The waitress raised one eyebrow, and a swift look passed between them.

'She's not paying for it anyway,' the waitress said. She bent down nearer to John. 'But don't tell the boss.'

John looked disappointed. 'Oh,' he said.

'Oh, what a shame,' the waitress mocked, but her tone was friendly, motherly almost. 'Pay for it if you want. If it'll make you feel better.'

'No, no,' John said quickly. 'Eh, what do you mean anyway, *make me feel better*? Do I look that bad?'

'As a matter of fact you look terrible,' she said. 'Heavy night last night, was it?'

'How about leaving the teas off the bill as well?' I said. I liked her style and thought I could be equally arch.

She looked at me dismissively. 'Chancer,' she said. This pleased me greatly: I'd never been called a chancer before. I tried to make something of it.

'That's a fine thing to call your customers,' I said.

'Och, wheesht,' she said, 'your patter's rotten.' She turned back to John. 'And anyway, what time is this to be having your breakfast?'

'How do you know it's our breakfast?' John said.

'Because I do,' she said. 'I'll just away and fetch it.'

Her name was Alison Crichton, but everybody called her Elsie. Her friend was Jenny Watson. Jenny was waiting for Elsie to finish her shift so they could go shopping on Princes Street. Elsie worked in the café every Saturday from eight till two, and the rest of the week she was doing a course in librarianship at Napier College. Jenny was doing a secretarial course there, but she didn't seem to care about it very much. Her family – her mother, father and a younger sister – had moved from the south of England when she was thirteen, and she lived with them out at Blackhall, off the Queensferry Road. Elsie was in a flat in Canonmills, and Jenny often stayed with her at weekends. We established all this information over our late breakfast, talking mostly to Jenny and occasionally to Elsie when she passed by, and by two o'clock all three of us were waiting for Elsie's shift to end so we could take them for a drink before they went shopping.

It developed from there. We used to meet at the café and spend Saturday afternoons wandering around the boutiques on Cockburn Street, where you could get a ten per cent discount if you showed your matriculation card. Then we'd walk through Princes Street Gardens or explore the Old Town, stopping for a drink in old-fashioned bars where hard-faced men eyed us suspiciously over their whiskies and fags. These men merely tolerated John and me, but they always liked the lassies. Sometimes we'd split up and arrange to meet later. If any of us had heard of a party to go to, we'd share the information and meet there. When we did, it was as if we hadn't seen each other for weeks.

Elsie was the more outgoing, warm, carefree one. She could light up any room with her friendliness. She was practical too, a good cook, a swift and efficient worker whatever the task: always on the go, full of energy, never settling. She was training to be a librarian but didn't really have the patience for books. She dipped in and out of them, lost interest, started something else. She preferred conversation to reading.

Jenny was quieter, more pensive. She wasn't as tall as Elsie, she wasn't fat but was rounder, cuddlier. She had the most beautiful, unblemished skin, and thick black hair, which in those days she wore in a perm. Later she let it grow out and it fell naturally around her face with the kind of haphazard grace that a stylist would charge a fortune to create. There was a sleepy comfortableness about her that everybody found endearing. Her quiet, dreamy English voice was very easy on the ear. She read everywhere and all the time – newspapers, books, magazines – and seemed to be able to enter and leave the imagined world of a novel from one minute to the next without any difficulty or irritation. I couldn't imagine her as somebody's secretary. I used to think that she and Elsie had somehow got mixed up, that each should be doing the other's course.

This easy four-way friendship went on for several weeks. Somehow John and I managed not to spoil it by making a wrong move. Like me, John was fed up with unsatisfactory brief encounters: there was something about Elsie and Jenny that made us wait, without either expecting or hoping too much. Nothing happened, and then, in December, Elsie and her flatmates decided to have an early Christmas party before everybody went their separate ways for the holidays.

There'd been a mood in the air for days beforehand, a kind of awkwardness with the girls, a difficulty of communication that was quite new. Early in the evening, before many people had arrived, I found myself alone in the kitchen with Elsie. She was wearing a black dress and looked stunning. When I leaned close to her, I could smell her skin under her perfume.

'What are you going to do about Jenny?' she asked abruptly.

'What am I going to do about her? What do you mean?'

'You know.' She smiled teasingly and touched my arm.

'No, I don't.'

'You do like her?'

'Of course I do. I like you too.'

'Aye, but Jenny. She's lovely.'

'She is,' I said. I felt something slipping from me: Elsie in her beautiful black dress looking at me with great tenderness, slipping away.

'She's waiting for you,' she said. 'She's all yours if you want her.'

I felt a thrill, excitement and disappointment mixed in equal quantities. I didn't want to be set up with Jenny, not by Elsie, but I knew that she was telling the truth. I wondered briefly if she was toying with me. Jenny *was* lovely. And yet . . .

All night I was on the move. I kept my distance from Jenny, and when she wasn't looking I watched her and the men hovering about her. I saw how they wanted her, and how she didn't want them, but I held back in case I'd misinterpreted Elsie's meaning. I didn't want to commit myself – I wanted the possibility of something else.

At one point I found myself standing next to a man I didn't know, whom I'd never seen before in fact. Elsie and Jenny were in a group across the room, talking and laughing. John was with them. I noticed the body language between him and Elsie. Unmistakable. I thought, how have I missed that before? And just then the man beside me spoke.

'Nae chance there, eh?'

I turned to him. He was tall, thin, hollow-cheeked and with a moustache that trailed down either side of his mouth. He could have stepped out of a Western.

'What was that?' I said.

He lifted his beer-can, indicating Elsie. He didn't look at me.

'She's spoken for. Nae chance there. Better going for the other lassie.'

'Eh?' I said. 'What the hell's it got to do with you?'

'I'm just making an observation. If it was me, like. I'd hae the dark-haired lassie. Otherwise I might end up without either of them.'

I was furious and embarrassed that he had been watching me watching the girls. If I'd been drunker I might have hit him. But he looked very tough, and I did not want to be responsible for spoiling the night. I said nothing, knowing that he was right. He drank the dregs from his can and left the room. I never saw him again. Sometimes I wonder if I imagined him.

At the end of the night, when there were just half a dozen folk still standing, and the music was down to the last, slow track on the first side of *Rumours* (it was the age of punk, but that winter it was Fleetwood Mac that was playing at most of the parties I went to), Elsie and John started to dance, and as they danced they started to kiss, and I knew that there was no longer any hope of my being mistaken. Then she took him off to her bedroom and the door closed, and I wondered if I'd blown everything, if Jenny would decide that I'd had my chance and lost it. We stood there awkwardly, Jenny and I and a couple neither of us knew, and the needle clicked on the innermost groove of the record. One of the others moved to take it off.

'Well,' Jenny said, 'looks like my bed may have gone for the night.' She shared Elsie's room when she stayed over. 'Do you feel like some fresh air?'

'Aye, okay,' I said.

'Going to walk me home then?' she said.

We put on our coats and headed out into the cold, clear night, walking past the colonies and through Stockbridge and Comely Bank, holding hands and talking, and not talking, until under a streetlamp on Craigleith Road we stopped and turned to each other and I kissed her.

That kiss went on for a long time. Wonderful though it was, even as it was happening a voice in my head was telling me that it was not what I really wanted but it was the best I could hope for. The voice was that of the moustachioed man at the party and it spoke with great conviction. I did not challenge it.

Afterwards Jenny and I didn't say much. I took her home and we kissed again. I watched her let herself in and then I was faced with the long walk to the halls of residence on the other side of town. It was about four o'clock when I left her, and I didn't get back till nearly six. I can see myself walking even now. The occasional taxi went rattling over the cobbles, there were a few late wanderers, the streetlamps and the stars, but mostly it was just me and Edinburgh.

Walking through a deserted city in the hours before dawn is sobering way beyond the undoing of the effects of alcohol. Everything is familiar, and everything strange. It's as if you are the only survivor of some mysterious calamity which has emptied the place of its population, and yet you know that behind the shuttered and curtained windows people lie sleeping in their tens of thousands, and all their joys and disasters lie sleeping too. It makes you think of your own life, usually suspended at that hour, and how you are passing through it as if in a dream. Reality seems very *un*real. We had only kissed, Jenny and me, we hadn't fondled or seen each other naked or had sex, but we had started something that wasn't going to stop after the weekend. I was dog-tired by the time I got into bed but what I felt more than tiredness was relief. Things had been decided for me. I thought of kissing Jenny and it felt good. If there was disappointment in there I managed to minimise it. It wasn't hard to convince myself that what we had started could be sustained, and that it would be enough.

XV

After that Christmas party, John and Elsie were one item, and Jenny and I were another. As soon as this was established, it seemed as if it was how things had always been going to end up.

I did not love Jenny as I should have: I was not capable of doing so. Walking through Edinburgh that night I should have felt delirious happiness rather than relief. But if there was a raging passion waiting to be released in me I did not let it out. I kept myself clamped down. And Jenny, too, seemed to adapt easily enough to our new life. How deeply did she love me? How do you measure love? It was as if we woke up and found that we'd been together for longer than we could remember. It was – or it seemed – very, very simple.

And yet I made a complicated lie of it. She asked me why I'd blanked her signals, and I said I hadn't even seen them, that because I'd thought she wanted me just as a friend I couldn't have seen them. Had I not fancied Elsie, she wanted to know? No, I said, *she* was the one I wanted to be with; I just hadn't allowed myself to hope I ever could be. I don't know why I said these things, except that it was easier than telling the truth.

To outsiders we must have seemed a pretty boring foursome. The changed relationships didn't seem greatly to reduce the amount of time we spent together as a group. We had other friends, but none with whom we shared so much of ourselves. The next summer we saved up enough money to go on holiday to Greece, the first time I'd ever been abroad, and the fortnight we spent there reinforced our self-sufficiency as a group. We were mutually supportive, we liked our own company, we laughed a lot, we felt secure. What more did we need?

One of Elsie's flatmates moved out that summer and Jenny took the empty room. John and I still had two years of study left, but the girls had finished their courses and found themselves jobs. Elsie worked in a bookshop and Jenny had some incredibly dull job with the local council – I never did understand exactly what it was, nor did I care much. John and I moved out of student halls and into a flat. Jenny and I were sleeping together, of course, and hardly a night went by when I wasn't at hers or she wasn't at mine, and the same was true of John and Elsie. It seemed so exciting and new, and for me it was also rebellious. How feeble that sounds now. Some rebels had Kalashnikovs and revolutionary manifestos; others were into punk rock and anarchy. I had a girlfriend who was on the pill.

I was taken to meet her parents, and that went smoothly enough; I found them boring and insular, but I was, as ever, adept at concealing my true opinions. The trickier introduction was always going to be the one between Jenny and my parents. I put it off for as long as I could, but finally, one cold weekend in November, we took the train to Stirling and then the bus to Ochtermill. My father was by then sixty-six but seemed twenty years older. He'd offered to come to Stirling for us in the rust-eaten Morris Minor, but I'd said we weren't sure which train we'd be on: I couldn't bear the thought of being driven by him. As Jenny and I trudged hand in hand up the brae to the manse, my heart sank a little; a lot in fact, and at least as much for my sake as for hers.

We would have to endure separate, freezing bedrooms, grace at the start and end of every drab meal, no alcohol, and church on Sunday morning before we left – the general threadbare discomfort of my upbringing; all these things Jenny was prepared for. No amount of preparation, however, would make my father any easier to meet for the first time.

He was still entirely grey, except for his hair and collar, which had both turned a yellowish white. His speech had become even more deliberate – not because of the stroke, now long in the past, but as if, in protest against the speed at which everybody else lived, he'd chosen to put the brakes on his own existence (and, by extension, on my mother's). You had to listen carefully for the full-stops in his sentences, otherwise you found yourself interrupting him, your own words sandwiched between two portions of whatever he was saying. I found all this infuriating: it seemed wilful and antiquated and purposeless. Now, in retrospect, it makes more sense. He saw himself tramping up the narrow path to salvation, while in the opposite direction godless humanity rolled down the highway to destruction.

'She seems very nice, Gideon,' my mother said, as I helped her take dishes through to the kitchen after dinner on Saturday night. She'd made a real effort – a chicken casserole followed by apple pie with cream. The cream was thin and had tasted slightly off. My father had taken Jenny through to the drawing room, where, astonishingly, a fire had been lit in her honour. I was nervous about leaving them together for too long.

'Thanks, Mum,' I said. 'She *is* very nice.'

'Your father thinks so as well,' she said, though I couldn't see when they'd had a chance to discuss it. 'Level-headed,' she added. 'And bonnie, too, not that that matters.' Jenny had put on a longish skirt and not too much make-up or jewellery, so as not to alarm them. It appeared to have worked.

We took a tray of tea things into the drawing room. My father had put more coal on the fire than he would usually get through in a week, and the room had actually reached a reasonable temperature. I sat down on the sofa next to Jenny and she took my hand. My father from his armchair spotted this at once but said nothing.

'Your father's been telling me about what you might do after you graduate,' Jenny said.

'Oh?' I said.

'How the Church is still an option,' she said, fixing me with a smile. I had more than once dismissed this possibility in Edinburgh.

'Well,' I said cautiously, 'I suppose it is. We haven't talked about it for quite a while, though, Dad. I still intend to teach.'

'Yes, of course,' he said, as if this were a childish whim of mine, not to be taken too seriously. He set his cup and saucer on the chair arm. 'But, as we said before, one starts best from a position of doubt. You feel you want to be a teacher, but you haven't ruled the Church out. That gives me confidence that you may yet end up in the ministry.'

No doubt as he intended, his presumption made me angry.

'Why?' I said. 'Why do you keep thinking that? I've told you, I'm not cut out to be a minister.'

'Cut out,' my father said, as if he'd never heard the expression before. The way he said it made me think of paper ministers in a chain. 'I thought the same of myself,' he added.

'Gideon has always been headstrong,' my mother said to Jenny. Her hand was trembling, making her cup rattle in the saucer. 'He goes his own way.'

'No I don't,' I said. 'I've always tried to please you.'

'I hope I never taught you to go through life trying to please other people,' my father said.

'"Honour thy father and thy mother,"' I said. 'It's one of the ten commandments, you'll recall.'

'Your wit is beneath you,' he said coolly, and I was stung, because I knew he was right.

'He refused to go to Scouts when he was twelve,' my mother continued, as if oblivious to these exchanges. There was something like pride in her voice. 'He said it was trivial. He's always been a serious boy.'

'I'm nearly twenty-one, Mum,' I said.

'He's like his father,' she said.

'I could wish he were more so,' my father said.

This was intolerable. I felt trapped, sitting there beside Jenny, with my parents batting me back and forth like a ping-pong ball. I decided to throw something of my own into the discussion. It was an idea that Jenny and I had talked about, briefly and indecisively, but which now suddenly became a fully formulated plan in my head.

'I'm thinking of going abroad again this summer,' I announced. 'Jenny too, but she would only be able to come for a couple of weeks. She'd join me over there.'

'Over where?' my father asked. He'd shown no interest in the Greek holiday whatsoever: if one journeyed to other lands it should be to work, to preach the Word, or for some other necessary reason like war, not in order to lie on a beach. As for the sexual adventures that might occur during a fortnight in Greece, my parents must have barred them from their minds.

'America,' I said. 'You can get work in these summer camps they run for kids over there. They pay for your flight and your accommodation, then you get some time at the end to go travelling.'

The American Child: Is He a Monster? The ads were headlined like this, and I had sent off for the information. I didn't fancy working with children much, monstrous or not, but if it got me into the USA and gave me time to hitchhike over to California and back, I thought I could thole it. It was nothing more than a vague idea, but at that moment all I wanted to do was retaliate.

'America,' he said. 'A-mer-i-ca.' He looked sadly at Jenny, as if to say, look what you have landed yourself with, young lady. 'Gideon's weakness is an infatuation with America.'

'*Your* weakness is an infatuation with America,' I retorted. 'Nothing American can ever be any good. Nothing good can ever come from America.'

'Broadly speaking, I would concur with that,' he said.

'Narrowly speaking would be closer to the truth,' I said.

'We seem to have touched a raw nerve,' he said.

My mother's teacup rattled again. Jenny looked my father full in the face.

'You obviously have strong views about this,' she said. 'What is so wrong with America?'

My father didn't usually sit in the drawing room – nobody did – and he didn't fit comfortably into his armchair. He was all angles and jutting limbs, and his cup and saucer threatened to crash at any moment. Now he placed these on a side-table and unfolded himself on to his feet. 'What is so wrong with America,' he repeated, as if it was the title of a lecture. As indeed it was. He stood in front of the fire, blocking the heat, hands clasped behind him, and I could hear the back of one slapping into the palm of the other as he answered Jenny's question.

'The Americans sentimentalise anything they touch,' he said. 'And because they dominate the world, they have done their best to sentimentalise our understanding of it. This will not do. It enfeebles the intellect. It gives the most banal aspects of human existence a spurious significance purportedly on a level with, or surpassing, the great truths of revealed religion.' I glanced at Jenny: her wide eyes were threatening to pop out of her head altogether. 'Stupidity is rife in this world, and its wellspring is the United States of America. This stupidity and this sentimentalism derive from a document which says that humans have an inalienable right to the pursuit of happiness.' He paused, as if to see if there was anybody in the room stupid or sentimental enough to defend the Declaration of Independence. 'They don't. The chief end of mankind is to glorify God.'

'An end and a right are different things,' I said. I don't know why I spoke, it was only going to encourage him.

'Yes, you're correct, but the Americans have obliterated the difference, and so, in turn, infatuated by America, has the rest of the Western world. They have turned the pursuit of happiness into an end in itself. Happiness! What is happiness but the flicker of a struck match in the vast expanse of God's creation? It is nothing. You cannot measure it but by false measures – a well-paid job, a nice house, a new car, a loving spouse.' He held up a finger, as Jenny seemed about to interrupt. 'Wait. All these can be taken from you in an instant. Where is your happiness then? You *cannot* sentimentalise the valley of the shadow of death, but the Americans do their best, and what they fail to sentimentalise they brutalise. How else could Thomas Jefferson have written those words and yet owned slaves? Ever since Jefferson the Americans have blundered on, pursuing happiness, though it may lead to the destruction of the planet, the starvation of millions, though it means war and crime and incalculable waste and misery – they will pursue happiness to the ends of the earth. But they will find only wormwood and gall, because happiness is a false god.'

In the aftermath of this outpouring the only sound came from the fire hissing and cackling behind my father. My mother's mouth hung open in the way it often did in kirk. Jenny looked as though she'd received some terrible news by telegram. Eventually she managed to say, 'That is certainly a very powerful argument. It doesn't hold out much hope for us, does it?'

My father gave her one of his long, unblinking stares. 'There is no hope,' he said, 'without Christ. You are English, Jennifer. Did your parents give you a Christian upbringing?'

'Yes, they did,' she said.

'In the Church of England?'

'Yes.'

'Dad . . .' I said, but he ignored me.

'You've been in Scotland only seven years or so, is that right?'

'That's right.'

'And to what church do you now belong?'

'Dad, this is outrageous,' I said.

'What is?'

'Cross-examining Jenny like this.'

'Nonsense,' he said. 'I want to know. You brought her here so we could meet her, didn't you?'

'I wish we'd stayed in Edinburgh,' I said.

'Well, you didn't. You're in Ochtermill now, and I am the minister of Ochtermill. Is it not perfectly reasonable in the circumstances to ask my son's friend to what church, if any, she belongs?'

'Yes it is,' Jenny said. 'But the answer is, I don't go to church any more. My parents are in the Episcopal Church now. They go to St Mary's Cathedral, but I don't go with them. I'm sorry, but I don't believe it any more.'

'I'm sorry too,' my father said, 'although not surprised. You're young, though. I had doubts when I was young. I came through them.'

I facetiously wondered if he was going to suggest that she enter the ministry too, but said nothing.

'It's more than doubts,' Jenny said, with a great deal more honesty than I'd ever demonstrated. 'I simply don't believe any of it. I don't wish to offend you, Mr Mack, but you did ask.'

'Yes, I did. Well, I am not a monster, despite what Gideon may have told you. I'm not going to throw you out of the house for being truthful. And I hope you will still come to our service tomorrow. You may not think it worthwhile, but I do. There is nothing more terrible than that you lose your faith.'

'Yes, there is,' I said. 'You can lose your humanity. That is far more terrible.'

'Fine words, Gideon,' my father said, 'but they mean nothing. You go to America, and that is what they will tell you there. It won't help you when you have to confront your own immortality.'

Jenny and I glanced at each other, but we'd heard correctly: *im*mortality was the word he had used. I have never forgotten that phrase. Of course it has a resonance now that it did not have then. This is what the last few months have been about, and what the rest of my days will be for: confronting my own immortality.

My father excused himself after this relaxing post-dinner conversation and went off to his study, saying he had to put everything in order for the morning. I thought his retreat cowardly, but was also glad to see the back of him. My mother left us shortly afterwards, and Jenny and I sat on the rug in front of the fire, cuddling, and talked over the evening. She was remarkably calm about everything, but then one of Jenny's qualities was that nothing ever seemed to disturb her.

'So you're going to be a minister,' she said.

'I am not.'

'Your father thinks you are.'

'He can think what he likes.'

'And I agree with him,' she said.

I screwed up my face at her. 'Come on, Jenny, I've no more faith than you have.'

'Oh, you do,' she said. 'You might deny it, but it's in you, deeper than you think. Anyway, I wouldn't mind if you did become a minister.'

'You're not serious?'

'Yes, I am. It would be okay. It might even be fun.'

'Fun?'

She laughed. 'You see, you're shocked. You're just like him.'

I shook my head. 'But you don't believe any of it. And neither do I.'

'So you say. But even if you don't, times have changed. Why do you have to believe in God to be a minister?'

'I expect it's still an essential qualification.'

'In this day and age? Why? A minister's a kind of social worker with an extra qualification in rhetoric. You could do that. You'd be better at it than teaching.'

'Away you go.'

'I mean it. You don't like kids very much. All that stuff about going off to Camp America – you'd hate it.'

'You still have to deal with kids if you're a minister.'

'Yeah, but not all the time, every day, dozens of them.'

'You can't just walk into the Church of Scotland and say, I want to be a minister, give me a job. They check you out. They'd soon see through me.'

'I very much doubt it. You're one of them already. You could convince them. They need young blood like yours.'

'Aye, but why? What would be the point?'

'A job for life,' she said. 'Not many of them around these days. A roof over your head. The chance to help people, make their lives better. You wouldn't have to convert them, all you'd have to do is be a decent human being. All right, not a great income, but not poverty either. It could be an interesting life. You could *make* it interesting. *We* could make it interesting.'

'I can't see you as a minister's wife,' I said.

'Is that a proposal or a rejection?'

'Neither,' I said. 'But can you?'

'If I can see you as a minister, I can see me as your wife,' she said. 'But we wouldn't be like your parents. We'd be ourselves. If we ended up in a house like this we'd do something with it, make it our own. I'm fantasising,' she said, 'but what else are you going to do?'

'Teach,' I said.

She looked at me. I said it again, to show I was sincere. 'Teach.'

'Yeah,' she said. 'I know. That's what you've always said.'

'Don't you think I mean it?'

'You know yourself you don't mean it,' she said. 'It's in your eyes. You don't want to teach, you never have.'

'That's good, coming from you. Rushing off to that office every day with such enthusiasm.'

'That's how I know,' she said.

'I do want to teach,' I said weakly.

'Okay,' she said. 'Let's wait and see what happens.'

We kissed for a while. I was thinking of having to go to our separate rooms, and whether I would dare to creak across the landing and into her bed. I pulled away.

'I'm sorry, Jenny, putting you through this. Do you want to just head off first thing?'

'No,' she said. 'I want to see him in action in church. Anyway, we said we'd stay. It wouldn't be fair on your mother. We'll go after lunch, like we said.'

'What do you make of her?' I asked.

'She's nice,' she said. 'But she's sad.'

'Yes,' I said, 'she is, isn't she? He did that to her.'

'No,' she said, 'I don't think so. I think she's always been sad.'

XVI

I didn't slip into Jenny's bed that night, I didn't offend my parents by missing church in the morning and I didn't go to America the following summer. Instead I stayed in Edinburgh and got a job in the city's tourist accommodation office matching visitors and their budgets to hotels, guest houses and B&Bs. I didn't realise it at the time, but from the moment Jenny and I walked down the brae to the bus-stop I was moving towards a life in the Kirk.

It was a year of change, and not just for me. On 1st March 1979, a referendum had been held, asking the Scots whether they wanted a devolved Assembly in Edinburgh. The result was a resounding *maybe*, with roughly one-third of the population voting for devolution, slightly fewer against, and the rest, the biggest proportion, abstaining. I confess that on the day of the vote I managed to represent all three of these positions.

Jenny, John, Elsie and I had discussed the subject at length. John was the most nationalistic among us, and although what was on offer fell far short of complete Scottish independence, he thought it was a step in the right direction. We all felt, Jenny included, that the country needed to be better governed, that something was preferable to nothing, and that an inadequate Assembly could be built on and strengthened, so on the day we all went out and voted in favour.

At least, we said we did, and I've no reason to doubt the others. It was the first time any of us had been able to vote for anything more than a local councillor or a student representative, so there was at least that excitement on a day that seemed strangely muted. But at the last minute, standing in the polling-booth, I felt a sudden queasiness in my stomach. What was I actually voting for? Would it really be an improvement? And what if we were starting something we couldn't stop? My left hand hung in the air, clutching the stubby pencil. I thought, I'm not ready for this. But I could not vote against. I panicked for a second, before putting one X on the paper in the 'yes' box and another in the 'no' box, thus invalidating my vote. Then I fled from the booth.

A clause had been inserted into the devolution legislation which required at least forty per cent of the registered electorate to vote in favour in order to bring the Assembly into being, and the 'yes' vote fell some way short of that hurdle. We were furious: Scotland had been cheated. I was as vociferous in my outrage as the others. I admitted nothing, but I almost came to believe that I'd been duped into spoiling the ballot paper against my will.

This depressing debacle was followed a few weeks later by a General Election which saw the Labour government swept from office and the arrival at 10 Downing Street of Mrs Margaret Thatcher. At least I didn't vote for her. But I was on safer ground by then – it was clear that the Tories were going to win without my help. Meanwhile I continued on the road to the Kirk, and perhaps my moment of humiliating self-denial in the polling-booth made it easier to contemplate that future. If I could be so false-faced when it came to a vote on the future of my country, why should the fact that I didn't believe in God debar me from the ministry? Not only might faith be unnecessary in a modern minister, it might even not be desirable. There was so much talk about how churches needed to connect with people who had lost their faith or never had any: perhaps what the Kirk needed was an influx of faithless ministers. And if faith *was* essential, I would find out. I would *be* found out. It was in this frame of mind that, midway through my fourth and final undergraduate year, I began to explore the option of staying on at Edinburgh to study Divinity.

Because of my first degree, I would be able to complete the Bachelor of Divinity with Honours course in three years. This was the usual academic training for anyone wanting to be a minister in the Church of Scotland. The question, though, was how I would maintain myself as a student for three more years. I investigated further, studying the prospectus for the Faculty of Divinity and looking up various directories and manuals at the library in New College. I found an obscure fund, established in the 1860s, the George Mylne Foundation,* which existed solely to provide financial support for the sons of ministers of the Kirk who were themselves training for the ministry. The trustees of this fund were named as a small firm of solicitors in Greenock, and I duly wrote to them for further details.

I sensed, from the slightly surprised tone of the letter I received in response, and from the rust on the staple holding the application form together, that mine was the first such request for some time. The conditions were stringent – the father of the applicant had, for some undisclosed reason, to be more than forty and less than seventy years old at the commencement of the training, the son had to be an only child, born and wholly educated in Scotland, and there were various other strange clauses of inclusion and exclusion the rationale for which eluded me – but I read through them, ticking them off as I went, and found that I was a perfect candidate. Indeed I suspected I might be almost the *only* person in the country eligible to apply for a George Mylne Foundation bursary. There was even a codicil which stated that, should the recipient bear the same initials as the founder, he would be entitled to an additional sum representing five per cent of the award. As the bursary was worth £3,000 per annum, being named Gideon Mack would earn me a further £150. Bizarre though this seems, it was true, and I have since learned that such oddly constructed bequests and funds exist the world over, each with their own idiosyncratic requirements which must be met before anyone can benefit from them.

I did not discuss my plans with anyone except Jenny. We plotted my new life – our new life – in secret, keeping it hidden even from John and Elsie, as if it was something to be ashamed of. In truth, I was ashamed, but I was also excited. That I might actually become what my father was, be so like him on the surface yet so different

* Despite extensive research, I have been unable to find any record of this fund, nor indeed any reference to or information on its founder. – P.W.

beneath it, appealed to me like a smutty joke. It seemed a kind of revenge.

It was at this time that I started running again, for the first time since I was about seventeen. At school I had run in cross-country competitions against other schools, and I had joined a club in Stirling and gone running with men twice my age along the roads and through the fields, woods, farms and industry of much of central Scotland. But during my first three years at Edinburgh I took virtually no exercise at all. Now, as life with Jenny became more routine and settled, I felt the urge once more. I didn't want to compete, I just wanted to run. I slipped back into it without any difficulty, finding routes along cycle tracks, canal paths and old railway lines that liberated me from everything but myself. Within a week I was managing five-mile runs. After a month I was running ten, twelve, fifteen miles, three times a week. And while I ran I thought about being a teacher, and not being a teacher, and I thought about being a minister. *Minister, minister, minister, minister.* The word ran round in my head like a locomotive. I would be able to do it with my eyes shut, I was tailor-made for it, and there was a bursary with my initials on it waiting for me. A sign from God? No, I did not think so. But I knew there was a glut of teachers of History, English and the other arts. The education authorities wanted teachers of Maths and Science, not of literature. The Kirk, on the other hand, was desperate for people to become the next generation of its flockmasters.

I made an appointment to see the Dean of the Faculty of Divinity. My father's name was known to him, but it took a little effort to persuade him that I was James Mack's son, not his grandson. After half an hour the Dean stepped out of his office and returned a few minutes later with a colleague. Coffee arrived. I engaged them with my intelligence, my understanding of the realities of modern Scotland and the world, and my deep-seated Christian convictions. I was quietly evangelical, moderately and modestly political; my heart was Christ's but my feet were on the ground. I was just the kind of young man – *of* the Kirk but not blind to its problems and the challenges it faced – they were looking for. We shook hands, and I left New College with their enthusiastic farewells ringing in my ears.

The next day I applied to study Divinity, and the day after that I sent off my application to the George Mylne Foundation.

XVII

My father's second and fatal stroke occurred in June, on the day of my last exam, which meant that I didn't get the message from my mother until I came in, very drunk, that evening. It was too late to go home even if I'd been in a fit state, but the next morning, with a sore head and an upset stomach, I took the train to Stirling and met my mother at the infirmary there.

She had found my father lying at the bottom of the stairs in the middle of the afternoon. His head was badly bruised and cut where it had collided with the banister's cast-iron newels. He couldn't tell us what had happened, for he had quite lost the power of speech. We sat on either side of his bed, almost as mute as he was. The ward was hot; I was sweating out the alcohol of the night before. I probably didn't look much healthier than my father.

His greyness had drained away completely, and he looked shrunken and dry and horribly white apart from the stormy bruise on his forehead and the crusty blackness of the wound. Various tubes and wires were attached to him, and he was on a drip. His mouth was slightly open and crooked, and his breath came in short rasps that sounded like somebody inexpertly sawing logs in the distance. His head didn't move, and although his eyes were open they didn't seem to see anything. They were still blue, but had finally lost their brightness. I found myself counting the white hairs sticking out of the top of his pyjama jacket. I'd never seen his bare chest before, had had no idea if it was hairy or smooth. The hairs didn't seem real. My flesh was his flesh, yet I felt no connection between us.

My mother kept on her wool coat in spite of the heat. She'd had that coat for years but now seemed too small for it. Her neck stuck out from the collar like a tortoise's. Like my father she had shrunk. But I noticed also that the collar was shiny with wear and dirt, and that the hem, dragging on the floor, was frayed. She looked not just tired and worried, but poor.

There was a constant background muttering of visitors at other bedsides, the scraping of chair legs on the floor, and somewhere out of sight a door banged loudly and often. My father's breathing got under my skin like an itch. I needed to speak, to scratch it out.

'I've not had time to tell you,' I said. 'I've been accepted to study Divinity next year at the University.'

My mother frowned. 'But you've only just finished,' she said. 'You've just sat your exams.'

'I'm going back to do another degree,' I said. 'I'm going to study for the ministry, Mum.'

She stared at me. I could not read what was in the stare, whether she was pleased or horrified or simply couldn't comprehend my news. Her head turned from me to the slumped body of my father.

'Tell him,' she said. There was an urgency in her voice, a ferocity even. 'Tell *him*. I don't know if he'll hear you, but if he can hear anything he'll hear that.'

I leaned over the bed until my face was just a few inches from his. I tried to focus on the glimmer of light in his eyes, as if I could get the words in that way.

'Dad,' I said, 'you were right all along. I'm going to follow in your footsteps. I'm going to be a minister in the Kirk.'

His breath rasped in and out at me, curiously odourless. Nothing. Nothing in his eyes, nothing from his mouth. I sat back again.

'I don't think I got through,' I said.

My mother exhaled, something between a sigh and a laugh, and her shoulders sagged as if she had let out a lifetime of wondering the same thing.

'I wouldn't be so sure,' she said.

He died the next day without – I was going to write 'without regaining consciousness' but perhaps 'without becoming unconscious' is more accurate. His eyes stayed open all the time, but I could only detect in them a fleeting movement, as if someone was roaming the empty rooms of his mind, someone whose presence at the windows I was forever just missing. When the breathing stopped, and then the pulse, and the doctors and nurses began to switch things off, my mother patted the great veiny hand at the end of the arm on her side of the bed, and said, 'Good night, James. God bless you and keep you. Amen.' Then she turned to me. 'So you're taking your father's place, Gideon. Will we go and get a cup of tea?'

At the funeral she was quiet and reserved, buttoned up for those inhabitants of Ochtermill who attended the funeral. My father was only sixty-eight when he died but latterly he had looked older even than the octogenarians who came to pay their respects. A good number of elderly parishioners gathered like a circle of crows round the grave as we lowered him in on a hot June afternoon, peering over each other's shoulders as if curious to see how far down their ex-minister would go. Afterwards they were served tea and sandwiches in the church hall, where I had to endure many questions about my future – questions to which I gave vague, evasive answers – and then Jenny and I took my mother back to the manse.

We sat round the kitchen table, drinking more tea. I realised that my mother, though she knew many people to nod and say hello to, did not have a close friend in the world. Jenny fluttered about like a butterfly in a box made for a moth, finding biscuits and spoons and plates, and I tried to imagine her as the minister's wife, my wife, in a manse of our own. My mother sat with an elbow on the table, and her head resting on her hand.

'Are you all right, Mum?' I asked.

'Yes, Gideon, I'm all right. I just have to get used to it, that's all.'

'It'll be hard,' Jenny said.

'Oh, I don't think so,' my mother said. 'It won't make much of a difference to me.'

And then, for the first time in my presence, her life with James Mack gushed out of her. For the first time, she told me about my father.

'He was a very strong man, Gideon, but he had a great weakness. No, I know what you're thinking, the football. That was about as important to him as sucking a sweetie. His weakness was that he was afraid of himself, his own feelings. Feelings lead you into fallacy, he told me, early on. They get in the way of the purity of thought. I watched that fear for ten years before he asked me to marry him. He'd sit in our house and talk of the Kirk and the troubles of the world, and there was a great passion in him for truth and justice and faith, but his own feelings, well . . . I used to watch his tea getting cold, willing him to drink it, and then when he did his lip curled up as if he didn't really want it anyway. His feelings had gone cold, like that tea. But it wasn't really his fault.

'It was the war that did it to him, I'm sure. I didn't know him before it, but I think he must have been different. He was away the whole time, seven years. Of course most of that time the men were just preparing, waiting. But then the waiting was over, they were over there in France, and I think he saw some terrible things. He didn't talk about it much, but a lot of men were like that when they came back. They couldn't talk about it. They had rooms in their heads where they kept the things they had done and the things they had seen. Your father's room was a cellar. There was a cellar in a town in Germany somewhere, near the Rhine. He only told me about it once, in the middle of the night. He kept it locked up after that.'

'What do you mean?' I asked.

She shook her head. 'Too awful,' she said. 'I don't think he even meant to tell me.' Her mouth clamped up for a minute. Then she went on again.

'Your grandmother thought the world of him, it was embarrassing the way she pushed me forward every Sunday after church to shake his hand, as if I would be a great catch, when in her eyes he was the catch. She thought his coldness made him more of a saint. I'm not saying he wasn't a good man, but he was no saint. He didn't want to be a saint, he was a human being cursed with the sin of Adam, and he didn't want a saint for a wife either. I wonder sometimes why he wanted to get married at all, but he thought it was what he should do, and in a funny way if he got married to me he would never have to worry about his feelings – *those* feelings – again. He wanted someone who would look after the house and be obedient, and that's what he got. I knew he would ask me years before he did, I just had to wait, there was nothing else I could do, there was nothing else I was waiting for, I couldn't have run away even if I'd wanted to. He asked me as he was leaving the house one night. It was March, a cold evening, my mother had gone in but I'd come down to the gate with him and he turned suddenly and took my hand, grabbed it really, a thing he'd never done before, and he asked me, and I said yes.'

'Why?' I said. 'Did you want to get married? Did you love him?'

'It wasn't like that. I was the same as him, I thought it was what I should do. Take myself off my mother's hands. He was the first man to ask me, and I knew he'd be the last, so I said yes. He looked like a frightened rabbit, just for a moment, but that was enough for me. I'm a timid soul, I thought, but I'll never be as frightened as that. We were married in June, and you arrived nine months later. I never saw that face on him again, and do you know something, I never wanted to.'

She picked up her teacup and drank from it with a soft slurp. There was a calmness about her, an absence of nerves, that was new.

'That's what he didn't like about the Americans. They showed their feelings too much. And he feared for you in case your mind wasn't strong enough, in case it would be blown hither and thither by your feelings. He wanted you to succeed, you see. He didn't worry about me, because my mind wasn't good enough in the first place, but he feared for you. And then there was the manse, and being a minister, a respected man, not a wealthy one but not poor either. He had a good childhood in Glasgow, but he saw so many poor people there, children and women and men struggling to survive, and he always thought it was just the width of a wall away, it could come back in a moment. He was a strong man, Gideon, but he was full of fear.'

Then she turned to Jenny. 'Do you remember when you came to stay with us, dear? It's the only time we've met, of course you remember. He told you that happiness was a false god. I saw how that shocked you, it must have been such a hard thing to hear when you were coming to meet us for the first time. But I'm afraid he was telling the truth. Happiness is nothing. It has no substance in itself.'

'Have you been happy, Mum?' I asked. 'Were you happy with Dad?'

'You don't understand what I'm saying, do you?' she said. 'Your father and I were suited. This life isn't about happiness. It simply isn't important.'

I looked at Jenny, and she was looking at me. We gave each other a smile, to reassure ourselves that it wouldn't be like that for us. But some deep and unspeakable part of me sensed that my mother was right.

It turned out that my father must have worried about my mother a little, because he'd been making provision for her for years. He had taken out two insurance policies and had saved enough money to enable her to buy a small flat in the village. Then there was the Kirk's Widows' Fund, which would keep her in reasonable comfort. All this meant there wasn't anything for me, but I considered not having my mother on my hands a generous legacy. In that long speech she made at the kitchen table she was the most articulate I'd ever heard her, as if her mind had been suddenly liberated, but soon after she left the manse I began to notice that her sentences were tripping her up, that she was becoming forgetful, and confused by the simplest things. She found it difficult, almost impossible, to adjust to normality. Within a short time she began to lose her mind.

We helped her to move to the flat, taking the opportunity to replace some of her ancient furniture with new things, and we emptied the manse of my father's presence. I packed several boxes with his theological books – now that I was going to be a minister they had a new relevance – and put them into storage until I had somewhere with space for them. (I took the Waverley Novels back to Edinburgh with me, but I never reread them.) By the end of that summer the Ochtermill congregation had selected its new minister and he and his family were preparing to move in. To an outsider, it must have been as if my father had never existed.

I passed my English exams and was awarded a 2:1, which satisfied the requirements of the Faculty of Divinity. I graduated in July, and soon after that the George Mylne Foundation offered me a bursary. In September Jenny and I got married. I would have waited, and gone through with a church wedding in order to keep her parents and my mother content, but Jenny was adamant that we should get it over with quickly and quietly in a civil ceremony. 'I couldn't face a big wedding,' she said, 'and if we don't control it that's what we'll get. My mum and dad will insist on paying for everything and they'll want a hundred and fifty guests, St Mary's Cathedral, a three-course meal, a cake, a frock, bridesmaids, the works. Do you want all that? I can't stand the thought of all the fuss. And we can use your father's death as an excuse not to have it.'

'They'll say he wouldn't have approved of a registry wedding,' I said.

'What do they know?' she said. 'They never met him. Would he have married us in *his* church, knowing the bride was a fraud? I doubt it. He might actually have respected us for not being hypocrites.'

Jenny's parents were upset at being deprived of the chance to spend thousands of pounds on their daughter's 'big day', but they deferred to our wishes. They were English, middle-class and polite, and I think they were a little afraid of my Presbyterian inheritance and that I might explode into righteous anger at them. And they had another daughter, after all. We were married at the registry office in Victoria Street, with John and Elsie as our witnesses, and afterwards we went to Spain for a week. When we came back, we rented a one-bedroom flat in Gorgie and there we lived for the next three years, frugally but, I suppose, more or less contentedly.

We told John and Elsie about our longer-term plans. John said he'd known something was afoot when I prevaricated about applying for Moray House, the education college, where he was going, but he'd never suspected I was intending to enter the Church.

'I don't get it,' he said. 'You're not religious. You don't believe in any of that stuff.'

'I've changed my mind,' I said. 'Or maybe my mind was always made up, but I was fighting it, kicking against the pricks. Like Saul on the road to Damascus. He was blinded by a light and he heard the voice of God saying, "It is hard for thee to kick against the pricks."'

'Sounds painful for the pricks,' John said. 'So what happened, did you hear the voice of God?'

'Something like that,' I said.

He looked totally unconvinced. I said, 'It's all right, I'm not going to change. I'll still be the same Gideon and I promise I won't try to convert you. Listen,' I said. 'Fuck, bastard, bugger, shite, cunt. See? I won't embarrass you. I won't become some ghastly born-again evangelical praising the Lord and saying hallelujah every five minutes. It's not like that.'

'What is it like then?'

'It's like Pascal,' I said, 'only when you toss the coin and call *heads* you know that's how it's going to land.'

He shook his head. 'What about you, Jenny?' he asked. 'What do you think?'

'It's going to be fine,' she said. 'It's an adventure, really. I'm with him all the way.'

'I still don't understand it,' John said.

'Neither do I,' Elsie said, 'but actually I'm quite impressed, Gideon. I like the idea of someone doing something different and nonconformist.'

'It's hardly nonconformist,' John said, 'being a *meenister*. Especially if your father was one before you.'

'Aye it is,' Elsie said, 'in this day and age. How many other people do you know who are going to be ministers?'

'Elsie, thank you,' Jenny said. 'You're such an optimist.'

'I have to be,' Elsie said, and cocked a thumb at John. 'I'm with him.'

By the end of those three years – years of lengthening dole queues, war in the Falklands, splits in the Labour Party and a second Thatcher election victory – we'd all moved on. John was a teacher working in a fierce inner-city school in Dundee, being made ever more cynical by the hopeless task of instilling some enthusiasm for history into teenagers who cared nothing about the past or, for that matter, the future. Elsie and he were married, and she was working in the Dundee city archives. They'd had a church wedding, the cause of some gentle mockery on my part. As best man, I made a speech notable for its impeccable balance of spiritual uplift and risqué humour. Jenny had left her council job in Edinburgh and was working for a law firm in Charlotte Square, which paid better but was just as boring. And I had graduated as a Bachelor of Divinity, was a licentiate in the Presbytery of Edinburgh, and was looking for a probationary post in one of the city's charges.

I'd been one of the best students of my intake. I'd worked hard, but I'd enjoyed it too, the biblical analysis, the theological arguments, the history of the Christian Church: my brain was stimulated by the greatest story ever told and the greatest philosophical and metaphysical questions ever posed. I believed none of it, but intellectually I had thrived. It was generally assumed that I would soon be an assistant minister, and that at the end of my probationary period I would be ready for my first calling.

XVIII

One evening in the summer of 1988, when I was an assistant minister in Leith, thirty years old and still looking for my first sole charge, I came home to Jenny with the news that I had found the ideal place for us to go. I'd been in Leith for more than four years, much longer than anyone expected, because the minister of my church there had been seriously ill, and I had effectively taken his place. Now he was back, and I wanted my own parish. That day I had learned that the incumbent minister of Monimaskit was retiring at the age of seventy.

'That was going to be *my* news,' Jenny said. 'Elsie's just been on the phone. She said I was to tell you, in case you hadn't heard.'

John and Elsie had been two years in Monimaskit by then. John had had enough of Dundee and had seized the chance to escape when a vacancy came up in his old school's History department. The head of department was a crusty dame of fearsome reputation called Miss Craigie, who had terrified him as a pupil but had also, he said, been the best teacher he'd ever had and the reason he'd studied History at Edinburgh. He was still in awe of her, but reckoned they could work well together. If they did, he anticipated her job coming his way before too long, for she was not in good health. So he went back to his home town, and Elsie found a part-time job at the local library. We'd been going there regularly for months, helping them do up the run-down cottage they were converting, and we liked what we saw of Monimaskit and the surrounding area. I'd even met the retiring minister, Mr Cathcart, who remembered my father – 'Formidable, formidable,' he kept saying – from encounters at the General Assembly. Cathcart had talked about his retirement, and how he planned to go when he reached his threescore years and ten. And so, when the vacancy was announced, I applied and in time was called to preach to the congregation.

What did I preach? Was I safe? Yes and no. I was safe by being unsafe. I didn't think mere safety would win me plaudits. If you opt to spend your Sunday mornings in a church, you want a bit of stimulation in return. This idea, of course, was not original to me. Thousands of ministers have thought the same thing. But it happened that I'd recently finished reading Lewis Grassic Gibbon's *Scots Quair* trilogy. In the second volume Chris Guthrie's new husband Robert Colquohoun, the minister of Kinraddie, is trying for the kirk in the mill town of Segget. On the day he is to preach, Robert is tempted to butter the congregation up, just to get their vote, but decides instead to give them a good-going sermon from the heart, socialism in biblical dress. So he does, and though the Segget folk don't rightly know what he's talking about, he comes top of the leet because they like how he sounds. I took a leaf out of that novel, fancying myself a bit as Robert Colquohoun and Jenny as Chris, and the ploy worked for me too.

Throughout the 1980s a nationwide argument had raged over the retention and development of British nuclear weapons, the presence of nuclear submarines in the Firth of Clyde, the deployment of American Cruise missiles at Greenham Common, and so on. My text was the passage from Psalm 27: 'Though an host should encamp against me, my heart shall not fear: though war should rise against me, in this will I be confident. One thing have I desired of the Lord, that will I seek after; that I may dwell in the house of the Lord all the days of my life, to behold the beauty of the Lord, and to inquire in his temple.' I preached on the utter immorality not just of the so-called first-strike capability, but of the possession of nuclear weapons at all. There were no circumstances, I said, when their use could be justified. The Psalmist was challenging us not to be afraid, not to fear the Soviet host encamped against us. The Russians might be atheists and Communists, but they were as nervous as we were, as trapped by the false logic of nuclear deterrence as we were. It was a fatal error to fix our stare on their fixed stare and see who blinked first. That was why the Psalmist set his mind on God. The Lord's temple was the world he had created, whole and not divided by ideology, the world in which we all lived. Contemplation of the beauty of God, inquiry into his temple, freed our imaginations from the futility of the nuclear stand-off. I didn't, I said, expect everybody to agree with me, but this was where I stood, and these were the things I would say from any pulpit.

I genuinely did hold these views, but Robert Colquohoun, for all that he was a character in a novel, was a man of far greater moral courage than I. The Kirk's General Assembly had passed motions condemning nuclear weapons, and many other churches were speaking out against them, so I wasn't exactly a lone voice in the wilderness. Nevertheless, I don't think the congregation of Monimaskit had heard such a sermon in decades. When I started there was an audible insucking of breath all round the old building, a creaking of pews as folk sat up in them. These were good signs. I had their attention, something the genial, gentle Mr Cathcart probably hadn't had for years.

There were two other candidates for the charge. Both were men in their late fifties whose age, I felt, would count against them, for surely the vacancy committee wouldn't want to go through this process again in just a few years. I was young, and though I might express strong views on great matters, I also showed myself, after the service, to have a sense of humour. A man, a local farmer, accosted me at the door and said, 'I enjoyed your sermon, Mr Mack, but there's a flaw in your argument. The Russians dinna hae meenisters like you preaching against *their* nuclear weapons, and the reason is they've shot them all.' 'Ah, well then,' I said, 'if I get the job, you'll just have to bring your guns to kirk with you and keep the safety catches off.' He roared with laughter, and I knew the story would go round the whole congregation.

It was a pushover. By the beginning of January Jenny and I were installed in the manse, and John and Elsie were helping us to remove the old décor. The Cathcarts had retired to their home town of Kilmarnock, and I wasn't sorry to see them go. I didn't want my predecessor's shadow following me as I went about my business.

Monimaskit is like many towns in this part of Scotland: its centre somewhat run down, its edges pushed out by new housing and industrial estates where half the units are empty and nothing much seems to happen, its traditional shops hit by competition from supermarkets and retail parks in Dundee and Aberdeen, its older people proud of the past but uncertain of the future, its younger ones bored, and envious of anyone who comes from anywhere else. There is a Monimaskit entry in the online *Gazetteer of Scotland** which I downloaded some days ago:

* The *Gazetteer* may be found at www.scotgeog.com. This downloaded page, the legend of the Black Jaws which appears below on pp. 188–95 (evidently photocopied from Menteith's *Relicts and Reminiscences of Old Monimaskit*) and the typed pages of his recorded interview with William Winnyford on pp. 269–97, are the only parts of Gideon Mack's testament not in his own handwriting. – P.W.

MONIMASKIT

A market town and fishing port on the east coast, Monimaskit has been a burgh since 1403. It has associations with William Wallace, who as a boy, according to legend, killed three English soldiers there after disputing with them the ownership of a bannock; and with Sir James 'the Black' Douglas, who destroyed the now vanished castle and its English garrison in 1311. In the 16th, 17th and 18th centuries Monimaskit's modest prosperity was based on the export of wool, skins and fish to the continent, and it was also a market for the surrounding fertile land, particularly after widespread drainage and other agricultural improvements carried out by Sir William Guthrie of Keldo in the 18th century. The North Sea herring boom caused the town to expand rapidly in the early 19th century, and it was subsequently a centre for fish-curing and -processing, although today the fishing industry has all but disappeared, and only a few small vessels operate from the harbour. New industry related to North Sea oil, tourism and food-processing are important sources of employment in the area. The town has a secondary school which also serves the surrounding villages, and two primary schools.

Historic buildings of note in or near the town include Monimaskit Old Kirk (CoS) dating from 1565, Keldo House (16th century, largely reconstructed and enlarged in the 1760s), the Corn Exchange (1860, now the town museum) and the Municipal Buildings (1876).

The area is rich in ancient monuments, including souterrains, hill forts, cup-and-ring marked rocks and, most notably, twelve standing stones, all of which are within a five-mile radius of the town.

Augustus Menteith, the folklorist and mountaineer, was born in Monimaskit in 1853 and after studying at Aberdeen was minister at Myreside before translating to Monimaskit Old Kirk in 1883. He wrote the definitive *History of the Parish of Monimaskit*, published in 1887, and *Relicts and Reminiscences of Old Monimaskit* (1892). He died in a climbing accident in the Alps in 1895.

Four miles west of the town the Keldo Water flows through an impressive geological formation known as the Black Jaws, a narrow chasm with cliffs some one hundred and fifty feet in height.

Population (2001): 4650

National Grid Reference: NO 999578

The Old Kirk* is a five-minute walk from the High Street, but on the other side of the Keldo Water. In the early nineteenth century the town centre was moved from south to north of the river in a grand plan of improvement, leaving the kirk and its more recent, Victorian manse marooned in what is now a quiet residential area. The once bustling harbour a few hundred yards away is used more by pleasure craft than by working boats. At night, especially in winter, you can sit in the manse and hear nothing of the world outside, as if you are deep in the countryside instead of a short stroll from pubs and chip shops, buses and cars, and groups of listless teenagers. After Edinburgh, it felt to Jenny and me as though we had stepped back thirty years.

I worked hard, for there was plenty to do. Cathcart had relied on the congregation renewing itself, and this, as at Ochtermill, was no longer good enough. Like other places up and down the country, Monimaskit was in the throes of change. The economic developments of the 1980s were uprooting many people, sending some in search of new work and bringing others in from outside. I had to reach out to the general populace, but it seemed futile to try to persuade non-churchgoing people to become churchgoers in an increasingly irreligious age. Instead I set out to persuade them that what the church and its minister did might have some relevance to their everyday lives. I was not going to manage this by force-feeding them God, but by doing things which their better instincts approved of. I believed that most people approved of helping those less fortunate than themselves, and it was therefore to charity that I decided to devote my energies.

But I must explain myself more fully. The fact that I did my job under false pretences, that I lived a lie on a daily basis simply by

* Following the Disruption of 1843, the Free Kirk raised funds for and constructed a church north of the river, and the original Church of Scotland building acquired the adjective 'Old' to distinguish it from this upstart. In 1960 the Free or 'New' Kirk, having in the interim become the United Presbyterian Church before closure in 1952, was demolished to make way for public toilets. The Old Kirk, despite now being the only Presbyterian establishment in the town, retains its familiar appellation. – P.W.

donning a clerical collar, that I, who was without faith, took God's name in vain week in and week out by invoking it at Sunday services, christenings, weddings and funerals – none of this meant that I intended to be idle. My time in Leith had taught me that it was possible to be a Christian without involving Christ very much. People with problems generally welcomed any support that was offered, and if they were at first sceptical, fearing perhaps that my help would be conditional on them coming to church or professing religious faith, I soon made it clear that there were no such conditions. I simply did not discuss religion, and if they raised the subject I changed it as soon as possible. If anybody was particularly insistent, I would make an apology for all the mistakes and miseries perpetrated in Christianity's name. The great age of religion had passed, I said, and if there was to be a role for religion in Scotland's future those of us who were the messengers of God would have to earn our right to be taken seriously by showing that we were, first and foremost, human beings.

Even if I'd believed my own argument, I was, theologically speaking, skating on thin ice, which was what earned me the rebukes of folk like Peter Macmurray. There are some, in the Kirk and out of it, who have always been suspicious of skating ministers. Macmurray thought I was undoing the work of 450 years, by opening up that old debate between justification by faith and justification by good works. 'Without faith,' he said once, when the Session was discussing my latest plans for fund-raising for this or that cause, and he felt that too long had gone by without God getting a mention, 'without faith, we are nothing. I think we need to remember that.' 'Faith, hope and charity, Peter,' I replied. 'We need all three, according to Paul. But the greatest of them is charity.' 'Yes,' he said, 'but you know perfectly well it doesn't mean *charity* in Corinthians, not in the way we use that word. That's your Authorised Version again, old-fashioned, misleading. It should really say *love*.' 'I don't think we need worry about the semantics too much,' I replied. 'Charity, love, what difference does it make what we call it?' 'What I'm saying,' Macmurray insisted, 'is that charity for the sake of charity is not enough. It must come from faith.' 'It does,' I lied, quietly and firmly. Others in the room looked embarrassed at the implied criticism of their minister's motives. My cheating heart did not miss a beat. Macmurray had no option but to drop the argument, but I could see that he saw through me, and that he was my enemy.

Fortunately Macmurray was only an elder. Had he been, say, Session Clerk, life would have been intolerable for both of us. The Clerk was a man then in his mid-sixties, John Gless. Quiet but determined, his first loyalty was always to Monimaskit Old Kirk, and he accepted me as his minister on the basis that so long as I was working in the Old Kirk's interest he would stand by me. And he did, until very recently. A minister cannot operate without a good Session Clerk, and John Gless was, and remains, an excellent one. He is now eighty, and still in post: an onerous task, as he is also Treasurer, but he does not want to relinquish his role and nobody else appears to want to take it from him.

There were only twelve elders at the time of my induction, all of them men, even though women have had the right to be elders since 1966. The Session needed new blood, and I made it a priority to persuade several members of the congregation to become elders. In particular, I sought out younger candidates, especially women – people I believed would be willing to change the old ways of doing things. Within a couple of years the eldership was up to twenty-five, and included ten women. Most of these already knew each other: one, Nancy Croy, was an English teacher at Monimaskit Academy, who taught the children of some of the others and ran a reading group in the library to which a couple more belonged. Once I had Nancy on board, the others followed easily. The Session became livelier, lighter of mood and much more energised. The women met in each other's houses and organised events and the division of tasks with consummate ease. Once, when they came up with a scheme for a series of summer barbecues in different parts of the parish, to which every child (and their families) would be invited, I jokingly referred to them as a coven, a term which did not offend them but deeply shocked Macmurray and his allies. I used it quite a lot thereafter. The other new elders were family men who smiled often but said little and were usually content to follow my lead.

I threw myself into raising money for charity, and so did Jenny. She'd made it clear that she would support me in her role as minister's wife, participate in what she felt she could and do nothing to jeopardise my position – 'So long as I don't have to go to church,' she said, 'or join the Women's Guild.' We talked about whether she should attend church at all, and decided, since she had no wish to, that she shouldn't. Coming and going, appearing one week and not the next, would merely get the tongues clacking faster. 'A matter of conscience,' I said. 'We'll call it a matter of conscience, and anybody who wants to make an issue of it can just bugger off.'

We were lucky to be of the generation we were: it would have been unthinkable for my mother not to have attended church. But Jenny stayed away, and very soon the fact that I had an irreligious wife was seen as a quirk of *my* nature. The Macmurray faction disapproved, but that was only to be expected.

Meanwhile Jenny joined with me in getting that first charity campaign off the ground. We talked to the schools, to shopkeepers and publicans, to the Roman Catholic and Episcopalian Churches, to all the local organisations, from the Women's Institute to the local football club, asking them to join with us in putting Monimaskit on the map as one of the most generous places in the land. At first the responses were muted. The other churches were happy to work with us in principle, but in practice they already had their own strategies and ways of doing things. Among the secular groups there was much debate about what causes should be supported, and some resistance based around the fact that they needed to raise money for themselves. I argued that if they ran events – coffee mornings, bring-and-buy sales, dances, fêtes, whatever – with the proceeds being divided between themselves and some other cause, they would widen the appeal, increase the turn-out, raise their own profile, attract more members and, in the long term, make themselves more viable.

I suggested that a number of organisations, including the Old Kirk, agree to fund-raise for one 'outside' cause for a period of six months, then choose another, then another, each time extracting the maximum publicity by pooling our resources. We managed to get eight organisations to sign up for an experimental run in the spring and summer of 1990, with cancer research as our first designated cause. Nobody, I thought, could argue against that. We laid down a plan of action, making sure that activities and events didn't clash or duplicate, and we set ourselves a target figure of £40,000, half of which would go to the selected cancer charity. I told the charity of our plans and they responded enthusiastically, providing publicity material and spreading the word to places we could never have reached. I promised to run in two marathons, London near the start of the six-month period and Moray near the end, to demonstrate the Church's commitment.

The whole thing could have fizzled out for any number of reasons, but it didn't. The target seemed so vast and unattainable – we needed to raise nearly £9 for every man, woman and child in Monimaskit – that everybody pulled the stops out to try to get close to it. We seemed to catch the imagination of people not just in Monimaskit but further afield. I put sponsorship sheets for my marathons in the kirk and took them everywhere I went. It is amazing how two-, three- and five- pound pledges mount up when almost everybody makes one. I became so focused on raising money that other events – poll tax riots in Trafalgar Square, a government minister feeding his five-year-old daughter a hamburger to show that he wasn't afraid of mad cow disease, the Iraqi invasion of Kuwait – almost passed me by. I felt as I did when I went running in the woods: immune to the world and its problems.

I'd never run an official marathon before, although I had covered distances approaching twenty-six miles several times for the pleasure of it. I put in some extra long runs in the weeks leading up to the big London event, but I never had any doubts about not being able to complete the course. I wasn't even that bothered about what time I achieved. Under three and a half hours would be good, I thought, but I didn't want to do too well as I intended to improve at the Moray marathon in Elgin.

I took the train down to London on the Saturday, having arranged for a Reader to take the Old Kirk service in my absence. I should have been prepared for the hordes of competitors milling about at Blackheath for the start – I was designated runner number sixteen thousand and something – but you never really get used to the vastness of such events. Every conceivable size, shape and age of runner was present: there were men in dinner jackets, women in nurses' uniforms, even a man dressed as a carrot. There were a few vicars too, who turned out, when I asked them, not to be vicars. I made a mental note to wear my clerical shirt and collar in future runs. (I did too: it chafed my neck, but it was good publicity.) It rained most of the way, and the first two or three miles were hard work until the crowd thinned out a bit, but after that I settled into a good rhythm, and found myself steadily working my way past other runners. I surprised myself by knocking half an hour off my anticipated time when, tired but exhilarated, I crossed the finishing-line.

I caught the train to Edinburgh at five o'clock and was back at the manse by midnight. Jenny had stayed up for me, although she'd had a bath and was in her dressing-gown. I never saw her looking as happy as she did that night. She was pleased that I'd run the race in a good time and glad that I was home. She'd put a bottle of champagne in the fridge and she cracked it open, and we drank it sitting holding hands across the kitchen table while I told her about the day. I, too, was happy. We went to bed and made love, and settled into our spoons position, me slotted against her back. I thought from her breathing that she had gone straight to sleep, but a few minutes passed and then she said drowsily, 'It would be good, wouldn't it, if it could be like this.'

'If what could?' I said. Her shoulder was warm against my mouth.

'Being dead,' she said. 'If being dead could be like this. For ever and ever.'

I kissed her shoulder. 'It would be great,' I said. She wasn't being morbid. I knew exactly what she meant.

She fell asleep and I must have drifted off too, but I woke an hour later with my left arm twitching furiously, trapped between our bodies. I turned away from her and lay on my back. There was not a sound outside. I listened to Jenny's regular breaths, while my arm jerked and shuddered of its own accord, as if it was jealous and wanted my attention. I lay there for ages – not worried, for I was used to it by then – but wondering what it meant. When I think back, I see that we were at a peak of happiness then, from which we began, imperceptibly but steadily, to descend. Whether this proves that my mother was right – that happiness does not matter in the greater scheme of things – I cannot say. Nor can I say that it was mostly my fault, or mostly hers, that we made our way down from that peak, but the sad truth is that we did not see what was happening, that it happened almost as if to two other people who were not us, who had nothing to do with us.

XIX

I raised £800 in sponsorship from the London marathon, and I learned a simple truth about campaigning over that summer: once something begins to roll, everybody wants to jump on board. Local businessmen competed with each other, donating cases of wine, televisions, washing-machines and foreign holidays as raffle prizes at different events, or writing cheques for £50, £100, £200. I did my best to make sure all these donations were recorded in the local paper, *pour encourager les autres*. The football club ran a disco, persuaded the bar staff and DJ to work for nothing and charged £5 a ticket and an extra fifty pence on every drink – the money raised came to an astonishing £3,200, half for the club and half for cancer research. This was a wonderful effort, but someone in the Macmurray clique complained at the next Session meeting that the Kirk was being associated, albeit indirectly, with a scheme to relieve people of their money while they were under the influence of alcohol. It is too tedious to detail how we countered this petty-mindedness. We won the argument, but Macmurray insisted on the objection being minuted.

As September and the Moray marathon approached, it became clear that we would exceed our £40,000 target. I wanted to do it in style. I wrote to NessTrek, the outdoor activities retailers, and followed up the letter with a series of phone-calls to their head office in Inverness. I talked to a secretary, a marketing assistant and the marketing assistant's boss before finally someone calling himself an operations manager called me back. He'd read my letter, he said. He thought he might be able to arrange a meeting with the company's founder and managing director, Iain MacInnes. Was I likely to be in Inverness in the near future? I said that that could be arranged. He booked me in for an appointment in a couple of weeks' time.

The operations manager's name was Douglas Sim. He was pleasant enough, but a kind of smirk appeared at his mouth whenever he thought I wasn't watching. There was something I wasn't being told. We were making polite conversation in a reception area while Mr MacInnes finished another meeting. The next time the smirk happened I decided not to let it go.

'Is there something funny?' I asked.

He blushed. 'No, no,' he said.

'You probably don't get many ministers in here,' I said.

'No, we don't. That should be him now,' he added. The sound of voices and laughter came through the door.

'Sounds promising,' I said. 'He's in a good mood.'

'Don't be fooled by that,' Sim said. 'He's a businessman first and foremost. But he's very generous to charities he likes. A word of warning. He likes your cause, but he might give you a hard time. You personally, I mean.'

'Oh? Why's that?' I asked, and the door opened and a large, red-bearded man in an open-necked checked shirt filled the space.

'Iain,' Sim said. 'This is your next appointment. The Reverend Gideon Mack, from Monimaskit.'

MacInnes took three strides and stood in front of me. He was very tall and very wide, and any remnant of laughter was gone from his face. I held out my hand. He took it for half a second. 'You'd better come through,' he said. 'Thank you, Douglas.'

MacInnes turned around and headed back through the door. I looked at Sim, who stretched out his hand to indicate that I should follow. Then with the same hand he briefly grasped his throat as if to throttle himself, and the smirk turned into a full, unpleasant smile. He was, I realised, referring to my collar.

I followed MacInnes down a corridor, and we went into his office, a big airy room with a window looking out on to the river. He shut the door behind me. 'Take a seat,' he said. 'I've read your letter. Talk to me.'

I told him about our activities, the people we'd involved, the way it had snowballed. He seemed to be listening, but he didn't look at me. He doodled on a sheet of paper, swivelled in his chair, glanced out of the window. I came to the crux of the matter.

'Have you ever been to Monimaskit?' I asked.

'No,' he said.

'It's not a big place,' I explained. 'Population four and a half thousand, rural, quiet, unassuming. But in six months we've managed to raise £40,000 – half of it for cancer research. To wrap the campaign up I'm running in the Moray marathon and I'm going to do it in my dog-collar. I want to buy a pair of running shoes from NessTrek, and at the end of the race I want NessTrek to buy the dog-collar from me.'

'Why?' MacInnes asked. 'What's in it for us?'

'Masses of press coverage,' I said. 'TV too – *Reporting Scotland* are interested. So are Grampian Television. Association with a cheque for at least £25,000 going to cancer research. It certainly won't do you any harm.'

'And what kind of time do you anticipate finishing in?' he asked. 'We wouldn't want to be associated with a five-hour hirpler. Or a non-finisher.'

'I did London in just under three hours,' I said. MacInnes looked impressed. 'I'll be quicker this time. The scenery's better, and so is the air.'

'Okay,' he said. 'How much do you expect to get for your efforts?'

'Five thousand pounds,' I said. 'That's why the cheque for cancer research will be at least £25,000. I'm counting on one last big donation, to be made at the end of the marathon.'

'That's a lot of money for a dog-collar,' he said.

'Yes, it is,' I said. 'But that's the price.'

'And you're the Church of Scotland minister in Monimaskit?'

'Yes, I am.'

Something passed over his eyes, like an icy breeze over a loch. I tried, and failed, to anticipate what was coming.

'I hate the Church of fucking Scotland,' he said.

'Oh,' I said.

'I hate religion, I hate all churches, but I hate the Church of Scotland the most.'

I was, as I was supposed to be, thrown. This was what Douglas Sim's smirk had meant. But it didn't make sense. Had Sim got me all the way up there, knowing that my request would be rejected out of hand, just so that his boss could let off steam at me? And why had MacInnes agreed to see me at all? It had to be some kind of test, to see how I reacted.

'I'm not so keen on it myself,' I said. 'But don't quote me on that.'

He seemed barely to hear me. 'I grew up in Wester Ross,' he said. 'A beautiful, bleak bog of a place. My parents were members of the Church of Scotland. Believe me, we were on the liberal wing of Christianity in those parts. Other folk thought we were worshippers of Baal. Not that you'd have noticed in our house – religion oozed out of the walls. We all had to go to church, of course, every week, me and my brother and sister. Sundays that went on for days. No escaping them.'

'I can believe it,' I said. I was about to say something about my own upbringing, but he spoke again.

'Our minister's name was Mackenzie. He was a miserable bastard. There were only two more miserable bastards than him in the whole district. Do you know who they were? The Free Church minister and the Free Presbyterian one. In Wester Ross there's something like one sheep to every three acres of land. There are more fucking ministers to the acre than sheep, did you know that? Do you know how long the services go on there?'

'A long time, I've heard,' I said. Maybe I was wrong, maybe this wasn't a test, there would be no donation and I'd been summoned just so that he could get this stuff out of his system.

'If you started your marathon when Mackenzie entered his pulpit,' he said, 'it would be a close thing who would finish first.'

'Is he still alive?' I asked.

'God, I hope not,' MacInnes said. 'Why?'

'It's just that the Moray marathon is on a Sunday, so if he was we could put your theory to the test.'

'You'll run on a Sunday?'

'Why not?'

'The Lord's Day. It's supposed to be sacred. A day of rest.'

'Yes,' I said, 'and that's the way I prefer it. I don't usually run on a Sunday, it's true, but it's a working day for me anyway. If I want to raise this money I'm going to have to compromise.'

'That's a very dirty word in some circles,' MacInnes said. 'You might find Wee Free ministers lying down in front of you.'

'Not in Elgin, surely.'

'They might be bussed in specially. You might have to tread on them.' He made it sound like I'd be stepping in dung.

'It would be painful,' I said, 'but I'd grin and bear it.'

He laughed. Quite a friendly laugh, as if he couldn't be bothered trying to wind me up any more.

'Nice image,' he said. 'I'll treasure that. And you really are a minister?'

'Guaranteed,' I said.

'That's not fancy-dress you're in?'

'It is in a way,' I said. 'But yes, I really am a minister.'

'Aye,' he said, 'you are, aren't you? You've got that same burning light in your eyes as the ones that plagued me as a child. The same but different. How much of this £40,000 is going to your church?'

'None of it,' I said. 'The other organisations keep half of what they've raised. We take nothing.'

'My father died of cancer,' he said. 'Did you know that?'

'No,' I said. 'I'm sorry to hear it.'

'You didn't check up on me first? I wouldn't put it past you people.'

'I don't know anything about you,' I said, 'except that you own a successful group of sports shops and you're based here in the Highlands.'

He looked out of the window again.

'It was a bloody nightmare. Cancer of the arsehole. Can you believe how impossibly difficult and painful that is?'

'No,' I said, 'I cannot.'

'It was the last time I ever tried to pray,' MacInnes said. 'Seven years ago. I'd sworn I'd never go anywhere near a church again, and I didn't, but I prayed for my dad because he was in so much pain. I said to God, just make it hurt less for my dad, and I'll believe in you again. That's what I said. And my dad prayed too, because he still believed in God, and if my mum had still been alive she'd have been at it as well. Do you know what good it did?'

'None at all,' I said.

'It got worse,' he said. 'The pain got worse. He'd be talking to you and he'd suddenly freeze up completely, go white. White as fucking Dulux. Sweat on his forehead. Tears springing from his eyes. Then it would pass. "Sorry," he'd say. *Sorry!* I stopped praying then. I thought, well I always knew there wasn't a God. Either that, or he's a complete fucking cunt.'

'I know how you feel,' I said.

'How can you?' he said. 'You're one of his lackeys. You think he'll make everything all right for you in the end.'

'No,' I said. 'That's why I'm trying to raise the money for cancer research. We're the only people that can make things better. Human beings, I mean.'

'So you don't object to me calling him a cunt then?'

I shrugged. 'That's your prerogative. I wouldn't do it myself, but there's plenty of folk who have good reason to.'

He looked at me for perhaps half a minute, an unblinking, searching stare. Thirty seconds is a long time to hold a stare like that. I thought, I bet he drives a hard bargain with his suppliers. I thought of his father, and I thought of my father, and I did not blink.

'Five thousand pounds,' he said at last. 'It's a hell of a lot of money.'

'I'm running the marathon whatever you decide,' I said. 'And I'll be selling the collar to somebody.'

'You've got some bloody nerve,' he said. And then: 'I'll think about it.'

He stood up. The interview seemed to be over. I stood up too. We faced each other across his desk.

'One thing I'd like to know,' he said. 'Right to the very end, my father never wavered, he never lost his faith. Now why the hell would that be?'

'Maybe it was all he had left,' I said.

'Aye,' MacInnes said, 'that's what I thought too.' He shook his head. 'Bleak, eh?'

I nodded. I knew not to offer any platitudes. We did not shake hands. I thanked him for his time.

'That might be all you thank me for,' he said. 'I'll let you know.'

He did, two days later, in a letter promising us £5,000 provided I completed the marathon in less than three hours. Also, he would only write the cheque out to the charity, not to the Church of Scotland. He kept his word, and came to Elgin to hand me the cheque in exchange for my dog-collar at the finishing-line, in front of a bank of press photographers. I held up my NessTrek shoes as I took the cheque. I'd come in in two hours and fifty-three minutes, the best time I ever did. I believe the dog-collar still hangs in a frame in their Elgin branch.*

Back at Monimaskit, when we had done all our sums, we found that, including the NessTrek contribution, we had raised £26,470 for cancer research. There were a lot of laughs and a lot of tears in our different groups when we announced that sum. I still remember how good it felt. Even watching Margaret Thatcher resign as Prime Minister a few weeks later didn't match it.

* NessTrek's Elgin branch closed in 2001, and the company was bought by a competitor in 2002. I have been unable to find any information with regard to the present whereabouts of Gideon Mack's collar. – P.W.

XX

We spent the winter months planning our next campaign. After the success of that first season, more people and groups wanted to be involved, which led to a few logistical problems and some personality clashes. We set up a steering committee, to simplify the decision-making, and raised our target to £50,000. I pushed for us to choose an overseas charity this time, on the grounds that it would be beneficial to show our small Scottish town reaching out to the rest of the world. There was some dissent – 'charity begins at hame' being the commonest objection – but we eventually settled for an organisation that builds wells and provides clean drinking-water in Africa. I sent off the forms to run in two more marathons, dates were fixed for other events, and we girded up our loins for the task.

By October 1991 we had raised £15,000 more than we had in the first year. The newspapers were full of us: headlines like WEE TOWN WITH A BIG HEART, MONIMASKIT KEEPS ON GIVING and MARATHON MACK HITS THE ROAD AGAIN. I lost count of the number of times I was interviewed for radio and the press. We received donations from all over the world, and unsolicited letters and phone calls from prominent charities wanting to work with us. It was invigorating and daunting at the same time. Nancy Croy and a couple of her friends were the stalwarts who kept going, even when fund-raising fatigue affected some of the others. I reassured people, as individuals and groups, that it was all right for them to take a rest, that nobody was obliged to go on year after year. But I'd started something that I, at any rate, couldn't stop. And Peter Macmurray's warning rings in my head now as I think of it. I was like a Munro-bagger who doesn't stop to admire the view, but charges on to the next summit thinking only of the names he will tick off his list at the end of the day. I realise now that the money, the actual amount, became more important to me than the cause for which it was being raised.

Jenny had played much less of a role in the second year. She'd done some temping when we first came to Monimaskit, but by then she'd found permanent part-time work, three and a half days a week, as a receptionist at a dentist's surgery. It gave her a life outside the manse, and we needed the extra income. It meant, however, that we saw less of each other, especially as I was out virtually every evening, either running or at meetings or on pastoral visits. Often she would be asleep by the time I came to bed, and one of us was usually up before the other in the morning. We talked, we looked after each other, we still laughed together, but more and more we led separate lives. I thought, if I thought about it at all, that this was normal, it was what happened when you'd been married for a while. Compared with my own parents, the Reverend and Mrs Gideon Mack seemed to be getting along fine.

One rare night when I wasn't due to go out, after we had washed and dried the supper dishes together in what felt to me like an easy and companionable silence, I left Jenny in the kitchen, settling down in the Windsor chair with a book, while I went through to my study to catch up on some administration. It was November, about eight o'clock. I drew the curtains against the dark outside and put a match to the fire. In doing these things I was making a kind of subconscious statement to myself, that I would be there for some time, probably till after midnight. I had at least that much of my father in me: I would never light a fire just for an hour's comfort.

I had an electric typewriter on my desk – it would be another year before I made the technological leap to computer – and a half-written response to some tedious bit of bureaucracy from 121 George Street was sitting in the machine. I read it over. It was the sort of thing I should have been catching up on, but I had neither the energy nor the desire to finish it. I looked at the shelves of books, so many of them my father's, and I looked at the catching fire and the armchair beside it. I'd so often wondered what my father got up to in his study, night after night alone with all those books. Had he done what I was doing? Had he looked around and wondered what on earth was the point? Or had he been past doubting by then? I had dutifully preserved his books, thinking that they *might come in useful*, and some of them had, but others I'd never opened, not once. What was the point of all those millions and millions of words?

I sat down in the armchair and stared into the flames, reached forward to the basket of logs and put a couple on. I suddenly felt exhausted. I remember thinking, I'll just sit here for a minute, close my eyes and gather my thoughts. Ten minutes. Then I'll work.

I came awake when the door opened and Jenny entered carrying a mug of tea. She saw at once that I'd been asleep. She usually put the tea on a coaster on the desk but instead she brought it over to me.

'Tired?' she said.

'Aye. A wee bit.'

She stood in front of me, looking down. For a moment her face looked odd, the face of a stranger, then it reassembled itself into its familiar shape.

'What?' I said.

'Do you think this is it?'

'What do you mean?'

'You and me. Like this from now on. You here in one room sleeping, and me in another reading but not really taking it in. Is that where we are?'

I didn't know what to say. I began to mumble something about it being a phase, that we were both tired, but she stopped me.

'Do you love me, Gideon?' she said. 'Do you really love me?'

I put the tea down on the hearth and made to stand up but she dropped to her knees in front of the fire and put her hands out to stop me.

'Sometimes I wonder if you ever have,' she said.

I started to protest, 'Jenny, that's a terrible thing to say,' but she interrupted before I could shift the responsibility on to her. 'Or if I've ever loved you,' she said. 'I mean, really and truly. Because whatever this is, it doesn't feel like love.'

I couldn't speak. She said, 'Do you think we'll get back to being lovers?'

It was the first time either of us had admitted the fact that we weren't having sex any more; hadn't made love for weeks, for months in fact.

'Yes, I do,' I said.

'I don't. Not until we stop living like this.'

'Like what?' I said.

'Emptily. Our lives are supposed to be full and mine feels empty. And I think yours must be too. And I worry that it's because of what you're doing, what we're doing. Because we're not being truthful.'

'We are, to each other,' I said. 'Aren't we?'

'You know what I mean. You're not being honest now, saying that, you know you're not. Can you be dishonest in one part of your life but not in another? Maybe we shouldn't be doing this.'

'We can't stop it now,' I said.

'We can,' she said. 'We can start again.'

'What do you mean?' I said. 'Do you want me to give up the ministry?'

She gave a laugh that threatened to turn into a sob.

'How can *you* give it up?' she said.

'You mean, how can I give up something that I don't believe in in the first place?'

'No, I mean, how can *you* give up being a minister? It's in your blood. It's me I'm talking about. How can I be with you when this life is so false?'

'I don't understand,' I said. 'Do you want to leave me?'

'No, Gideon, I don't.'

'Well, then. I thought you were happy. I thought *we* were happy.'

'You know we're not,' she said. 'We're just going through the motions. We're living a lie, and it's killing us. Gideon, I don't want to lose you, but I think maybe I already have.'

I put my arms around her and she began to cry. 'You haven't,' I said. 'You haven't lost me.' But inside I felt a horrible queasiness, as if she'd found me out.

'I don't even know if I ever had you,' she said through her tears.

'Don't,' I said. 'Don't think that. We'll be okay. I'm sorry, I've just been so caught up in everything. Please don't cry.'

I got out my handkerchief and she blew her nose and wiped her eyes.

'I need to ask you something,' she said. 'You'll hate me for asking it, but I must.'

'What is it?'

'Will you be truthful? I don't care if it hurts, but I want the truth.'

'What do you need to know?' I said. 'Ask me, and I'll give you a truthful answer.'

'Is there someone else?' she said.

I didn't understand. 'What do you mean?' I said.

'Someone else. Is there?'

'You mean, am I having an affair?'

'Yes. Are you?'

'Like who?' I said. 'Who would I be having an affair with, even if I had the time?'

'I don't know who, Nancy or someone.'

'Nancy Croy?'

'Why not? You see such a lot of her, you get on well, she's nice-looking . . .'

'She's an elder.'

She puffed sceptically at that.

'No,' I said, 'no, no.' I started to laugh, stopped myself. 'Jenny, I'm not having an affair. Not with Nancy, not with anyone. I swear it. You're the only one. We've just drifted a bit, that's all.'

'The truth?' she asked.

'The truth.'

She managed a smile. 'I'm sorry,' she said. 'I don't know why I was thinking it. I'm sorry I asked.'

'It's okay,' I said. I had a fleeting image of Elsie. Jenny carried on, cutting across that brief thought.

'This has just been building up for ages,' she said. 'We shouldn't have let it get to this.'

'I know,' I said. 'I'm sorry too.'

'I mean, when was the last time we had sex? Either I'm asleep, or you're too tired. We should have sex more.'

'Yes,' I said. 'Well, we will.'

'I want to have a baby,' she said.

We'd talked about it before, then let the subject slip away, and now it was back. We'd been together fourteen years, she was thirty-two, of course she wanted a baby. But if we had one everything would change. A little chill went through me, followed by a little hope. Maybe a baby would make it all right.

'What do you think?' she said.

'Well, maybe we should. If you want to, we should try.'

'But do you want to?'

'I don't know,' I said. 'Aye, I do, why not? But there's plenty of time.'

'Not so much any more. Not for me.'

We stayed there in front of the fire till it died down, talking it through, apologising, and then, for the first time in weeks, we went to bed at the same time. We didn't make love that night, we were both drained, but it felt like some kind of fresh start. But maybe it wasn't, maybe we were just perpetuating a lie. Either way, we didn't have much time left to find out.

XXI

She'd gone to Edinburgh for the day to do some shopping. It was 8th January 1992, a Wednesday. The sales were on. I returned home from a round of visits at half-past six. Normally when I came in for the evening my first act was to remove the clerical collar and change into casual clothes. On this occasion I went straight to the television to catch the Scottish news: somebody had told me that British Steel had made the long-expected announcement that the Ravenscraig steelworks at Motherwell were to close, with the loss of 1,500 jobs. A reporter read out the company's statement, which was terse and to the point: market forces dictated that the plant was no longer viable. Adding insult to injury, the chairman, Sir Bob Scholey, was not available to comment. Various Conservative politicians appeared, stammering about sad truths and hard facts; they looked ashen, as if 'Black Bob', as he was known, was an old buccaneering crony who had tipped them the black spot. Union officials and red-faced MPs from other parties talked of betrayal, economic disaster, social devastation. But they'd all known it was coming: Ravenscraig, a symbol of the former might of Scottish heavy industry, had been taking cuts and blows for years, and now the big axe had been wielded. Somebody said something about the plant having finally been put out of its misery. Workers driving away wound their windows down and said they were gutted. 'Nae comment,' one said, with a face that commented all too plainly.

I was watching this with a kind of futile anger when the doorbell rang. Irritated, I went to answer it. The fact that Jenny was late back hadn't even entered my mind.

The policeman at the door was one of my congregation, a young lad called Andy McAllister. I said, 'Oh, Andy, come in. I'm just watching this Ravenscraig shambles.' Andy had his hat under his arm. He said, 'I'm really sorry, Mr Mack, I've some bad news for you.'

The accident had happened ten miles from Monimaskit, on a twisty stretch of road known as the Glack. Andy didn't know the exact details, but it seemed that her car had skidded on a downhill bend, maybe on some black ice, and gone into a spin. A lorry was coming the other way. The car slid, driver's side first, into the front of the lorry. The lorry-driver was unhurt. He scrambled out of his cab to help but couldn't reach her. It was the days before the ubiquitous mobile phone: he had to run a quarter of a mile to the nearest house to make the call. By the time the emergency services arrived – actually, long before that – Jenny was dead.

We stood in the hall with the TV still going in the background and me staring at Andy in disbelief till suddenly something snapped in me. 'I'll just turn that fucking thing off,' I said, which I did, giving Andy time to recover from one of the biggest shocks in his life. He was well meaning but had a conventional mind: he probably thought ministers had such language scrubbed out of them at college. I came back and said, 'Sorry, Andy. Are you all right?'

'Actually, it's the first time I've had to do this,' Andy said. 'I just wish it didn't have to be you, Mr Mack.' At which point it struck me that he was telling the truth; that what was happening was real, it wasn't an item on the news about someone else, it was about Jenny, my wife, she was dead, and I was going to have to deal with it.

I leaned against the wall. 'Yes,' I said. 'I see. I wish it wasn't me too.'

'I'm not to leave you alone,' Andy said. 'Not unless I'm sure you're all right.'

'Where is she?' I asked.

'Dundee,' he said. 'Ninewells.'

'I need to go there.'

'Are you all right to drive? I don't know if I can take you all the way to Dundee . . .'

'I'll get John Moffat to come with me. I'll go via his house.'

'I'll follow you,' Andy said, 'make sure you're okay. Make sure he's in.'

'Andy, you don't need to do that,' I said, but I could see that he wanted to, that it would make him feel better to be the minister's escort at least for the first leg of this difficult journey. 'Okay,' I said. 'Maybe you're right.'

We drove in convoy down the coast road. The night was clear and cold: the moon threw a long yellow rope of light across the dark water of the firth. Because it was a minor road the gritters hadn't been on it yet, and I kept my speed down. I felt as if I was in a motorcade, a funeral procession already. Everything in my life seemed to be in the past. I looked in the mirror and saw the police car keeping a respectful distance behind me. I half-expected Andy to put his flashing blue light on. This is an emergency, I thought. Why are we travelling so slowly? But of course it wasn't an emergency. The emergency was already over.

John was alone in the house, making the tea; Elsie was on a late shift at the library and wouldn't be in for another half-hour. Andy came to the door with me. 'John, something's happened,' I said. I turned to Andy and said, 'Thanks, Andy, we'll be fine now.' 'Okay,' Andy said, 'I'm really sorry,' and he nodded at John, got back in his car and drove away. 'What?' John said. 'What's happened?' 'Jenny's been in an accident,' I said. 'I need you to come to the hospital with me.' I couldn't bring myself to say what I had to say. 'Is she badly hurt?' he asked. 'I'll tell you in the car,' I said. He turned the oven off, scribbled a note to Elsie and came outside. 'Do you want me to drive?' he said. 'No,' I said. 'I'll drive there, you drive back. I'll need you to drive back.' It wasn't till we were moving that I told him, 'John, it's the worst thing you can imagine.' I needed to be driving. I gripped the wheel so hard I thought it would come off in my hands. 'Jenny's dead.'

It took us forty minutes to get to Ninewells Hospital in Dundee. You think, on such occasions, there will be hours of sitting on plastic chairs in hospital waiting-areas; hours of waiting. But she was dead, there was nothing to wait for. We were there around half-past seven. By nine o'clock we had seen her, spoken with everybody we needed to speak to. A doctor explained that there was nothing the people at the scene could have done to save her: she'd been crushed between the lorry's engine, her steering-wheel and the car's bodywork. The fire brigade had had to cut her free. What must it be like, I found myself thinking, working away in those circumstances, to free somebody already dead?

One of the ambulance crew was still there, he'd finished his shift. 'I ken this isna much comfort,' he said, 'but it would have been over in a second. She probably didna even feel it.' I thought of that second. I'd never been in an accident but I imagined it to be something like what I'd experienced that time with my arm, only more intense: I imagined the slow unravelling of everything, the helplessness, the dreamy horror of waiting for the impact. The ambulance man was trying to make it seem better, but I knew a second could last a long time.

The lorry-driver, who was being checked over at the hospital for shock and whiplash, had been breathalysed. He was not at fault, the police said. They'd be making a full report, of course, but their view was that the accident was simply that, an accident: a momentary lapse of concentration, a loss of control on a tight bend, maybe some ice; nobody was to blame. John and I listened, and I knew what they were really saying, as kindly as possible: if anybody was to blame, it was your wife. 'It's just one of these things,' one of the policemen said.

We identified her together, John and I. I'll always be grateful to him for that. She was in a little room in A&E, a room where hundreds of bodies must have lain prior to being taken to the mortuary. There were cuts on her cheeks and forehead – ten, I counted them – and some bruising, but they'd cleaned her up and she looked astonishingly unhurt. I began to turn the sheet down below her neck, and the doctor put a hand out to stop me. I closed my eyes. I thought, how do I want to remember her, remember this? The doctor was right. When I opened my eyes she was still lying there, unhurt, the red lines of the cuts like bits of thread placed artistically on her creamy skin.

Then without warning I was outside myself looking down, just as I had been on that previous occasion. I saw my hand touching the dark, thick hair that framed her face. My fingertips touched her lips. 'Oh, Jenny, what have you done?' I heard myself say. Tears that had nothing to do with me poured from my eyes. John was crying too. I saw us clinging to each other like two old drunks. We staggered from the room, and as we did so the sensation ended, and I was back in my body again. I could not speak. Seconds after it was over I wasn't even certain it had happened.

There were forms to sign. The hospital staff had taken off her rings, earrings and a bracelet and put them in an envelope. I had to sign for them too. John fetched some tea in two polystyrene cups and emptied several sachets of sugar into each, even though neither of us took sugar. He called Elsie from a public phone in the corridor. Then he took my arm and led me away.

At the main entrance to the hospital a man and a woman were standing in a clumsy embrace. They were middle-aged, in their fifties maybe, and were both haggard and pale, as though they'd just been told that their son or daughter had not come through some difficult operation. Even in the midst of what was going on I could not help noticing them. The man was in a blue boiler-suit. He was much taller than the woman and leaned over her like a sick tree trained to a stake; he wore a neck-brace and he was weeping, dabbing at his eyes with a filthy handkerchief. She was short and fat, in a tweed coat; she had her arms around his waist and was speaking quietly, trying to draw him towards the exit. Between dabs the man saw us approaching. He broke away from her and said, 'I need to speak to you.' It took me a moment to realise that he was addressing me.

'No, no, Duncan, no,' the woman said, but the man said again, 'I need to speak.' He bent sideways to try to look into my eyes. 'You are the minister, aren't you?'

I shook my head. I'd never felt less like a minister in my life. John said, 'The chaplain, you mean? I'm sorry, this isn't the chaplain. This is another minister. I have to take him home.'

'But you *are* the minister,' the man said, more definitely. 'It was your wife in the car, wasn't it? It was my lorry. I was driving the lorry.'

'Not now, Duncan,' the woman said, but he couldn't stop. 'I could see it was you,' he said. 'From your collar and that. And your face. They tellt me she was a minister's wife. I kent it must be you. I'm so sorry. I'm so sorry. But I couldna do a thing. She was on to me before I kent what was happening. I couldna do a thing. I'm so sorry.'

I let go of John and stood in front of the lorry-driver. He was solid and broad-shouldered, about my height. His eyes were red with weeping and there were snotters hanging from his nose. He was like a big, blubbery, giant-sized bairn.

I said, 'Please don't distress yourself. I know it was not your fault.'

'No, it wasna my fault,' the man said. 'No. Thank you, thank you. I'm so sorry.' He seemed rooted to the floor. The woman tugged at him as if he were an obstinate weed in her garden.

'I need to go now,' I said. 'I need to go home. You should go too.'

'Come on, Duncan,' she said. 'Let the minister go home.'

And so we went, they to their house of misery, and I to mine.

XXII

We hardly spoke all the way back to Monimaskit. John drove with infinite care, as if somehow that would help. I thought, someone is killed in one of these things, and the first thing we do is get in another one and drive to see the body, then drive away again. We have no option: our lives depend on machines that kill us. And I remembered an image from the news item about Ravenscraig, a rush of molten steel coming at the camera.

'She looked very beautiful, Gideon,' John said. 'She looked like she was at peace.'

'Aye, John, aye. Fine words. She looks like that because she's dead.'

After a minute I said, 'I'm sorry, that was uncalled for. You're right. I hope you're right.'

There are two routes between Monimaskit and Dundee, both about the same distance. We had gone one way, and drove back the other. We were halfway through the Glack, with its wooded slopes running steeply down to the road on either side, before I realised where we were. It was very dark. 'It was here somewhere,' I said. 'Can you see anything?' John slowed down, and on a short bit of straight before one of the sharpest bends he came almost to a complete halt. Had it been here? From what the police had said I thought so. We stared, but there was no evidence. The wreckage had been cleared away and the road in the headlights' glare looked as it always had done. Nothing was different. Everything had changed. I heard my mother saying, 'This life isn't about happiness. It simply isn't important.' My father's voice thudded against the inside of my forehead, his phrase about confronting one's own immortality. I stared into the darkness. Jenny's body was lying in Ninewells Hospital, but was a part of her wandering out there somewhere? I felt like getting out, going to look for her, but John picked up speed again and I said nothing.

Elsie met us at the manse, red-eyed. She hugged me, then I got out the house-keys and gave them to her and we went in. The house was more than just empty; it was as if no one had lived there for years. Elsie wanted to collect some clothes, a toothbrush. 'You're coming back with us,' she said. 'You're not staying here tonight.'

'I've got things to do,' I said. 'I'll need to phone people. Jenny's parents. My mother.'

'Tomorrow,' Elsie said. 'It's half-past ten. It's too late and there's nothing they can do. Let them sleep.'

The light on the answer-machine in the study was flashing. I moved towards it.

'Get in the car,' Elsie said. 'There's nothing there that can't wait.'

John and I went out, and Elsie followed a minute later, switching off the lights and locking the door behind her. John had the engine running. 'Let's go,' Elsie said. The wheels spun on the gravel. You'd have thought we were in a gangster movie, that we had a plan, except that when Elsie got in the back with me and took my hand and squeezed it hard we both started crying as if we were children lost in the forest in the middle of a horrible fairy tale.

XXIII

A fairy tale. These two stories are running in my head, converging, separating again, but one seems remote and unreachable now, slipping away from me even as I recall its details and write them down. The other, the one that began with the Stone and is not yet over, is the one that feels real and true.

I was tired when I got back from the Moffats' house that Sunday evening, after telling them about the Stone, so I went to bed early, but I did not relax. Usually I slept well – 'the sleep of the just about eight hours' Jenny had called it. She'd been a good sleeper too. We would hardly move all night. Only for a few weeks after she died had I suffered from insomnia. I'd reach for the shape of her and find myself awake, clutching at space. The feeling had reminded me of my childhood sleepwalking phase, and, like that phase, it had passed. But that Sunday night I was restless, waking every hour or so to find the Stone massively present in my mind.

At three o' clock, mouth a little dry from the whisky I'd drunk,

I found myself mulling over John and Elsie's different responses to what I'd said. John's had been typical of him. He was Monimaskit born and bred. He had stepped out into the wider world for a while, then come home again. He'd worked with Catherine Craigie for a couple of years, fully expecting to take over her job in due course. Not long after Jenny and I came to Monimaskit, Miss Craigie had taken early retirement because of her increasingly debilitating ill health. John had applied for the principal teacher's post, but hadn't got it. Gregor Wishaw had. They were friends of sorts, and some difficult days had followed. Then John seemed to overcome his disappointment, shrugged his shoulders and got on with doing what by his own account he enjoyed most, classroom teaching. He developed a jauntiness in his step, a barely disguised disdain for educational policy, and a reputation for encouraging his pupils to be outspoken and awkward. The open-ended nationalism he had espoused in the 1970s seemed to me to have shrivelled into something less wholesome. After years of political frustration Scotland had at last gained a Parliament, but when John mentioned it now it was to sneer at its cost and the uselessness of its members. He had the bitterness and boldness of a home-grown boy on his own territory; but under that boldness was insecurity and a sense of failure. So John's response to my story of the Stone was entirely predictable – friendly but dismissive. But what about Elsie?

She'd been more open-minded, and that was typical of her too. I knew that things weren't always good between her and John: they saw the world differently, and he didn't appreciate her as I thought she deserved. I ran a little fantasy through my head, of telling Elsie about the Stone when we were alone together. She'd listen, her hand would come over my hand, those long, graceful fingers like the fingers of a pianist. I'd tell her about the Stone and she'd picture walking up there with me, and then I wouldn't stop, I couldn't, I'd go on to tell her how I felt about her. Her fingers would touch my cheek. I'd be looking in her eyes, still speaking, she'd put her fingers to my mouth and then she'd start to kiss me, soft and hard and long. Elsie, Elsie, Elsie!

It was three-thirty in the morning and the minister of Monimaskit, lying on his back in the double-bed he'd not shared with anyone for eleven years, had an erection. I told myself I was needing a pee, it was bladder pressure that was causing it, but it wasn't, it was Elsie Moffat.

The blood in my penis beat like a drum. I tried to think about the Stone instead. Who else could I speak to about it? Telling my mother hadn't achieved anything, not for either of us. Who else? Amelia Wishaw was too straight. Gregor Wishaw would ridicule it, do *Twilight Zone* theme music at me. John Gless or Peter Macmurray were complete non-starters. There was, however, Lorna Sprott.

Lorna's rural parish, adjacent to mine, is actually composed of three former parishes – Meldrick, Easton and Kingallie – amalgamated into one as a result of the decline of population in the glens. She manages two dwindling congregations, taking services on alternate Sundays in the tiny kirks at Meldrick and Kingallie. She is always guaranteed an attendance of at least one, because her very friendly but irredeemably dim black Labrador, Jasper, accompanies her and lies on a cushion for the duration.

What can I say about Lorna, that won't sound patronising or disparaging? She means well. She does her best. She is brimful of faith but entirely lacking in confidence, which makes her, for example, the worst driver I've come across. She is always in earnest, a constant worrier. When people meet Lorna in the street they tend to address Jasper first. This is not because they find Lorna intimidating, but because they feel sorry for her, and in these circumstances it is easier to make a fuss over her pet. Without God and the dog, they feel, this rather shapeless, untidy person would cut a very lonely and sad figure indeed. And there, I have patronised and disparaged her as I knew I would.

Yet Lorna was the only minister I knew who was also a friend. Naturally I associated and worked with other ministers, but at a personal level I kept them at a distance. I did not want to be sucked into a whirl of Kirk get-togethers. Jenny and I had avoided that, and after Jenny's death I wanted it even less. But Lorna was different. She didn't fit either.

She had a lot of spare time on her hands, and especially since

Jenny had died she'd spent much of it in Monimaskit, her nearest town. John Moffat used to say she was stalking me. 'She's wanting into your Presbyterian pants, man,' he insisted. It was true that I did see a good deal of her at Presbytery meetings and community events, and she'd participated in some of the charity work as well. She often called at the manse, seeking my advice on anything from the failure of her car windscreen washers to an interpretation of a passage of Scripture. But I wasn't convinced that John was right. I thought she might not be interested in men at all; or women for that matter; I thought she might be asexual. Whatever the truth was, I didn't want to confuse the issue, for me or her.

I liked her, but her bulk and her tendency to knock things over were oppressive indoors, so we'd take her dog for walks, usually on the beach, sometimes in the woods along the Keldo, two or three times a month. I imagined myself talking to her about the Stone on one of these outings. We could even go and look at it. But the scenario wasn't appealing. Lorna would never laugh at me, she'd listen with a sympathetic ear, but she'd be too intense, *too* concerned, too damned nice. I didn't want her mooning all over me with her big cow eyes. Because even if the Stone were there in front of her, even if she actually touched it, she would not understand. She'd want us to pray to God together, seek his views on the matter. She wouldn't deal with it until she'd had a message back from God. The trouble was, Lorna was always receiving messages from God. She believed every one of them, but they didn't enable her to act with any more efficiency or clarity of purpose. God simply muddied the already murky waters for her.

I needed someone quite unlike Lorna. Someone who wouldn't pussyfoot around, and who knew, when it came to standing stones, what she was talking about. There was, in fact, only one person to speak to. I'd looked up Catherine Craigie's book when I'd got in, and sure enough there was nothing in it about a stone in Keldo Woods, but there must be a reason for that. Catherine would set me right. That she would doubtless take the opportunity to pour dismissive disdain on my story was probably why I'd been trying to think of someone else to talk to instead.

The Stone slid away from my mind again. Someone was beside me in the bed. I half-turned. It was Elsie. I sat up, wide awake, alone, turned the pillow, and lay back down again.

Be grateful for Elsie, I told myself. Beautiful, down-to-earth, warm, kind Elsie. And be grateful for John. They'd made me stay with them on the night of Jenny's death and again after the funeral, when we came back from Edinburgh, which was where, at her parents' request, it had taken place. For two nights John had supplied talk and whisky, and Elsie talk and cuddles and food, till I began to feel ungrateful because I was drowning in their kindness. On the second morning I said I wanted to go back to the manse. They came in with me, made sure I was all right, and in the following days dropped by with so many cooked meals that I had to plead with them not to bring more or I'd have to start throwing stuff out. And, ever since, they had remained loyal (leaving aside recent times). I hated the way my imagination wormed its way between them, but I couldn't help it.

Weeks or maybe months after the funeral, I don't remember exactly, Elsie had made me an offer. 'Gideon, whenever you feel like sorting out Jenny's things, her clothes I mean, I'll help if you like. If it would make it easier, just ask me.' I didn't take her up on it until later in the summer. One weekday afternoon, for no particular reason – certainly not because I'd planned it – I'd found myself taking black bin-bags up the stairs and staring at the chest of drawers, the wardrobe and the press, wondering where to start. It was late August, I think. I know it was summer because the bedroom window was open, the air was hot and making me feel lazy, and a lawnmower was going in the distance. I stood in the middle of the room and said, 'Time to go, Jenny. Your clothes, I mean.' I went to her dressing-table and opened one of the wee drawers under the mirror and a fat bumblebee flew out, bumped into the mirror twice, hovered for a few seconds and then droned across the room and out through the window.

History. You can't get away from it. What the bee made me think of was one of those things that is half-myth, half-history: Archbishop Sharp, dragged from his coach on a moor in Fife by nine vengeful Covenanters, pushed to his knees and slaughtered.* When they ransacked the coach they opened the dead man's snuffbox, and a bee, his supposed familiar – for Sharp, they believed, was not just their enemy and persecutor but a warlock who counted Satan among his friends – escaped from it and drifted away over the heather. Why would a man keep a bee in his snuffbox? How had a bee got into that closed drawer? I sat down heavily on the edge of the bed, Jenny's side, and wondered if there was a message in it; any kind of meaning at all. I thought, this is going to be hard, maybe I should have called Elsie. And at that moment the doorbell rang.

I knew it would be her even before I reached the foot of the stairs. It was about three o'clock, she'd just finished a half-shift at the library, and as it was such a fine day she'd come by to see if I fancied a walk. 'So long as I'm not interrupting anything,' she added. 'Well, you are,' I said, 'but it's all right, I was just thinking about you. Come in.' And in she came.

She was wearing a khaki cotton skirt, calf-length, and a white tee-shirt, and her arms were brown from the sun. I explained to her what I'd been about to start. 'I didn't think I'd need your help, but I do,' I said. 'Part of me just wants to stuff everything into bin-bags and take it to the charity shops. But it seems so final.'

Elsie said, 'I know it's a cliché, but this is about moving on, Gideon.'

'Aye, but I feel there should be something more to it than just emptying the drawers out. A ritual of some kind. Anyway, maybe I was subconsciously looking for some kind of signal to get started, I don't know, but this strange thing just happened.' And I told her about the bee.

Perhaps it was inevitable: the fact that I shared that story with

*James Sharp (1613–79), Archbishop of St Andrews from 1661, was one of the most hated opponents of the Covenanters, who saw him as having betrayed the Church of Scotland by reintroducing Episcopacy following the Restoration of Charles II. An unrelenting persecutor of religious and political dissent, he was murdered in the presence of his daughter on Magus Muir, near St Andrews. – P.W.

her; the fact that she'd appeared at that moment on the doorstep; the fact that the day was hot and still; the fact that her arms were so brown; the fact that I took her hand as I led her upstairs; perhaps all these things combined and made what happened one last unavoidable fact. Perhaps it was inevitable; but it certainly wasn't planned.

We went into the bedroom. 'Maybe there are clothes you'd like,' I said. 'Jenny would have wanted that. You're welcome to anything.' 'No,' she said, 'I couldn't. Anyway, I'm not the same size. Her stuff would be a bit big for me.' 'Scarves,' I said. 'Handbags. Things like that.' I felt clumsy and ignorant and out of my depth. I wanted her to take the responsibility away from me and she saw that. She said, 'Look, you bring things out, and I'll sort them into piles on the bed, then we can get them away.'

I started with the wardrobe. She'd not had a lot of clothes, Jenny, we didn't have much money and she made things last, but I was still surprised at what came out. Coats and dresses I'd never seen her in or forgotten she had; shoes she never wore; pairs of jeans and shorts she probably couldn't have got into any more; jumpers still heavy with her scent; I took them from the hangers and the shelves of the press and passed them to Elsie, who folded and piled them and then started filling the black bags with them. The clothes I didn't recognise were like surprises, and as I checked the pockets of one coat I thought, will there be any secrets in this surprise? But there were none, and I said nothing, while Elsie kept up a quiet commentary from beside the bed – a dress she remembered some occasion by, a top Jenny had looked good in. I listened and looked and nodded and sometimes laughed. And all the time as we were working together my hands were shaking, and I thought at first it was because of the task, the emotional difficulty of it, but then I realised it was Elsie's presence in the bedroom, her handling of the clothes, her moving around the bed. I excused myself and went to the bathroom. I was half-erect. What on earth was I thinking of? But it was involuntary, I wasn't thinking of anything. I had a pee, washed my hands and face, checked in the mirror that it was really me. Then I went back.

Elsie had run out of clothes and had started on the chest of drawers. She was sitting on the bed surrounded by Jenny's underwear. It was mostly white: bras and pants and a suspender belt she hadn't worn for a while; balled up tights and stockings and a couple of nightdresses. Elsie was holding a slip with a lacy hem and delicate shoulder-straps. She had shaken it out and was holding it draped across her arms, looking at it almost as she might look at a sleeping child. She brought it to her face and breathed in. 'Oh, I can smell her,' she said, and she started to cry.

I knelt down in front of her and lowered my face to the white slip and breathed in its smell. My dead wife in the arms of her friend. My hands found Elsie's through the material and they gripped. I thought, I cannot stop this, only she can stop it. Elsie leaned towards me and began to kiss me. I shifted on my knees to come closer to her and felt my erection straining so hard I thought my trousers would burst. Elsie's hands, one of them still holding the slip, came round to the back of my head and she pressed her mouth down on mine. I felt the cool slide of the material on my neck and the hot softness of Elsie's lips and tongue. I pulled away from her and she looked surprised and yet not surprised, her eyes were wet but she was smiling.

We both stood up together and she dropped the slip on the bed behind her. We kissed again. Then quickly we took off our clothes, there was no time to undress each other, and she lay down on the bed among Jenny's underwear and I knelt with one knee between her legs. Elsie's breasts were rounder and firmer than Jenny's, the nipples were red and hard. I had never experienced an erection as big or urgent as the one I had. I heard myself saying, 'Elsie, Elsie, Elsie,' as if it was half a declaration of love and half an apology, and she said, 'It's all right, be quiet, come on,' and I pushed myself into her without needing to be guided, feeling her wet and tight around me, and began to thrust. Her legs lifted about my waist and squeezed and we kissed again, our tongues going deep into each other's mouths, I could hear myself grunting with effort and Elsie groaning in time with me. I felt myself about to come and some distant alarm sounded in my head, making me hold back, but she felt the hesitation and grabbed my buttocks and pulled me in again. 'Do it, Gideon, do it,' she said angrily, and I emptied myself into her in a series of long tremors, my face buried in the hollow of her neck and shoulder.

After a while I came out of her and rolled on to my back. Elsie said, 'I'm leaking,' and reached for the nearest thing to hand, which was the slip, and put it between her legs. 'Would she mind?' Elsie asked. 'About that?' I said, meaning the slip. 'No,' she said, and started to laugh, 'about this,' meaning what we had done. 'Would she be surprised?' 'No,' I said, 'I think, somehow, she'd approve.' Elsie said, 'I don't think so.'

We lay staring at the ceiling, holding hands, shoulders and thighs touching. 'Will it be all right?' I said. 'I mean, we didn't use anything.' 'Aye,' she said, 'don't you worry about that.' And a little later she said, 'This can never happen again, you do know that, don't you?' 'Of course,' I said, trying to keep the disappointment out of my voice.

I fell asleep for a few minutes, but woke to the movement of her getting off the bed. She gathered up her clothes and went to the bathroom and when she came back she was dressed. I wanted her naked again, I stood up and tried to kiss her, she returned the kiss but was pushing me away at the same time. 'Come on, Gideon,' she said, 'let's quit while we can.' 'I love you, Elsie,' I said. 'No you don't,' she said. 'I do,' I insisted, 'I always have.' 'Okay,' she said. 'I love you, too. I love Jenny and I love John. Be kind, Gideon, be fair. Go and get dressed.'

I went to the bathroom and washed quickly and put my clothes on. I wondered if anything remotely like what we had done had occurred before in the manse's 120-year history. When I went back, the bed was tidied, all the underwear gone. Elsie had folded the slip and laid it apart. 'I'll wash it at home,' she said. I was about to say I'd deal with it but she seemed very definite, as if she wanted to remove all trace of herself, of what had happened, from the manse. She would not make eye contact with me. We went through the rest of Jenny's clothes without any more reminiscing. In ten minutes we had everything sealed up in bags. I began to take them down to the hall.

'I'd like some tea, do you want some?' Elsie asked. I nodded and she went to the kitchen to put the kettle on.

The manse has a south-west-facing courtyard at the back door. We took a couple of chairs from the kitchen and sat out in the sun, drinking our tea. There was no danger of being overheard, but we didn't say much.

'I don't want this to come between us,' Elsie said. 'Or between me and John, or you and John. It shouldn't have happened but it did and it was special and lovely. But it can't happen again. We have to move on.'

'Yes, we do,' I said.

'Don't feel awkward about it,' she said. 'I don't, really I don't. It's a good thing to have happened, a necessary thing. A secret thing we'll always share. But I don't want it to change anything.'

'Hasn't it changed everything?' I said.

'No,' she said. 'It hasn't. You understand that, don't you?'

'Yes,' I said. I was lying already. I wanted to tell her again that I loved her, had always loved her, but I saw that she didn't want the pain and difficulty of that – the awkwardness, as she put it. The sun was hot, but I felt cold inside.

'I'll never tell John, and you mustn't either,' Elsie said. 'Okay?'

'Okay,' I said. She smiled at me, sexy without meaning to be, the way it would always be from then on. And after she'd finished her tea she kissed me on the cheek and went away, and I went indoors. In the gloom of the manse hallway, the black bags containing Jenny's clothes sat waiting to be taken to Oxfam and Cancer Research.

XXIV

Memory: a tricky substance. Sometimes I wonder if that brief but impassioned encounter with Elsie ever took place at all. It was never mentioned again, never alluded to by word, touch or look – not until the Stone came. There were so many times when we were alone together, so many moments in company when our eyes connected across a dinner table, across a room, but Elsie's communicated nothing about that summer afternoon. I looked and looked, but her eyes admitted nothing.

Did I imagine it? The only evidence, the slip soaked with our DNA, was taken from the scene. But you can't erase an event like that. Of course I know it happened. And she knows it too. The memory is too strong, too rich in detail to be a fantasy. It was, in a way, both fact and fantasy; it was like a dream, but it was not a dream.

Something happened to me between losing Jenny and making love with Elsie. It wasn't that through these crises I found God again, but it did occur to me that God might have found me. I had not loved Jenny well enough: she had been taken from me. I wanted to love Elsie: no sooner was that desire realised than it too was denied me. Perhaps God had noticed my indifference to him and was repaying it in kind. Or perhaps all this was not a punishment, but a test. For the first time in years, I entertained the possibility of a divine plan, a system of rewards and retributions. All my reason objected to the idea, but all my childhood fears were reawakened. What had I done, or not done, to deserve my failures in love? And where were Elsie, Jenny and John in this scheme? What about the man MacInnes in Inverness, and his cancer-ridden father? What about my own father, and my mother? Were we all part of some vast, intricate machinery of weights and balances, some perpetual morality calculator? None of this led me to God, but I could not stop my mind from dwelling on it.

I think of my mother again now. Is she lying awake in the care home, and if so what pack of wild half-sentences, dreams, misremembered memories and unlabelled pictures are roaming in her head? Is what she sees in the dark hours any different from what she sees in the daytime? Maybe it's all clear to her – maybe she's cracked it, life, the plan, knows the code to the combination lock that lets you in, or out – and the smile on her face is one of contentment, the sly delight of knowing the answer. I hope so, I really hope so.

Outside in the hall I hear the grandfather clock's mechanism whirring as it reaches the hour. I count the chimes: one, two, three.

Then silence again. The world is asleep, I am alone in the ticking silence of the manse, and I am not far, I believe, from knowing the answer myself.

XXV

When the Stone first appeared Catherine Craigie (*Miss* Craigie to all but a few) was sixty-two, and though ravaged by rheumatoid arthritis unquestionably the town's most formidable female inhabitant. She had a reputation for terseness and for intolerance of stupidity and triviality that made Amelia Wishaw seem like a flibbertigibbet. Catherine could utter a word like 'flibbertigibbet' straight-faced and still be taken seriously, whereas used by anyone else it would have caused sniggering or outright guffaws. Many admired her, but few professed to liking her. She had left her mark on hundreds of children, through thirty years of teaching at the Academy, and through her involvement in the Local History Association, the Community Council and the Monimaskit Museum Trust. Nobody knew more about the topography, the social history and the archaeology of the area. And – the crowning glory of her reputation – she had published a book. There were three copies of this book* in the public library, and others could be found in the houses of all respectable indwellers of Monimaskit. Most people, finding the material too academic, had given up after a few pages, but this only increased rather than diminished the general awe of the Craigie brain. The book was out of print by the time I came to Monimaskit, but I had acquired a second-hand copy and read it. It was hard going in places, and I said so in an unguarded moment. The news was around the town in no time, and was marked down as a triumph for Miss Craigie. It was pretty obvious that to write a book that just anybody could read – a detective novel, say, or a Mills & Boon – couldn't be that difficult, but to write one that

* *The Ancient Stones of Monimaskit and Surrounding District* (Dundee: The Ballindean Press, 1983). – P.W.

defeated even the new minister, well, that smacked of real intellect.

I had not, in fact, been defeated by *The Ancient Stones*. True, I had skimmed some of it, but elsewhere I had become quite engrossed by the subject matter. Of all the abundant archaeological remains to be found in the parish, the twelve standing stones. Some of them are prehistoric, some Pictish, but together they seem to make some kind of pattern, to relate some indistinct, fragmented or unfinished story – a story that Miss Craigie's book tried to tell. I was especially intrigued by her description of how the later, Christianised Picts seem to have incorporated their ancestors' symbols into their own cruciform carvings.

I must write now of the first time I properly met Catherine. It was the summer after Jenny's death, June or July, a month or two before Elsie and I had our 'incident'. After three and a half years in Monimaskit, I was still regarded as being on trial, and the fund-raising activities had annoyed some who thought I wasn't showing enough decorum as a minister. How little they knew! But my wife had died, and somehow that put me beyond censure, at least for the time being.

I knew Miss Craigie by reputation and soon after my calling to the Old Kirk had seen her, on sticks and clearly in pain, at one or two civic functions, but we had not been introduced, perhaps through design on her part. Since then her physical condition had deteriorated, and she seldom went out. I decided one evening to pay her a visit, to ask her more about the Pictish stones. An ulterior motive was that I wanted to meet her face to face: there was something about her that appealed to me. I was fed up with mealy-mouthed sympathy, with people pigeon-stepping around my feelings; I was frustrated by polite kindness that prevented real conversations; I couldn't tolerate any more sanctimony about God's mysterious ways. I knew there'd be none of that from Miss Craigie, for I'd been told that she was Monimaskit's most outspoken and inveterate atheist. I'd also heard that she wouldn't donate to any of our fund-raising activities because of my involvement. Whether she approved of other charitable causes I did not know, but for a certainty she didn't approve of ministers.

Her house was in Ellangowan Place, a long, curving Victorian terrace lined with cherry trees and overlooking the park, with neat front gardens behind low stone walls bearing the marks of cast-iron railings removed during the war. I opened a small wooden gate and walked up a path that needed weeding. My legs were brushed by various healthy-looking shrubs and bushes I didn't know the names of. There was a small patch of thick grass with a circular rose-bed in the middle, and honeysuckle spreading from under the two bay windows that flanked the front door. The garden looked as if it were on the verge of going on the rampage, but the house was freshly painted and seemed in good condition. One of the storm-doors was open. I pushed the bell and waited.

Nothing happened. Perhaps she was out, or in the back garden. I rang the bell again. I remembered being sent on errands by my mother or father, delivering messages or Communion card envelopes or pots of jam to various houses in Ochtermill, standing on stone doorsteps just like this one, anticipating the stilted conversation I would have to endure if somebody came to the door, knowing that if nobody did I would not be absolved from my task but would have to return later. Scents from the garden, wood-pigeons cooing like stuck records, the buzz of insects: I was almost that boy again . . .

I became aware of a voice calling and snapped out of my reverie. Through the etched glass of the inner door I saw a shadowy figure moving awkwardly.

'Just come in, for heaven's sake. It's not locked.'

I leaned forward to open the door and noticed a handwritten card taped to the wall of the vestibule: *Please ring and enter. If locked go away.*

'Can't you read?' the voice said as I let myself in.

'Sorry,' I said, 'I only just saw it. I'm sorry if I've interrupted you.'

'You shouldn't have rung the bell if you didn't want to interrupt me,' Miss Craigie said. 'I don't sit around waiting for visitors all day, you know. Oh, it's you.'

She said these last words not apologetically but with added

distaste. It was dark in the hallway, and I could not make out the expression on her face, but the tone of voice told me all I needed to know. I'd been well warned by various members of my flock: Catherine Craigie thought that the Kirk, by and large, had been, was and always would be a scabrous outbreak on the flesh of Scotland.

I was wearing my dog-collar – I was planning to make some other calls that evening – and assumed that this was the cause of her aggravation. I tapped it with my forefinger.

'It doesn't make you a bad person,' I said.

'Hmph,' she retorted. 'It doesn't make you a good one either. What do you want?'

'I've come to say hello, Miss Craigie. I've been here nearly four years and I feel we should have met by now.' This didn't seem to impress her. 'And I want to ask you some questions about the standing stones. I've been reading your book.'

'Well, it's all in there, so I don't see why you need to come bothering me if you haven't taken the trouble to read it properly.'

'Supplementary questions,' I said. 'Arising out of what I've read.'

'I know what a supplementary question is,' she said. 'Such as?'

I'd had the forethought to compose something beforehand.

'Well, it seems to me, in all this debate about pre-Christian and Christianised Picts, that we forget that they were under pressure from two rival Christianities, the Celtic and the Roman – the Scots in the west and the Northumbrians in the south. And I wondered what bearing that might have had on the symbols on the stones.'

During this speech her head inclined towards me like a bird's listening for danger, or for a worm. Later, I realised that this stance was in part due to her illness, which prevented her from moving her neck very much. She was standing halfway down the hallway, holding on to a tall wooden plant-stand positioned in the middle of a large rug. There was no plant on the plant-stand and it took me a moment to understand the reason for its location: the lay-out of the hall, from the front door to the foot of the stairs and on towards the back lobby, was a kind of domestic rock-face, with hand-holds and rest points along the way, some pre-existing and some strategically placed: the plant-stand, a chair, a table, a stool, a shelf, the banister end, radiators. This horizontal climbing-wall was how Miss Craigie managed to get around her house.

'You'd better come in,' she said. 'You have me at a disadvantage out here. I shall deal with you in the drawing room. But I warn you, Mr Mack, if you have come with the intention of either converting me or extracting money from me I shall be very, very cross. Follow me.'

She launched herself from the plant-stand and began ricocheting from one point to the next like a ball on a bagatelle board, out of the hall and into the drawing room, until she performed a neat pirouette in front of an expensive-looking black leather orthopaedic armchair and landed in it with what was evidently practised accuracy. I, plodding after her like a dog, felt awkward by comparison. She pointed at another chair and obediently I sat in it.

The room was obviously where she spent most of her time. There was an electric fire in front of the open fireplace, a big old sofa covered with rugs where she possibly took naps, a dresser displaying various bottles and glasses, a television and VCR, a stereo system, bookcases stuffed with books and journals, and a large desk covered with paper, pens and an Amstrad computer. On a table beside her chair were remote controls for the electrical equipment, and a telephone.

'Now,' she said, 'my foot is on my native heath, or at least my backside is. Ask me your questions about Christianity and the Picts, and I will answer you as best I can. You must know, though, if you really have read my book, that we know a great deal less about the Picts than we do about Christianity, a circumstance which, in my opinion, entirely favours the Picts.'

There was something in these remarks, from the mild crudity at the start to the dig against my professed faith at the end, that suggested I'd made some progress, although I didn't know quite why or how. Later I learned that Miss Craigie had numerous visitors, who for the most part came seeking information about the town or out of some sense of duty, rather than because they liked her, and that this was how she maintained a vast and meticulous knowledge of the affairs of Monimaskit. She'd been expecting me to call for months and had always planned to give me a hard time, to see how I would react. Cautiously, I began to talk to her about my understanding, or lack of it, of the Picts and their culture.

Caution, I soon discovered, was not the best approach with Catherine Craigie. She could detect wishy-washiness in the first few words of a sentence and would interrupt to tell you what it was you really meant. Her briskness and impatience should have been infuriating, but I found myself warming to her, to her precision of thought and to the clipped voice that was halfway to being gentrified but carried in it her years of teaching and, still, a good dose of her Monimaskit childhood. She tolerated no prevarication, no 'whittie-whattieing' as she called it, and I liked her for it.

'Don't tell me, Mr Mack, that you have some romantic notion that Columba and his Iona gang were soft and cuddly while the Northumbrians were hardened criminals. It was all about conquest, military or ecclesiastical, whichever was more effective. There's a pithy saying that if you have a man by the balls his heart and mind will follow, but the reverse is also true. It doesn't much matter which Christianity won out in Pictland in the end – the biggest losers were always going to be the Picts.'

Her efforts to offend me amused me. 'I don't think you could really survive in the sixth century by being cuddly,' I said. 'Columba was a warrior before he was a saint. Whatever you think of his faith, he comes across as somebody quite heroic.'

'And what do *you* think of his faith?' she demanded.

'I think he was a man of his time.'

'Don't equivocate. What do you mean?'

'I don't know what his faith consisted of,' I said. 'My recollection is that he'd killed someone in battle, and had to get out of Ireland for political reasons. Your pithy saying works for Columba too. His balls took him to Iona and he found something there that satisfied his heart and mind. I think he was doing what most of us do, searching around for meaning. Maybe it was easier and simpler then, but I doubt it.'

Miss Craigie smiled. 'Well,' she said, 'at least you have an opinion. But you don't sound very convinced.'

'It was a long time ago. I wasn't there.'

'I don't mean about Columba. I mean about faith.'

'I'm *not* convinced,' I said. 'I have huge doubts and misgivings. If you forced me to choose at this point, as to whether I was for or against religious belief, I'd probably be on the same side as you.'

'Against it?'

'Yes.'

A look of glee filled her face. 'Well, what on earth are you doing being a minister?' she shouted. 'If that's how you feel about it, get out!' I shifted awkwardly in my chair. 'No, stay where you are, I don't mean here, I mean out of the Church. Make room for a genuine, dyed-in-the-wool hypocrite!' She started to laugh heartily which, judging by the way her shoulders suddenly hunched up, caused her some pain. 'Actually, on second thoughts, cancel that. You're a kind of fifth columnist, aren't you? You've been – what do they call it in espionage? – *turned*. Goodness knows how or who by, but you'd better stay where you are. The whole rotten edifice will come down a lot quicker if people like you stick on the inside. Oh – wait a minute. This isn't about your wife, is it?'

'I beg your pardon?' I said.

'You haven't fallen out with God because he took your wife away from you, have you?'

It was an astonishingly crude, even cruel question. For a moment I could not speak.

'Because if you have, I can tell you, you're mistaken. God had absolutely nothing to do with it.'

'I'm aware of that,' I said quietly. 'I fell out with God, as you put it, long before Jenny died. But I'm wondering why *you* take so strongly against him. If you're an atheist, why does he bother you so much?'

'He doesn't bother me in the least,' she said. 'It's you lot that bother me – regurgitating stories about God and heaven and hell and causing endless misery as a result. Anyway, who told you I was an atheist?'

'It seems to be common knowledge,' I said.

'Common ignorance,' she said. 'I'm not an atheist, I wouldn't be so presumptuous. How do I know what's out there and after this? I'm an agnostic. I'm only concerned with what we know, what we *can* know.'

'Me too,' I said.

She stared at me evenly. I thought she might even be about to apologise.

'Look,' she said, 'that decanter on the dresser has a rather excellent single malt in it. Do you drink whisky? Good. Then fetch a couple of glasses and pour us both a drink. Do you mind if I call you Gideon? It's a hell of a name, but "Mr Mack" sounds like something out of a children's television programme.'

'Gideon's fine,' I said, and got up to fix the drinks, still somewhat shocked by the way she'd mentioned Jenny, but also struggling not to laugh. Maybe that was a nervous reaction. I did not ask if I could call her Catherine.

When I came back with the glasses she was beaming at me. I seemed to have passed some test. We spent the next couple of hours arguing happily, as John and I had once done, and before we were finished she'd asked me to use her first name. The decanter had been half-full when I arrived, and it was empty by the time I left, quite incapable of any more pastoral duties.

That was my first encounter with Catherine Craigie, and soon I was dropping in regularly, usually on a Wednesday after visiting my mother. My calls did not go unnoticed by the Session. 'You're wasting your time on her,' Peter Macmurray commented. 'She's a God hater and nothing you can say will change her.' 'Oh, I'm not trying to change her,' I said. 'I'm rather fond of her as she is.' Macmurray's face sucked in on itself. He said no more about it, at least not to me, but it was another black mark against me.

There was something else about Catherine that Macmurray did not know, that if he had would have confirmed his worst suspicions of both of us: she smoked cannabis. She'd discovered that it alleviated some of her pain, and had used her local knowledge to get herself a regular supply through a man called Chae Middleton. Chae did a bit of gardening for her, mowing the lawn and pulling weeds, and every month he'd bring her a quantity of cannabis, and she'd add the price on to whatever she owed him for his chores. She smoked the occasional cigarette, so there was no difficulty for her about inhaling: her problem was that her swollen fingers made rolling joints almost impossible. She mentioned this frustrating situation to me a few months after I started going to see her. Although I hadn't smoked any dope since I was a student, and didn't want to again, I could roll a joint with ease. It became one of the things I did on my Wednesday visits – make up half a dozen to keep her going through the week. How Peter Macmurray would have loved to see me at work! I can imagine the joy with which he would have contacted the police.

It made complete sense to speak to Catherine about the Stone when it appeared, but her very expertise and knowledge also made me hesitate. She was so incapacitated these days that it was a struggle for her to get down to the shops, let alone into the depths of Keldo Woods, but she had a detailed picture of the locality in her head, she had the Ordnance Survey's maps and she had her book, and my standing stone wasn't in any of them. If I tried to tell her about it she would have every right to denounce me as a drivelling fantasist.

XXVI

Another week passed. I went back to the woods in the interim and the Stone was still there. My courage failed me when I saw Catherine that week, but I made a vow to myself to tell her on my next visit. Before that, however, I myself had a visitor. William Winnyford, the artist, called early one morning. We had previously met at a reception for him hosted by the council. He was a small, sandy-haired man who boomed when he spoke.

'Good morning, Mr Mack. I hope this isn't an inconvenient moment. Do you remember I said I would call on you?'

I didn't remember this at all. All I remembered, as soon as I heard him, was his loud, bouncy voice. He'd made a short speech at the reception about how excited he was to have the commission, and his enthusiasm had been painful to witness. I wondered if I was as irritating when I was fund-raising.

I let him in anyway, took him through to the kitchen and put the kettle on. 'Take a seat,' I said, indicating the chairs around the table. He sat down in Jenny's Windsor chair. He wasn't to know, of course. She'd been dead a long time.

'What can I do for you?' I asked.

'That's what I've come to discuss, what you can do for me. You know I'm working on this big project at the museum.'

'Yes, I do. How's it going?'

'Early days, early days. It takes time to engage with the material. Human or otherwise. The thing is, I'd like you to be part of it.'

'Oh, I don't think so,' I said.

'Let me explain,' he said, and was off without drawing breath. 'I'm interested in the spaces people occupy and how the spaces affect them and how they affect the spaces. I'm building up this multi-layered experience, creating, or *re*-creating is more accurate, the world in which people live, bits of it that are always there but which they don't always pay attention to. I see the world as multi-dimensional, I mean you've got the physical, spatial world and the metaphysical of course' – he made a sort of half bow at me from his seat – 'but then you need to factor in time, the past, present, future, I mean does the past exist at all for most people, not just their personal past but the community's, history? Some would say yes, it's what the present is built upon, others wouldn't recognise those foundations at all, and as for the future, *well*, if you catch my drift. So what I want people to focus on, but obliquely subconsciously, in an *un*focused way, as they walk round the exhibition I mean, are the things they normally only deal with subliminally or not at all in fact, so they'll see, hear, touch, interact with aspects of the man-made and natural environment which are seemingly alien but which are in fact integral to the fabric of the context in which they exist, the people I mean, and by doing this the people will feed their own energies back into the context, social, environmental, historical, whatever, the *en*tity, do you follow me?'

This is only an approximation of what he said, because his words ran into each other and changed direction in mid-flow so much that it wasn't at all clear what he *was* saying. The kettle came to the boil. I made coffee, asked if he took milk or sugar. It gave me a few moments' grace.

'Milk no sugar, thanks,' he said. 'So are you with me so far?'

'Well . . .'

'Good.' He stormed off again. 'I'm building items into the whole that are self-reflecting, recyclable. Echoes that are sometimes natural sometimes manufactured sometimes a mixture of both. Echoes, connections, continuities. Sometimes if you're lucky or clever you get what I call a *conjunction* – space, time and narrative overlap. An example. Two men are sitting drinking in the bar down at the harbour. You know the one, the Luggie?'

'Yes, but I've never been in it.'

He looked at me in surprise, as if he'd not expected me to answer. My intervention had the effect of making him slow down a little.

'One of them is in old torn jeans and a filthy jumper, the other is in a heavy green herring-bone tweed suit. A big man. He's a water-bailie on the Keldo. His companion is a well-known poacher. Generations of poaching in the family. But they're both off-duty, they get on fine over a pint, they respect each other. Above them on the wall is a photograph of the herring fleet in Monimaskit harbour in the 1880s. The poacher is telling the story of the time his grandfather nearly drowned trying to land a forty-pound salmon, which got away. The bailie knows this story, but the poacher doesn't know the story of the *bailie's* grandfather. He skippered a fishing-boat out of Monimaskit in the 1880s. The boat was lost at sea with all four members of the crew. You can see the boat's bow just sticking out from behind another vessel in the photograph. It is identifiable because of its name: *Escape*. That's what I mean by a conjunction.'

'A coincidence, in other words,' I said.

'No,' Winnyford said. 'Everything's connected but by conjunction not by coincidence. We just don't see the connections most of the time.'

'I don't know about that,' I said, 'but I do know the men in your wee scenario. Keir Anderson and Chae Middleton.'

'Chae's quite a character,' Winnyford said. 'He's been very helpful. Claims he can get you pretty much anything you want, for a price.'

'I've heard that,' I said, non-committally. 'He once brought a salmon to the back door for us, when my wife was alive. Unfortunately I was out, and Jenny sent him away with it because she didn't like fish. He's never been back with another, I'm sorry to say. And I wouldn't want to run into Keir Anderson up the Keldo on a dark night, he's a right bruiser, but he brings his kids to church once in a while and is as meek as a lamb. Coincidences, conjunctions, whatever you want to call them, they're pretty thick on the ground in a place like this.'

'That's why the space for this exhibition is important. It will be circular, a circuit, ideally there should be no fixed entry or exit to the experience. Of course there is in fact, has to be, the main entrance, can't avoid it – fire regulations, school parties, all that – but once you're in it'll be like one of those round wooden puzzles with silver balls. The people are the silver balls, the space is the puzzle, with openings at various points within concentric circles, are you with me?'

'I think so,' I said.

'Good. So you'll do something for me?'

'Such as?'

'It's not much I'm asking, Mr Mack. I've been reading up the history of Monimaskit from ancient times to the present and finding all kinds of artefacts to put into this exhibition, but my main collaboration is with the people, the people are the source, the material and the interpreters even if subconsciously. And what I want from you is this chap Augustus Menteith, splendid name isn't it, who recorded all these legends about the town. Do you know his books?'

'I've dipped in and out of them,' I said.

'Then you'll know he was the minister here a century ago. I just thought it would be marvellous if you would read a short extract from one of his stories. I want to record it. Today's minister reading something written by the Victorian minister about something that happened centuries before. Reputedly. I imagine the tableau, the setting if you like, I've not built it yet but I have it in my head, as a room like a study or a library lined with books . . .'

'Perhaps you'd better have a look at *my* study then,' I said.

'Rather not just now. Would interfere. Later perhaps. I envisage this room all very civilised sedate Victorian, but through a window at the back will be this trompe-l'œil drop into the chasm up in the woods there, a sort of gaping view into the depths of the earth.'

'The Black Jaws,' I said.

'Yes, the Black Jaws. Astonishing place. Went to look at it myself – slipped, nearly fell in. I've brought a photocopy of the relevant pages from Menteith's book in case you're not familiar with the legend. I've highlighted the bit I'd like you to read. It's only a few lines, can't do more than that or the natives get restless, attention span deficiency, what do you think, you'll do it?'

He handed me some A4 sheets with one passage marked in yellow. I glanced over it.

'You'll need to leave it with me, Mr Winnyford,' I said.

'Bill, please.'

'Bill,' I said. 'I'll have to read the whole thing and see. It might not be appropriate . . .'

'Nothing to worry about there, no filth, no blasphemy just a spooky legend, I hear you're not afraid to stick your neck out anyway but no need in this case, a bit of fun, *highly* appropriate if *you* would read it.'

He drained his coffee and stood up. 'I'll leave it with you, Gideon, may I call you Gideon? You can leave a message at the museum or here's my card, mobile number, I usually remember to switch it on.'

I showed him out, this torrential man, half of me wanting to kick his backside, half of me wishing to humour him and involve myself in his exhibition. There was something in his description of the Victorian study with its window looking down into the void that made me think he had at least some imagination. But when I sat down to read the photocopied story that evening, I realised that the imagination, or nine-tenths of it, belonged not to Winnyford but to my predecessor, the Reverend Augustus Menteith:

The Legend of the Black Jaws

The flat coastline north and south of Monimaskit, the rich, rolling farmland surrounding it, and the douce, settled sandstone streets of the town itself, give, to the innocent stranger, little indication of the rugged, wild and inhospitable interior to be found only a score of miles distant, where the lower slopes of the Grampian range commence. On these slopes, tradition has it, the lost battlefield of Mons Graupius lies, where, some maintain – and this in defiance of Tacitus, who was but a Roman after all – the legions were put to flight when the Caledonian tribes gathered together, and, setting aside their differences, dared, under the leadership of the warrior chieftain Calgacus, to resist subjugation. The Keldo Water flows from these hills to Monimaskit, and, where it passes through the town and enters the sea, it presents a steady and stately face to the world; yet, between its source and its mouth this river takes at times a tumultuous course, and at no point is this more the case than a mere four or five miles upstream from Monimaskit, and but two from Keldo House. Here it rushes and roars through a gulf of great depth known in the locality as the Black Jaws.

This ravine, split originally perhaps by ice and subsequently scoured by the torrents of millennia, consists of walls two hundred feet in height which are always soaked black with the spray of the foaming water, and which are home to a dense mass of vegetation – mosses, ferns and grass, and trees clinging with the most tenuous grip to clefts and cracks in the rock. Above this gloomy drop the land is so thickly wooded with birch and pine that, were it not for the constant booming of the water, the unwary visitor would be almost over the precipice before he realised its existence. It was once the supposed sport of town lads to traverse the gorge on the trunks of trees which, uprooted in winter storms, had fallen across it, but in truth these narrow and slippery bridges are so dangerous that few must have dared such an adventure, and certainly I have never heard of any boy in the present time who had courage enough to essay that dread crossing. Even from the path which wends its way along one of its sides it is quite unnerving to peer down into the chasm, where the warmth and light of the sun never penetrate, and to see forest birds flitting in and out of the foliage and through the spray like seagulls on a dizzy, over-beetling ocean cliff; and it is easy to imagine that the echoing din is a chorus of lost souls cast into the awful void, or the triumphant roars of the demons that persecute them. And this, perhaps, gave rise in former times to a story, which I might myself relate, but which, by good fortune, I am able to reproduce just as it was told to me in my youth by an old woman of the town, now long dead, whose stock of lore was as rich as she was poor, and whose imagination, perhaps, was as broad as her cottage was narrow.*

'Weel dae I ken the Black Jaws,' old Ephie Lumsden would quaver, 'for mony's the time as a lassie I wad ga'e to the woods aboon it wi' my freens to gaither bluebells an' primroses in the springtime. But tho' it was a bonnie-lik' place to wander, nane o' us wad daur to frequent it alane, bricht an' blue tho' the day micht be, an' as for the nicht, weel, ye could ne'er ha'e persuaded ony o' us to gang there efter dark, no' for a' the gowd in Edinbury. The place had an unco' souch aboot it, an' tho' I'm owre auld to hirple up there noo, I dinna doot but it'll aye feel the same to this verra' day.

'Lang lang syne, in the days whan Keldo Hoose was in the hands o' the Guthries, an' hadna passed owre to the present faim'ly, there cam' a bonnie leddy to be the wife o' the laird. She was a dark, fremmit craitur' frae anither pairt o' the warld – frae Spain, some said, frae France said ithers, while still ithers tauld o' Hungary, Romania, Poland an' sic'like distant lands. Whan she spak', it was wi' a saft, queer-lik' lilt, but in a pure English that a'body marvelled at. Even the laird himsel', a guid an' generous man weel-lo'ed by his people, didna speak English as braw as she. Hoo he had cam' by her naebody kent, save that he had been on a great tour o' Europe an' maun ha'e met her while he was awa', but she

* For the sake of readers not familiar with the Scots language, I supply a glossary of some of the words employed by Ephie Lumsden (or Augustus Menteith!) on this and the following pages. – P.W.

---

gowd: gold; *an unco' souch*: a strange feeling; *hirple*: limp; *lang syne*: long ago; *fremmit*: foreign; *weel-lo'ed*: well-loved; *braw*: fine; *kent*: knew; *maun ha'e*: must have

was thocht an awfu' fine jewel for him to bring hame to a quait place lik' Monimaskit.

'Yet, for a' her beauty, or maybe on accoont o' it, she wasna weel likit at the muckle hoose. She was proud an' aloof, an' her speech set her apairt, as did her foreign ways, an' forbye thae things it was whispered that she was a papist. Certain it was she was never seen at the kirk, tho' the laird wad come his lane an' sit in his pew wi' a glower on him as if they had focht aboot it owre their disjune. An' that was anither mark against her, for she was cauld an' distant to the laird an' a', an' he that should ha'e been in the prime o' life seemed a doun-hauden an' weariet man sin' e'er the hamecomin' wi his new bride. Her a'e companion was the maid she had brocht wi' her, an' she *wes* French, an' a fykie, pettit-lipp'd, ill-to-please jaud juist as ye'd expeck o' a Frenchwoman. Jean, her name was. She wadna mix wi' the ither servants, nor wad she answer ony questions aboot her mistress, save to say that she an' the laird had been merriet abroad an' in her view the laird had the better pairt o' the bargain.

'The twa were in the habit o' takin' lang walks in the gairden o' Keldo an' beyond, an' in partic'lar they wad gang up the glen that leads to the Black Jaws. In dry weather, as I ha'e tauld ye, this is a fine place, wi' a path windin' up the brae, the birds chantin' in their innocent glee, an' deer grazin' shy-like amang the trees. But in winter, or on days o' weet an' wind at ony season o' the year, the Black Jaws is dour an' ugsome, an' wad fleg a squadron o' dragoons, never mind a pair o' weemen on their ain. But the leddy somehow seemed to like it best whan the weather was at its maist dismal, an' wad tak' the French lass up there mair an' mair. Whiles they wadna return till lang efter dark, whan the laird was growin' frantic for their safety an' the men were aboot to be turned oot wi' lantrens an' dogs to seek them. Syne, in they wad come, drookit an' shiverin', an' gang strecht to my leddy's chaumer wi' scarce a word or a

---

quait: quiet; *muckle*: big; *forbye*: besides; *his lane*: on his own; *disjune*: breakfast; *an' a'*: as well; *doun-hauden*: downcast; *a'e*: one; *fykie*: troublesome; *pettit-lipp'd*: sulky, with a protruded lower lip; *jaud*: wilful woman; *dour an' ugsome*: grim and ugly; *fleg*: frighten; *ain*: own; *whiles*: sometimes; *lantrens*: lanterns; *syne*: then; *drookit*: soaked; *chaumer*: chamber

look, forbye ane that said the laird was naethin' but a glaikit fule for fashin' his heid aboot them.

'Noo, in the autumn o' the year, as the days grew short an' the leaves fell frae the birks an' made the path by the Black Jaws mair treacherous than usual, it was noticed that Jean seemed to seecken, an' to shrink frae her mistress as she had never done afore. Whaur she had aince walked willingly wi' her to the gorge, noo she ga'ed wi' a falterin' step an' a fearfu' face. But she had nae freen's amang the hoose servants, an' naebody socht to speir at her whit ailed her. Syne, a'e nicht, the mistress cam' hame alane, pale an' distracted, wi' a tale that pit the hale hoose in a steer. The lassie, it seemed, had gane owre near to the edge o' the chasm, her denty fuit had slippit on the leaves, an' afore the leddy could gang to aid her she had plunged doun into the roarin' flood. Nae man kens the depth o' the water as it rins through the Black Jaws, an' nae man kens whit twists an' turns it tak's till it flows oot at the tither end, but it has aye been a truth that naething that fa's into the Black Jaws – tree, deer, dog or lass – is ever seen again.

'Weel, some said it was only whit they had expeckit frae the start, while ithers were suspicious o' the leddy's version o' events, an' said there was mischief an' foul play in the business. The leddy retired to her rooms, an' seldom ventured furth again, an' wadna thole ony ither servant to tak' Jean's place. But it was said that whiles the leddy's bed lay empty at nicht, an' a licht had been seen flichterin' amang the trees o' the glen, but folk were owre fear'd to follow it an' see if it was her.

'A'e day, a week or thereawa' efter the maid's disappearance, a young lad, a fisher frae Monimaskit, chapped at the door o' Keldo askin' to see the mistress. His name was Dod Eadie, an' he was wont to bring fish to sell to the laird's kitchen, fresh frae his faither's boat. Noo the laird was awfu' fond o' fish, an' likit to ha'e it at his table, but his leddy didna care for it ava', considerin' it coarse an' unclean: if she happened to be there whan Dod ca'ed, she wad send him aff wi' a flea in his lug, an' the laird

---

glaikit: silly; *fashin'*: bothering; *birks*: birches; *seecken*: sicken; *aince*: once; *ga'ed*: went; *socht to speir at*: sought to ask; *steer*: stir; *denty fuit*: dainty foot; *the tither*: the other; *furth*: abroad; *thole*: suffer; *flichterin'*: flickering; *owre fear'd*: too frightened; *thereawa'*: thereabouts; *chapped*: knocked; *ava'*: at all

wad get nae fish to his supper that nicht. But Dod wasna cairryin' ony fish wi' him this efternune. He threapit that he had an important message to gi'e to the leddy, an' he wadna gang hame till he had seen her; an' as proof o' his seriousness, he handed to the servant that was to tak' word to her a locket on a chain. Noo this locket had belanged the French lass, an' as sune as the leddy saw it she ordered for Dod to be admitted an' brocht afore her, an' this was the tale he tauld her. He an' Jean had been secret lovers for months, an' she had gi'en him the locket as a keepsake. He kent that she had become unhappy an' fearfu' on the visits to the Black Jaws, an' that it was on accoont o' a tryst that the leddy kept wi' a foreign man, but she wadna tell him mair. An' noo Dod begged the leddy o' Keldo to tell him if Jean was yet alive, an' whaur she micht be found, an' he wad gang to fetch her an' never breathe a word o' the leddy's indiscretion to anither soul.

'Weel, at first the mistress o' Keldo raged at him, an' syne she said that Jean was deid an' nae mair could be done aboot it, an' syne she grat, an' at last she composed hersel' an' tauld him a story o' her ain. On ane o' their first walks in that gloomy place, she an' her maid had stumbled upon a hidden path that led doun an' doun into the verra' he'rt o' the chasm. An' there they had come across a black-avised gentleman, dressed in the finest cla'es, danderin' aside the breengin' torrent an' smokin' his pipe as if he did it every day o' his life. He greeted them, but they couldna hear a word, sae he led them into a cavern whaur the water ran slow an' silent an' black as tar. There was a table an' chair made o' iron fixed into the rock, wi' a chain attached to the chair, an' twa great slaverin' hounds sleepin' i' the mooth o' the cave. An' faur, faur ben, they thocht they could see the faint licht o' a bleezin' fire, an' even imagined they could hear voices – but that surely couldna be!

'Jean was gey fear'd, but the stranger spak' wi'a gentle voice, an' speired efter the leddy's health in her ain native tongue. "You are sad, and far from home," he said, "but I have the power to transport you there, where

---

threapit: insisted; *grat*: wept; *ane*: one; *black-avised*: dark-featured; *cla'es*: clothes; *danderin'*: strolling; *breengin'*: rushing; *faur ben*: deep within; *gey fear'd*: very afraid

you may be happy again." An' the leddy o' Keldo confessed to Dod Eadie that, tho' she had merriet the laird, she had done it for siller, no' for love, an' that she had anither lover in her ain land that she green'd to see. She had jaloused by noo wha the gentleman o' the cavern micht be, but she didna care. She said that she wad dearly like to be joined wi' her lover aince mair. "That may be done in an instant," said the gentleman, "but your companion must wait for your return at the head of the path." The maid pleaded wi' her no' to bargain wi' sic' a frichtsome craitur', but her mistress ordered her to withdraw an' attend her at the path heid. Syne the man sent the leddy o' Keldo owre the sea, by what means she never related to Dod, an' she was reunited wi' her lover. Whan she cam' back, tho' she felt she had been awa' for days, only an 'oor had passed. "Whenever you wish it," the stranger said, "I can arrange for you to make that journey, but there is a price, and that is that you sign a bond assigning your soul to me." He had the document a' drawn up, an' a pen ready for her, on the iron table. Eagerly she sat doun to sign, but there was nae ink. The De'il – for ye may be sure it was he – produced a pocket-knife frae his coat. "Since you will supply the soul, you may supply the ink also," he said, an' nicked her airm wi' the blade sae that the blude trickled oot. She dipped the pen in the wound an' bent to sign, but again she hesitated. "It is a fair bargain," she said, "but I would fain make another with you. I pledge to settle the account with a human soul, but let the name be blank. Either, when you redeem the pledge, it will be mine, or it will belong to one far more innocent than I." By this she had Jean in mind, an' the De'il, kennin' her meanin', wi' a canny look agreed to her proposal. Whan Dod heard this, he cried oot, "An' had ye nae he'rt that ye could sign awa' my dear Jean for sake o' your ain sinfu', selfish ways?" "Alas, that I had not!" lamented the leddy, "for I was consumed with my own desires, and thought that I would find some way to outwit him ere the time of reckoning came. And when he claimed her some weeks after, I tried to prevent him taking her, and wrestled with him at the mouth of that horrid cave, but he was too strong and dragged

---

siller: money; *green'd*: yearned; *jaloused*: guessed; *craitur'*: creature.

her beyond the dripping teeth of his hounds where I could not reach her. I pleaded with him, and took from my wrist a gold bracelet and threw it over the hounds to him, and said if he would only release her he would have all the gold he desired. But he laughed at me for a fool, saying that he had more gold than he could wish for, and that it was nothing compared with the two souls he had gained – for, he said, by my deeds I was surely bound for his kingdom in any event. And he kicked the bracelet from him as if it were but worthless trash." An' the mistress flung hersel' at the feet o' Dod Eadie, an' sobbed for what she had done, an' begged his forgiveness, an' tauld him that if he wad gang wi' her, she wad plead again wi' the De'il for the lass's release, an' if need be wad offer hersel' in her place, an' Dod wad ha'e Jean back an' lead her to safety.

'They set aff athout a moment's delay, tho' the day was near its end, an' at the entrance to the gorge the leddy bade him stop. She must gang on alane, she said, an' he must wait for Jean to be returned to him. Dod was laith to let her awa', for he didna a' thegither trust her, but whit else could he dae but stand at the fuit o' the gorge whaur the water rins oot frae't, while she warsled up the secret path to the gloomy yett o' hell? An 'oor passed, an' syne anither, till it was quite dark, an' Dod had gi'en up hope o' seein' either maid or mistress again. But the mune rose clear that nicht, an' by its licht he suddenly saw, floatin' in the dark water, a figure a' in white. He plunged into the river an' cairried oot his ain Jean, half-droon'd wi' ha'ein' come through the waters o' the Black Jaws. In a while she recovered eneugh to speak, an' tauld how her mistress had arrived at a time whan the De'il was awa' to his kingdom to look owre the torture o' ither lost souls, an' his muckle hounds were asleep. She had found the keys to unchain Jean frae the iron chair on which she was bound, an' urged her to rin for her life, but afore she hersel' could follow, the hounds awoke an' lowpit upon her, haudin' her to the ground till their maister should return. Jean had been keepit as a slave an' a drudge to the De'il, cookin' for him an' servin' him an' aye chained to the chair whan he was awa', an' she little doubted but that her mistress wad ha'e

---

athout: without; *laith*: loath; *a' thegither*: altogether; *warsled*: struggled; *yett*: gate; *lowpit*: leapt; *haudin'*: holding.

ta'en her place. An' frae that day on, the leddy o' Keldo was never seen by earthly craitur' again.'

XXVII

Catherine Craigie was not impressed that I was thinking of helping William Winnyford with his exhibition. It was my usual Wednesday-evening visit, and I was determined this time to consult her about the Stone, but rashly mentioned my encounter with Winnyford as I was pouring the whiskies at the dresser. She gave a little sigh of disapproval.

'Don't be taken in by his nonsense,' she said. 'He's a charlatan. He was round at my door the other day, looking for other people to do his work for him. He got short shrift from me, I can tell you.'

'What did he want?'

'He wanted to know all about standing stones. Not like you, Gideon, the first time you called on me. You had a genuine interest in the stones. You wanted to hear what I had to say. This Winnyford character already had his opinion of standing stones, and nothing I said was going to budge him from it. He kept coming back to druids, human sacrifices at the solstice, that kind of thing. Eventually I lost my temper and told him where he could stick his bloody druids. What does he want you to do?'

'Read a paragraph from Augustus Menteith's "Legend of the Black Jaws".'

Catherine snorted.

'Well, that simply underlines my point. Menteith always appeals to people like Winnyford. Can't tell the fact from the fantasy.'

'Who, Winnyford or Menteith?'

'Winnyford. Oh, Menteith knew the difference all right. He just exploited his resources better. Well, slightly better.'

'I thought he was recognised as the authority on Monimaskit. If it wasn't for him wouldn't we have lost half our information about the place?'

'If it wasn't for Gus Menteith we might not be wallowing in

fairies, ghosts and devils underground. I grant you there is some useful stuff in his *History of the Parish*, but *Relicts and Reminiscences*,* which is the one everybody reads, is just tosh.'

'I rather liked the story of the Black Jaws.'

'That's because you're soft in the head, Gideon, a necessary qualification in your line of work. That story of Menteith's is perfectly all right for children, I suppose, but deconstruct it and it just doesn't add up. He pretends he knew this old woman Ephie Lumsden who told him the story when he was a boy. Well, he was born in 1853 so let's say she told him it before he was twenty, that would make it 1873 at the latest. Now there have been Lumsdens in Monimaskit certainly, but you can search the parish records all you like and you'll not turn up an Ephie, Euphemia, Phemie or anything else Lumsden between 1850 and 1880. The Lumsdens were fisherfolk and they caught the cholera in the epidemic of 1831 and every last one of them died. The next time you see a Lumsden here is 1887, by which time Menteith was thirty-four. This Lumsden was a man from Aberdeen and he was hired as a gardener at the manse. His first name was Adam and I'll bet everybody knew him as Edie. Coincidence? I don't think so. I think Menteith invented the whole Black Jaws legend and then stuck a convenient name on it to give it a bit of provenance. His book is the only place the legend, so-called, is ever mentioned.'†

I was, as ever, impressed by Catherine's astonishing knowledge and powers of recall. Local historians are so often like that: they are

* Neither volume has been in print for some years, although a facsimile of *Relicts and Reminiscences* was issued in the 1970s by Messrs Nimmo & Grant, Forfar, in a limited run of 500 copies, and a new paperback edition is under consideration by myself at the time of writing. – P.W.

† It has been drawn to my attention by Dr Hugh Haliburton of the University of Stirling that Menteith's 'Legend of the Black Jaws' bears a striking resemblance to the tale of 'The Lady of Balconie', related by Hugh Miller (1802–56) in his *Scenes and Legends of the North of Scotland* (first published in 1835), a source of folklore with which Menteith would certainly have been familiar. Miller's story is associated with the Black Rock of Kiltearn, near Evanton in Easter Ross. Catherine Craigie, however, appears not to have been aware of this similarity. – P.W.

walking libraries of information, but with their own idiosyncratic cataloguing systems. Still, I felt it incumbent on me to raise an objection.

'But why would he make it up? Are you saying he made up all the stories in his book?'

'A number. You can tell which ones from the style. The genuine items are often incomplete, ragged at the edges, they lack precise details, they are quite unsatisfactory as crafted stories. The fakes are the highly polished ones. Take the Black Jaws tale. He might have started with some scrap gathered from some old wife, but he simply couldn't resist dressing it up. Look at the language he puts in Ephie's mouth. All derived from some ghastly genteel concept of what the *guid Scots tongue* should look like on the printed page. Those apostrophes all over the place, as if someone's slammed the book shut on a plague of corn lice. But when Ephie gets to the bits when the Devil and the Lady of Keldo speak, she turns to perfect English. The whole thing's just not credible as a piece of genuine folklore.'

'What happened to Menteith?' I said. 'All I know is that he was killed in the French Alps in 1895. I presume he's buried in France.'

'You presume wrong,' Catherine said, 'at least on a narrow definition of the word "buried". They never found him. He was trying to get up Mont Blanc. He'd been there several times before – used to climb with all those terribly fierce johnnies in plus-fours and fore-and-afts like Albert Mummery and Geoffrey Hastings and Norman Collie, but they got bored with the Alps and went off to the Himalayas that year, so Menteith went to Mont Blanc alone and climbed with a local guide. It was ironic really, because Mummery was killed in the Himalayas and Menteith was killed in the Alps about the same time. Apparently he and his guide took a wrong turn and fell several hundred feet down a crevasse in a glacier. Presumably they're still in it, making a very gradual descent.'

'Catherine, that's terrible.'

'No it isn't, it's the truth. Gussie Menteith had no business clambering about the Alps. He should have been tending his flock. And the guide knew the risks of his occupation. Actually I don't think Menteith was much missed back here. What with his summer mountaineering and his winter scribbling he can't have got much flock-tending done. I believe there'd been a few polite expressions of dissatisfaction from some of the congregation, but not much more than that. When Menteith didn't come back from his Alpine adventures, they replaced him with a mild-mannered chap who had giddy turns just going up the pulpit steps, so that was all right.'

'So,' I said, 'you have no sympathy for how Menteith met his end, and not much regard for his expertise as a folklorist.'

'That summarises my views very well, Gideon. Which is why I see red when someone like Winnyford seizes on the sort of thing Menteith produced, as if it's the key to understanding how a community functions. Dabbling, that's all it is. I don't know why you want to get mixed up in it. Have you seen what he's done so far?'

'No, I didn't think it was open to the public yet.'

'It isn't – at least the whole exhibition isn't, and won't be for months – but he's building bits of it in a unit on the industrial estate and he's put two or three items into the museum already, to monitor audience reaction, so I'm told. I thought I'd go and react. It cost me most of a morning and a great deal of inconvenience to get there, but I was determined to see what he was up to. A lot of nonsense, as I suspected. I had to put him right on a few things. Eventually, whenever this blasted exhibition opens . . .'

'September, I think,' I said.

'Yes, and that's another thing, why he needs so long to prepare is quite beyond me. Anyway, eventually he's going to take over the museum or a large part of it and turn it into a parody of a museum.'

'Perhaps that's the point,' I suggested. 'Perhaps it's irony.'

'Mr Winnyford wouldn't recognise irony if it slapped him in the face with a fish. He's going to set up a whole lot of *installations*. The ones on display already are sound installations, which is what he's roped you in for. Do you know what a sound installation is?'

'No.'

'Well, I'll tell you. It's a loudspeaker hidden behind a pot plant. A tape-recorder in a fish-kettle. Mr Winnyford has gone around recording different people talking about Monimaskit and taken the bits he considers *meaningful* and made loops out of them, and the resulting gobbledegook booms out at you from a speaker, so that you can't look at a painting without the idiot mumblings of a schoolchild or a man from the pub interrupting your thoughts telling you why *they* like the painting.'

'What man from the pub?'

'I have no idea. It sounds like he's in a pub, you can hardly make out what he's saying. The ones he's done are all like that – inarticulate, ignorant, inane – even when you *can* hear them. I can't imagine how he selected the people he recorded. Perhaps he stood outside Woolworths one Saturday morning with a sign round his neck saying, "Please help. I am not a junkie, I am not an alcoholic, I am a struggling artist." Honestly, Gideon. Fetch me another whisky and take my mind off it. What have you been up to since the New Year?'

I refilled the glasses. 'I'm not sure that you'll want to know,' I said. And I told her about the Stone.

Ten minutes later I was kneeling by Catherine's chair holding one side of an Ordnance Survey map of the area, while she gripped the other side between knotty fingers and thumb. I traced the tracks through Keldo Woods with my free hand. 'There,' I said. 'Definitely just about there, I would say.'

Catherine leaned over, peering through reading glasses, and I got a fousty whiff off her, not unpleasant, like an old empty wardrobe.

'Well, you can see as well as I can, there's nothing there.'

'There's nothing marked on the map,' I said. 'I agree. But there is a stone there.'

'Impossible.'

'I know it's impossible. But it is there.'

She released the map and sat back in her chair with a groan.

'Gideon, this map is only five years old. How many years ago do you think all the standing stones in Scotland were identified and marked on maps? The Victorians did it all. You know perfectly well there is no stone at that location.'

'There is,' I said.

'Are you calling me a liar?'

'Of course not. Are you calling me one?'

'You're mistaken. You must be.'

'I'm just telling you what I know. It's there. I've seen it. I've touched it.'

'You're imagining things. Standing stones don't just appear out of thin air.'

'This one seems to have.'

'Well, there has to be a logical explanation for it. Either you were hallucinating, or you dreamt it, or someone is playing a trick on you. Who might want to play a trick on you?'

'A pretty elaborate trick. It's not cardboard, Catherine, it's solid rock. And it's not a dream, it's real.'

'Next time, take a camera,' she said. 'Bring me proof.'

'I'll do that,' I said.

'Good.'

We had become abrupt with each other. Well, she was always abrupt, and I had become so. I got off my knees and folded the map, thinking as I did so how total is our trust in maps. We believe what they tell us about solid ground, about earth, rock, water, forests, buildings. We trust in maps because when we test them out, on a walk or a drive, we find, generally speaking, that they are telling the truth. Even if some detail is wrong it doesn't shake our general confidence in maps. And yet they are only pictures. They are not the real terrain, only representations of it. But our inclination is nearly always to believe the map.

I looked at Catherine and she was eyeing me over the tops of her glasses. Suddenly she laughed. 'I'm always suspicious of you, Gideon,' she said. 'After all this time I should take you at face value, but I can't. It's the dog-collar, whether you're wearing it or not. Actually it's worse when you're not wearing it. I feel you're in disguise, trying to catch me off guard and mystify me. Especially when you come out with something like this.'

I said, 'The day I manage to mystify you Peter Macmurray will convert to Catholicism. You've reacted exactly as I knew you would. I don't blame you. It doesn't make any sense.'

'Quite. Now, let's talk about something else. And I need you to prepare my pain relief ciggies. And let's have another dram.'

XXVIII

Although I still ran three or four times a week, I'd given up marathons a few years earlier when my right leg had developed a muscular weakness in the thigh that became unbearably sore if I ran for more than twelve or fourteen miles. I remember the day I was forced to acknowledge this as a permanent injury: I had to limp the last two miles home after going out on a deliberately long route to test it to the limit. With each step, what felt like a shower of red-hot sparks shot through my leg. And then, for the last mile, my left arm began to jerk and swing, as if jealous of being usurped. It was raining lightly as I hobbled into town, and I must have presented a sorry sight to the few people who were about. Is this it, I remember thinking, as I dripped sweat and rainwater the last few yards to the manse. Is this when the body parts start to rebel and refuse to function?

So I'd learned to pace myself. In the same way, as the year progressed, I willed myself not to run in Keldo Woods, as if by not going there I could *manage* the Stone, keep whatever it signified at bay, possibly even make it disappear. Loops of thought went round in my head as my shoes beat the earth and the tarmac: when nobody sees the Stone is it there, is it there when anybody is present but me, has it always been there but visible only to some, is it there at all? Then, after avoiding the route for two or three runs, I would have to go back to check on the Stone. And there it would be, and I would be compelled to go and touch it. It was a comfort – a cold, wet comfort often enough, but that was how it felt, comfortable. Sometimes I'd lean with my back to it and close my eyes. Once I even fell asleep like that for a few minutes. It no longer felt alien or unfriendly. I liked it. And – there is no other way I can put this – I felt that it liked me.

Meanwhile John and I never managed to arrange a time when we were both free to go to Keldo Woods. It was January, then February. The days were still short, he was in school Monday to Friday and I was busy at the weekends. No doubt if I'd really tried we could have fixed something up, but there was another factor: I didn't want him there. I didn't want him *not* to see the Stone, and thus disbelieve me, but neither did I want him to see it. My attitude had shifted. It was *my* Stone.

I still wanted proof of its existence though, for myself if for no one else. Maybe for Catherine, who couldn't physically get to the site. The only person I wanted now actually to see and touch the Stone was Elsie, but I had to be sure before I took her there. This was why I took up Catherine's suggestion about photographing it.

I'd forgotten I possessed a camera. It was Jenny's originally. We took it on holidays and days out, used it at some of our charity events. We'd had no need for family snaps, evidence of children growing, ourselves changing, so it recorded places we'd visited more than people. Since her death I'd not touched it, but I knew where it was: in a cupboard in one of the spare bedrooms, along with a backgammon set, packs of cards and some board games. I'd had no use for any of those things since her death.

The camera was an old Kodak model, with three settings for the light – cloudy, fair and bright – and a detachable flash bulb. It was virtually an antique but it had one thing in its favour: it didn't need a battery. It still had a film in it too, a 24-shot cartridge with eight exposures still to be used. I'd no idea if the film would still be usable, but I didn't see why not. It had lain undisturbed in the camera, in dry darkness, and there was no obvious sign of deterioration. My father's parsimony came out of the shadows at me and told me just to get on with it. Getting the Stone on film was all that mattered. I only needed a couple of successful shots. On a sunny but windy day when I had no other pressing business, I got in the car and drove to Keldo Woods.

There was nobody about. I had put on my outdoor jacket and

boots, but the ground was hard and dry, the paths thick with pine needles. I found myself walking briskly, as if to a meeting, and the closer I got the quicker I walked. The east wind was chilly and pushy, and I did the last hundred yards at a trot. I knew I was behaving irrationally, that my impatience and excitement would be foolish in a child, let alone a man in his forties. But I couldn't help myself.

The Stone looked like an old friend waiting for me. I put my palm against it. Nothing had changed. I carefully inspected the ground round about. No sign of disturbance, no sign that anybody else had been there. I felt pleased about that.

I took the camera from its hard plastic case and stepped back far enough to fit the whole Stone into the frame. I moved slightly so that a patch of sky, rather than a solid rank of trees, was behind it, and pressed the button. The wind in the tops of the trees gave a gusty roar of approval. I wound the film on and took another picture from the same angle; moved round a bit, stopped, snapped again. I did a complete circle, taking six photographs all together, then went back to the path and took two more from there, to give a better sense of the location. The camera seemed to be fine. If the film was no good, I'd buy another and come back.

I drove home, picked up some letters for the post, took the film out of the camera and walked across the river with it to the High Street. I recognised the woman at the photography counter in Boots: she'd been at the watchnight service on Christmas Eve.

'Haven't had one like this in for a while,' she said, taking the film. She caught my eye and looked mildly embarrassed. 'Oops. You could have said the same about me at Christmas, couldn't you?'

I made light of it, since she had. 'Not at all. You're one of my regulars. Only once a year, but very regular. Can you still develop this kind of film?'

'Oh yes,' she said. 'It's mostly digital stuff and disposables these days, but we can do this no bother. Looks a bit old, though.'

'It is,' I said. 'Eleven, twelve years, something like that. Think it'll be all right?'

She looked doubtful. 'The colour will have faded,' she said. 'You'll have to be prepared for the quality to be quite poor. But there's no reason why the pictures shouldn't come out. Could be a few surprises in there, eh?'

'That's what I'm hoping,' I said.

She gave me a puzzled look. 'Do you want it done today? I can have the prints ready in a couple of hours.'

'That would be fine,' I said. 'I'll come back later.'

She wrote my name on an envelope, dropped the film in and handed me the tear-off collection slip. 'Any time after four then, Mr Mack.'

I walked along the street to post my letters. Lorna Sprott was coming out of the post office just as I got there.

'Oh, Gideon,' she said. 'I was on my way to see you. I'm parked just along here. Perhaps I could give you a lift home? Actually, I've got Jasper in the car. I don't suppose you'd like to go for a walk?'

This was always her way. Hesitant questions that meant she needed to talk about something. I weighed up the terror of getting into Lorna's Fiesta against her coming to the manse and staying for hours, and managed to quell the terror.

'How about the beach?' I said.

We reached the beach car park, half a mile away, without incident, and let Jasper out. He immediately started to dash about as if he'd been in prison for years. The wind was colder and stronger here, whisking the tops of the waves and sending a succession of miniature sandstorms across the beach. There were only a few people out, mostly walking dogs.

It is not a very beautiful beach. There is always a fair amount of debris, and the sand is gritty, more brown than golden, but you can walk for a mile and a half before black, slippery rocks jutting into the sea prevent further progress. I've always liked its bleakness, its inhumanity. When you walk that space between land and sea, you get a proper perspective on your own insignificance.

Lorna, Jasper and I had walked it dozens of times. The dog never tired of it, and I never tired of seeing him rush about from one smell to another, snorting and snuffling around every stone, every bit of driftwood, every scrap of feather, empty crab shell and bleached gull bone, hoovering information from the ground with a frantic urgency, as if all the walks in his life were never going to be enough to take in and decipher the world and its mysteries. Watching Lorna's dog tearing around at full speed just for the fun of it, for the release of all that excited energy and unfocused marvel at the world, gave me great pleasure. There was no method, no calculation in it. Jasper would gallop along the beach and plunge in and out of the sea, fetching the same thrown stick countless times from the crashing waves, not because there was any point or meaning but because his nature obliged him to. Such stupidity, such mindless pleasure in life: I loved to watch it, but it made me envious.

'Gideon,' Lorna said, or rather shouted above the wind, 'do you mind if I confide in you?'

I'd been half-expecting this. 'No,' I shouted back. 'Of course not.'

'Somebody's asked me for some advice,' she yelled, 'and I wanted to ask you what *you* thought before I spoke to them. That's pathetic, isn't it? I mean, somebody needs some help and support from a minister, and the first thing the minister does is run and ask another minister.'

'Mutual support,' I said. 'Nothing wrong with that.'

'Oh,' she said, 'good point. Anyway, I did in fact try to help them, but I don't think I did very well, and I need to go back and speak to them again. Sooner rather than later, probably. And I'm up to high doh about it. Why do I always get into this kind of mess?'

'Because you take it all too personally, Lorna. When somebody comes for help, they don't always expect an immediate solution. Just having someone who listens can be a huge relief, and you're a good listener. What's it about anyway?'

'What did you say?'

'I said, what's it all about?'

'Oh,' she shouted. 'It's that usual dilemma of deciding what's best – keeping quiet or telling the truth.'

'Do you want to be more specific?'

'You know what I mean. We're always supposed to be truthful, but sometimes the truth doesn't help much, can cause complications, damage. So is it better to leave it unspoken?'

'What kind of damage?'

'Hurt. Emotional damage. Damage to a friendship. You can't unsay things once they're said.'

'What kind of truth are we talking about, Lorna?' I asked. 'Family secrets? Past crimes? Hidden desires?'

'Yes, I suppose you could say that. Hidden desires. Acknowledging them. Nothing wicked, you understand. Feelings. Powerful feelings.'

We were striding into the wind, with the dog some distance ahead of us. When we spoke the wind whipped our words inland, and I imagined them being trapped miles away, caught in the branches of trees like plastic bags. I thought of the trees beside the Stone.

Lorna and I kept our heads lowered and didn't look at each other. This suited us both. I knew what this was about. It was about Lorna. She was too embarrassed to look at me, and I didn't want to catch her gaze in case it provoked something, tears or a lunge in my direction. We soldiered on across the sand.

'So,' I said, 'you have a person who's got this dilemma. To speak or not to speak. Am I right?'

'Yes, that's pretty much it.'

'And if they speak, it might all be okay, but it might go horribly wrong. And if they don't speak, it'll just continue to gnaw at them, and they feel time slipping away, and they can't concentrate on anything else until they've sorted this out.'

'That's it, Gideon, you've summed it up perfectly. You're so good at this sort of thing.'

'It happens all the time. The same old issues.' I decided to push things a little further. 'But why have they come to you about it? That's not a question of faith, that's about – well, what is it about? Is it a marital thing?'

'No, no, not at all,' she said, a little too hastily. 'There's no one else involved.'

'Then let me hazard another guess. We're talking about a minister. One who's single.'

'Yes,' she said. She still wouldn't look at me. 'Yes, we are. And if you're a Christian, if you're a minister with a minister's responsibilities, you have to ask yourself: is this all a diversion from one's work? Shouldn't one exercise some self-restraint? Sublimate these feelings into higher things? Especially if the other person, the *other* person, is, well . . .'

She staggered as a particularly fierce gust knocked her off balance, and I instinctively reached out an arm and caught her. I regretted it immediately, as she grabbed it and held on tight. It was my reward for being cruel, perhaps.

'Is what?' I shouted.

'The same,' she said. 'If the other person's the same.'

Suddenly I was less confident of my diagnosis. By 'the same' did she mean, if the other person was also a Christian, or a minister? Or was she talking about the same sex? Maybe this wasn't, as I'd presumed, about Lorna and me. Maybe it was about Lorna and somebody else. Or maybe I was *completely* wrong and it was just about somebody else.

I felt somewhat ashamed. I really did not want to hurt Lorna's feelings. 'What have you suggested so far?' I asked.

'Prayer,' she said. 'That seemed an obvious place to start.'

'I'd have thought they'd have thought of that. Being a minister, I mean.'

'Yes, they had, of course they had. But it wasn't working. They kept praying for help and it wasn't working.'

'No reply?'

'Lots of replies. One minute this, one minute that. Conflicting answers. No answers. Just more questions. Oh, Gideon, look at that!'

She let go her hand from my arm. We were a hundred yards from the rocks, and a huge white wave had just broken over them. Jasper was trotting happily towards this mayhem, barking with enthusiasm.

'Better call him back,' I said. 'He's daft enough to try to go out into that.'

We shouted and clapped and whistled for half a minute until we caught Jasper's attention. He came bounding back towards us, and Lorna went down on her hunkers to greet him.

'Gideon called you daft,' she said, hugging his neck. 'You're not daft, are you? You're just a bit too brave for your own good.'

We turned our backs to the wind with some relief. It was as if we'd moved behind a wall, the way the noise dropped and my face began to lose its stiffness. The sea pushed long fat tongues of foam far up the beach, and the lowering sun gave them a lovely pinkish tinge. The two or three figures ahead of us, and beyond them the roofs and spires of Monimaskit, seemed to hover in the light.

'Isn't that beautiful?' I said.

'Fabulous,' Lorna said. 'Thanks for listening, Gideon.'

'I hope it was some help,' I said. I didn't think I'd been any help at all, but Lorna said, 'Oh, yes, you always help. Would you say, then, that the best advice I could give this person is to keep on praying? The answer will come eventually, won't it?'

'Keep on praying,' I said. 'Well, that certainly won't do any harm.' I was hoping that the discussion might be at an end, and indeed for a few minutes she was silent. Then she spoke again.

'Prayer's a wonderful thing, Gideon, isn't it? But you have to be careful with it. You have to really listen to what God's telling you, not what you want him to tell you. But sometimes they're the same thing.'

It was the kind of thing I used to hear from Divinity students in the library café. There was something very comforting in such an innocent approach to religion, and I played along with it – up to a point.

'Head versus heart,' I said. 'That's another old dilemma, for human beings and ministers. Maybe Jasper has got it right. Doesn't give a damn so long as it smells interesting. But then, he won't go to heaven.'

'Oh, he must,' Lorna said. '*I'm* not going to heaven if there aren't any dogs there.'

'Lorna,' I said, 'look at him. He's already *in* dog heaven. It doesn't get any better than that.'

We followed Jasper back to the car park, and she drove me back to the High Street and dropped me off outside Boots.

The woman at the film counter gave me a mournful smile when I presented myself. 'Oh, Mr Mack,' she said. 'It hasn't gone too well, I'm afraid.'

She flipped through the box of envelopes until she found mine. It felt rather thin when she handed it over.

'You'll see on the negatives that quite a few are just blank, or black anyway. There's no charge for those because we haven't printed them. The ones that have come out have lost a lot of colour. I'm very sorry.'

I'd started to open the envelope, but something in her tone made me stop.

'Och well,' I said, paying her what I owed. 'Not your fault. You did warn me. I'll have a look at them when I get home.'

'That's probably best,' she said, and again, 'I'm very sorry.'

I hadn't been a widower all those years without becoming alert to the look of pity, the sympathetic tone. She'd seen the photographs. She knew who was in them. It simply hadn't occurred to me, in my keenness to get the Stone on the film, what might already be there.

I went home and spread the photographs out on the kitchen table. We'd gone away for three days that November of 1991, after she'd confronted our failing marriage. It had been a quiet, gentle time. A lot of walking, a lot of talking. The weather had been mild and dry. And there we were, faded but still recognisably the Reverend and Mrs Gideon Mack. Jenny in Glencoe. Me in Glencoe. Jenny at Fort William. Jenny in front of Ben Nevis. Ben Nevis on its own. Jenny at Glenfinnan. Both of us at Glenfinnan (the only other visitor at the monument, a German, had insisted, when he saw me taking Jenny, that we let him take us together). Me trying to look manly in front of the Commando memorial at Spean Bridge. Jenny at Loch Ness. She was wearing a black coat and a red tartan scarf, and her thick black hair was tucked in under the scarf and the upturned collar of the coat. The colours were tired, she looked tired, and her smile was a little forced, but she was trying.

The woman in Boots hadn't wanted me to get upset in the shop. I felt a prickle of tears in my eyes, but I was thinking about Elsie. I should show her these pictures. They would make her cry. If she saw them they might trigger something else in her, just as had happened before.

I held the strips of negatives to the light. There we were in the Highlands, and there were the pictures I'd tried to take that afternoon. Darkness, darkness. Fuzzy haze, fuzzy haze, fuzzy haze, fuzzy haze. Darkness, darkness. The camera had kept Jenny all that time, but had failed to capture even a hint of the existence of the Stone.

XXIX

The phone rang one morning some time after this. 'Gideon? Bill Winnyford here. Have you had any thoughts about our little project? Time's wearing on, you know.'

'I'm sorry,' I said. 'I was supposed to get back to you, wasn't I?'

'Can't remember. No matter. I was speaking to a friend of yours, John Moffat up at the school.'

'Is John doing something for you?'

'He's selected some passages from the burgh records, and we've recorded some of his pupils reading them. Fascinating stuff. Your name cropped up. Wheels within wheels. Thought I'd give you a ring.'

'I don't think I've a very good voice,' I said feebly.

'Perfect voice. Pulpit voice. Anyway that's not the point, I want real people real voices not people acting. And you're the link with Menteith. I presume he lived in the manse? The same house you're in?'

'Yes,' I said. 'As a matter of fact he was the first minister here. The old manse was knocked down and this one built in its place in 1880.'

'Perfect again,' Winnyford said. 'He must have written his books there.'

'I suppose so.'

'You mentioned before that you have a study?'

'Yes, all manses have studies.'

'Would that room have been his study?'

'Oh, yes. Apart from the light fittings and plugs, I don't suppose it's changed at all. The bookcases must have been put in when they built the house.'

'Better and better. We could record there. How about that?'

There was no arguing with him. I decided to get it over with and asked him round for eight o'clock that evening. He was delighted.

'Brilliant, Gideon, brilliant. I'll look forward to it.'

'Fine,' I said. In spite of myself, I was beginning to like Bill Winnyford's breezy idiocy. 'I'll see you then.'

He came at ten to eight armed with a compact but weighty DAT recorder, a microphone and a set of headphones. I'd lit the fire in the study and showed him in. He could barely contain himself.

'This is wonderful, Gideon, wonderful. I mentioned the tableau I'm designing? I've only done sketches so far, but in my mind it's this to a T. The fireplace the desk the books. Glad I didn't see this before. Confirms my instincts are on the right track. The only thing that'll be different is the window. Yours – lovely proportions, sash and case, overlooking pleasant garden. Mine – narrow, slanting, funnel into the pit. Let me set this thing up.'

He put on the headphones and played around with the recorder for a minute, making sure it was working properly, listening to the background noise. A log in the grate spat, and he asked if he could pile some more wood on. 'Nice fireside crackle,' he said. 'Homely sound but hellish too. Now when you're ready, off you go. Just speak naturally.'

The passage he'd selected was from the introduction to Menteith's story, that is to say, it was in Menteith's own 'voice'. As I read, I glanced up occasionally and found Winnyford nodding at me encouragingly, a beatific smile on his face. This was one of his 'conjunctions', the present-day minister reading the words of his predecessor in the very room in which they had been composed. Except, of course, that we didn't know for sure if Menteith had written his books here. I thought about that as I read: 'The Keldo Water flows from these hills to Monimaskit, and, where it passes through the town and enters the sea, it presents a steady and stately face to the world; yet . . . a mere four or five miles upstream . . . and but two from Keldo House . . . it rushes and roars through a gulf of great depth known in the locality as the Black Jaws.' The recorded voice always sounds different from how one usually hears it, and I wondered what I sounded like to Winnyford through his slightly ludicrous headphones; and then I found myself contemplating what Augustus Menteith would have sounded like, how broad or how refined his accent would have been, and what kind of man he had been. 'It was once the supposed sport of town lads to traverse the gorge on the trunks of trees which, uprooted in winter storms, had fallen across it, but in truth these narrow and slippery bridges are so dangerous that few must have dared such an adventure, and certainly I have never heard of any boy in the present time who had courage enough to essay that dread crossing.' He was a mountaineer who had perished, according to the online gazetteer, in the Alps. What dread crossing had he essayed? I read on to the end of the paragraph. 'And this, perhaps, gave rise in former times to a story, which I might myself relate, but which, by good fortune, I am able to reproduce just as it was told to me in my youth by an old woman of the town, now long dead, whose stock of lore was as rich as she was poor, and whose imagination, perhaps, was as broad as her cottage was narrow.'

That was where Winnyford wanted me to stop. I waited while he held up his finger for a few seconds. Then he switched the machine off.

'One take,' he said. 'You're a natural, Gideon. I should come and hear you preach.'

'You'd be welcome,' I said.

'I'd come for the performance, not the message,' he said. 'The performance is everything. Being a minister must be like being an actor, is it?'

'There are certain similarities,' I said. 'People think we didn't have theatres in Scotland for centuries because the Church suppressed them. Well, perhaps. But you could also argue that we had theatres in every town and village in the land: they were called kirks, and every week folk packed in to see a one-man show about life, death and the universe. But I want to ask you something. Why that passage? I can see that it's where Menteith is writing in his own voice, but it stops just as the story starts.'

'Precisely. The whole story would be too long to use, and it's impossible to lift an extract that stands on its own. This passage is setting the scene, and that's exactly what my installation is – scene-setting. There'll be a direction to visitors to read the legend in Menteith's book, if they wish. If they don't, and let's face it most won't, they go away with a scene in their head – a minister's study with a view into hell.'

'Yes, I see,' I said. Winnyford had more brains than either Catherine Craigie or I had given him credit for. 'Look, if our work is done, do you fancy a whisky?'

'That would be nice.'

'Well, stay where you are, since the fire's lit in here, and I'll go and get some.'

I went through to the kitchen for glasses, some water and a bottle of malt, and carried them on a tray back to the study. Winnyford, naturally enough, had been looking at my books. He'd taken one down and was slowly turning the pages. 'What on earth's this?' he said.

It was a slim blue book in a grey dustjacket, about six inches by eight. *The Secret Commonwealth of Elves, Fauns and Fairies* by Robert Kirk.

'Where did you get that?' I said. I must have spoken sharply, because Winnyford looked startled and shut the book like a schoolboy caught reading something smutty. 'Sorry,' he said. 'It just kind of fell out. I was actually reaching for something else.'

He pointed out the space where it had been, wedged between two of my father's leather-bound reference works.

'That's bizarre,' I said. 'I haven't seen this for more than thirty years.' I reached out my hand, and Winnyford passed me the book.

It was undoubtedly my father's copy, the one I thought he had hidden away from me. But maybe he hadn't: maybe it had been stuck between those two great unopened volumes all this time, and I'd merely lifted them together from place to place and never spotted it. Maybe. But it seemed incredible that Winnyford should come across it so easily.

I opened it and glanced at a page or two: *Their Bodies of congealled Air are some tymes caried aloft, other whiles grovell in different Schapes, and enter into any Cranie or Clift of the Earth where Air enters, to their ordinary Dwellings . . .* And a little further on, *no such thing as a pure Wilderness in the whole Universe.* I read these words, and I remember them now, and they are a mystery and a strange comfort to me.

'You didn't . . . ?' I began. I was about to suggest that he had brought the book with him and set up his little scene as soon as I left the room. But that was ridiculous. It was my father's book, complete with the inscription and the initials G.M.

'I didn't what?' Winnyford asked.

'Nothing,' I said. I poured the drams, large ones, and put some more fuel on the fire.

'That book,' Winnyford said, 'is ringing a vague bell in my head. Remind me who Robert Kirk was.'

When I was studying at New College I had come across a reference to Kirk, which had rekindled my interest, and a little research in the college library had yielded another edition of *The Secret Commonwealth* and a great deal of information about its author. I remember being mildly disappointed, unpacking his books a few years later, not to come across my father's copy. I assumed that he must have destroyed or discarded it. Now I found myself telling Bill Winnyford, just as my father had told me, about Kirk's Gaelic Bible, and about his interest in fairies.

'My father was a very straight kind of man,' I said. 'He refused to discuss the fairies with me. He dismissed it all as a lot of nonsense.'

Winnyford had an eager, puppyish expression on his face. 'What happened to Kirk?' he asked. 'Didn't he disappear or something?'

'That's one story,' I said. 'The credible one is that he simply died.'

He laughed. 'Well, don't tell me that one!' he said.

I couldn't help but laugh too. 'All right,' I said, and I told him the legend of Robert Kirk as nearly as I could remember it, glancing occasionally at the introduction to the book for verification. He was the seventh of seven sons, a fact which he made something of, seventh sons being, as any student of folklore will tell you, strongly susceptible to magical influences. After twenty years as minister at Balquhidder, he transferred to Aberfoyle, his father's former charge. It was there that he wrote *The Secret Commonwealth*, and there that in 1692 at the age of about fifty he fell into a dwam or swoon while walking on a little hillock, supposed to be a fairy-mound, near to his home. He was found stretched out on the ground, apparently lifeless. A funeral was held, and he was buried in his own kirkyard. His wife was pregnant at the time and she duly gave birth to the child. Shortly after this the form of the minister appeared before a cousin, saying that he was not dead but a captive in Fairyland. Only one chance remained for him to escape: at the christening of his new child, he would appear in the room, and a knife must be thrown over his head. This would enable him to be restored to society. If the knife was not thrown, he would be lost for ever. In the event he *did* appear, but the man entrusted with the knife was so astonished that he failed to throw it, and Robert Kirk was seen no more upon the earth. And it is said that to this day he is held a prisoner by the inhabitants of the fairy netherworld, who resented the fact that he had disclosed so much information about them in his manuscript.

Winnyford listened intently. He seemed to forget about his whisky while I was speaking, but as soon as I had finished he picked up his glass and knocked back the contents. I reached over with the bottle.

'Thanks,' he said. 'I thought I recognised the name, but I haven't heard that story before. It's odd, because I pick up tales and legends like that all over the place. It's my trademark: the overlap of myth and history. Pity there isn't some kind of specific connection with here.'

'Or conjunction even,' I said. 'You could make one, though, couldn't you?'

He shook his head. 'You can't make conjunctions, you can only reveal them. Menteith, the Black Jaws, you – that's plenty to be going on with.'

In the firelight he looked a curious mixture of young and old, fresh-faced and haggard, puppy and old dog. I felt myself on the verge of telling him about the Stone, and how not a single one of the eight photographs I'd taken of it had come out. I'd tried to make myself believe there was a logical explanation – something to do with chemicals in the film – that the already exposed film had been preserved while the rest had deteriorated beyond use. I'd tried to persuade myself that with another film, or another camera, I could go into Keldo Woods and fire off a hundred photos of the Stone and they'd all come out. But I knew that, however reasonable this was, it would not happen. The Stone did not *want* to be photographed.

I no longer wished to share the Stone with anybody. Not Winnyford, not John Moffat, not Catherine Craigie. Elsie was the only one who might understand. I wished that I'd never mentioned it to anyone. And that night, while we sat and chatted about his work, his interest in legends and folklore and how people interpret them, and why communities remember or forget them, I said nothing about the Stone to Bill Winnyford.

XXX

I am thinking of a particular night seven months after Jenny was killed, and just a week after Elsie and I had our moment of truth, if that's what it was, in the bedroom upstairs. The occasion was a dinner party at Amelia and Gregor Wishaw's. Amelia had phoned me. 'Gideon,' she'd said, 'we all want to see you again. Yourself, not the Reverend. I know it's hard, but you need to do it. Come and have dinner on Friday and share some good company with us. Nobody intimidating, nobody you have to put on airs for, just a few friends.'

'Who?' I said.

'Gregor and myself, and John and Elsie. Can you handle that?'

'I think so,' I said. 'Yes, okay.'

'I thought I'd ask Nancy Croy to make up the numbers,' Amelia added smoothly. 'You get on well with her, don't you?'

'Well enough,' I said. 'I hope you're not matchmaking, Amelia.'

'Of course I'm not.'

'I'm not interested.'

'It'll be fine, I promise.'

Elsie and John were already there when I arrived. Elsie greeted me as if nothing had happened between us. I detected no fear, no resentment, no shame and, worst of all, no residual smouldering passion in her gaze. Her smile was the smile of an old friend. John, too, was his usual self, both to her and to me. He and Gregor were drinking beer and beginning to compete with each other at jokes and stories. I did not want to be part of their game. I chose to drink red wine.

Nancy joined us a few minutes later, wearing a short tweed skirt and an olive-green silk blouse. I tried to think of her as a woman I might want to be with: she was bonnie, intelligent, kind, active, enthusiastic, creative; she was dedicated to the children she taught and the causes she espoused; she was liberal-minded and a Christian. But, try as I might, I could not find it in my heart to lust after her.

In the Wishaw household it was Gregor who did the cooking. Amelia was far too busy as a GP, or rushing from one conference to another, to have the patience for it. Gregor on the other hand was obsessive about meticulous preparation and artistic presentation. Each of the five courses he served us looked beautiful and tasted momentarily delicious, but there wasn't much substance to any of them; and I cannot now remember what they were.

As the drink flowed, we all became more voluble, Gregor and John especially. There were a few differences of opinion over politics (John Major's Tory government had, against all our expectations, won the General Election in April), the rumbling crisis of UN arms inspections in Iraq following the Gulf War, and the state of the National Health Service. We had reached the coffee when in a lull in the talk Nancy looked across the table at me and said: 'I'd like to raise a glass to absent friends. One in particular. We all wish she was here. Here's to Jenny.'

There was an awkward silence, as if Nancy had done something exceptionally gauche, but she was only articulating what we were all feeling: that Jenny's ghost was at the feast and we were ignoring her.

'Thank you, Nancy,' I said. 'I appreciate that, and so would she. Here's to Jenny.'

Everybody joined in the toast. I smiled at Nancy and then at Elsie. She smiled back, unabashed. I thought about lying naked on the bed beside her. It probably looked to everybody else as if I was thinking fond thoughts of Jenny.

'I mind the first day we met her,' John said, 'as if it was last week. Do you mind that, Gideon, in that café in Forrest Road?'

'Of course I do,' I said. 'We met Elsie too.'

'She was reading the *Guardian*,' John said to the others. 'Jenny I mean, not Elsie. We sat at the same table and got talking to her. Then Elsie came over, she was the waitress, and we got talking to them both. Didn't we, Elsie?'

'A right pair of patter merchants, I bet,' Gregor said.

'No, they were hopeless,' Elsie said. 'It was quite touching actually.'

'I can see her now,' John said. 'A red jumper and that lovely hair of hers. Remember, Gideon?'

'Yes,' I said. 'It's as if she's still there. I imagine we could walk into that café and she'd be in the same seat. Does that make sense?'

'Yes, it does,' Elsie said.

'You must miss her so much,' Nancy said.

I shrugged. 'I catch her out of the corner of my eye sometimes, or I hear her telling me something. But other times I can hardly remember what she looked like.'

'That's sad,' Nancy said.

'It's normal,' Amelia said. 'It's completely normal. Real. It's what happens.'

There was a brief silence, as if we were all trying to picture people – parents, grandparents, lovers, friends – whose faces were fading or already gone from our memories. And into this silence John's voice came again.

'Sometimes,' he said, 'I think we don't lead real lives any more. Do you ever think that?' He didn't seem to be addressing anyone in particular.

'No,' Gregor said. 'Never. My life is intensely real. Trying to teach thirty wee shits stuff they don't want to know about five days a week is very real. And you're just down the corridor from me teaching a different set of wee shits, so I can't imagine it's less real for you. What do you mean?'

'Well, us, here, round this table,' John said. 'Forget the wee shits for a minute. Our daily lives are so much less physical than they would have been a generation or two ago. Not just us – most people in this country, at this juncture in history. Hardly any of us do *real* jobs any more – I mean hard physical labour. We don't get a grip on the world – a hard, sweaty, actual grip on it. We don't *feel* it. I'm not trying to demean the work any of us does but it's not how it was fifty or even thirty years ago.'

'Not true,' Gregor said. 'There were teachers then, and doctors and ministers and librarians. *They* didn't do the physical labour. Other poor bastards did it, but as soon as technology and more disposable income and upward mobility and all that made it possible, they stopped doing it too. Now it's poor bastards on the other side of the world that do the hard labour.'

'All right,' John said, 'maybe the lack of physical work is only a symptom. I just feel that we're not connecting with reality any more. I mean, when we went to war last year, when they were bombing Baghdad, it didn't feel like you were watching a real war, it looked like a film, a computer game. Nobody *feels*, nobody cares any more. There are no *causes* left. Even Scotland doesn't feel like a cause anybody's going to get angry about. How else could a man like John Major have won the election, for fuck's sake? Did he *bore* us into not caring? I mean, we don't even believe in God any more, most of us. Well, do we, Gideon?'

'Maybe not in this room,' I said, 'but all the opinion polls tell us the majority of people still believe in him. And in the rest of the world, well, there are plenty of folk out there creating misery and mayhem in God's name. He's a lot less popular than he used to be, though, which is probably no bad thing.'

Nancy looked shocked. 'There are plenty of people doing good work in God's name too,' she said. 'You should know that, Gideon. You're one of them.'

'Good and bad don't come into it,' John said, before I could answer her. 'It's historical change, you can't stop it. But we still have to make sense of our lives. If we don't do it through politics or religion we have to do it some other way.'

'Oh, and how's that?' Gregor asked.

'Film,' John said. 'I think we think of our lives as films. Movies. Moving pictures. Sometimes you catch yourself thinking – or you hear someone saying – "Oh, mind when that happened, it was just like that scene in such-and-such." If your life is like a film it gives it a kind of framework. I think we imagine our lives as movies because that's the only way left to understand them.'

'Speak for yourself,' Gregor laughed. 'You're talking mince, John.'

'Actually I don't think he is,' Nancy said. 'You're saying films, John, but it could be fiction, it's the same thing. When I think of all the novels I've read, I do wonder if it's been a sensible use of my time. Why would I fill my head with all those made-up stories if it wasn't to try and understand my own story? Every month my book group discusses a novel and its characters as if they were real people making real choices. Life is a story. It doesn't matter whether it's a book or a film, it's still a story.'

'Maybe that's why everybody thinks they have a novel in them,' Amelia said. 'Every bloody game-show host or model or has-been politician or weather forecaster for God's sake seems to be writing a novel these days.'

'It's a refuge from confusion,' Nancy said. 'If they can just tell a story where all the loose ends tie up, the whole world will make a lot more sense.'

'Aye, but with a film it's visual,' John said, the only person at the table, as far as I was aware, who was writing a novel. 'Your head is filled with images without you having to be literate or without you having to make the effort of reading. You just sit in the cinema and it washes over you. Imagine what it must have been like the first time you went to the pictures, back in the silent era, when you had no experience at all of film. You're in the stalls watching a huge train hurtling towards you. There's a woman tied to the tracks. There's a chortling villain, but you can't hear his laugh, you can only imagine the sound it makes. You know the train must be making a hell of a noise, but you can't hear it. And the woman's screaming but you can't hear her either, you just see her mouth opening and shutting and you know she's screaming. There's a pianist bashing out dramatic music to go with the pictures. You'd start screaming yourself. How could you *not* be caught up in that? How could you *not* imagine your life differently once you'd had that experience?'

'You're talking shite,' Gregor said. 'I don't know about novels, but cinema, film, TV make things *more* real, not less. It's true now and it was true in the silent era too, as you've just eloquently proved.'

'Aye, right, Gregor,' John said.

'You can't deny it,' Gregor said. 'The camera brings you face to face with stuff that you might otherwise never experience or know about. Think of that footage of the concentration camps being opened up in 1945. Horrible, horrible, horrible images, but utterly real. One of the reasons people know all that happened is because we have the pictures, we have the evidence on film.'

'That's not what I meant,' John said, but Gregor had more to say.

'I'll tell you what's real,' he said. 'When I was a kid, my two brothers and I used to have this thing about who'd use the loo first in the morning after our dad had been in there. It was hellish – basically, his shit stank.'

'Gregor!' Amelia said.

'Oh, come on, we've finished eating. It was unbelievable, at least it was to us wee boys whose bowels were still unadulterated by bevvy and middle-age. Going in after him was a kind of endurance test. We'd have a right laugh about it, holding our breath and everything. Then I guess we grew up and forgot about it. And one day recently I was in the bathroom having a crap and I went back in five minutes later, and the smell hit me. My dad's smell. The exact same. You know how your sense of smell can take you back decades in just a split second? I was eight again, holding my nose. And I thought, Christ, if even your shit smells the same as your father's, what chance have you got? Against your genes, I mean, your inheritance. No chance. Now *that's* real.'

All six of us present that night were well into our thirties, and at the time it didn't look like any of us were going to pass our genes on to anybody. I thought of my father and realised that I had no recollection at all of what the toilet had smelt like after he'd been in it. The same for my mother. I tried to think of my father's ordinary, everyday smell, and came up with nothing. I imagined it as dry, bookish, but I was remembering the study, not him. If film was evidence of existence, so was smell. I had neither photographic nor olfactory evidence that my father ever lived. The best proof I had of him was myself.

At the end of the evening, when I stood up to go, Nancy said that she too must be off. Her house was on the way back to the manse. It would have been churlish, indeed impossible, not to offer to walk her home.

It was about one o'clock, and although there were few clouds and many stars in the sky it was a warm night. Amelia and Gregor lived just round the corner from Catherine Craigie, and Nancy a couple of streets beyond. My visits to Catherine were well established by this time. Her house was all in darkness as we passed. Nancy said, 'Do you know what they're saying about you going to see Miss Craigie so often?'

'They?' I said.

'Peter Macmurray and his friends. They say it's the ungodly communing with the godless.'

I laughed. 'Which is which, I wonder. I really don't care what they say.'

'No,' she said. 'It's all nonsense, of course.'

A little further on she said, 'I hope you didn't mind me mentioning Jenny.'

'Not at all. I meant it when I thanked you.'

'And did you mean what you said about belief in God?'

I knew at once what she was referring to, but pretended otherwise.

'What did I say?'

'That it wasn't a bad thing that God wasn't so popular these days.'

'It's a fact of life,' I said. 'A lot of people just can't accept the idea of God any more. It's not because they don't want to, it's because intellectually they can't. I don't think it makes them worse or lesser beings. It's like what Amelia said about Jenny. It's normal. People are forgetting what God looks like. Sometimes he's still there, but often he's not. It's a natural process.'

'That makes it sound as though it doesn't matter.'

'Oh, it matters all right. It causes all kinds of anxieties. But to individuals, to human beings. I don't think it matters to God.'

'Oh, Gideon, that's a terrible thing to say, that God doesn't care. How can you say that? "The very hairs of your head are all numbered."'

'Don't quote Scripture at me, Nancy, it's far too late for that. Anyway, I didn't say he didn't care, I said it didn't matter to him. There's a difference.'

She didn't reply. We reached her garden gate and came to a stop.

'Do you want to come in for a coffee?' she asked.

'No, thanks. I'll just head for home, I think.'

'Okay,' she said. 'I'll see you at church on Sunday then.'

'Tomorrow.'

'Yes, tomorrow.'

We both hesitated. If I changed my mind, she would let me come in. I was tempted, but only for a moment. It wasn't Nancy that I wanted.

'Good night, then.'

'Good night.' She opened the gate and went through it. I looked up into the night. Countless stars winked down at us and didn't give a damn what we believed.

'Gideon,' she said, as I turned to go.

'What?'

'God cares,' she said. 'I know he does.'

XXXI

Catherine Craigie's rheumatoid arthritis had developed aggressively in her late forties, and since then she'd had only brief periods of remission. She'd tried everything, from physiotherapy and homoeopathy to a vast range of drugs, ingested and injected. Some of these treatments gave her temporary pain relief, but none helped much in the long term. Her knees and ankles were bolted up as if enclosed in some medieval instrument of restraint, her fingers were thick, deformed and stiff, her shoulders were twisted and she could hardly turn her neck. It had even got into her jaw, which made chewing her food difficult. A home help came every morning to clean the house and make her lunch and dinner, but Catherine ate very little. 'Too much bloody hassle,' she said. Her swollen joints were red and angry, bulging out because she had lost so much weight. Everything was an effort, from making a cup of tea to holding a book. Every movement had to be conducted at a snail's pace, but she didn't complain much. Complaining didn't get you very far, in Catherine's book.

I poured the whiskies and asked her how she was, a question which invariably drew a facetious response.

'I'm dying,' she said. 'By degrees, some days faster than others, but definitely dying. So are you, of course. So are we all. Actually, that's something I've been wanting to talk to you about. My funeral arrangements.'

'Really?' I said.

'Don't look so surprised. I'm very poorly, Gideon, and I'd rather get everything settled while I'm still *compos mentis*.'

'I don't think I've ever met anybody of sounder mind.'

'No, of course you haven't. But one of the nastier aspects of this blasted disease is that it lurks in the shadows waiting to mug you. It's likely to finish me off when I least expect it, because it's turned my immune system against me. I'm so wasted away, you see, that my body can't support its own vital organs, even if they hadn't been seriously compromised by the amount of steroids I've had pumped into me over the years. I shouldn't be drinking this stuff but frankly if I'm going to incapacitate my liver I'd rather do it with a decent malt than a cocktail of drugs that don't appear to do any good. Well, anyway, I won't bore you with the details, but sooner or later my liver, my heart or my kidneys are going to give out, possibly all of them at once, and that will be that. I hope so anyway, I don't want to hang about on some ghastly life-support system, thank you very much. Cheers.'

'That's better,' she said after she'd raised the glass to her mouth with two hands, swallowed a mouthful and got the glass down on the table beside her again. It was hugely tempting to try to assist, but she hated that. 'If I want help, I'll ask for it,' she would snap.

'Sometimes I can feel my heart creaking away like an old boat on its moorings,' she said. 'And sometimes I'm sure it's a clockwork spring just about to burst. That's why I want to make sure everything is properly in place if I should suddenly drop dead.'

'What can I do?' I asked.

'Well, I want you to run the show, of course.'

'Me?'

'Yes, you.'

'Where?'

'In your church, for heaven's sake, where else? And afterwards in the church graveyard. Why else would I ask you to get involved?'

'I don't know,' I said. 'Out of badness?'

She grinned at me like an elf.

'You're not supposed to turn me down, you know,' she said. 'I'm one of your parishioners.'

'I wouldn't dream of turning you down,' I said. 'But I'm surprised, given your lifelong aversion to churches. Why not book into a crematorium and have done with it?'

'Well, there's the family plot for a start. My father and mother, paternal grandparents and great-grandparents are already in it, and a few aunts and uncles too, but I think there's room for one more. Why go to the extravagance of lighting a fire when there's a perfectly good hole in the ground waiting for me? Not that I have to have your blessing to go in there.'

'No,' I said. 'That's the local council's concern, not mine. And you know there's no legal requirement for any kind of service or ceremony at all, religious or otherwise. But this isn't about religion, is it?'

'No,' she said. 'If you look on the desk beside the computer, you'll see a sheet of A4 printed out with your name at the top. Instructions. That's what it's about.'

I went over to the desk. Her old Amstrad was long gone, and she now had a sophisticated-looking laptop. Before I could even glance at the paper, she was speaking again.

'No, no, wait, don't read it yet. Remind me what happened to Jenny. She's not buried here, is she?'

'No, she was cremated. She thought humans were taking up enough space as it was. We'd talked about it once or twice so I was pretty sure that's what she wanted. The funeral was in Edinburgh. Her parents wanted that, and it took the pressure off me.'

'And what did you do with her afterwards?'

'I brought her back here, and one day John and Elsie Moffat and I went for a walk on the beach, and we scattered her there.'

'For any particular reason?'

'No, not really. I think we thought she'd blow away easily on the beach. I remember feeling a bit awkward at the time, guilty almost. As if we were dropping litter or something.'

'But she wasn't from here,' Catherine said. 'I am. I feel rooted, four generations deep. That's why I want to do it through your church. I haven't gone to church for forty years, Gideon. I don't believe any of the claptrap you no doubt come out with every week, I don't believe it any more than you do, but . . .' She looked at me steadily, and for the first time in our acquaintance I thought she was about to shed a tear.

'But,' I repeated.

'One doesn't abandon it all on a whim. The kirk, the kirkyard, my family, me, you – there's something much bigger than religion going on in all that. Much bigger. The religion was just a phase, and it's coming to an end. Do you understand what I'm saying?'

'I think so,' I said. 'Like the Picts putting Christian signs on their ancient stones, but the stones surviving the Picts *and* their new religion.'

'Something like that. When you've spent all your life steeped in history, learning it, teaching it, absorbing it, it becomes a very solid thing. It's like this disease – it gets into your bones. It isn't ephemeral or theoretical, it becomes part of you, and you part of it. And I feel a very strong obligation to that idea. If I believe in anything, that's what I believe in, do you see?'

'And you want me to ensure you remain part of it, after you're gone?' I asked.

'Exactly.'

'I'll do everything I can to see that you do.'

'Thank you. I knew I could rely on you, Gideon.'

'That's not what you were saying a few weeks ago. You couldn't bring yourself to trust me, you said.'

'That's different. It's your thinking I don't trust. As a functionary you are totally reliable. Now I typed that out laboriously, using two semi-functional fingers, because it's important that you know exactly what is to happen. My lawyer will get a signed copy, too, but first I need to know if you have any objections. I hope not. If you officiate, I imagine that will prevent any busybody official from the council coming along and putting a ban on proceedings.'

'That's hardly likely, is it? Unless you're planning a riot or to be lowered in by helicopter or something.'

'You'd better read it,' Catherine said.

'Who is your lawyer, by the way?' I asked.

'Mr Stewart in Montrose,' she said. 'A sound man. I recommend him if you ever need a lawyer. His details are there too.'

I read the sheet she had typed out. It was quite a read. I shall come to the details of it at the appropriate place in this narrative, but Catherine's words described a funeral like none that had ever been held in Monimaskit.

'I've told you about my trip to Mexico in the sixties, haven't I?' she said. I nodded. She'd gone there in 1962 after finishing her teacher-training, to take part in an archaeological dig and visit some of the Aztec and Mayan ruins. 'That's where this comes from,' Catherine said. 'Some of it, anyway. Mexico made a huge impression on me. Everything there is loaded with symbolism, weighed down with it. The ancient ruins loom over the whole country, or at least they did for me. I went to Chichen Hza and Uxmal and Palenque, and seeing those places changed my life. Human beings are at one and the same time utterly splendid and utterly insignificant. I got a sense that everybody in Mexico understands that in some deep way. We were there on the first of November, when they celebrate the Day of the Dead. It was unforgettable. I gather it's become something of a tourist attraction nowadays in certain areas, but back then we knew we were watching something special, this weird mixture of Indian and European, pagan and Catholic, ancient and modern, life and death. It was spectacular and powerful and strange but it wasn't dressed up for foreigners, it wasn't for us. We were privileged to see it. Mexico was pretty rough and ready in 1962, especially for a young girl. The people were delightful, but desperately poor, except for the landowners, who were horribly rich.'

She'd told me all this before. Each time I heard it I was envious of what she'd experienced.

'Basically, Gideon,' she said, 'I'd like a bit of Mexico in Monimaskit when I die.'

'It will cause some tongues to wag,' I said.

'Let them wag,' she said.

'It might upset a few people.'

'Fine.'

'And get me into trouble.'

'It's possible. Do you care?'

'Not really. It would probably be remembered for a long time.'

'Good. That's why I want the children there, so that they grow up remembering it, so that they remember it when they're old and grey and about to die themselves. But I want them to enjoy it. I don't want them running amok, but it shouldn't be a solemn occasion, it should be fun.'

'Yes, I see that.'

'I've always liked graveyards. They're peaceful, unrushed places. The pace of change in a graveyard is very gradual. I've never thought of graveyards as gloomy, and I don't like the idea that they're places one should only visit out of a sense of obligation, or when there's a funeral. People should be able to go and sit or sleep or read a book in a cemetery without being thought odd. I'd like people to have picnics in them if I thought they would behave properly and not leave their litter behind, but I'm afraid that's a forlorn hope.

'When I was physically able, I used to spend a lot of time wandering about graveyards, reading the stones, but I talked to the people under the ground too. That didn't come from Mexico, that was in me from a very young age. I've had some excellent conversations with the dead, and I've learned a lot from them. I don't think people should creep around them as much as they do, do you?'

I laughed, waving the paper. 'This certainly isn't creeping.'

'I hope you don't think it's silly. It's not intended to be.'

'No, not at all. It's an attractive idea. I've just never considered such a thing before. Graveside entertainment.'

'Perhaps you should have it debated at the General Assembly,' she said drily. 'The entertainment, as you put it, is in the hall cupboard under the stairs. There's quite a lot of it. My home help kindly put it away, and I haven't been able to go through it. The perishable items aren't there, of course, they'll have to be bought at the time, and Mr Stewart will reimburse any expenses. I bought the kites from a catalogue that came with one of the Sunday papers. I'd be grateful if you would try one out. It would be a bit of a flop if they didn't work properly.'

'I'll take one when I leave,' I said. 'The weather may be a factor, of course. Or the school holidays, or something else quite unforeseen.'

'Oh, have a little more faith, Gideon. Monimaskit won't let me down. It'll be fine. Splendid, in fact. I wish I could be there to see it.'

'That's the trouble with funerals, isn't it? One of the biggest days in your life and you can't be there.'

'Not if you think like a poor benighted Scot. Think like a Mexican and you never know, you might make it.'

'You sound almost as though you're admitting the possibility of something beyond the grave.'

'That's not a possibility, that's a certainty. All the dead are still here. But are they conscious of it? On the available evidence, in spite of what I've just said, no. Evidence, Gideon, hard evidence. You may think I'm turning into someone who believes in ghosts and fairies, but I'm not. I believe in the dead. I believe in history.'

We sat in silence for a minute. It was after ten o'clock, and I began to think I should go home. But it was good just sitting there with Catherine, saying nothing. For all that she ribbed me, I felt that we understood each other.

'You'll notice,' she said, 'that I haven't mentioned your mysterious stone.'

'You have now,' I said. I'd hoped she might have forgotten about it, but Catherine forgot very little.

'*That's* ghost and fairy stuff,' she said.

'How do you know, you who've not even seen it?'

'I just know,' she said. 'Perhaps *because* I haven't seen it. But I also know you, which does make me wonder just a little. Did you take any pictures yet?'

'No,' I said, 'I've not managed.' Which wasn't a complete lie. 'The thing's still there, though. At least, it was a couple of days ago.'

'Hmm. Well, humouring you for a moment, perhaps your friend Winnyford is responsible. Perhaps it's another of his installations, but one he hasn't finished yet. And you're part of it. You've probably been recorded running past it, touching it, staring in amazement. I hope you haven't been doing anything too embarrassing. Sprinkling it with holy water, that sort of thing,' she added with a grin.

'I'm not even going to dignify that with a response,' I said. 'But in any case, it isn't an installation. It's not made out of cardboard or polystyrene and there aren't any sound effects. It's a piece of solid rock.'

'If you say so,' she said. I felt aggrieved that she had raised the matter only to dismiss it again, but I wasn't sorry to let it go at that. I had become protective of the Stone. It was no longer a mystery. It was *my* mystery.

I left Catherine's that night carrying a red and yellow kite in a clear plastic case. It was, as I discovered the next morning when I assembled it, a traditional diamond-shaped kite with a long tail. I tied the string to two hooks on the cross-spar and took it out into the garden to test it. There was enough lawn for me to get a run at launching it, and enough wind to give it some height. I don't know whether anybody was paying attention to the sky above the manse that day, but I like to think that somebody noticed the red and yellow diamond twisting and diving like a swallow in the breeze. Maybe they even smiled to themselves and thought, 'Ah, that must be the minister playing with his kite.'

Kite-flying is a double-edged experience, at once liberating and a reminder of your earthbound nature. The kite is a part of you and yet not a part of you, it is like having your soul on a long string tugging at you, attached to your body and yet with a life of its own. The temptation, of course, is to let go.

XXXII

In writing all this down, I have hardly touched on my parish activities: given what has happened to me, they seem unimportant in the scale of things. Yet I have been a busy and conscientious minister for most of my time at Monimaskit, just as I was at Leith. It is only in the last year or so, since the advent of the Stone, that I have been less thorough in the performance of my duties. Until that time, I fulfilled my parish obligations, attended, as far as I could, to the spiritual needs of my congregation and made myself available to the wider community, as is requisite of a minister of the national Church. I performed baptisms and administered Holy Communion; I prepared people, young and old, to become communicants; I married couples and buried the dead – all with an acceptable dignity and expression of faith, however disengaged my heart may have been. Funerals, as any minister will tell you, are difficult and draining events both for the family of the deceased and for the minister; and you cannot schedule them to fit with your other commitments. I once conducted five in as many days and I have heard of a minister who did thirteen in one week. It is hard to preach the life everlasting to distraught people whose only sure knowledge is that their loved one is gone for ever; doubly so when you yourself don't believe what you are telling them.

And then, on top of this work, came the bureaucracy and constant round of committee and group meetings that characterise the Presbyterian system of Church government. I attended Presbytery and Session regularly, of course, and three times I have gone to the General Assembly, that gathering of ministers and elders in the spring that I've always thought must, from the air, make the Mound in Edinburgh look like a gigot of lamb swarming with bluebottles. All this reminds me of how demanding these years have been, and how tired I became latterly. The charity work, it is true, gradually fell by the wayside, till the amounts raised were just fractions of those early sums: our steering committee was shrunk by resignations, our army of helpers dwindled, those of us left simply didn't have the energy we'd had at the start, and – predictably, perhaps – as Monimaskit became a more prosperous place in the late 1990s, so the willingness of the people to give their time and money to good causes seemed to decline. I used to think that most people were instinctively charitable towards the less fortunate. Now I'm not so sure. Perhaps charity is simply a way of putting distance between yourself and misfortune. Perhaps Peter Macmurray was right all along, and a collection box proffered without love is an empty shell of a thing, no matter how much money is put into it.

In other respects, the work-load of my ministry remained constant, or grew. I felt increasingly isolated – a situation largely of my own making. And another factor in my tiredness was that in 1997 my mother came to live with me in the manse. She was then nearly eighty, and had been a widow for seventeen years. In that time she had become increasingly wandered in her mind. Her neighbours in Ochtermill kept an eye out for her and had my phone number, but she was always a source of worry. Jenny and I tried to visit her every fortnight, but it was hard to make the time, and often Jenny ended up going herself because I was too busy. After Jenny's death, I regret to say, I took to telephoning her instead.

Her senility was curious. Some days she could be reassuringly lucid, conduct a normal conversation and appear to have reasonable control of her everyday life. Other days she would phone six times in the space of an hour to ask me something I'd already told her. She would also talk to me as if I were my father, which I found difficult: at what point do you interrupt your mother to tell her that the husband to whom she imagines she is speaking has been dead for years? I can't imagine that they'd ever had a phone conversation in their lives: I used to wonder if she pictured him at the other end of the line, or if she simply forgot she was on the telephone and saw him beside her. It became obvious that she could not go on living on her own. She was becoming a liability to herself and to her neighbours. Finally they had to call out the fire brigade because she'd forgotten to take her dinner out of the oven.

I packed up her things, sold off most of the furniture and put the flat on the market. She'd been to stay in Monimaskit a few times when Jenny was alive, but not since then. She came to me in September, not long after Princess Diana was killed and the Scots voted, decisively and overwhelmingly (I among them), for a Parliament in Edinburgh. My mother was only ever sporadically aware that these things had taken place. I'd hardly settled her in one of the spare rooms when she began seeing Jenny everywhere – in the garden, on the stairs and especially in the kitchen in the Windsor chair. Sometimes we both saw her simultaneously. At first I didn't mind this. It made for interesting three-way conversations. But after a while I resented it. I resented my mother for seeing Jenny more than I did, and I resented Jenny for not being there to help look after her.

I am not proud of myself. I went to the Monimaskit Care Home, where I was a regular visitor, and special-pleaded my mother to the top of their waiting-list. I did in fact have a case: I was in and out all day and often at night, and she wasn't fit to be left alone. I would come home on a chilly winter's day, and all the windows would be wide open, or I would find that she had bolted the doors and gone to bed. She wasn't capable of making an edible meal, so I had to cook for both of us. Latterly we existed almost entirely on oven-ready meals – they were safer and easier. I did my best to keep her out of the kitchen, but lived in constant fear that she would burn the manse down. After nine months of this, my nerves were in ribbons.

Then one day a place at the home became available. I took her in that week, and she went without a word of protest. The care she got there was better than anything I could provide, and visiting her four or five times a week, as I did at first, seemed like a luxurious saving of time. She was still quite lucid and articulate some days; on others, as one of the staff remarked, she didn't know if it was Tuesday or the tatties. Gradually my visits shortened and reduced in number. As I say, I am not proud of myself. I think of her as Tantalus, unable to drink from the waters of one reality and with the grapes of another always just out of reach.

Enough, however, of these past troubles, which seem so diminished now. I must write of the events of the autumn months of this year 2003, the year of the Stone. Other events distracted the world in this year: the invasion of Iraq by American and British forces, and all the dreadful consequences of that misguided policy; but I cared about such matters less and less. The seasons moved on from spring into summer, and still the Stone was mine and mine alone. If anybody else had discovered it, they said nothing to me. And I said nothing to anybody else. I went to see it now, as a matter of course, once a week, on a Tuesday or a Thursday in the late afternoon. It never changed, which was a source of reassurance.

Madness, terror and devastation scarred other parts of the world. Deep in the woods of Keldo the Stone was more permanent, and seemed more real, than the shifting turmoil of human affairs.

I had not seen anything of Elsie and John for some months. John's visits to the manse had become very sporadic, and there'd been occasions when the doorbell had rung, and I hadn't answered it, suspecting it would be him. Then he did not come at all. I do not know why I thus shunned my oldest friend: guilt, I suppose, because of the desire I still felt for his wife. But nor, from March to September, did I see Elsie. They didn't invite me for a meal, and I didn't bump into her on the street. I drove or ran past their house often enough, but either there was no one there or I did not care to go in. I was astonished at myself: I had always been able to play the hypocrite so well. I suspected the Stone's influence. It seemed somehow to have changed us all, even though only I had seen it.

And then, one Saturday morning, I saw Elsie at last. It was the first week in September, and William Winnyford's exhibition was finally ready to open. I had received an invitation, and when I arrived at the museum at eleven o'clock the entrance hall was already crowded. Orange juice, apple juice and wine were being served; there were tiny oatcakes adorned with fish paste, greasy vol-au-vents and sausages on sticks. I made my way around the hall, shaking hands and having my ears dinned by the usual aimless chatter of such occasions. There were only a few noticeable absentees. One of them was Catherine Craigie, who had certainly been invited – I had seen the card on her mantelpiece – but who had declined, whether on grounds of incapacity or of ideological opposition I did not know.

From a podium squeezed between the reception desk and the postcard stand, the museum director Alan Straiton made a speech. The museum, he said, could not and would not have missed the opportunity to celebrate the 600th anniversary of the granting of Monimaskit's royal charter, and originally the plan had been simply to stage an exhibition of the town's history. But there was a problem: the museum's permanent exhibition, housed in the main or inner hall, *was* the town's history. Some extra dimension was needed to mark such a special occasion. And so the unique talents of the conceptual artist William Winnyford had been enlisted. Mr Winnyford, known for such works as *Steam Ghosts* at the East Midlands Rail and Road Museum, *See Out 2 Sea* at various locations around the Humber Estuary, and *The Monkfish of Burntisland*, was the leading, possibly the only true exponent of mythohistoriographical art, and he, Alan Straiton, felt proud and privileged to have collaborated with him. Bill Winnyford then spoke, using many superlatives, of the huge personal satisfaction he had gained from working in this wonderful community: he only hoped that the artistic experience that was about to be unveiled would be equally satisfying to the people who came to see it. Finally, the convenor of the council, a tiny woman weighed down by the chain of office that sat on her shoulders, was called upon to declare *Echoes: 600 Years of Monimaskit Memories* open.

People began to move through to the exhibition space, and the crowd thinned considerably. A photographer from the local paper was taking pictures of the three speakers. I saw Winnyford look in my direction and give me a wave. A few minutes later he bounded up to me.

'Gideon, so glad you've come, marvellous turn-out, have you seen any of it yet? You must have a quick look at the Black Jaws. Won't be able to see a thing of course but just a glance tell me what you think.'

'What do *you* think?' I asked.

'Delighted, works a treat, so grateful for your contribution. Best come back another day when things have quietened down, though, get the full effect. Runs through till Christmas so plenty of time.'

Somebody I did not know came up to speak to him and I slipped away. I didn't fancy the jostle and crush of the crowd, so went outside and took a walk up the High Street. By the time I returned people were beginning to leave. I passed through those who were still in the entrance hall drinking wine, and entered the exhibition.

Winnyford had constructed *Echoes* pretty much as he'd described it to me months before. There were five concentric circles with plasterboard walls, about eight feet high, fixed to a timber framework, and you worked your way round the corridors that were thus created and came across installations, panels and tableaux representing different aspects of Monimaskit's long history. The walls themselves were covered in paintings, photographs, extracts from historical documents and transparent cases containing artefacts of the town. At various places there were gaps in the walls through which you stepped to enter the next inner circle. It was not unlike being in a maze: you could only get to some parts of the outer circles by first going deeper in towards the centre, and you came across dead ends too, which obliged you to retrace your steps to the next gap. At each of these dead ends was one of Bill's installations, and at various points around the circles there were others set in small alcoves or bays. The one based on the conversation in the Luggie between the poacher and the bailie had a full-length mirror at its back, so that it was not until you got quite close, and saw your reflection in an elongated version of the pub, that you realised that the way was blocked. Another dead end was made to look like the outer wall of a house, complete with a small nine-paned window. When you looked through the window you saw the interior of a fisherman's cottage, which you had seen from the other side only a few minutes before. The journey that Bill had constructed was full of such tricks and double-takes, and I began to see why it had taken him so long to create it.

And through the whole exhibition echoed a cacophony of words, music and other sounds – bells ringing, hammers hammering, birds singing, wheels rolling over cobbles, young voices reading extracts from the old burgh records. At first all this was noisy and distracting, but again, as you approached each installation, you were able to distinguish the voices and sounds associated with its particular subject reasonably clearly. I wanted to be alone, to hear what the voices had to say. Once again, I found myself having to reassess Bill Winnyford. What was he really telling us, the inhabitants of Monimaskit, about the place we called home?

I moved on, pondering this, doing my best not to stop and be talked to. Some people wore expressions of distaste, as if *Echoes* was not what they'd expected – or perhaps entirely what they'd expected. Others seemed to be getting more out of the experience: they looked studious or puzzled or dreamy as they took in scenes depicting Picts, Vikings, William Wallace, wool merchants, fishwives, farmers, soldiers and schoolmistresses. What Catherine Craigie had derided was there too – a scene of some ceremony being performed by druids in front of a menhir which had neither the solidity nor size of my Stone in the woods. Bits of folklore, fragments of history and soundbites from the present mingled in people's ears as they looked and listened. A boy loudly inquired of his father, 'Why's it like this?' 'I'm no sure, son,' the father replied. 'Maybe if we keep going we'll find oot.'

I reached, quite unexpectedly, the centre of the exhibition, a room with four doors leading back into the outer circles, and a bench in the middle. On its walls was a much-enlarged, continuous 360-degree photograph, taken from offshore – one half a panorama of Monimaskit, the other an expanse of grey sea and overcast sky. There was nothing else in the room, and no installed sound. When you sat on the bench the camera's point of view made you feel as if you were in a boat. It was peaceful, but I stood up again, realising that I had missed the thing I most wished to see.

I left the central room by the door opposite that by which I had entered, and found myself in a part of the exhibition I had already seen. I returned and tried a third door. The curved passage I went down had nothing in it or on its walls, as if Winnyford had run out of time and left the section uncompleted. But a few feet further on I found what I was looking for – the Reverend Augustus Menteith's study. I had been on the point of turning back, and wondered how many people had done so, and whether this too was what Winnyford intended – that only the most daring or curious would find Menteith's den.

There it was in front of me: the shelves of dusty books, the desk scattered with papers, the leather chair, the coals glowing in the grate, the minister's spectacles, the minister's tea and biscuits, the minister's slippers, and beyond all this a deep-set window through which, I imagined, one could look into the Black Jaws.

A voice was speaking. It took me a few seconds to recognise it as my own, intoning the passage from Menteith's book. The effect of the voice and the room together was like waking from a dream and finding myself back in my own manse, or perhaps more like being in a dream itself, for this study, though familiar in some respects, was also quite definitely not mine: the dimensions were wrong, only a few of the books were real (the rest were painted), there was no telephone and no computer. And, standing on a wooden step with her back to me, her hands cupped around her head as she stared through the little window, was Elsie.

There was nothing to stop you stepping into this odd little half-room, and this was what Elsie had done. She might have been a life-size model of herself, part of the tableau: she might have just stepped in to get a pen, or a book; she might have been looking for me and, finding the study empty, gone to see if she could see me through the window. For a few seconds any of these things might have been true, and I stood still, unwilling to break the slightly disturbing comfort of that scene. Nobody was there but us. My recorded voice was coming to the end of its routine. I heard it saying, 'whose imagination, perhaps, was as broad as her cottage was narrow' and the tape fell silent. I cleared my throat quietly and she swung round in surprise.

'Hello, Elsie,' I said.

'Gideon. I was just thinking about you. Listening to you in fact. This' – she made a gesture that took in the whole scene – 'this is uncanny, don't you think?'

'It's a little odd. I didn't know you were here.'

'I was invited. All the library staff were, but none of the others came. They're either working or can't be bothered.'

'Is John here?'

'No, he was invited too, through the school, but we didn't think the girls would be welcome, so he volunteered to stay at home.'

'There are other children here.'

'They're older. Katie and Claire would have been bored in five minutes and a nuisance in ten. I'll bring them when it's quieter.'

'What do you think of it? The whole thing, I mean. Do you like it?'

'I can't make up my mind. It's interesting.'

'And this?'

'Like I said, uncanny. It disturbs me, I don't know why. Anyway, I was just thinking of you. We've not seen you for ages. John said Bill Winnyford had got you involved, but I'd no idea how.'

There were two explanatory panels on the wall of the passage beside me, one giving a brief summary of Augustus Menteith's life and achievements, the other a physical description of the Black Jaws. Of the legend itself, the only mention was that it could be read in Menteith's *Relicts and Reminiscences*.

'You should have a look through this window,' Elsie said.

She moved towards me and to one side so that I could get past, and I took the opportunity to kiss her cheek. 'Nice to see you,' I said. 'You too,' she said. She was wearing a white shirt and stretchy black trousers and black boots of soft leather with neat little heels and was carrying a raincoat over her arm. She looked fabulous. I breathed in her perfume as our bodies brushed.

'It's a wee bit spooky,' she said.

I got up on the wooden step, and this seemed to trigger the tape, for a few seconds later my voice began its reading again. The window was about two foot square and surrounded by a rough wooden frame. It was set at an angle, so that you looked down through it rather than straight out. The glass appeared to be slightly warped, distorting the view. I instinctively cupped my hands, just as Elsie had done, in order to block out the light behind me. I was peering down a kind of enclosed chute, which began as the whitewashed sill of the window and became, as it got further away, a rocky, slimy-looking crevasse. At the far end it opened out into a wider space, a cave of some sort lit with an eerie, flickering green light. I strained to see what was going on. There appeared to be two figures down there. One was standing, the other seated, but they were shadowy and indistinct. Tantalised, I found myself stretching forward, out of the fake study, trying to make out more of what was going on in that fake netherworld, but the glass prevented me. My own voice droned its insistent narrative in my ears.

I came away and returned to Elsie, who was reading the panels.

'Well,' I said, 'that'll give folk something to think about. It's quite oppressive.'

'That's what I thought,' she said. 'In fact I could do with some fresh air.'

'I've seen enough,' I said. 'I'll come with you.'

We made our way back to the museum entrance. It had rained the previous night and the day was grey and uncertain. We stood to one side as people came and went. Elsie took deep breaths.

'Do you want go for a drink, something to eat?' I asked.

'What time is it? I've forgotten my watch.'

It was just after one. 'I'll need to get back soon,' Elsie said. 'John'll be wanting off duty.' She stood, looking up the street for a moment. 'Oh what the hell, he can manage a bit longer. I've done all the shopping already, everything's in the boot of the car. Buy me a coffee, then.'

'I've got a better idea,' I said. 'Come back to the manse and I'll make you a coffee and a sandwich. I want to show you something.'

She looked doubtful, worried even. Then she said, 'All right. I'll go and fetch the car and drive round.'

'I'll see you there,' I said.

I hurried home, cleared up the breakfast things piled in the sink, and put the kettle on. The air in the manse seemed stale and tired, and I went round opening windows. I was seized by a sudden restless energy: I was building up to something, a declaration or an action of some kind. I found the photographs of Jenny and put them on the kitchen table. Usually I make do with instant coffee, but I got out the cafetière in Elsie's honour and had just poured in the water when the doorbell rang.

'Come in,' I shouted, and she let herself in and came through to the kitchen. She stood by the door, nervous and hesitant. 'Come in,' I said again. 'Sit down.' But she stayed where she was.

'How have you been?' she said. 'I don't know where this year's gone. I'm feeling guilty that we've not seen you, but you haven't dropped by either. The girls are growing up so fast it's terrifying. Katie especially. You should come and see them.'

'Aye, or you could bring them to church,' I said, and then, seeing her face fall, hastily added, 'I'm joking, Elsie.'

'I would,' she said, 'but John won't hear of it. I wouldn't come for the religion, you know that, but I think they should see the inside of a church, see what goes on in there, how people behave.'

'The young kids love it,' I said. 'They just think it's a show. They have no inhibitions about it. They have to be taught those.'

'Well,' she said, 'maybe we'll manage one Sunday.' At last she came into the room properly and sat down at the table, putting her bag at the end. I brought over the coffee and milk, mugs and a plateful of biscuits.

'But they're fine, are they?' I said. 'The girls?'

'They're great,' she said. 'It gets to me sometimes. I love them so much but there's always this terrible fear something will happen – they'll be harmed in some way, die in an accident. Maybe it's because of Jenny, I don't know, but I fear they'll be taken away from me before they have time to see the world, to really live, and then I worry that I'll try to limit their experience because of my fear.'

'All love has fear in it,' I said. I poured the coffee.

'I suppose so,' she said. Then she laughed. 'By the way, Friend's gone.'

I didn't understand her for a second. 'Friend?'

'Katie's imaginary pal. The invisible pain in the neck. He'd not been much in evidence for a while and then the other day someone had been drawing on the wall with crayons and then made a bad attempt to rub it off. I stood Katie in front of it and said, I suppose Friend did that, and she looked down at her toes and said, no, Friend's gone away. Where's he gone, I said. He's gone to Spain, she said, and he won't be coming back, it was me. And then she started crying, and so did I.'

'She's growing up right enough,' I said. 'She's learning guilt.'

'I know, it's awful,' Elsie said.

'You can't stop it. Anyway, guilt's a pretty good tool to have in the box. It breeds responsibility.'

'Sometimes you really do sound like a minister,' she said. 'When

I told John what had happened he said, well, just because he's gone to Spain doesn't mean we need to forget him. We can tease her about him when she's older, he said.'

'Sounds like John,' I said. 'How is he?'

She shrugged. 'Constantly knackered. Teaching's wearing him down. The other night he said he was glad Gregor got the principal teacher job and not him, the admin would have killed him by now. That's the first time he's ever admitted that.'

'That was ten years ago,' I said.

'Twelve actually,' Elsie said. 'Things simmer away in John for a long time.'

'Like his novel,' I said.

'Aye, like his novel,' she said, and again the worry lines formed on her brow.

'What's wrong?' I asked.

'Nothing,' she said. 'My imagination.' She breathed out heavily. 'I think he's having an affair.'

'Ah,' I said. I assume my face must have looked concerned because I *was* concerned, but even in that instant, I couldn't help my heart beating faster, my mind flooding with possibilities.

'I mean, I don't know,' she said, 'I don't know anything for certain, but some things haven't been making sense, his behaviour, his schedules at the school, unexpected meetings in the evenings, that kind of thing, and suddenly one day it struck me that if there was a woman involved it would explain it all. But I don't have any proof. I don't *want* any proof.'

'Who do you think the woman is?' I asked.

'Nancy Croy,' she said, and her eyes filled with tears. I stood up and began to come round the table to hug her. 'No, don't,' she said. 'Please, Gideon. I don't trust myself.' I felt giddy with excitement at the import of those words. She went on rapidly, 'I shouldn't have told you. I can't afford an emotional collapse just now. Forget I said anything, will you?'

'I can't,' I said. 'You have to face the truth, Elsie.'

'The truth is, I'm not going to confront him with it, so I have to get myself through this. He loves the girls too much. If there's anything going on it'll end. He won't lose the girls for Nancy Croy.'

I sat down again. Our coffees were untouched and growing cold. I asked her how long she thought it had been going on, and she said, 'I don't know. I don't even know if it *is* going on. But they're colleagues, they see each other every day, she's single and interesting and bonnie-looking . . . Do you think she's bonnie?'

'Yes,' I said, 'up to a point. But she doesn't do anything for me. Plus she's a kirk elder.'

'I thought you got on well.'

'Tolerably. We used to get on better, but she suspects me of infidelity. The religious kind, I mean. Elsie, if John's having an affair with Nancy he must be insane. She's got nothing on you.'

'That's very sweet of you, Gideon. Well, maybe there's something between them, maybe there isn't. I know there's not much between John and me just now. That's another reason we've not seen you, we haven't seen anyone really, it's been pretty bloody awful. But I have to believe it will come back. It always has done so far. We've had our ups and downs.'

'You've been together a long time now,' I said.

'Twenty-six years,' she said. 'And we've known Nancy for half of them. I wake up in the night and think, what if it's been happening all that time? Or since before Katie was born? It took so long for me to get pregnant. Was he having an affair with Nancy then? And he's lying there beside me dead to the world and I can't believe there's anything going on. But there are other times . . . He works late a lot, and sometimes he says he's going to drop in on you but I know he hasn't seen you. I'm a coward, I don't want to challenge him. I think people can sometimes have flirtatious relationships with work colleagues for years and it never comes to anything. Do you think that's true?'

'Of course,' I said. 'It happens all the time.'

'I know what you're thinking,' she said. 'You're thinking about us. And that's another reason why I don't want to confront John. Maybe he guessed about that. Maybe he's known all along. And now it's his turn.'

I didn't want to hear any more about John. I pushed the envelope of photographs towards her.

'Have a look at these,' I said.

She wiped her eyes and took the pictures out. I watched her as she looked at them in turn. Her slim fingers slid the top one to the bottom of the pile, slid the next one, and the next. I was mesmerised by the movement of those fingers.

The pictures provoked a few more tears. 'How come I've not seen these before?' she asked.

I explained how I'd found the camera with the film still in it. 'They're a bit faded,' I said.

'It's like seeing a ghost,' she said. 'I remember you going away that time, over to the West Highlands.'

'Did she tell you why?'

'No.'

'We were making a fresh start. We'd drifted apart. We were getting back together again. That was the idea anyway.'

'Oh, Gideon.' And now she reached her hand towards me, and I took it.

'So it can happen,' I said. 'People can make a fresh start. People who once connected can get back together again.'

She frowned at me. I looked at the table.

'I went to take pictures of the Stone,' I said. My fingers were playing with her fingers. I looked at them, not at her face because I knew if I looked at her face she would take her hand away. 'With the rest of the film. Months ago. I took these pictures of the Stone but they didn't come out.'

'What stone?' she said.

I couldn't believe she'd forgotten, but I explained patiently. 'Remember, back at New Year, I told you about the standing stone I'd found when I was out running? In Keldo Woods? I went to photograph it, to prove it was there.'

'It just went out of my mind,' she said. 'You never mentioned it again, and we haven't seen you . . . Is it still there?'

'Yes,' I said, 'but it didn't want to be photographed.'

She frowned again. 'What do you mean?'

'Just that. The photos came out blank. Look, you can see on the negatives. These are all pictures of the Stone and there's nothing on them.'

She held the strip of negatives to the light.

'Gideon, the film's faulty.'

'No,' I said. 'The film was good. It took me and Jenny. Why not the Stone?'

'I don't know. Because the film was too old?'

'Because the Stone prevented it.'

Elsie put the photos and negatives back in the envelope. She shook her head as she did so.

'Don't do that, Elsie,' I said. 'Don't be like everybody else. You didn't disbelieve me before. And anyway, it doesn't matter that the photos haven't come out. It's better that way. Nobody else has seen the Stone, and I don't want anyone else to see it. Except for you.'

Now we looked at each other. I could tell she was afraid. I held on to her hand.

'It's all right,' I said. 'There's nothing to be frightened of. But I want to share it with you.'

'Share what?'

'The Stone. Elsie . . .'

'Why are you looking like that, Gideon?'

'Like what?'

'You look strange. Are you all right?'

'I'm fine,' I said. 'I love you, Elsie.'

'Don't say that.'

'Elsie, remember what happened here,' I said. 'I've always loved you.'

She stood up suddenly, pulling her hand away and picking up her bag.

'I think I'd better go.'

I stood up too. 'No, not yet,' I said.

'I have to,' she said.

I reached out, tried to hold her, but she slipped past me. 'No, Gideon!' she said, quite loudly, as if I was a dog. 'What do you think you're doing?'

‘I’m not doing anything,’ I said, and forced myself to stand still. ‘I just want you to see the Stone. I want us to see it together.’

‘What are you talking about? You keep going on about this stone. I don’t think there is a stone. I think it’s all in your head.’

She went quickly to the hallway and then she was at the front door and then outside and half-running towards her car parked in the drive behind mine. I followed her. I wasn’t chasing her. I only wanted to tell her, but she wouldn’t listen.

Her car wasn’t locked, and she’d left the keys in the ignition. She got in and slammed the door and pushed down the lock. I saw her fumbling to turn the key, and then the engine started, and she revved hard as she swung the car round in reverse. I stepped back, raising my hands as if in surrender. I was saying, ‘Wait, wait, wait,’ and trying to apologise with my face.

She opened the driver’s window a crack.

‘You frighten me, Gideon,’ she said. ‘I think you need help. You’ve probably needed it for a long time. You’re depressed or something. Go and see Amelia, or if you don’t want to see her go to another doctor. But you scare me when you’re like this.’

She put the car into first gear and drove off, spraying my legs with gravel. I half-thought of driving after her, but saw it was futile. She was in no mood to listen. She thought I was ill, that I had invented the whole thing about the Stone. But I knew I wasn’t ill. She’d panicked because I’d said I loved her, and because she loved me too. *That* was what frightened her.

XXXIII

A crisis was upon me. I was sweating, seething with energy. If I didn’t do something the energy would burst out of me and leave me wrecked on the floor. My left arm was twitching as if in contact with an electric fence. I wanted to go to the Stone, yet at the same time was afraid to go. It seemed to me that the Stone had provoked this crisis, had engineered it in some way. I paced round the manse, in and out of every room, up and down the stairs. I’d just decided to get changed and head off for a long run, to try to calm down, when the bell rang again. I thought Elsie must have come back and rushed to the front door. A car had pulled up in the drive, but not Elsie's. It was Lorna Sprott.

'Gideon,' Lorna said. 'I've been at the museum. I missed the exhibition opening but I've had a good look round.' Something in my expression stopped her. 'Is this an awkward moment?'

'Actually, I was about to go for a run.'

'You wouldn't like to come for a walk instead? I've got Jasper in the car. I was thinking we might go to the Black Jaws.'

I opened my mouth to make an excuse, but she didn't notice.

'The exhibition surprised me,' she said. 'I didn't think it would be my cup of tea at all, and I can't say I understood everything, but it was quite thought-provoking. I saw old Menteith's study and listened to you reading while I was looking down through that window. That's what put me in mind to go to the Black Jaws, the real place. I haven't been there for ages, and Jasper could do with a change from the beach.'

She looked pleadingly at me. How could I resist? Lorna stood on the step, inexorable and solid, and I knew I'd never get rid of her. Even if I slammed the door in her face she wouldn't leave me alone. I imagined her scraping and chapping at the windows until I let her in. 'Wait a minute,' I said, and went to get my boots and a jacket.

Perhaps I was meant to go for a walk with Lorna, to talk to her about what was going on. Perhaps the Stone was wielding some strange power over events and had brought her to my door at this moment. In the minute or two it took me to get ready I made a decision. I would go with Lorna to the Black Jaws and, depending on how things went, I would swear her to secrecy, take her to Keldo Woods, and show her the Stone. I could trust her thus far, I knew. If Lorna acknowledged that the Stone existed, then I would know I was neither hallucinating nor mad and I would go to Elsie and John. I would confront them with the misery and mockery of our lives and ask them to have the courage, with me, to change them. If, on the other hand, Lorna could not see the Stone, then I would have to admit that what Elsie had said was true, that I needed help.

I didn't know, as I locked the manse door and got into Lorna's car, that I wouldn't be back for nearly a week. Nor could I have foreseen that I would return utterly transformed. Nor indeed, as I strapped myself in and gritted my teeth against Lorna's terrible driving, and was greeted by Jasper's happy squeals and licks from the back seat, could I have guessed that it would not be Lorna who would trigger what happened next, but her dog.

Beside the narrow road that goes past the gates of Keldo House and then winds its way up into the hills, there is a muddy lay-by with space for three or four cars. There was no other vehicle there when we stopped and let Jasper out. A wooden signpost pointed along a path through the trees: TO THE BLACK JAWS. KEEP DOGS ON LEAD. But Lorna, unless there were sheep around, never heeded such instructions, and I couldn't blame her, as Jasper pulling and lunging on the lead was more trouble than he was off it. Anyway, my head was so full of other things that it didn't occur to me that the dog might be a liability to himself or anybody else. He bounded off, snorting and sniffing as if this new world of scents were even more fabulous than the beach.

The rain came on again as soon as we set out. The trunks of the birches and beech trees were slick and shiny, the grass and shrubs at their feet beaded and dripping. The path was muddy and narrow in places, so that at times Lorna and I had to walk one behind the other. I was following her blue cagoule-draped back and wondering how to begin to tell her about the Stone when, as I had half-expected, she spoke first.

'Gideon, I hope you won't think I'm imposing on you again, but I'm having a bit of a crisis.'

'So am I, Lorna,' I said.

She stopped and turned to stare at me. 'You?' she said. 'Whatever about?'

'I'll tell you later,' I said. 'You go first.'

At that point the path widened again and I was able to come up alongside her. I feared that Lorna might read something symbolic into this, and I wasn't wrong.

'You're so polite and unselfish, Gideon,' she said. 'You always put others before yourself. But look, I don't have to go first, we can do this together. Walking side by side, you can help me, and I hope I can help you.'

It sounded like a thought for the day from the Scripture Union. I squirmed inwardly, but something had got into Lorna. As if moved by some heavenly impulse, she suddenly broke into song:

> 'Yea, though I walk in death's dark vale,
> yet will I fear no ill:
> For thou art with me; and thy rod
> and staff me comfort still.'

She was not blessed with a good voice, and the words did not so much drift as crash unmelodiously among the trees. Not wishing to encourage her, I didn't join in. It was a mercy to me that we were alone, although also worrying: if Lorna could launch herself at a metrical psalm with such vigour, might she not also launch herself at me? I began to wonder why I was even considering telling her about the Stone. At the same time I had a brief and unexpected image of us as characters in *The Pilgrim's Progress*: Lorna stumping on up the narrow path as Christian, with her burden on her back, and me smirking along beside her as Mr Worldly Wiseman.

At the sound of her singing, Jasper came bouncing back to us and planted his front paws all over her cagoule. She shooed him off, and I picked up a piece of broken branch and threw it into the wet undergrowth. He rushed after it, spent a frantic half-minute trying to locate it, then lost interest and raced up the path out of sight.

Lorna said, 'Gideon, do you remember last time we went to the beach, we talked about truth, and how sometimes it was hard to know whether the truth should be spoken out loud or kept to oneself?'

'Yes,' I said, 'I remember.' There was a breathlessness in her voice which I could ascribe to neither her psalm-singing nor the slight incline of the path. She stared resolutely ahead, and went on speaking.

'And you advised me to keep praying, that an answer would come if I prayed long enough.'

'I don't think I quite said that,' I said. 'And Lorna, you told me you were speaking about someone else.'

'Well, Gideon, that's where I was deceitful, for which I am truly sorry. I went away and thought about what you'd said and I realised that I would never be at peace unless I was honest, with myself and with you. There *was* no other person, Gideon, no other minister. I was talking about myself.'

'I see,' I said.

'I know that must astonish you. I know how furtive it must seem, but it was the only way I could sound you out.'

'Lorna,' I said, 'I'm not that astonished. I did suspect, you know.'

'Really?' she said. 'Was I that obvious? Well, I took your advice, and I prayed again, and the answer came back as clear as anything this time, that the only way forward was the truth. And although this is very difficult, and I may make a fool of myself and regret it, I must tell you the truth, Gideon. I can't not tell you the truth any longer.'

She stopped walking and turned to me and looked directly into my eyes, and I looked back. I steeled myself against what was coming. She was going to declare her feelings, and I was going to have to hurt them. But even as I realised this, I saw that she realised it too, that she could see the rejection in my eyes, and that all she'd achieved by forcing herself to advance this far was to make a retreat inevitable. And I saw that she'd probably known all along how hopeless her planned confession was, how doomed, and that this walk to the Black Jaws would be just one more stage in the hard bloody slog that was her unhappy journey through life. And I felt something I'd never felt before, huge admiration for her. She was courageous and honest, she always believed in trying to do her best, and I was ashamed of my own cynical, calculating life. And there was something else: I envied her. I envied her futile, sad, stubborn optimism, that she would recover from this blow and carry on just as she always did, bumping and jerking her way into the future. In that moment of Lorna not saying what she'd built herself up to say, I respected her more than I ever had, and I saw why, in spite of her irritating ways and in spite of myself, I had always liked her.

She started to cry, and I put my arms around her and hugged her. 'I'm sorry,' I said, and through her sniffs and tears she said she was sorry too, and then Jasper, coming back to find out what was keeping us, began to leap up at us, barking and whining for attention. It was impossible to ignore him. I started to laugh, and so did Lorna. She pushed herself away from me, fumbled under her cagoule for a handkerchief, blew her nose and petted Jasper. 'Sorry,' she said again. 'I'm okay now, Gideon, honestly.'

'Come on,' I said, and I put my arm through hers. 'Let's go and see the Black Jaws.'

We could already hear them. The last few days of rain had poured off the hills and swollen the upper reaches of the Keldo, and now thousands of gallons of water were being funnelled through the ravine every minute. The black cliffs were drumming with the sound of it. It was difficult to tell if the haze surrounding the trees was part of the fresh rainfall or spray rising from below. The path took a turn to the right and dropped a little towards a wooden bridge stretched across the ravine – an innovation since Augustus Menteith's day. Immediately to our left, at the path's turn, the ground fell away ever more steeply, with trees stretching from it at odd angles, some almost horizontal, their roots like clawed hands clutching fiercely at the earth. The roar and reverberating boom of the river seemed to be coming up through the soil itself, through the layers of rock, through the trunks of the trees and the very soles of our boots. Even Jasper, who had shown only curiosity towards the crashing waves at the beach, trembled a little and slowed to a walk, keeping himself within easy reach of us. If he hadn't been behaving like this, I would have suggested to Lorna that she put him on the lead. As it was, there seemed little risk of him doing anything daft.

But I had reckoned without the appearance of the rabbit. As we came down to the bridge, there was a sudden burst of movement to our right, and a brown shape shot across the path and into the undergrowth on the other side. Jasper was after it in a second. Lorna and I both yelled at him, but he was oblivious to anything but the rabbit. I have never seen a dog move so fast. The pursuit was over in seconds, however, because the rabbit, plunging down through wet grass towards the wetter ferns and creepers which marked the edge of the cliff, took one leap too many as it strove to outpace the dog. Suddenly it was in flight, launched from the last scrape of rock into the spray-filled air. It hung there for a long second and then dropped out of sight like a flung toy. We could not hear above the din but we could see Jasper's desperate efforts to halt, the shower of mud and twigs and grass his back claws threw up as he skidded down the slope, and then he too disappeared. For one ghastly moment we waited to see his taut black body also flying into space, but there was nothing. Lorna let out a long scream, 'Jasper, O God, Jasper, O God, O God.' Nothing. And then, faintly above the terrible roar of the Black Jaws, a pitiful howl came back to us. Beyond our vision, but evidently perched somewhere on the edge of the precipice, Jasper was still alive.

Lorna started to scramble down from the path, and slipped on to her backside almost at once. I pulled her back. 'Stay here,' I said. 'No, see if you can climb along a bit further up, spot where he is. But keep back from the edge. It's absolutely treacherous. I'll try and reach him.' And getting down into a sitting position, gingerly I began to work my way down the slope.

The slight outcrop of rock from which the rabbit had jumped was only twenty feet away, but it felt like half a mile. The vegetation was completely soaked, and there was no grip on the slimy rock which it covered. Easing my crablike way across this horrible surface, clutching at clumps of grass as if they were anchored ropes, I finally made it to the outcrop. Here the noise from below battered still more loudly and relentlessly around my head, so that it was almost impossible to think. I shifted myself into a forward-leaning position and inched my way over the lip of the rock. On the other side, no more than ten feet away, was Jasper.

He was crouched on a bare patch of quartz-speckled rock surrounded by sickly green, slippery-looking foliage. He teetered on the very edge of the chasm, unable to go either forward or back, issuing whimpering sounds that were halfway between barks and sobs. His back was arched and his feet scrabbled constantly as he struggled to keep his balance. 'Jasper,' I called, 'I'm here,' but in his overwhelming fear he didn't hear me. I had no option but to push myself along those last few feet towards him.

By leaning into the cliff-face, almost smothering myself in the thick wetness of ferns and leaves, I got to within a couple of feet of him and reached out my right hand to support him. It was the first knowledge he had of my presence. A splash of urine squirted from him on to the rock, and he gave a startled but grateful look over his shoulder. My hand on his side allowed him to rest his paws, but his whole body was still quivering miserably. I tried to calm him. 'All right, Jasper, all right, it's all right.' But it wasn't all right. I felt desperately insecure, with one hand holding the dog and the other, my left, clinging to stalks and roots that might give way at any moment. I had little idea what I was going to do. I couldn't carry him under one arm back the way we had come. The only possibility I could see was to try to turn him, then get enough purchase under his body to push him to safer ground directly above us.

Stones rattled down over us, and from somewhere up there – presumably not far or I wouldn't have been able to hear her – Lorna called, 'Can you see him?' 'I've got him!' I bellowed back, but my face was pressed into the vegetation and she obviously didn't hear. 'Gideon! Can you see him?' she shouted again. Jasper heard her and restarted his frantic scrabbling. I did my best to calm him, but my right arm was getting tired. I knew we couldn't stay the way we were for very much longer.

Lorna shouted again. 'Have you got him? What can I do?' The faint sound of her voice set Jasper off again, whining and shaking. He lurched outwards, and it took all my strength to hold him back. I summoned what breath I could into my lungs.

'Lorna,' I yelled, 'you're panicking him. You'll have to be quiet.'

'What?' came her voice, and Jasper howled. 'Have you got him?'

'Will you shut the fuck up?' I screamed, but whether this was directed at Lorna, Jasper, the Black Jaws or our hopeless situation I don't know. I doubt whether she heard me, but it didn't matter anyway, because something in the despairing tone of my voice must have penetrated the dog's brain and made him decide that, however many canine years or minutes were left to him, here was not the best place to spend them. He made a sudden furious scramble up off the patch of rock, into the foliage, and in so doing managed to turn himself to face me. 'Good boy!' I said, and my right hand slipped round his rump, along his back and gripped the scruff of his neck. I hauled him up over me, felt his back paws push on my right shoulder and then lift as his front paws found some kind of leverage, and in a second he was away, sending a mini-landslide of loose pebbles, mud and dead leaves down on my head. Some grit got into my eyes and temporarily blinded me. I held on. I was almost certain Jasper had got far enough up the slope to get himself out of danger, but I no longer cared if he hadn't. I had done all I could for him, and now I had to rescue myself. But a moment later I was beyond rescue.

After years of toying with me, my left arm chose this moment to deliver its *coup de grâce*. With a sense of helplessness, knowing what the feeling was and that there was nothing I could do to ward it off, I felt the fuzziness coming on, the clouds gathering in my head, the roaring sound of water all around me that was both more and less than the thunder of the river below. I felt the slow spasm of the arm's independence as it began to shake the grip of my fingers from the foliage. I tried to hang on, but the arm wouldn't let me, it was pushing me out, away from the cliff. I felt the cliff coming away in my hand. I went through a flailing, swimming motion with my right arm, clawing at anything that might hold, but now my legs were dragging me down faster than my fingers could work while the left arm went into its mad conductor mode. I thought of car crashes. I thought of Batman and Robin as the credits rolled. I thought, this really is it this time, Gideon, and the cliff moved two, three, four feet away from me and I was falling, still clutching bits of greenery in my right hand, my left still urging on its manic orchestra, falling, falling, falling into the black and white frenzy of the waters below.

XXXIV

How to describe what followed? It is not easy. I could tell of these events in the order, as it is clear to me now, that they must have happened, but who would accept the veracity of such a telling? I myself would not have in previous times. Better, therefore, to reveal these strange marvels as they were revealed to me – as the record of memory, accessed *after* they were over. That they happened is not in question: I have the proof. The only point at issue is what they signify.

I remember this: I fell into a roaring mouth that instantly became a cold, wet, hard throat sucking me down and down into itself. Nobody but I knows how apt the name *the Black Jaws* is for that dreadful place, for nobody else has been devoured by it and lived. I fell, as helpless as the rabbit that had gone before me, and at some point all my senses were smothered in the darkness. I don't know when this happened, whether I was still in the air or had hit the water, but I have no memory of hitting the water. The last thing I remember thinking was the mundane fact that I had eaten nothing since breakfast.

Then there was a tremendous, freezing pressure all around me, and I was being churned and spun like a sock in a washing-machine, carried along by an immense, frothing, surging force. Something hit me, or I hit it. I was caught for a second, snagged, then I was moving again. This is all I can remember of however long I was in the Black Jaws.

Somewhere in my head was the knowledge that I couldn't possibly have survived the fall; that even if I had, the river would have killed me; drowned, broken, battered, chilled and crushed me to pulp. I was of the opinion, therefore, that I must be dead.

And yet I remained in the body that had been Gideon Mack. It was as if the essence of me was trapped in that now useless shell, that rudderless vessel spinning like a barrel in the flood. I was moving very rapidly in black water through a long black tunnel. My head kept going under, coming up again. I tried to breathe, but there was no room for breath in my lungs. The tunnel must have been dimly lit because I could see the black rock of its roof and walls, and the horrible, sickly race of the water rushing me along. I tried to see where the light was coming from. I couldn't possibly swim in such a current, but as I travelled I was turned by it and whenever I was facing in the direction of the flow I saw a tiny speck of yellow far in the distance. This was the light that cast just enough of itself to illuminate the tunnel, and I was moving towards it. The tunnel was very straight, the river more like a mill-lade than a natural river. I felt that I was being propelled along at hundreds of miles per hour.

And yet I did not panic. There was no point in panicking. I could do nothing. Everything was out of my hands. I could only be taken by the water wherever it was going. The water was very cold and did not seem quite real, it was thick and viscous yet at the same time it flowed as freely and fast as a burn; it was both solid and liquid at the same time. And it was carrying me towards the light.

The light grew brighter. My sense of calmness grew with it. I did not want to be calm, I felt I ought to be fighting for my life – but at the same time I thought I was dead. And as this thought intensified, became a certainty, in some indefinite moment the essence of me slipped away from my physical self. And my consciousness was with the essence. I was the kite I had flown in the garden, centuries before it seemed, attached but at a distance, outside, above, looking down on my body as it was swept along the tunnel. I was hovering above it, keeping pace and yet not moving at all. I had a memory of watching myself on the bedroom floor all those years before, the sounds of Jenny working in the kitchen below. Then I had other memories: Elsie and me in that same bedroom making love, me and Buzz arguing in the school playground with part of me outside myself looking on, John and me identifying Jenny at the hospital, my mother watching me sleepwalking, my father's vicelike grip on my neck in front of the television, my mother kneeling beside my father on the floor, the little pile of yellow vomit at his mouth. These and other images appeared as if I was looking at them in a flicker-book. I thought, *this is a ridiculous cliché, my life is flashing in front of me*, but it was true and I could not stop it. And all the while the light was growing brighter.

Soon it was so bright that I thought it would blind me, but it was not like staring directly into the sun, it was more as if sunlight were all around me, illuminating everything with a wonderful clarity. The light changed from yellow to brilliant white. I was sinking into it. Angelic, celestial light. I could see every detail of the tunnel, every ripple and swirl in the racing water, the head of Gideon Mack bobbing up and down in it, Gideon's limbs as lifeless as the limbs of a rag-doll. I realised that I was on the point of being for ever separated from that body. Its fingers were numb and limp and letting go of whatever filament still linked us. I looked around from my vantage point in the air, and every fissure and bulge and fold in the rock walls was perfectly clear and defined. And it was this that returned me, with a shock, to my physical self, for it made me think of the Stone.

The Stone was unfinished business. Elsie was unfinished business. I had left too much unresolved. The calm that had been overwhelming me splintered, and I began to panic, trying to make my heavy arms and legs move, reach, seize. I felt as though I was falling again, banging into things, being hurt: I was back in my own body. The tunnel was no longer a tunnel, but a twisting, jolting chute of crashing white water and black undercurrent. There were branches and pebbles and stones and other debris. Gideon Mack was debris. The constant battering of water and rock felt distant and dull, and I was frozen but I understood that I was being bashed about like a log, and it was only a matter of time before I received a fatal blow to the head or chest.

I was suddenly flushed over a long, smooth rock into a deeper, less turbulent body of water with a head of foam rotating on it. I submerged again and came back up into relative tranquillity. The roar of water seemed much diminished, and I had the sensation of having been washed many feet from the source of that tumult. I could feel no bottom beneath me, but then my feet were too numb to feel anything – I didn't even know if I still had my walking-boots on. I had the will but not the strength to swim and felt myself sinking again. And at that moment a hand reached to me, pulling me from the water.

A hand, yes. That much is clear. Now comes the tricky part. Picture me, as I slowly pictured myself, my mind gradually infilling blocks of the scene like a clumsy child painting by numbers. I am blinking my way out of darkness. A white background with patches of yellow, grey, blue. The colours blur, separate, overlap. Shapes emerge from them. I am lying in bed in a room full of beds. Linoleum on the floor. Wires and tubes and screens around me. I am aware, vaguely, of men and women coming and going, of kind but brusque attention being paid to me. I come and go too, only without moving. Smells: coffee, sweat, urine, air-freshener, disinfectant. Then comes a time when I stay a little longer. I hear myself breathing. I sense light through my eyelids and open them. My left arm lies peacefully on the covers, extending from the sleeve of a pyjama jacket I do not recognise. My right arm is there too, with something attached to it, a plastic bracelet round the wrist. And on either side of the bed, a shadow that becomes a person, familiar, leaning forward. Voices that say, 'Hello, Gideon.'

Elsie on the one side, John on the other. John's hand touches my hand. Elsie stands up and bends to kiss my forehead. I move my head against the pillows, take in the rest of the ward. Three other beds: men of various ages, all grey of complexion, two sleeping, one staring into space. A woman is sitting next to one of the sleeping men, holding his hand.

'You had us worried for a while there,' John said. 'We thought you were never coming back.'

'I was in the river,' I said.

'Yes,' Elsie said. 'You fell. You saved the dog, do you remember that?'

'Jasper,' I said. 'Yes, I remember it all.'

But of course I didn't, not then. The real memories, sharp and shining as crystal, came later.

'You should have died,' Elsie said. 'Nobody knows how you didn't, but you didn't.'

This is what they told me: that Lorna had raised the alarm, and assorted police, firemen and rock-climbers, and local men who knew the Keldo, hurried to see what could be done. They lowered men on ropes into the Black Jaws as far as they could and found no trace of me. They tried to scramble their way past the raging water from the lower section of the river but couldn't penetrate to the deepest part of the chasm. They searched till nightfall and in the morning they searched again, but to no avail. The next day's papers carried the story of the lost minister, who had died rescuing a fellow minister's pet dog, and whose body would never be recovered from the secret course of the river.

'They say some nice things about you,' John said. 'Generally speaking, the view is that you were a pretty decent kind of guy. Certainly not bad for a minister.'

'John,' Elsie said quietly. He threw her a look of disdain, and I realised that they were talking to me as individuals, not as a couple. But something else was puzzling me.

I said, 'I'm in hospital. Where?'

Elsie said, 'You're in Ninewells, in Dundee.'

'How long have I been here?'

'A day and a half,' she said.

'What day is it?'

'It's Wednesday. You've been asleep since you came in.'

'But I only saw you yesterday, at Bill Winnyford's exhibition.'

'That was Saturday,' she said. 'You saw me at the museum, and then later you went for a walk with Lorna Sprott at the Black Jaws. You were missing for three days, Gideon.'

'Three days? That's impossible.'

'No,' John said, 'but it's close to what some folk might call a miracle. We don't believe in miracles, do we? But the river kept you for three days, and then it spat you out, which is pretty miraculous. A bit like the guy that was swallowed by the whale.'

'Jonah,' I said.

'Aye, him,' John said. He knew perfectly well who was swallowed by the whale. He was just testing me.

'Three days,' I said. 'Who took the service on Sunday?'

'Don't worry about any of that,' Elsie said. 'The elders handled it, so I'm told. It was short and simple, and John Gless gave a five-minute sermon, and they prayed for your safe return.'

'And hey, it worked,' John said.

'And Lorna Sprott's going to cover for you for the next couple of weeks,' Elsie continued. 'You can put your mind at rest on that front.'

'What about her own congregations?' I asked.

'Gideon, it doesn't matter,' Elsie said. She saw I was not satisfied. 'She says she has somebody who can look after them. A Reader, is that the term? Anyway, he's going to take the services at Meldrick, and she wants to come to Monimaskit. She says it's the least she could do, all things considered. Don't worry, it's taken care of.'

I waved a hand to show that I wasn't that worried.

'She's been here too,' Elsie went on. 'Yesterday and this morning, but you've been asleep. She's very fond of you, Gideon.'

John made a face. I responded to neither of them. I was trying to fill the gaps.

'I remember being in the water,' I said. 'Being battered about a lot. Somebody fished me out.'

'That was Chae Middleton,' John said. 'Chae the poacher. He was out for one of his strolls up the river and he spotted you floating in the water. Thought you were a dead sheep at first. He waded in and got you up on the bank, saw who you were and phoned for help. You really would be dead if it wasn't for him.'

'I'm grateful,' I said. 'I mind him getting me out. At least, I think I do.' But the memory didn't seem quite right. I closed my eyes. A gravel bank, but before that the sensation of bumping into or being bumped by something. Something that wasn't Chae Middleton.

'Gideon,' Elsie said, 'we're going to leave you now. You need to rest. It's so wonderful that you're alive. And you're in good shape too. The doctors are amazed at you. You've been incredibly lucky.'

Everything else from that Saturday was coming back to me. I didn't feel that I needed to rest at all. I tried to hold Elsie's gaze, and she looked away, which was understandable with John right there.

We talked for a few more minutes before they left. My adventure had made quite a splash in the news. 121 George Street had put out a statement expressing delight that I had been returned to continue in the service of the Lord. John was collecting the press cuttings, including a couple of brief obituaries, and would keep them for me. 'You're in danger of becoming a celebrity,' he said, as he stood up to go.

I lay for quite a while after that, wondering about the missing days of my life. It was like waking from a deep and dreamless sleep, and yet I was clutching at some kind of memory from within that sleep. A nurse came and talked to me, made sure I was comfortable. I asked her what had happened to my clothes.

'They had to cut most of them off you,' she said. 'You'll not be seeing them again. Anything else you came in with is in your locker there – the personal possessions you arrived with. Was there something special you wanted?'

'I don't know,' I said. 'I don't know what's there.'

With her help I was able to swing my legs out of bed and sit on the edge of it in front of the locker. I felt pretty good, apart from a lump on the side of my head and a general stiffness in my limbs. My right leg was aching, and the thigh seemed rather swollen. When I pushed down my pyjama bottoms to inspect it I saw it was purple and black with bruises. 'How did that happen?' I asked.

'You were in a raging river getting hit by rocks, that's how,' she said. 'It's not broken, though.'

'Oh,' I said. Some other conversation nudged at my mind. 'I thought it must be.'

'You're a very lucky man,' she said. 'You shouldn't even be alive, let alone in one piece.'

My watch was there, its glass bleary and scratched. It had stopped at 3.37 on the sixth day of the month. There were a few coins, and my house-keys, which had apparently been retrieved from my trousers before they were thrown out, but no wallet or paper money. The nurse was about to leave me when I pointed to the bottom of the locker. 'What are those?'

'Your shoes,' she said. 'They were the only things you were wearing that survived. I'd have chucked them out too, but we can't do that with patients' things, not unless they're completely ruined.'

'My shoes?' I said. I was about to protest, to say that some mistake had been made, but I held my tongue. I asked her to hand them to me. They were still a little damp. And as I held them, sitting there on the edge of the hospital bed, a door unlocked and the missing days came rushing through to me. For the shoes the nurse gave me were not my old walking-boots, the ones I'd had on when I fell into the Black Jaws, but a mangy, battered, cracked and laceless pair of old trainers. They were not mine, but I recognised them. I knew whose they were, and I knew where I had last seen them.

XXXV

I lay awake all that night, reliving in my head what had happened. In the morning I was stiff and sore, but this, I felt, was more from lying so long in bed than from any injury I had acquired. I got myself up and went to wash my face. The lump on my head was a little tender. Sitting on the toilet, I examined the plum-coloured bruises on my right leg. Although it didn't give me much pain the leg felt distinctly odd. When I walked back to my bed I realised that I was pitching like a boat in a rough swell. I could not help it: I was walking with a pronounced limp. Another half-memory came to me, and I felt uneasy in my heart.

Later in the morning the consultant came on his rounds and spoke to me from a great height. I was extremely fortunate to be alive, he said. If I really *had* spent three days and nights trapped in the Keldo Water he was at a loss to explain how I had survived. Hypothermia, heart failure, drowning, multiple lacerations and blows to the head and chest – any one of these ought to have finished me off. Yet apart from some cuts and bruises, and the fact that I had been unconscious for thirty-six hours, and probably a good deal longer, I seemed unharmed. Did I not have any memory of what had happened after my fall? No, I lied, I did not. Perhaps it would come back to me later. Yes, he said, sounding doubtful, perhaps it would.

'When can I go home?' I asked.

'Well, Mr Mack,' he said, 'given what you have *apparently* undergone, I wouldn't have anticipated your leaving us for quite some time. But the restorative powers of sleep appear to have worked wonders with you. You're going to have a few aches and pains for a while, and I certainly wouldn't advise going back to work for a couple of weeks – but, frankly, there's no reason I can see why you can't go today. We will of course be in touch with your GP, who'll be your first point of liaison once you're home, but you appear to have a very robust constitution. Home is probably the best place for you – so long as you don't work. Rest, Mr Mack, plenty of rest. Rest is what has pulled you through so far.'

His tone suggested that I was little more than an idle layabout. I said I would take his advice and do nothing for at least a fortnight.

'There is one thing I wanted to ask,' he said. 'Your right leg, as you'll no doubt be aware, has some very severe contusions. It looks pretty dreadful but there's nothing to worry about – that will all heal with time. But we did wonder, have you ever broken that leg?'

'No,' I said, 'never.'

'Didn't break it as a child, no accident you can remember?'

I shook my head. 'No. Why?'

'It looks as if there's been some kind of fusion in the femur. As if the bone has contracted. Your right leg is a good inch shorter than your left. We x-rayed it but there's no obvious explanation. Perhaps you can offer one.'

'It's been a bit dodgy these last few years,' I said. 'Too much long-distance running. I must have cracked it against something in the river.'

'But you didn't break it. The image the x-ray gives us is more like the sort of thing one might find in human remains after a very intense fire – an air crash, perhaps, or an explosion. The bone appears to have been subjected to extreme heat. It's very unusual.'

'Maybe it'll sort itself out as the bruising goes down,' I said.

'Maybe,' he said, 'but I don't think so. We might get you back for a further examination, once you've recovered a bit. Did you walk with a limp before this accident?'

'No,' I said.

'Well, you've got one now. I can't explain it. You're a bit of a mystery all in all, Mr Mack.'

He was obviously irked by the problem and seemed on the verge of accusing me of being some kind of charlatan, not a real patient at all.

'Look,' I said, 'if a limp is all I'm walking away with, I'm happy. I should be dead, so people keep telling me.'

'Yes,' he said. 'I agree with them, you should be. Which is why a period of convalescence is essential.'

There was a public phone down the corridor from the ward. I used a couple of the coins from my locker and managed to get Elsie in. She was surprised when I said I was coming home. I said I would have discharged myself if they'd tried to stop me. I felt fine, I said. A little tired, but basically fine. I wanted to get back to Monimaskit. Could she or John go to the manse and bring me some clothes? She said she'd come down for me in the afternoon, once John got home from school. She offered, somewhat reluctantly, for me to go and stay with them. I insisted on going back to the manse. If she could buy me some milk and bread I would be perfectly all right there. It would, I added, be easier for all of us.

'Okay,' she said, 'if that's what you want.' She sounded relieved.

'Elsie,' I said, 'see if you can get hold of Bill Winnyford. Ask him if he'd mind dropping in to see me. Tonight if possible. Ask him to bring his tape-recorder.'

'Tonight?' she said. 'Hold on a minute.' I could hear one of the girls shouting in the background, Elsie quietening her. She came back on. 'You want him to come round tonight?'

'It's very important. If not tonight, tomorrow. Something amazing has happened and I need to record it while it's clear in my head.'

'Gideon, you need to rest.'

'And I will,' I said. 'But I won't be able to until I've got this off my chest.'

'Got what off your chest?' she said.

'I've remembered where I was these days that I was missing,' I said. 'I've remembered what happened.'

'I don't understand,' she said. 'You were in the river.'

'Yes,' I said. 'But not all the time. I'll explain later when you fetch me.'

Perhaps there was something too much like a threat in those last words. Perhaps she was still frightened. At any rate, it was not Elsie but John who came for me at five o'clock that afternoon. He brought me clothes that Elsie had collected earlier. She had also, he told me as I got dressed, stocked up my fridge with basics and a few oven-ready meals to keep me going. I'd be able to shut myself away from the world, if that was what I wanted.

'Although the world won't be too happy if you do,' he said. 'I think a few newspapers are hoping for your story.'

'They'll have to wait,' I said. 'They can have my story when it's ready.'

'What is your story?'

'It's complicated. You'll have to wait too.'

We walked through the hospital concourse together, and I thought, as no doubt he did, of the last time we had done that. But we said nothing, and no distraught lorry-driver accosted me with his need to be absolved of blame. We reached the car without incident.

I was glad, really, that John had come and not Elsie: it made things easier. We didn't speak much on the journey. I was tired, and closed my eyes. John was also withdrawn. I didn't know what Elsie might have told him and I didn't try to find out. My mind was too full of other things to deal with that.

At one point the twists and turns of the road woke me. John glanced at me as he negotiated the corners. We were in the Glack, and again I thought of that previous time, and again we said nothing. But as we emerged from that snakelike stretch, John said, 'Are you all right, Gideon?'

'I'm fine,' I said.

'You fell, didn't you?'

'What do you mean?'

'You fell in the Black Jaws, didn't you? You didn't jump?'

'What are you suggesting?'

'I haven't seen you for a while,' he said, 'but Elsie was saying – she said on Saturday in fact, after she'd seen you at the museum – that you were acting strangely. She thought you were ill, stressed.'

'What else did she say?'

'She was upset. She said she'd never seen you like that.'

'Like what?'

'I don't know, Gideon, I wasn't there. A bit mad, was what she said if you must know. And the next thing we hear you've gone up to the Black Jaws and fallen in.'

'And you think I jumped?'

'No, I don't. But it did occur to us, both of us, that if you weren't well, you might, you know, not be thinking straight.'

'And I might subconsciously try to kill myself,' I said. 'Accidentally on purpose.'

'We're concerned, that's all.'

'I'm not suicidal, John,' I said. 'I'm not even depressed. Believe me.'

'Fine,' he said. He sounded annoyed, as if I'd proved him wrong, made him look stupid.

I might have got angry too, but I was thinking of what had really happened to me. It made any misunderstanding with John utterly insignificant.

XXXVI

John delivered me to the manse and left with an assurance from me that I would contact them if I needed anything. We both knew I wouldn't be doing so, and that was fine by both of us. I locked the door and turned out the lights at the front of the house. I wanted no callers, or rather I wanted only one.

There were thirty-seven messages stacked up on my answer-machine, some no doubt of hope, some of joy, some of relief, perhaps some of curiosity and some of demand. The tape, in fact, was full, and the machine had stopped recording calls. It didn't matter. I had no interest in them and deleted them all without listening to them. Then I phoned Bill Winnyford. He picked up the receiver almost at once.

'Bill,' I said. 'It's Gideon. Did Elsie Moffat contact you?'

'Gideon! Yes she did. Gideon! Astonishing news dramatic in fact I mean . . .'

I cut him off in mid-flow. 'Can you come round with your tape-recorder? Now?'

'Absolutely,' he said. 'Elsie said you were most insistent. Was about to call you myself. Wouldn't miss this for anything. God knows what you want to tell me. Is it what you'd call an exclusive?'

'Yes, it is,' I said. 'But you have to promise me something.'

'What's that?'

'That you shut up while I'm speaking, otherwise I'll lose the thread. You can drink as much of my whisky as you please, but you must let me talk. And afterwards, you must give me the tape.'

'That's not much of an exclusive,' he said.

'Bill,' I said, 'you're going to be the first person to hear what happened to me. What *really* happened to me. Believe me, it's an exclusive.'

'Okay,' he said. 'I'll be on my best behaviour.' But after he arrived, and once we had settled ourselves in the study, got the fire going and set up the drams and his equipment, and as I began to speak of the things that were surging through my brain, it proved impossible for Bill to remain silent. I told him about my fall and my journey through the tunnel, and he couldn't stop himself from offering suggestions and explanations at every turn. I asked him to pause the recording.

'We need to lay down some ground rules,' I said. 'I've asked you here because I want to speak about things before I forget them, and because I can't write or type fast enough to keep up with everything that's buzzing around in my head. That's why I've asked you to record me. I've got an old cassette-player and I daresay I could find a microphone for it somewhere, but that's not the point, there's another reason why I want you here. I want you as a witness. If anyone should ask you in the future, whether it's in two weeks or twenty years, I want you to be able to testify that what you heard tonight came from the mouth of a sane human being, not some gibbering lunatic. Do I strike you as being a sane human being?'

'You always have done.'

'Now, though? At this moment?'

'Yes.'

'Good. So now what I need you to do is just listen. Don't interrupt me to insinuate your own views. Don't say anything unless something I say needs clarification. Just listen. Can you do that?'

He nodded. It was hard for him, but after a while he settled down. At the end of the evening, he left me the cassette, and over several succeeding nights I typed out the transcript, stopping and starting and replaying the cassette so often on my own tape-player that I thought one or the other would break. And so what follows is a true and faithful account, as related by me to Bill Winnyford, of the time I spent in the netherworld, deep below the Black Jaws, in the company of one who until then I had presumed to be a figment of the human imagination.

GM: Until yesterday, I had no recollection of the three days during which I was missing, presumed dead. I remembered falling into the Black Jaws, and I've already described to you, Bill, the way in which the water carried me, the light that I saw, the sense that I was floating above as well as in my own body.

WW: Everything you've said is absolutely characteristic of an NDE. Sorry, a near-death experience.

GM: You think that's what was happening? That I nearly died, and then I came back?

WW: You want me to answer that? I thought . . . Okay, yes, I do. There are hundreds, probably thousands of documented examples of this sort of thing. The bright light, the out-of-body sensation, the dreamlike quality of what you were undergoing . . .

GM: But the point is, it wasn't a dream. And then there was this gap in my memory. Until yesterday everything was a blank prior to being hauled out of the water by Chae Middleton. I remembered Chae pulling me out, or at least that's what I *thought* I remembered. But there *was* something before that. Seeing the shoes in the hospital brought it all back to me.

WW: What shoes?

GM: These. This ratty old pair of trainers. The nurse said I was wearing them when I was brought in. Well, it seems I must have been, but they're not mine. I was wearing boots when I fell in the river. My own boots. At some point, somebody swapped my boots for these.

WW: Chae Middleton?

GM: No, somebody else. Look, let me take it from the moment I came out of that near-death experience, if that's what it was. Let me tell it to you exactly as I remember it.

WW: Go ahead.

GM: I was back in my body, in the water. I didn't want to die. There was too much I had left to do. I'm back in my body. I'm trying to grab something, to stop myself drowning, but there's nothing to grab. And then suddenly I'm in a different part of the river. It's calmer, the water isn't as violent as it was. I try to swim, but I'm not strong enough. And then, just as I'm going under again, my head bumps against something. Something hard and yet soft at the same time.

The white light's gone and instead there's this reddish-orange glow. I stretch up my right hand to this light, and to whatever it is I've hit, and a hand reaches down to me, a man's hand. Somebody is leaning over me. Strong fingers close around my wrist and pull. I hear a voice – 'All right, I've got you, you're all right now', something like that – and then a splashing, creaking noise. My head hits the soft-hard object again. Now I'm being towed behind a boat of some kind. There's a scraping sound – the boat has grounded. *I've* grounded – there's something beneath me other than water. Then I'm being pulled from the water. I'm lying on my front on a tiny beach. Silvery gravel that sparkles in the orange light.

I don't know how long I lay there. It might have been minutes, it could have been hours. I drifted in and out of consciousness. I was vaguely aware of a person near me, and this was a great comfort. I assumed it was a man – I remembered the maleness of the hand. He seemed to be busying himself around my body and his boat. Also, he was going back and forth to another spot a little distance away. These sounds were immensely soothing. It was like listening to a nurse from your sick-bed. I could have stayed lying there for ever, even though it was cold and wet. I felt safe. Well, I was. I had been saved.

At some point I opened my eyes and was able to keep them open. Beside me on the shingly beach was a sticky, translucent mess of vomit, which must have come from me. I heard a scooping sound and some gravel landed on top of it. This happened a few more times until the vomit was all covered up. I managed to sit up. The man who had helped me from the water was crouched beside me. He looked at me without smiling, without frowning, without any trace of emotion on his face.

He said – I can hear his exact words, it's uncanny how precisely I remember what he said – 'You've had quite an ordeal. I thought it best to leave you where you were, since you were no longer in danger of drowning.' Then he bent down and got me on my feet and helped me away from the beach.

WW: What did he look like?

GM: Well, not what you might expect in a place like that – not some bearded, ragged wild man. For a start he was absurdly well dressed for his surroundings. He had on sharply creased black trousers and a black polo-shirt buttoned up to the throat, and a black jacket that looked like it was almost new. The only thing about him that wasn't immaculate was his footwear – a pair of tattered trainers, all bulging and broken and so filthy you couldn't even make out what brand they were.

WW: This pair of trainers?

GM: The very ones. I never set eyes on them before I saw them on his feet, and that's the truth. I remember watching them as he held me up and we started walking. And then I looked up. We were in this huge cavern with a ceiling stretching way beyond the penetration of the light. The pool he had taken me from was long and looked very deep. At the far end I could see the white torrent which I'd been thrown down, but it was about seventy or eighty yards away, and the noise was dulled by the distance and the sheer size of the cave.

There was a small rubber dinghy pulled up on the beach, with a wooden board across it as a seat and a paddle lying on one of its sides. Where we were going the roof dropped to about twelve feet. The cave seemed to go back a long way under this roof. This was where the orange light was coming from. There were two sources. One was a great fire crackling away at the base of a kind of natural chimney, which sucked away all the smoke. The other seemed to have a brighter glow but it was a long way back in the recesses of the cave. I know that sounds impossible, but that's how it was. It was like the glow of the sun at dawn, just before it comes over the horizon. Distant but incredibly bright. Anyway, we were heading towards the nearer fire. We made pretty slow progress, but he showed no impatience. Every step reminded me of the dunts and blows I'd received in the river, although at the time I'd been mostly unaware of them. My right leg was the worst: I could put hardly any weight on it at all. When my right boot – and I can see this as clearly now as I did then, I still had both my boots on – when my right boot touched the ground it sent a bolt of pain shooting up my leg into my groin. I wasn't thinking very coherently but I realised I'd done something serious – I have an old injury in that leg from running, but this was of a different order all together. I didn't cry out, though. I was in shock. More than anything I was shocked that I was still alive.

There was all this stuff set out near the fire. Some bits of furniture: a settee covered in big cushions and a couple of rugs, a white square plastic table like the kind people keep on their patios, two cast-iron chairs with round seats and floral designs to their backs and a set of wooden shelves with various items stacked on it – kitchen implements, plates, mugs, pans. And there were a lot of bottles, jars and tins too. Everything looked old-fashioned and battered and dirty. It was like a junkyard, or as if somebody had been put out on the street with all their possessions. I didn't care. All I wanted to do was sit down and get a heat from that blazing red fire.

He guided me towards one of the cast-iron chairs, placed my hands on its back and left me to rest there for a moment. He pulled the matching chair in by the fire, came back for me and helped me to sit down on it. 'We'll put you on the settee in a while,' he said, 'but the first thing is to get you warm. If you'll allow me to undress you, your clothes will dry very quickly. I have no towel or other clothes, or I would offer them to you.'

How could I object? I hadn't said a word so far, but I was powerless to resist in any case. He began to undress me. I can't describe the tenderness, the care with which he went about removing my sodden and torn clothes, unzipping and unbuttoning me, easing me out of my boots and socks, jacket, jumper, shirt, trousers and underpants as if I were his child. When I winced in pain he empathised – not in words but with little reciprocal noises – and proceeded even more gently. He wrung out each item and spread my clothes on the other iron chair, which he moved near the fire opposite me. There was a pile of logs and branches, some black, some bleached, some stripped of their bark, and he lifted a couple of chunky pieces and threw them to the back of the fire, sending a swarm of sparks up the chimney. My clothes were soon steaming away. I slumped where I was, feeling the heat roll over me and through me.

At the front of the fire was a dip or hollow in the stone, full of hot embers, and over it was an iron grill on which pots could be placed, and a spit resting on two uprights, one at each side. The corpse of some small creature was skewered on this spit, giving off a wonderful smell, and the man of the cave turned it occasionally when he passed the fire. I've said he was very quiet and calm, yet he seemed not to be able to settle. He was constantly on the move, checking the fire, the clothes, the grilling carcase, going to the boat, then to the settee, sitting for a few seconds, then getting up and going back to the fire. The light of the flames picked up his movements and turned them into shadows flitting around the walls of the cave. This must have had a soporific effect on me, because I slipped in and out of sleep several times. Once I almost fell from the chair, and as I came awake and stopped myself I jarred my right leg. I cried out, and in a moment he was beside me.

'It's badly hurt,' he said. He lightly touched my thigh. 'The bone here seems to be sticking out.'

'I think it may be broken,' I said. It was the first time I'd spoken, and it brought on a fit of coughing. He went off and returned with a grimy glass and a dark, unlabelled bottle with a cork in it. He eased the cork out with a hollow pop.

'Drink some of this,' he said. He poured a small measure of what looked like water into the glass and held it to my mouth. The vapours coming from the liquid nipped my lips. It certainly wasn't water. I took a mouthful and swallowed. It sizzled its way down my throat, and a great heat spread across my chest. I didn't think it would stop the cough, but it did. I drank the rest of the glass and asked him what it was.

'It is of my own making,' he said. 'Be careful, it's powerful. Water might be safer, but I think you've had enough water for one day.'

His voice was soft and neutral and had no obvious accent – as if he had lived in different parts of the world for long periods and his tongue had lost whatever mark of his origins it might once have had. I wondered if he might have been raised by Highland parents in some isolated part of Canada or New Zealand. That was the kind of indefinable voice he had. It was so unremarkable that it was remarkable.

WW: I'm surprised you even noticed.

GM: I was still in a daze, but I was getting inquisitive about him. He asked me if I was hungry, and I said I was, and he lifted the spit from the fire and slid the meat from it with a fork, on to a plate. I saw him take a knife to it, slicing it, and tearing what he couldn't slice. Then he brought the plateful of cut meat over to me, and told me to eat.

It was like barbecued chicken but with a stronger flavour. I ate several bits with my fingers while he hovered and flitted around. I suddenly thought I might be eating his only food and offered the plate to him. He said he didn't need it: it was for me. I said it was good and asked what it was. Rabbit, he said. 'I was fishing earlier and I caught a rabbit.' And then he excused himself and went down to the beach again, pushed his boat out into the pool and paddled a few yards towards a dark object that was floating in the water. He nudged it back into the beach with the paddle. It was the limb of a tree. It was six feet long and must have weighed more than he did, but he carried it back to the pile of wood beside the fire and threw it down without any apparent difficulty. He didn't break sweat, nor did he spoil the neatness of his dress. Although he didn't look it, he was clearly immensely strong.

'Supplies,' he said. 'Firewood, fish, fowl and beast come to me that way. A sheep, once in a while. A dog or two. A man, like yourself, very seldom. Not by that route.'

I wondered if he ate the sheep, the dogs. I wondered if he ate people; if he intended to eat me.

I asked him about the furnishings of his kitchen-cum-living room, how they had got there. 'Built on site,' he said. 'Or dragged and floated from the other end of the river.'

This excited me. Was there a way out if you followed the river? There was, he said.

I said, 'And you can show me how to get out?'

He said, 'No, but I can help you when the time comes.'

I asked what he meant by this. He said when I left him it would be by the river and he would put me into it. I didn't like the sound of that at all and I said so. He said I would have no choice.

I persisted in questioning him: 'If you dragged all that stuff here by some route, surely it can't be too difficult to get out the same way.' For the first time his calmness deserted him. He glared at me angrily. 'I didn't drag anything anywhere,' he said. 'Do I look like someone who drags things around? Do I?'

I did my best to placate him, assuring him I was grateful for all he had done for me. I thought I'd fallen into the hands of a madman. Who else would make their dwelling in such a place? He went to check the state of my clothes. 'These are dry,' he said. 'We can get you dressed again.'

Between us we slowly covered up my nakedness, but my trousers wouldn't go back on over my swollen and crooked right leg, so he put these aside. My boots, too, were still steaming in front of the fire, but he eased my socks on to keep my feet warm. He helped me over to the settee, arranged me on it with my head resting on some cushions at one end, and covered my legs with a rug. Then he went to the chair I had just vacated, turned it so that its back was towards me, and straddled it. He sat with his chin in his hand, peering at me as if he didn't know what to do with me. He said nothing, so I began to question him again.

'Where am I?' I asked. 'And who are you?'

He scratched the back of his head and smiled. 'One at a time,' he said. 'There's no rush. Where do you think you are?'

'I assume,' I said, 'that I'm below ground, somewhere between the Black Jaws and where the Keldo Water comes out at the other end.'

'Well, then,' he said, 'that is where you are.'

I said, 'But that can't be right. This place can't be there. It's too big.'

'The earth is full of cavities and cells,' he said. 'Some large, some small. How can you say this is too big to be where it is? You know how you came here. Do you disbelieve what your own eyes see?'

'I don't know,' I said. 'It's not that long since I thought I must be dead. Maybe I am dead.'

'Do you feel dead?' he said.

'No,' I said. 'Not any more.'

'If you were dead, how could we be conversing?'

'I don't know,' I said. I returned to the subject of the cave. 'Why doesn't everyone know about this? It should be as famous as Loch Ness or Ben Nevis.'

'There is no tourist route to here,' he said.

'But it's not possible that somewhere like this could be unknown.'

'Just because you think something not possible does not make it so.'

'Who are you?' I asked again. 'How are you here? How can you live here?'

He held up a finger. 'One at a time,' he said again. 'You see for yourself how I live. How am I here? I know my way around, above and below the earth. As to who I am, well, I am the one who has plucked you, a stranger, from the river. Wasn't that good of me? So let me ask you who *you* are.'

His voice was still smooth and easy, but he was being evasive. I responded with directness.

'I am Gideon Mack,' I said, 'minister of the Old Kirk at Monimaskit.'

He laughed. 'You sound like one of the old school,' he said. 'Very sure of yourself. I've had some right battles with the old school. *Un homme avec Dieu est toujours dans la majorité*, isn't that right? But you're not so sure of yourself, are you, Gideon Mack? Yes, I know of you. I know about your good works, and your bad ones. I know your secrets. There isn't much I don't know about you.'

That was what he said. How could I hear such words and not feel menaced by them? Yet he still had the calm, kind tone to his voice – the menace was there for just a second, then it was gone. But it was enough to frighten me a little. For the first time I wondered not if he were a madman, but if he were a man at all.

WW: Not human, you mean?

GM: Not human, or more than human. How did he know about me, if he really did? Why did he live in that place? I was still coming to terms with the fact that I hadn't been killed by the river. All my physical senses told me I was alive, but maybe I wasn't. And if I wasn't, then what about him? Also, Bill, there's been something else in my life this year, something I've not talked to you about. This isn't easy to explain in a hurry, and I don't want to get distracted just now, but there's a stone in Keldo Woods, a standing stone that was never there before. I know this won't make any sense, but it just seems to have appeared out of nothing. And I'm the only one who's seen it. I'll tell you about it later, now's not the time. But if I can see and touch a stone that isn't there, in a place I know to be real, then how can I say what's real and what's imagined deep under the earth? That's what was going through my head, and because of that I began to think that this man, this being in the cave, might have something to do with it.

WW: With what? You've lost me, Gideon.

GM: With the stone in the woods. I was being confronted with things that were impossible, supernatural if you like, and this man – maybe – was at the heart of them. That's what I thought.

WW: But you're a man of faith. You believe in God, *ergo* you believe in the supernatural. Don't you?

GM: I'm a man of doubt. I always have been. I don't know what I believe. But I've always accepted what my senses told me. Now suddenly they were telling me things I couldn't accept. Can you understand why I was confused?

WW: Okay. Go on.

GM: I asked him how he knew anything about me, what secrets of mine he could possibly know. He shrugged. 'There are windows on the world,' he said. 'Don't you think we don't look through them from time to time?'

'Who?' I said. 'Who do you mean when you say "we"?'

'Who do you think I mean?' he said.

I was getting tired of this. 'Come on,' I said. 'Who are you? Give me a straight answer to a straight question, won't you?'

'Oh, surely,' he said, 'we are beyond straight questions and answers, you and I. This is not an examination in a classroom, is it? This is a conversation between equals.'

I didn't say anything for a minute. I felt that I was coming awake all of a sudden, and that I had to be on my best, most alert form. It was as if I hadn't realised that I was in danger. Not immediate physical danger like when I'd been in the river, a different kind of danger. Like when you're in a bar in a town you don't know, you sense that you're vulnerable, do you know what I mean? I live a very protected existence here, Bill, it's years since I've felt like that, but I did. I felt vulnerable.

'You have me at a disadvantage,' I said. 'Wherever I am, I'm on your territory, not mine. I nearly died back there. I'm injured. I don't know how to get out of here. No, I don't think that we are equals just now.'

This threw him into a kind of sulk. It was clear that he did not like to be contradicted. 'Suit yourself,' he said. 'I have business to attend to.' He flung another couple of logs on the fire and fetched the dark bottle from the table. He put it on the ground beside me. 'That'll keep you going while I'm away. Perhaps when I return you'll be in a better humour.' And he headed deeper into the cave and in a moment was lost in the shadows.

I'd been beginning to mistrust and dislike his company but I liked being alone a lot less. I almost shouted after him not to leave me. But he was gone and I was on my own, lying on that absurd settee in the glow of the fire, with the Keldo thundering in the background at the other end of the pool.

I dozed again. When I woke I had a terrible thirst. Even if I could have dragged myself to the water's edge I don't think I could have persuaded myself to drink a drop of that thick black river. The only other drink to hand was in the bottle. I resisted for as long as I could, but I kept thinking of the healing effect it had had before. Eventually I reached for it, took out the cork and let some of the liquid burn its way down my throat. I waited. Then I drank some more. I could not stop taking swallows of it. It eased the throbbing pain in my right leg, which had been becoming unbearable. The more I drank, the better I felt. I lay there in a kind of stupor.

I had no idea what time of day or night it was: there *was* no day or night in that place. I woke once and he was back again, building up the fire. Then he disappeared. At another point I came to with a start, drenched in sweat and shaking with cold. I was in the grip of a fever. I heard myself groan. I tried to turn on the settee, but had not the strength. Then he was there again, crouched beside me. 'That's it, Gideon,' he whispered, and the whisper was a horrible hiss in my ear, 'sweat it out, sweat it out. Here, let me help you.' I felt him lift me away from the back of the settee, and then a huge weight pressed on my shoulder and I knew he was climbing over me. He was thin and bony but I tell you he was heavier than three men, and harder too. He squeezed himself in behind me. I cried out, 'What are you doing?' but he only held me tighter. 'We'll sweat it out of you together,' he said, and I felt his arms going around my chest like iron bands. I struggled, but it was useless, I lay there in his grip and the sweat poured from me, and all I could hear was the crackling of the fire and his breath in my ear.

I don't know how long we were like that, but then I felt something against my buttocks, like a cold iron bar it was, rigid, I could feel it pulsing against my naked skin – remember, I was without my trousers – and I thought, is this what this is about, that I'm to be impaled on the penis of some deranged cave-dwelling monster and then flung back in the river? And there was absolutely nothing I could do.

WW: For God's sake, Gideon. He raped you?

GM: No, nothing happened. Don't look at me like that! I swear nothing happened. He seemed to fall asleep, and I felt the erection ease although his hold on me did not, and at some point I must have slept too.

I didn't feel him leave me but when I woke he was away over by the fire. I watched him boiling water, making tea in a pot. He must have taken the water from the pool, but when he brought me over a mug I took it nonetheless. He helped me to sit up and I saw that in spite of the activities of the night – if it was the night – he was as immaculate and clean-looking as ever.

He asked if I was feeling better. I said I was. My head was thick from the alcohol, but I was no longer feverish.

He crouched again and touched my right leg. 'I'll mend that,' he said.

I laughed. 'How do you propose to do that? Are you a doctor?'

'No,' he said, 'but I can mend things if I choose to.'

I let that go. I wanted to ask him something else.

'There is a legend about this place,' I said. 'Do you know it?'

'This place?' he said. 'Oh, does it exist then?'

'Yes,' I said, 'I admit it exists. I admit we are here. Do you know the legend?'

'I might,' he said. 'Tell me.' He sprawled in front of me on the ground like a scornful teenager.

I began to tell him the story of the lady of Keldo House. Within a minute he was yawning rudely. It was obvious that he already knew it. 'She made a pact with the Devil,' I said. 'He was supposed to live down here.'

'Was he?' he sneered. 'Who told you that?'

'I read it in a book,' I said. 'One of my predecessors wrote it down.'

'Menteith,' he said instantly. 'Meddling old fool. Well, a fine end he had, hadn't he?'

I asked him how he knew about Menteith, and he said the same way he knew about everybody. Ministers, priests, pastors, nuns, choirboys, bishops, popes, he knew all the Christians that had ever lived by rank, denomination and serial number. 'Baptists, Quakers, Lutherans, Mormons,' he said. 'Bloody millions of you. Tens of millions. Jews, Muslims, Buddhists, Hindus. Hundreds of millions. *And* all the others. Heathens, whatever you want to call them. Billions and billions. Atheists, infidels, pagans, sun-worshippers, all of you with your doubts and certainties and hopes and fears. There isn't one human being I don't know about.'

'And how did you come by this amazing knowledge?' I asked.

'I have a library,' he said. 'A great big library with books to the ceiling, and I read up about you all every day.' He held my gaze for a second, then burst out laughing. 'Do I fuck! I know about you because you're all the fucking same.'

'Really?' I said.

'Yes, *really*,' he mimicked. He got to his feet slowly. 'Oh, cut the crap, Gideon. You know who I am. Let's stop playing these tedious games, eh?'

'You started it,' I said, but before the words were out of my mouth my ears were assaulted by the most appalling noise. The rock walls seemed to shake with it. If you've ever been out walking, in a quiet glen say, when one of those low-flying jets suddenly comes out of nowhere a hundred feet above you, and if you can imagine that din multiplied ten times, that's what it was like. It was so loud that it drowned the sound of the river. I thought the roof was coming down on us and raised my arms to cover my head. It was only as the echoes were dying away that I realised that the roar had come from his mouth, and that there had been words in it. And my brain unscrambled the words from the echoes, and what I think they were was 'I SAID, CUT THE FUCKING GAMES!' But it didn't matter really whether there were any words or not. I just knew that it was not possible for a human being to make such a noise.

I feared for myself then, sitting there with him standing over me. He seemed to have grown taller, or I had shrunk. But then his fury vanished, and he hung his head like some unhappy giant in a fairy tale. 'I'm sick of the fucking games,' he said quietly. 'I'm sick, sick, sick of them.'

In his despair I saw quite clearly, as if the light of all the centuries were shining on him, his haggard weariness. He was not, as I had thought, a young man at all. I knew at that moment who he was.

'The legend is true, isn't it?' I said. 'You are the Devil.'

He turned away from me. 'Am I?' he said. Then he spun back again. 'Is that what you think?'

'I don't know,' I said. 'Yes, yes, that's what I think.'

'That's what I think too,' he said. 'Yes, that's who I must be. A miserable devil. So now we understand each other.'

I thought of the roar. I thought of the unbearable weight of him on the settee. I thought of his strength. What further evidence did I need? But still I could not stop myself.

'Prove it,' I said.

Now he looked at me as if I were the mad one. 'What?'

'Prove it. If that's who you are, prove it.'

'Oh, for fuck's sake,' he said. 'What do you want me to do, show you a cloven hoof? Horns in my head, a forky tail and live coals for eyes? Is that what you want? Do you want me to take you up some mountain and show you my empire? Make loaves out of these stones? Throw myself off the steeple of your church and land without a scratch? I can do all of those things. I can do anything you ask. Do you want me to speak in many tongues? I can do that. I know every language and every dialect of every language that's ever existed on earth. Do you want me to show you my supposed greatest achievements? Battlefields, wars, torture chambers, famines, plagues, snuff movies, blitzkriegs, child porn, multiple rapes, mass murders? I can do that too, but what's the point? You know it all already and you don't believe I'm responsible for it. So what is it you want me to prove? That I exist? Look, here I am. Do you think I'm doing this for fun?'

He looked totally dejected.

'You must understand,' I said, 'that I've never seriously thought you existed at all. It's a bit of a shock now, to find you just a few miles from Monimaskit.'

'Don't think you're privileged,' he said, sparking up a bit. 'Don't think I'm paying you some kind of special attention. I do like Scotland, though, I spend a lot of time here. I once preached to some women at North Berwick who thought they were witches. They were burnt for it, poor cows. I preached at Auchtermuchty another time, disguised as one of your lot, a minister, but the folk there found me out. Fifers, thrawn buggers, they were too sharp. But I do like Scotland. I like the miserable weather. I like the miserable people, the fatalism, the negativity, the violence that's always just below the surface. And I like the way you deal with religion. One century you're up to your lugs in it, the next you're trading the whole apparatus in for Sunday superstores. Praise the Lord and thrash the bairns. Ask and ye shall have the door shut in your face. Blessed are they that shop on the Sabbath, for they shall get the best bargains. Oh, yes, this is a very fine country.'

In spite of his claimed affection for Scotland, he seemed morose and fed up. Suddenly he brightened.

'I know what I'll do if you want proof. I'll do what I said I would. I'll fix your leg.'

This did not strike me as a good idea. 'No,' I said. 'A surgeon should do that.'

'Please,' he said. 'I'd like to.'

When I said no again I heard a low rumble growl round the cave, which I took to be the precursor of another stupendous roar. I made no further protest. He went over to the fire and I saw him put his right hand into the flames, deep into the middle of them. He was elbow-deep in fire but he didn't even flinch. His jacket didn't catch alight, and his hand and arm were quite unaffected by the heat. He stayed like that for fully three minutes. Then he turned and his whole arm was a white, pulsating glow. He came towards me and reached for my leg with that terrible arm, and I shrank away from him.

'It doesn't hurt me,' he said, 'and it won't hurt you. Don't move.'

I was too terrified to move. I was still clutching my mug of tea and he took it from me with his left hand and placed it on the ground. I closed my eyes and waited for the burning agony, but it did not come. I was aware only of a slight tingling sensation on my right thigh. I opened my eyes and looked down. There was intense concentration on his face. His hand was *inside* my leg. Where the bone bulged out the skin was sizzling and popping like bacon in a pan, but there was no pain, only this faint tickle. He was pushing and prodding the bone back into place, welding it together. Smoke and steam issued from my leg, but still there was no pain. I felt only an incredible warmth, like the warmth of the spirit in his black bottle, spreading through my whole body. His hand twisted something and my leg gave an involuntary jolt. 'Don't move,' he snapped. 'I couldn't help it,' I said.

Another minute passed. The hand was now red-hot, not white, and he began to extract it from my leg. Soon only his fingers were left, an inch or so deep in my flesh. He looked at me and smiled, and I smiled back. I didn't much like his smile, there was something lascivious about it. He pulled his fingers out, and, although every part of my body was warm, I was aware of a cold sucking sensation around the wound as he withdrew. I saw my skin sealing again, puckering then tightening up over the flesh and bone. I once saw someone in a unit on the Monimaskit industrial estate shrink-wrapping jars of jam in twelve-packs using a heat-sealing machine. That was what it looked like.

He stood with his right hand hanging down, fast returning to its normal colour. There was no damage whatsoever to his flesh or clothing. He let out a long breath and wiped his brow with his left arm. It was the first time I'd seen him affected by any exertion.

'You shouldn't have moved,' he said. 'I overdid it with the bone. Still, it's better than it was. You'll have a lot of bruising, that's all.'

I couldn't speak for some time. Eventually I managed the single word, 'Why?'

'I can heal as well as Jesus,' he said. 'I just never had the opportunities.'

He took our mugs back to the pot and refilled them. The tea was grainy and stewed when I drank it but I didn't complain.

I said, 'You're not how I expected you to be.'

'How did you expect me to be?' he said. He seemed friendly and relaxed again, and sat at one end of the settee. I pulled my legs up to make room for him and found that I could do so with relative ease.

I said, 'Not like this. I don't suppose I had any real expectation of ever meeting you, so I never thought about it.'

'You fell back on stereotypes,' he said. 'Why should I fit a stereotype any more than you do? You're not your typical Church of Scotland minister, so why should I be your typical . . . whatever. I've hardly ever known a "typical" minister, when I think about it. There's always something that marks you out. Menteith now, hardly a Christian thought in his head, but a good mountaineer till he slipped. Thomas Chalmers – one of the funniest men you could ever meet, even when he didn't mean to be. Knox – a beautiful singing voice, and not averse to a drink either. Kind to women and children too, unless they happened to be royalty. Robert Kirk – what a strange mixture he was . . .'

WW: He knew Robert Kirk?

GM: Apparently, yes. 'He went in too deep, and couldn't get out,' he said. I would have pressed him on this, but then he said something else: 'Your father, he was an odd one too.'

I suppose I ought not to have been surprised. I sat up still further, pushing myself away from him with my heels. I was aware of my naked legs, my socks, my absurdity. 'My father?' I said. 'What did you have to do with my father?'

'I watched him for years,' he said. 'A sad, frightened man. He was so like you, or you're so like him. You may have started off from different places but you've both spent your lives scuttering about in theological mud. Even if you think you haven't. The hours and hours he spent in that study of his, wondering where he'd gone wrong.'

'My father never thought he'd gone wrong,' I said.

'Didn't he?' he said. 'I used to watch him from the garden sometimes. He was a mess, Gideon. Even before the stroke he was a mess.'

'I don't think so,' I said.

'Don't you?' he said. 'I think you've known it all along. He was hiding. You don't think he was in there because he *believed*, do you? Don't you think he would have been out fighting the world if he'd really believed? He didn't. He didn't have a shred of faith left, not after the war, anyway. He pretended he believed, he tried to force himself and everybody around him, but he couldn't. He'd seen too much.'

'What do you know about it?' I said.

'I know everything,' he said.

'You're lying,' I said.

He shrugged. 'If you say so. Ask your mother next time you can be bothered to visit her.'

'My mother doesn't know anything any more,' I said. 'She never did and she certainly doesn't now.'

'Oh, she knows,' he said. 'She might not have the right words, but she knows.'

He stood again and took his empty mug back to the table. 'Find out, Gideon,' he said.

I lost my temper. I shouted at him, why couldn't he just tell me? He shouted back, hadn't he already done enough? He'd saved me from drowning, he'd given me heat, food, drink, he'd mended my leg. How much did I want from him? I said, 'I just want you to tell me what you know about my father.'

'That's not the way it works, Gideon,' he said. 'You know that. Speak to your mother. Look into her eyes and ask her. Do you hear me? Look into her eyes. There are reasons for you to go back and that's one of them. And now I have things to do. We'll talk later.'

And again, as abruptly as he had done before, he vanished into the shadows.

As soon as he'd gone I got to my feet. I had cramps in my legs and the blood beginning to flow through them was painful and pleasurable at the same time. It made me want to move, to act. He had folded what was left of my trousers and hung them on the back of the settee, and they had fallen to the ground behind it. I put them on – they were ripped and shrunken but at least they went on. My right leg seemed pretty strong. I couldn't put my full weight on it but I could certainly hobble. Next I looked for my boots. They had been by the fire when I'd last looked, but they weren't there now. In their place was his pair of beaten-up old trainers.

WW: He'd taken your boots for himself?

GM: So it seemed. I hadn't noticed, but he could be so quick, he could have lifted them in that last moment by the fire, slipped off his own shoes and put the boots on later, in the shadows. Anyway, there was nothing I could do about it. I eased my feet into the trainers. They didn't have any laces, but my feet were swollen, so they fitted quite well. They probably suited me better at that moment than my boots would have. Then I started to look around.

It was all so disappointingly mundane. Given the powers he obviously had, my Devil was living a very basic existence. I inspected the jars and bottles on his shelves and found only oats and lentils and tea. No sulphur or other diabolical substances. The plates and pans were old and worn and dirty, but all I had seen him consume was tea, so I didn't think they were much used in any case. Perhaps he lived in opulent splendour somewhere else. There was the matter of his immaculate turn-out, his coming and going at all hours. Time seemed different to him. Where did he go when he wasn't there? The ramshackle encampment in the cave was like the home of someone who had – almost – given up trying.

Next I searched for a route out of the cave via the river. I've said that the smoke from the fire went up a shaft in the rock. I tried to look up this to see if I could see daylight, but the heat was oppressive and the smoke obscured any possible view. So then I went down to the beach, pushed the dinghy into the water, grabbed the paddle and scrambled in. I wasn't keen to be back on the water, but if I could find a way out before my host returned, I would take it. I steered the boat across the black pool towards the cascade at the other end. The noise was thunderous but it seemed to me that the volume of water was less. Maybe the rain had stopped. As I approached, the boat began to spin in the eddy created by the water entering the pool and I had to paddle constantly to get in close. I saw that the pool was separated from the main course of the river by a jutting promontory of rock, and that at the foot of the chute down which I had been flung there was a large flat-topped rock sloping away on either side, constantly washed by hundreds of gallons of white water. Anything that came down the chute, it seemed, either slid off into the pool or continued its helter-skelter way down the other, much broader side of the rock, and then on, presumably to emerge wherever the Keldo did. It was hard to assess from the unstable boat, but I reckoned the chances of ending up in the pool, as I had done, were about one in ten.

I remembered that he had hinted that my exit route was to be by the river. I was determined that this would not be so. I paddled back to the beach, pulled the boat clear, and returned to the fire. I picked up a few logs and threw them on. Then I took a deep breath and set off to look for an alternative exit in the only other direction available to me. I headed deeper into the cave, towards that other, distant, red light.

(At this point Bill Winnyford asked me to stop as he needed to change over the cassette. We refilled our glasses. I'd had my eyes closed for much of the time I was speaking – I found it easier to recall details that way. Now, looking at him over my whisky, I asked him what he thought.

He shook his head. 'I've never heard anything like it.'

'You're not worried about being alone in the house with a man who says he's spent time with the Devil?'

'Not a bit.'

'Am I telling the truth?'

He spluttered a bit. 'Only you know that,' he said. 'Unfair question. Show me your leg.'

I stood up, undid my trousers and lowered them to my knees. Bill whistled and leaned forward to inspect the right thigh.

'Impressive,' he said. 'It looks like boiled marble. But . . .'

'Yes?'

'It doesn't prove anything.'

'As I've been learning, Bill, nothing does. You either believe or you don't.'

'The jury's out at the moment,' he said diplomatically.

'Okay,' I said. 'If that cassette's ready to go, I'll tell you the rest.')

GM: The roof of the cave was about twelve feet in height over the area by the fire. It was like this for another twenty yards or so, then it came down steeply to about seven feet, and the walls closed in around me so that I found myself in another long tunnel, a dry one. The rock was cold to the touch, the ground was firm. At first the light from the fire behind me showed me the way. When this faded, I was left with only the distant glow ahead as my guide.

I didn't know how far away that other light was, but I assumed that this was the route my host used, so I hirpled on. The exercise was good – I'd been immobile for too long. I kept peering to right and left in search of other exits, and I saw numerous recesses and crannies that might have been further tunnels – and in retrospect probably were – but they showed no sign of light. I carried on the way I was going. I tried to count my paces but after several thousand I gave up. For a long while I walked on the level, then the tunnel began to slope downhill. It got steeper and steeper. I wondered if I could have missed some turning, because this didn't seem likely to lead me to the outside world. I was heading down into the bowels of the earth. Hours, I guessed, must have passed since I'd set out. The only thing that kept me going forward was the light, which was growing stronger all the while, a deep orange-red glow like the sun at dawn or at dusk. And there was something else – a thudding, pounding noise like the engine of a huge ship. It was like the noise the Black Jaws made, and I began to think I had come by some roundabout way back towards the chasm, and that perhaps it really was sunrise or sunset. I broke into the nearest thing I could manage to a run, and the light grew still brighter. The temperature rose rapidly too – a dry heat like the blast from an oven when you open the door, except that there was no air movement. Soon I was sweating profusely and having to shield my eyes with my hand because of the glare. And then without warning my route was blocked. Before me was a solid wall of rock, behind me the tunnel I had come down. And below me, right at my feet, was the source of the light and of the engine-like noise.

It was a huge, bulging hatch made of some material that was like rock but was not rock, that was like iron but was not iron. It was smooth in some places and pitted and bumpy in others. It seemed to be fixed in some way to the rock floor, but round its edges were cracks and holes, and it was through these that the intense light poured. I felt, if I looked directly at it, that it would burn my eyes in their sockets. The hatch, if that's what it was, seemed to move with the terrible pounding that was coming from below. Balancing on my stronger leg I stretched out my recently repaired one and gingerly let the toe of its trainer rest for a moment on the top. The vibration nearly shook the teeth from my mouth. What incalculable energy was at work down there, what monstrous furnace was driving that deafening rhythm and throwing out that level of heat and light? I felt that I was standing over the molten heart of the earth itself, and some words came to me, words I must have read in some long-forgotten book: 'the abyss beneath, where all is fiery and yet dark – a solitary hell, without suffering or sin'. A poem? A sermon? I don't know.* I thought of the river rushing through the Black Jaws and that if I could divert it down there and somehow open that hatch I might douse the heat and see in. But I knew that even all that raging madness of water would vanish in a hiss of steam the second it arrived.

I could not bear to stay there a moment longer. I turned and fled, panting and scrambling my way back up the tunnel, which stretched ahead of me now without any inviting light, since the glow of the fire by the pool was too feeble to reach anything like as far as I had come – a long, dark, stony passage back to what now seemed both a refuge and a prison.

Hours and hours I walked and stumbled. My feet in the unaccustomed trainers grew great blisters, my right leg trailed and my left leg ached with the extra effort demanded of it. I think I was on the point of collapse when I began to perceive a dim glow ahead of me. Another few hundred yards made it certain: I was back in the cave. I staggered out from the tunnel and over to the settee, and threw myself upon it. I was almost weeping with exhaustion.

From the vicinity of the fire I heard the familiar smooth, soft voice. 'Well, did you find what you were looking for?'

I couldn't answer. He understood this. He brought me a mug of cold water and I drank it, this time without hesitation. He sat down on one of the iron chairs and waited for me to recover.

'I found something,' I said eventually.

'Oh, what was that?'

'I found a door,' I said.

* Once again I am indebted to Dr Hugh Haliburton for identifying the words quoted by Gideon Mack as being those of Hugh Miller, from 'Lecture Sixth' of his *Sketch-Book of Popular Geology* (1859). – P.W.

'A door?' He was supercilious again, smug in whatever knowledge he had. 'Is that what you were looking for, a door? A way out?'

'Yes,' I said.

'I told you, there is only one way out for you, and that is by the river. This door, though, I'm intrigued. Did you open it?'

'I did not,' I said. 'It was a door into hell.'

'I doubt it,' he said. 'You're still trading in stereotypes, Gideon. Next you'll be telling me you heard screams.'

'Is that where you go?' I said. 'Down there? To hell?'

'I don't know where you've been,' he said, 'but it wasn't to hell. Ask your mother about hell. She knows about it.'

Neither of us said anything. There seemed no point in starting that argument again. I started another instead.

'You took my boots.'

'Yes, I did,' he said. 'I didn't expect you to be going anywhere. Actually, I did, I knew exactly what you would do. They're very comfortable, your boots. How did you find my shoes?'

I ignored this. I said I wanted my boots back. This is what I was reduced to: asking the Devil if I could have my boots back. Of course I could have them, he said. Did I want them now? He stood up and bent down where I could not see what he was doing. 'No,' I said, 'not over there. Take them off here, where I can see you.'

He gave a long sigh. 'Still looking for evidence, Gideon? O ye of little faith! Still looking for goat's hooves?' He walked over and sat on the end of the settee, untied the laces and pulled off my boots. He wasn't wearing socks. 'Look, two perfectly formed feet. Satisfied? No, probably not. Of course I *can* do goat's hooves. I can do pig's fucking trotters if I choose. I can do anything. But I choose not to.' He leaned back, and I shifted to make room for him, just as I had earlier. 'Do you want a drink?' he said. 'Let's have a drink. Let's not fight any more, Gideon.'

He fetched the black bottle, uncorked it and took a swig. He passed the bottle to me and I did the same. We sat together on the settee, staring at the fire, and the bottle went back and forth between us. We might have been old pals. We might have been you and me, Bill, sharing a drink just as we're doing now.

'So is the legend true?' I asked him after a while. Meaning the legend of the Black Jaws, the one we used in your show. He knew what I was talking about almost before I said it. He was so in tune with me, in fact, that I felt I hardly needed to voice my thoughts at all.

'Well,' he said, 'it's a legend. Can a legend be true?'

'Did you buy her soul?' I said. 'The way Menteith says you did, with a deed made up and signed in her blood?'

He shook his head at me: what a ludicrous question. I couldn't stop myself asking more, though. 'Did you keep her as a slave? Where is she now? Is she still here? Is that where you go to? Was it her that dragged all this stuff here?'

'Gideon,' he said, 'you're becoming overexcited. It's a legend. It's a metaphor.'

I thought of the cold, sucking feeling of his hand withdrawing from my thigh.

'So when you were fixing my leg, was that a metaphor too? Or was something else going on? Did you take *my* soul?'

He drank some more whisky. 'Don't be absurd. Your soul doesn't live in your leg. What on earth did they teach you at New College? Do you think I keep souls lined up somewhere in demijohns? Do you think that's them over there? Fucksake, what a paltry collection after all this time.' He jumped up and began to open bottles and jars and show me the contents. 'Look – salt, pepper, oil, vinegar. Not a soul in sight. Oh, but you've probably already checked, eh?'

He might have said this in a mocking way, but it didn't sound like that. It sounded forgiving, like he just wanted to tell me he knew.

I said, 'Earlier, before I went off, you said there were reasons for me to go back. My mother, you said. But what else did you mean?'

'Isn't she reason enough?' He came and sat down again. 'All right, what are you going to do about Elsie? What about Lorna? What about all the lies and denials in your life? What about life, eh? What about that stone in the woods?'

I shouldn't have been surprised any more, should I? He knew everything. Why would he not have known about the Stone?

(At this point Bill asked me about Elsie and about the Stone. I got him to stop the tape and told him what he needed to know. I didn't go into detail about Elsie: I simply said that she and John and I were old friends and that we needed to work some things out. He accepted this, although he looked sceptical. He wanted to know who Lorna was too. I told him, and he said he'd met her once. 'Are you . . . ?' he asked. 'No, Bill,' I said. 'We are not.'

The Stone interested him more. He asked me why I hadn't mentioned it to him before, and I said I'd almost told him once, but then I'd got to a place where I didn't think anyone would believe me about it. 'And now?' he said. 'Now it's all different,' I said. 'The Stone's only part of it. It was a game. The Stone doesn't matter much any more.' Then we carried on recording.)

GM: Why wouldn't the Devil have known about the Stone? He knew everything. He was smiling at me now, inclining his head, inviting me to come to the right conclusion.

I said, 'It was you, wasn't it? You put it there.'

He nodded. 'I get so bored, Gideon. I have to do something to keep myself amused. I wanted to see what would happen. I like playing with people's minds. Crop circles, ghosts, poltergeists, UFOs, alien abductions. People need these things. If they didn't exist they'd invent them, if you see what I mean. So, yes, I put the stone there. I found it aesthetically satisfying, apart from anything else. Kind of Andy Goldsworthy. But by and large it's been something of a failure. You're the only person who's noticed it.'

'You mean, it wasn't for me?' I asked.

'No, not specifically. Don't look so disappointed. You make of these things what you will. I knew you went running in those woods, but other people go there too. Nobody else has paid it the slightest attention. They don't seem to care about their surroundings. At least you noticed it. But I suppose if you hadn't wanted to, you wouldn't have seen it either.'

'But I didn't *want* to see it,' I protested. 'It was just there.'

'Yeah, well. It's that old chestnut, isn't it? Is the stone there if nobody sees it? Just because it's there one day, will it be there the next? It wasn't always there, was it? What would old Davie Hume have made of that, I wonder.'

'But what does it mean?'

'At least you're asking the question. But maybe it doesn't mean anything. Maybe *it's* a metaphor. Or maybe I'm just fucking with your head.'

We both started laughing. 'I used to have conversations like this with John Moffat,' I said, 'when we were students. We could go for hours.'

'We can do that,' he said.

I came back to the Stone. 'Why doesn't it come out on film? I took pictures but they didn't come out.'

'Who can say, Gideon? Faulty film, perhaps?'

I was beginning to feel drunk. I know this sounds bizarre, but I was enjoying myself. I was alone with him, away from all my parish responsibilities, all my personal ones, away from the insanity of the occupation of Iraq and Muslim suicide bombers and American fundamentalists and the AIDS epidemic in Africa and whatever petty arguments were going on in the Parliaments in Edinburgh and London – absent from it all. It was me and the Devil, and we were having a drink and a crack together. And it occurred to me, for the first time, that everybody must think I was dead. Effectively, I *was* dead. I wasn't there any more. And that felt amazing, fantastic. And I was no longer afraid, not of the situation, not of death, not of him. I felt that we knew each other.

'Where's God in all of this?' I said.

'Now that *is* a good question,' said the Devil.

'Maybe *you* are God,' I said. 'Maybe you're God, and this is one big test.'

'Yeah, maybe.'

'You wouldn't tell me if you were, would you?'

'I'd probably want to hear what you had to say for yourself first.'

'That's the trouble with God. He's always one step ahead.'

'What would you say to me if I were God?'

I thought about this for a while. The Devil passed me the bottle meantime.

'I'd say I was sick of apologising for you. I'm sick of the bloody mess. Something like that.'

'You'd blame me for it?'

'Well, ultimately, who else is there to blame?'

'Then you don't blame *me*? I mean, me the Devil. If that's who I am.'

'No,' I said. 'I don't blame you. You're just doing what you do. What *do* you do?'

'That's another good question,' the Devil said. 'I used to have a purpose. We both had a purpose, God and me. Now? I just go from one window to another and stare out. Or stare in. Sometimes I do a few conjuring-tricks, push a button here, pull a lever there. But my heart's not in it. Basically, I don't do anything any more. I despair, if you want the honest truth. I mean, the world doesn't need me. It's going to hell on a handcart, if you'll excuse the cliché, without any assistance from me.'

'And does God feel the same?' I asked.

'Probably. I feel sorry for him actually. What's in this for him? If things are going well, people forget about him. They unchain the swings, turn the churches into casinos and mock anybody who still believes in him. He's a very easy target. And who does he get left with? Fanatics and maniacs of every faith and every persuasion, who want to kill the heretics and blow themselves to pieces in his name. I feel sorry for God, I do. I mean, what a thankless fucking job. It must be like running the National Health Service when nobody believes in it any more. What are you looking like that for?'

I must have been frowning. The alcohol was making it hard for me to concentrate. 'I'm trying to work out,' I said, 'if you *are* God, what my response to that should be.'

He gave a long chuckle. 'No more games, Gideon, okay? I'm not playing games. Like you, I'm sick of them. Do you think God would spend his time in a place like this? Okay, well, actually he might. He might like the solitude. The fact is, I don't know where he is. I haven't seen him for a long time.'

I found I was struggling to keep my eyes open. The Devil's voice carried on in my ear.

'Maybe he's had enough. I keep thinking we're bound to run into one another again but it doesn't happen. I reckon he's gone, Gideon.

Taken early retirement. Packed up, pissed off, vamoosed, vanished, *desaparecido*. I think he's done a runner. And you know what? I don't blame him. I don't blame him at all.'

'I have to go to sleep now,' I said.

'Of course you do,' he said. 'How's your leg?'

'Sore,' I said. 'Not from what you did. From what I did. How long was I away?'

'A long, long time,' the Devil said. 'I thought you were never coming back.'

I wanted to stretch out but I didn't want to push him off the end of the settee. He read my mind, or at least the movement of my feet. He leaned over behind me and gently eased me forward. In a moment we were lying slotted together again.

'Sleep well,' he said. 'You're going to miss me, Gideon, you know that?'

'Yes,' I said. 'But you're right. I need to go back.'

'Sweet dreams,' he said.

He came and went through the night, if it was the night, just as he had before, but often when I woke, or half-woke, he was there against my back. Nothing happened between us, Bill, I swear it. Nothing sexual, I mean. We were like soldiers camping out under the stars. Comrades. I felt a great comfort in his presence. And I did dream. I had three dreams that were of the utmost clarity.

In the first dream he and I were walking in the hills. I don't know where, Scottish hills somewhere. It was summer. We were just wandering. I had the most intense feeling of happiness. We saw a couple of people, a man and a woman, coming along the path behind us. It was obvious that they'd seen us, because they weren't that far away. He said, 'Let's give them something to think about.' So we hid, but we didn't really hide, we just waited. And they came up to where we were, and although we were just standing there they couldn't see us. They were looking around, confused, wondering where we were. We were laughing, and they couldn't hear us either. I felt like a magician. That's all I remember of that dream.

The second dream was about my father. I didn't see him but I know it was about him. There was a street with all the buildings in ruins.

Dust and rubble everywhere. Men standing around in army uniforms. There was a wooden trap-door under some of the rubble, and they cleared a space around it and opened the door. There was a lot of shouting and an explosion. Then my father, or me, it was like it was both of us, went down some stone steps. It was very dark and very hot. As our eyes adapted to the dark we could see shapes. The shapes were bodies, and bits of bodies. Women and children and men piled up in the corners, and arms and legs and lumps of flesh lying everywhere. Horrible. But the worst thing was the silence. There was no sound at all, no groaning or crying, nobody moving. Just utter silence.

WW: Gideon, the tape's about to run out.

GM: It's okay. Stop it. There's not much more to tell.

That is where the tape finishes. The rest I knew I would remember without having to record it. I didn't, in the end, tell Bill the third dream. He did prompt me, but I said I'd changed my mind, it wasn't important. The third dream was about Elsie and Jenny. I was in bed with Elsie. We were just lying sleeping together, the way Jenny and I used to lie. And she said to me, 'Is this it?' And I said, 'Is it what?' And she said, 'Just this. Is this all there is?' And I said, 'Yes.' And she turned to kiss me, and it wasn't Elsie, it was Jenny, and a huge wave of sadness rolled over me. If I was deliriously happy walking in the hills with the Devil, this was the opposite. Happiness missed. I knew the sadness was because of some fault in me, but I didn't know what the fault was. It was as if there was something I didn't have, a part missing.

When I woke up from that dream the Devil was up and about at the fire, making tea, and there was such a surreal domesticity about the scene that I felt comforted, but still there was a residue of sorrow. Anyway, as I said, I didn't tell Bill about that dream.

What I did tell him, I write down here. In the morning – I say 'morning' only because it felt like that, but I really don't know what time it was – the Devil made me tea, and then he told me it was time to go. I said I couldn't go into the river again. He said I would have to, it was the only way that I could leave. I suppose by then I trusted him, or I would never have got in the boat. I sat at one end, and he paddled us out into the dark pool. The flames of the fire made the gravel twinkle and threw long orange fingers across the water. The black rock loomed above us. I felt like some character in a Fenimore Cooper novel, or one of those brothers in Stevenson's *Master of Ballantrae*, deep in the American wilderness.

'Now, Gideon,' he said, shipping the paddle. 'Go and do what you have to do. It won't take long. Then we'll meet again.'

'What is it I have to do?' I said. I sat on the edge of that tiny vessel, trembling over the tar-black water, and the question came out like a whine. I sounded like a child bewildered by a classroom task he doesn't know how to perform. I did not want to go, nor did I know how to go. Did he expect me to slip into the water like an otter?

'You'll understand what you have to do when you're back there,' he said.

'But where will we meet?' I said. 'And when?'

'I fancy somewhere peaceful, away from the crowds,' he said. 'Away from the noise and confusion of life.' He looked up into the cathedral above us and then back at me with a smile. 'Does anywhere occur to you?'

'The Stone,' I said immediately.

'Ah, but will it be there?' he asked. 'Anyway, that's not very adventurous, is it? Let's have an adventure, Gideon. Let's escape from the world, you and I, let's go on the run.'

I felt again an uncertainty as to whether the next idea that appeared in my head had sprung there of its own accord, or had been put there by some power of his. Maybe it was simply because I'd thought of Stevenson a moment before. At any rate, I instantly imagined, when he suggested the two of us on an adventure, Davie Balfour and Alan Breck at large on Ben Alder, and I named that dismal mountain.

'An excellent idea,' he cried. '"Am I no a bonnie fechter?" and all that? Ben Alder it shall be, come wind, rain or snow.'

'But when?'

'Whenever,' he said. 'Don't worry about when. When you're ready. I won't let you down.'

'It's a big mountain,' I said. 'A big wild place. How will we find each other?'

'Gideon,' he said, 'trust me. If you go there, I'll find you. Do you think I couldn't be at your side in an instant? Trust me.'

Trust me. Those were the last words I heard him speak. He began paddling again, smiling at me all the time, and soon the boat was pushing in under the great flat rock where we could not hear each other. I couldn't see how, even if I'd wanted to, I could possibly get out of the dinghy and on to the rock. I reckoned, of course, without his mighty strength: now, looking back, I see that my willingness to co-operate in this procedure was completely irrelevant. I made a shrugging gesture at him, to indicate that I was at a loss what to do. He smiled again, and with the paddle indicated a point somewhere above my head. I glanced up to see what he was meaning. There was a sudden rocking of the boat, and when I looked back at him he was standing up on the wooden plank with a happy grin splitting his face, both hands were gripping the handle of the paddle and he was in the act of bringing the flat of its blade down upon the side of my head.

Bill said, 'And then what?'

I said, 'And then the next thing I know I'm waking up in a hospital bed. I don't remember Chae Middleton fishing me out at all. I thought I did at first, but it was the Devil fishing me out I really remembered. After he hit me with the paddle, he must have taken off my boots and stuck his trainers on my feet. Then . . . well, your guess is as good as mine. He was certainly capable of simply throwing me up on to the rock. From there the water would have washed me off on the other side and I'd have continued my way down the Keldo. After that – well, you need to ask other people about what happened after that.'

XXXVII

It was well after midnight when Bill, taking his tape-recorder but having surrendered the cassette to me, left the manse. He'd promised to say nothing about it for the time being. I'd asked him again what he thought of my story. He said he'd have to think about that. It was a lot to take in. Did I propose telling anybody else about it?

'Yes, of course,' I said. 'How could I not tell people? I've spent three days in the company of the Devil.'

Bill looked horribly uncomfortable. It was acceptable, it seemed, to tell my story into a tape-recorder – that was like the extract from Menteith I'd read for his exhibition – but saying it out loud as if I meant it, that was another matter.

'Be careful, Gideon,' he said, speaking slowly for once. 'You're only just out of hospital. Take your time, don't do anything hasty.'

'I'll do what I have to do,' I said.

I asked him if he'd like a copy of the transcript when I'd typed it up. He said he would, but he was leaving Monimaskit the next day and didn't know if or when he'd be back. He wrote down a London address for me.

'Should be down there already,' he said, becoming a little more upbeat, 'but I stuck around when I heard you'd been found alive. Can't wait any longer, though. Next commission has to be finished by January, show opens first of February. In Lewes – the Sussex Lewes, not the Hebridean one.'

'What's it about?'

'Piltdown Man,' he said. 'Famous case of Edwardian skulduggery – literally. Skull of missing link discovered in quarry.'

'I've heard of it. It was a hoax, wasn't it?'

'Absolutely. Rival archaeologists falling over each other with claim and counter-claim. Bit of a change for me, but still touches on the idea of myth versus fact, what people want to believe, that kind of thing.'

'Fabrication,' I said. 'Truth versus invention.'

'Absolutely.' He stopped suddenly, as if he had blundered. 'Don't think that's what I'm thinking, Gideon. About you, I mean. It's just hard to take in. Would you believe your story if you heard it from somebody else?'

'I don't know,' I said. 'All I know is it happened to me. I can't pretend it didn't.'

'Be careful,' he said again, and we shook hands. He headed off into the night. I did post him a copy of the transcript but I never heard back from him, and I never saw him again.

For the next two days, Friday and Saturday, I stayed shut away from the world while I typed up the recording. It looked a miserable concoction on paper, and reading it again now I see that my words inadequately express the intensity of what I'd experienced. Meanwhile the phone rang incessantly, but I ignored it, letting the messages stack up and eventually taking the receiver off the hook. The doorbell rang too, half a dozen times each day, and to get peace I was forced to answer the most insistent of these callers, a reporter from the local paper. She wanted the 'inside story' of my survival: I told her she would have to wait, but that all would be revealed in due course. I pled frailty and exhaustion and asked her to respect the fact that I was still recovering. To my amazement and her credit, she went away. She was a polite, pleasant young woman with no future in the newspaper industry.

I was visited also by the police, on the Friday, in the form of my old acquaintance Andy McAllister. Andy had been in his early twenties when he'd come to the door with the news about Jenny. He'd been rosy-cheeked and innocent then, a churchgoer with a young wife and a baby boy that I'd baptised, a young bobby who thought he could make a difference. Now he was in his mid-thirties, a sergeant, overweight, grey-faced, cynical and divorced. I hadn't seen him at the Old Kirk for years.

'I just wanted to check a couple of things with you, Mr Mack,' he said, 'about your recent accident. If you don't mind.'

I had to let him in. We sat in the kitchen and he asked questions and made laborious notes of my answers. 'I've got to put in a report,' he said. 'We had a lot of manpower out looking for you last weekend. Not just us: the fire service, mountain rescue. Anything you can tell me about where you were, how you got out, would be helpful. For future reference, in case anybody else ever takes a header up there.'

I said I couldn't remember anything after the fall until I woke up in hospital. A vague recollection of somebody taking me out of the water, that was about it.

'That was Chae Middleton,' Andy said grimly. 'That one would take anything out of the water.'

'I'll need to thank him,' I said.

'I wouldna bother,' Andy said. 'He's been fou all week on account of you. He's in the Luggie every night, getting stood drinks by all and sundry and telling anybody who'll listen how he saved the minister. I wouldna worry about thanking Chae.'

He asked me why I'd gone after the dog. 'We're always telling people not to have a go, not to tackle burglars, that kind of thing, but they dinna listen. You must have known how dangerous the cliff was.'

'It was instinct. I didn't weigh up the pros and cons, I just went after him.'

'A dog's a dog,' he said. 'I understand you weren't wearing appropriate footwear either.'

I did not contest this. The Devil's trainers were sitting by the back door. I fetched them, and he inspected them as if they might be a murder weapon. He started shaking his head and telling me about kids who got lost in the mountains in tee-shirts and wellies. I cut him short.

'Andy,' I said, 'I'm very tired.'

'I'll no be much longer,' he said. 'What about these three days, now? I don't see how you can have been in the river for three days. Nobody could survive that. You must mind something about that time.'

'I'm trying to,' I said. 'I'm writing things down as they come to me.'

'And?'

'Nothing so far. I think I was unconscious most of the time.'

He obviously wasn't satisfied, but I didn't give way. He asked a few more questions, some of which were reworkings of earlier ones, as if he was trying to catch me out. I looked at my watch. He looked at his. He said, 'Lot of water under the bridge since I was last here, sir.'

'Yes, Andy,' I said.

'How are you? In yourself, I mean?'

'I'm fine.'

'It was a terrible loss, Mr Mack.' I looked blankly at him. 'Your wife.'

'That was a long time ago,' I said. 'I've moved on.'

'Aye, of course,' he said. 'Some folk can. But still . . .' In his ham-fisted way, he was trying to build a psychological profile of me. He was trying to work out if losing Jenny had led me, eleven years later, to throw myself off a cliff.

'I got over it, Andy,' I said. 'Believe me.'

He stood up to go. 'Well, if you remember anything else, you'll let me know.'

I showed him out, promising full co-operation. It was five o'clock, a lovely September afternoon. I stood on the doorstep, absorbing the air and the light. I was just going back in when a car turned into the drive, honking its horn. It was Lorna Sprott.

'Gideon,' she said, virtually falling out of the car in her rush, 'thank God! I've been leaving messages and trying to phone you all day. I thought you might be sleeping. Then I thought you might be lying dead on the kitchen floor. Are you all right?'

She hugged me, and I hugged her back. It was the least I could do. Jasper was in the car, and she let him out so he could thank me in person for saving his life. He did this by throwing himself at my chest, causing me to stagger backwards. When he'd calmed down we went into the manse and through to the kitchen. I put the kettle on. Lorna expressed concern about my limp. I told her it was nothing.

'I'll never, ever be able to thank you enough,' she said. 'You shouldn't have done it but you did, and I'm so, so grateful. Can you imagine what it's been like? I blamed myself, I blamed Jasper,

I blamed you. It's been a total nightmare. I even blamed God. And then on Tuesday, when they said you'd been found! I mean, the joy! The sheer joy of it, Gideon!'

'I really didn't mean to put you through all that,' I said.

We had to go over everything, from the moment Jasper saw the rabbit to the phone call she'd received telling her I was alive. At first I played it as I had with McAllister, claiming memory loss for most of the three days. But Lorna was more persistent and gradually she got more out of me. I told her about what Bill Winnyford had called my NDE, and this led me to describe the first tunnel I'd been in, and then the pool, and then the cave. She listened intently.

'This is amazing, Gideon. Don't you see how important this is? You were so close to death. You saw what it was like. You weren't frightened until you started to come back. And the light . . . It's what people always hope it'll be like, but fear it won't be. Not outer darkness, but bright, eternal light. But it's even better than that: God didn't want you to die then. He sent you back to us.'

I remembered my friend's words: *no more games*. I bit the bullet. 'No, Lorna,' I said. 'It wasn't God who sent me back. It was the Devil.'

So I told her. Or rather, I went and got the cassette-recorder and rewound the tape and played it to her. We sat and listened to this voice that was mine and yet wasn't mine talking about my three days with the Devil. We might have been listening to a ghost story on an audio-book, but I knew we weren't. Jasper snoozed on the floor with his nose between his paws. The light began to go outside. We listened on, right to the end.

I switched off the machine. I told Lorna that the Devil had taken me out in the boat the next morning, hit me over the head with the paddle, stolen my boots and flung me back in the river. I didn't tell her that I'd arranged another meeting with him.

'I feel like I need a drink,' she said.

'I've got wine,' I said. That was all she drank, white wine. Two glasses made her squiffy.

'No, thanks. Not a good idea. I need to drive home.'

'There's plenty of room here,' I said, 'if you want to stay.'

I said it in all innocence. I don't know why I did: I'd never suggested it before and I didn't want her to stay. She looked at me sadly, as if I'd suggested we go to bed together. As if I'd made the offer too late.

'No, I have to go. Gideon, you must promise me something.'

'What's that?'

'Don't tell anybody else about this. What I've just heard . . . Gideon, it's mad. It's completely and utterly mad. It's also deluded, foolish, unpleasant and blasphemous. You're not well. You're clearly not well at all.'

'I'm completely well, Lorna,' I said. 'I'm tired, that's all. How can it be blasphemous? It's the truth. There isn't a word of a lie in what you've heard.'

'Of course it's blasphemous. It goes against everything we stand for. You simply mustn't repeat it.'

'I can't *not*. I have to. It's what happened.'

'I'm taking your services this weekend and next,' she said. 'I beg you to let me do that. You have to rest. Your mind is disturbed. You're a minister of religion. You cannot go around telling people that you not only met the Devil but you actually got on with him. That you slept with him, for God's sake. All that stuff about . . . I know you said there was nothing sexual in it, but don't you see how disastrous it would be to speak about such things? To claim that the Devil lives in a cave in your parish. That you walked to the centre of the earth or wherever you think you went. That you don't really believe in God at all, and he's gone off on holiday somewhere. You'll destroy yourself and bring ridicule on the Kirk if you breathe a word of this to anyone. Which, if there is any truth in what you say, is precisely what the Devil wants you to do.'

She was right, of course. Everything she said made total sense.

'It *is* the truth,' I said. 'I'm sorry. I have to tell the truth.'

'At least wait,' she said. 'Will you let me take the services? This week and next?'

'Yes,' I said. 'I haven't the energy for that. I haven't even thought about it.'

'Well, thank God for that at least,' she said.

She stood up, and Jasper stretched and got to his feet. Lorna's eyes were full of tears.

'I hate to see you like this,' she said. 'I don't know if I should leave you alone.'

'I'm fine. I promise you, I am absolutely fine.'

'No, you're not, you're not well.'

'Lorna,' I said, and I pointed behind her, 'there are the shoes. Was I wearing those when we went for that walk?'

She turned and saw the trainers, which I'd dropped on the floor after Andy had examined them. I could see the shiver that went through her.

'I don't know what you were wearing,' she said. 'I don't notice things like that. Maybe you were, maybe you weren't, what difference does it make?'

'It makes all the difference in the world,' I said.

'I'm going now, Gideon,' she said. 'I'll be back tomorrow. Are you sure you're not going to do anything daft? I don't mean about that tape. I mean, you won't do anything to yourself, will you? Hurt yourself?'

'Quite sure,' I said. 'I promise.'

She accepted my assurance, which was illogical on her part. Everything else she'd heard she thought profane, blasphemous, insane invention. But she seemed to trust me when I said I wouldn't do myself any harm.

After she'd gone, I took the tape-player back through to the study and continued typing.

XXXVIII

On the Saturday I had more visitors. The first, at nine o' clock, was John Moffat. He, too, had been trying to get me on the phone. Had I been ill? Did I need anything? No, I said, I was fine. He brought a sheaf of newspaper cuttings which he thought would amuse me. John was doing his duty, making sure I was alive. Having done it, he was off like a shot. I am being unfair, of course. He had, after all, visited me in hospital, and fetched me home.

I skimmed through the cuttings. The stories about my death were all based on the same statements from 121 George Street, the local police and John Gless, who had spoken on behalf of the Session with commendable restraint. One or two of my parishioners described me as a good man who would be sorely missed. Most of the papers gave a brief summary of my career: some had photographs of me completing one marathon or another; there was one of me handing my collar over to Iain MacInnes of NessTrek. The stories about my survival invariably included the word 'miracle'. I became bored reading about myself. Only I knew the true story, the real miracle.

A couple of hours later the bell went again. This time it was Amelia Wishaw, my GP, making house-calls after her morning surgery. She had been in touch with the consultant in Dundee and wanted to check me over. I showed her my leg, which still looked like the floor of a Venetian palace, and she asked if I needed painkillers. No, I told her. She took my pulse and shone a light in my eyes. I have no idea what she was looking for. She asked if I was sleeping well. If not, she could prescribe me something that would knock me out every night. I declined the offer. I was already, I said, sleeping the sleep of the just about eight hours. She looked quizzically at me. An old joke, I said.

'Take it easy, Gideon,' Amelia said. 'I have no idea why you're even still alive. The fact that you're up and about at home, pretty much unscathed, and not plugged into a life-support system in Dundee, beats me. Don't be surprised if you start to feel lousy in the next day or so. Delayed reaction. Any problems at all, pick up the phone. Call me at home. Don't try and tough it out.'

'Thanks, Amelia,' I said. 'Is that you finished for the day?'

'One more call,' she said. 'Your friend Miss Craigie.'

I had a sudden rush of guilt. I had completely forgotten about Catherine. Through her various sources she would surely know about my fatal accident and resurrection. I would have to go and see her. This in turn reminded me that I should also go and see my mother, who was presumably blissfully unaware that her only son had died and come back to life in the space of a week.

'Anything serious?' I asked.

'No. I like to go in once or twice a month and check she's okay,' Amelia said. 'As far as anyone in Miss Craigie's condition can be described as okay, that is.'

'I didn't know you did that,' I said. 'I knew you were her doctor, but she's never mentioned you visiting.'

'Well, she wouldn't, would she?' Amelia said. 'That's not her way. She expects the doctor to call, even if there's no particular reason.'

'That's a bit unfair,' I said. 'Her health's terrible.'

'There are plenty a lot worse off, or much the same, believe me,' Amelia said. 'She's still living in the 1950s, Gideon. I don't blame her actually, I'd be the same if I could, but the world's moved on. There aren't many Doctor Finlays left these days.'

'Looks like you're doing a pretty good impression,' I said.

'I do feel that I'm stepping back in time when I go into her house,' Amelia said. 'I quite like it, though. It smells the way I imagine the houses in Tannochbrae smelt. Everything's a bit musty, including Miss Craigie. Not that I would dare say so. She can be quite scary. Gregor was terrified of her when she was his boss.'

'You could tell her I'm all right,' I said, 'if she doesn't know already. Tell her I'll come and see her soon. Tomorrow, probably.'

Amelia said she would do that and left. I went to my study and spent another two hours completing the transcript of the recording. By then I was exhausted. Perhaps Amelia was right, and I was premature in thinking I was fully fit. I went upstairs and lay down for a nap.

When I woke up it was four o'clock. I'd been dreaming of the cave. The Devil was moving about in front of the fire. Occasionally he would glance over at me lying on the settee and give me a smile. I shook myself and went and splashed water on my face. Then I put on a coat and hat and lurched off to the Monimaskit Care Home, to see my mother.

I got a warm welcome from Betty and the other staff and those residents who'd registered that I'd had an accident. Everybody was so relieved, I was told. 'Not as much I was,' I said, trying to keep it light. I asked for Mrs Hodge, but she was off duty.

Betty said, 'You'll be wanting to see your mother, Mr Mack. She's in her room, I think. Come on, I'll take ye doon.'

'Has she been told anything?' I asked as we went down the corridor.

'Aye, I think Mrs Hodge had a word with her when we heard about the accident. I'm no sure how much went in, though. And then, when Chae found you, she had to go and tell her the *good* news. Your guess is as good as mine, Mr Mack, whether she thinks you're deid or alive. I'm sure she'll be pleased to see you anyway. I'll just make sure she's decent.'

She chapped the door and went in. 'Hello, Agnes, there's someone here for you. In you come, Mr Mack. Do you mind who this is, Agnes? I'll just leave you to it,' she said, and backed out.

'Hello, Mum,' I said. She was sitting in an armchair crammed in between the foot of the bed and a jutting-out wardrobe. The room was fine in its way, with a view out to the gardens, but you couldn't swing a cat in it. I kissed her cheek and sat on the bed.

'What are you doing in here?' I said. 'You're usually in the day room.'

'Too noisy,' she said, looking at me as if she knew me.

'I'm sorry I've not been in this week,' I said. 'Events kind of took over. Maybe you heard?'

She stared at me, saying nothing.

'I fell into the river, Mum, and they thought I'd been drowned, but I wasn't. Did they tell you about it?'

'Nonsense,' she said.

'No, it's true,' I said. 'It really happened.'

She looked at me as if I were six and telling her something that had occurred at school. I thought of the time I'd told her about the Stone, months before. A pointless exercise, and this one was just as pointless. But the Devil had urged me to speak to her. Find out, he'd said. Your mother knows about hell. Ask her.

'Anyway,' I said, 'I'm back now.'

'Oh, you're back,' she said.

'Yes.'

'I don't know where you go,' she said. 'I came in earlier but you were away. I brought you a cup of tea.'

'That was nice,' I said.

'It'll be cold now,' she said. 'Did you go for a walk? I thought you were here but you're always away.'

'I'm here now,' I said.

'It's cold in here,' she said. In fact it was roasting. 'Will you not let me light the fire, James?'

She said these things as if she'd recorded them earlier and was just replaying the tape. She accompanied them with no physical movement, no attempt to act out the things she was talking about. But at least I knew who she was talking to.

'It's Gideon, Mum,' I said. 'Not Dad. I did want to ask you about him though. About the war. You said once that he must have been different before the war. It changed him. Do you think, when he came back, when you first met him, do you think he still believed in God?'

'She seems very nice, Gideon,' she said. 'Your father thinks so too. She's bonnie. Anyway, that's enough of that.'

She made as if to get up out of the chair, but then seemed to lose interest in the idea. She gazed into space. She wasn't looking at me or out of the window. She wasn't looking at anything.

'Mum,' I said. I'd been frustrated at her in the past, been wearied and made impatient by her. I'd been made angry by what had happened to her. Now I just felt like crying.

I reached out and took her hand. She didn't resist. I tried to make her look at me, see me. She didn't say anything else.

'Do you mind when I was a boy and I used to sleepwalk?' I said. 'I'd wake up and go back to my bed. And you'd be there, watching me. Do you mind that?'

She seemed to be thinking.

'I never knew if you'd heard me get up and were making sure I was safe, or if you just happened to be there by accident. And now

I'm wondering if I just imagined it. Maybe you weren't there at all. Mum?'

Nothing.

And then I knew what the Devil had meant when he'd told me to ask her about hell. She had no secrets to tell me. She had no revelations about my father. She had nothing. Now, when I finally wanted to communicate with her, I was too late. Hell was looking into my mother's eyes and seeing what I'd seen in *his* eyes before he died: nothing. No, I was wrong. Hell wasn't looking into her eyes, it was looking out of them. Being trapped inside, looking for an exit; not even doing that, just wandering empty rooms in bewilderment. That was all the Devil had wanted me to do: to look in through the windows of this woman who had brought me into the world, and see absolutely nothing there.

XXXIX

Lorna had called while I was out seeing my mother. She'd stuck a note through the door to say that everything was prepared for Sunday's service and I didn't need to worry. 'If I don't see you at church, I'll call round afterwards,' she wrote. She made no mention of anything else.

I had a solitary evening in the manse that Saturday night. I read from the Bible, the Book of Jonah, and then I read a chapter or two of *Moby Dick*, Captain Ahab and his obsession with the whale. I watched the news: the Swedish foreign minister had died after being stabbed while she was shopping in Stockholm; an opposition newspaper had closed in Zimbabwe. I ate some toast. I drank some whisky. I thought about the women in my life: my mother, Jenny, Elsie, Lorna, Catherine. I thought about the Devil, and how ludicrous it was that that was the only name I had for him. I couldn't imagine calling him Satan or Lucifer or Beelzebub. The Scots have a dazzling array of names for him: he has been a familiar acquaintance of ours for centuries. Auld Nick, Sandy, Sim, Bobbie, Auld Sootie, Clootie, Ruffie, the Deil, the Foul Thief, the Earl o

Hell, the Auld Smith, the Auld Ane, the Wee Man, Auld Mishanter, Auld Mahoun. Yet none of these names suited my Devil either. My Devil was suave and fit-looking, though I'd also seen, when he let down his guard, the aged world-weariness of him. I wondered how I would address him when we next met. Maybe he'd be Alan, and I'd be Davie Balfour. Comrades. I went to bed and remembered the way we'd been together. I missed him.

On Sunday morning I woke late and ate my breakfast to the sound of the church bell calling folk to worship. It was odd to be in the manse and yet separate from that ritual. I wanted nothing to do with it. It had for so long been a sham to be praising God and preaching his Word that to be signed off from it in this way was an intense relief. I could no longer maintain the pretence. *No more games*, the Devil had said. If I had entered the kirk that morning, either to lead the service or to participate in it, I felt that my false face would have been obvious to everyone.

Instead, once the service had begun, I left the manse and set off for Catherine Craigie's house. I felt as I imagine Boswell did that day he skipped church and went instead to visit the great infidel David Hume, 'just a-dying'. Who was the worse sinner, the ordained minister who had communed with the Devil but not with God, or the Edinburgh lawyer who feared God but drank like a fish and slept with whores? I decline to pass judgement. I only know that of the three of us Hume, being untroubled by guilt, was innocent. Nor, in truth, did guilt much trouble me. I was too full of the story I had to tell – though how I would even begin to tell it to Catherine I had no idea. So I did not sneak through byways and closes or slink in the shadows of walls. Not that there was anybody about to observe me, but I went with my head held upright. I could not, however, correct the lurch of my shortened right leg.

The curve of Ellangowan Place, together with its profusion of trees and bushy vegetation, effectively prevents you from seeing much of any single house until you are directly in front of it. It wasn't until I was at Catherine's gate, therefore, that I saw that the front door, most unusually, was wide open. Beyond it, I could see that the plant-stand had been moved from its usual place in the middle of the hall. I walked up the path, rang the bell and entered, calling hello.

Amelia Wishaw came out of the drawing room. 'Ah, Gideon,' she said.

'What's going on? Is everything all right?' I asked. But Amelia's presence, let alone her expression, told me at once that it wasn't.

'No, I'm afraid it's not.'

'What's happened?'

'Bad news, Gideon. Catherine's dead.'

'Dead?'

'Yes, I'm sorry, it's the last thing you can have been expecting.'

'How can she be dead? You were on your way to see her when you left me yesterday. She was alive then, wasn't she?'

'Yes, she was. She seemed fine. She *was* fine. Nothing the matter that I could see. She said she was getting a tingling sensation down her arm, but she had so many aches and pains it didn't seem anything serious. I checked her over, couldn't find anything to cause concern. We sat and chatted for a while, and then I came away.'

I heard a noise from the back of the house, the kitchen. 'What's that?'

'It's Norah, the home help. She found her this morning on the couch. She'd been well schooled by Catherine, my direct line was on a board in the kitchen. I was here in ten minutes, but there was nothing to be done. Except get Norah a cup of tea. The poor woman's upset because she was late coming in and thinks it was her fault.'

'She just died?'

'Looks like it. No suspicious circumstances. It must have happened last night some time. Rigor mortis is quite advanced, so I'd say before midnight. Her heart just stopped – no question at all in my mind. It's been waiting in the wings for a while, you know. Her heart was under a lot of strain.'

'Yes,' I said, 'she told me about that not so long ago. But it just doesn't seem possible.'

'I know. She was a good friend to you. Do you want to see her?'

A woman emerged from the back lobby, holding a mug of tea. Her face was pale and her eyes a little red.

'This is Norah,' Amelia said.

'Hello, Norah,' I said. 'Are you all right?' In all my years of visiting Catherine, I'd never met her home help, nor did I recognise her from the town.

'Just a wee bit shocked,' Norah said. 'I'll be okay.'

Amelia led the way into the drawing room. Norah came behind me. Catherine was lying on the couch, a rug wrapped round her middle, her neck and shoulders propped up on several cushions. Her head was turned to one side, and her left shoulder, the one that had given her the most trouble, was twisted up like a tree-root. She was wearing a tee-shirt, and one leg sticking out from the bottom of the rug revealed a loose pair of trousers. Her eyes were closed. One arm was by her side, the other, the left one, lay across her chest. Apart from the twisted shoulder and the obvious stiffness she didn't look too bad. Comfortable even. There was a tumbler half full of whisky on a table beside her, along with a book and the remote control for her stereo system.

'Have you moved her?' I asked.

'Not much,' Amelia said. 'Just to check. We'll need to contact an undertaker.'

I went over to Catherine and knelt beside her. I put my hand over the hand on her chest. It was like a cold lump of rock. The others stood back a little. It must have looked like I was saying a prayer.

I stood up again. 'I wish I'd come round yesterday,' I said.

'You couldn't have saved her,' Amelia said. 'You couldn't have stopped it happening any more than Norah could have.'

'That's not what I mean. I just wish I'd come round. Spoken to her one last time.'

Amelia put her hand on my shoulder.

'Listen, Gideon,' she said. 'She was lying on her sofa on a Saturday night, she had a whisky by her side, she was listening to music, and she was reading a book. She'd been in a good mood when I saw her, and she was really, really looking forward to seeing you today. She said so. I know these last few years have been bloody awful for her healthwise, but on a scale of ways to go this scores pretty highly.'

I seemed to have entered a phase of my life where people kept telling me sensible things. It didn't make it any easier. Gentle counsellor was a role I too had once been good at playing.

'She hasn't any relatives, has she?' Amelia said.

'None that I know of. She has a lawyer. I have his details. I can get in touch with him.'

'Thank you. What about an undertaker?'

'She'd sorted that out with a firm in Dundee, I know that.'

'I'm impressed. Well, it makes things a lot simpler. We can give them a call. I'll make out the medical certificate tomorrow.'

'Won't there need to be a post-mortem?'

'No, I don't think so. This is entirely explicable.'

'I just thought, with it being so sudden.'

Amelia nodded. 'I know, but the fact is she's been dying for years. It's a surprise, yes, but it's not sudden. Believe me, if I had any doubts . . .'

I shook my head to indicate, I suppose, that I had none either. Amelia went on: 'If we can contact the undertakers today, the lawyer can start making the funeral and other arrangements tomorrow.'

'Yes,' I said. 'Although, as a matter of fact, I'll be handling the funeral.'

'Will you?' Amelia said.

'Absolutely. We discussed it in depth.'

'Well, that really does surprise me. Will you be able to cope with it?'

'Of course I will.'

Norah, who had been hovering in the background, asked if she was needed any longer. Amelia thanked her for what she'd done and told her to go home. After she'd left we found the Yellow Pages, got the twenty-four-hour number for the funeral directors in Dundee and arranged for them to come for the body. They said they wouldn't manage for a couple of hours. Amelia gave them her mobile number and asked them to call when they were on their way.

She said, 'I'm going home now. Gregor's playing golf all day, and I've got the house to myself. I'm going to have a big glass of gin. Care to join me?'

'I don't really want to leave her,' I said.

Amelia looked at her watch. Clearly her ideal way of spending Sunday afternoon was not in the company of a corpse. I said, 'She'll have gin here. I could do with one too. Would you mind? If you don't want to stay I'm happy to wait for the undertakers myself.'

'Okay,' Amelia said. 'Fix us a couple of large ones. I don't suppose she'd mind us helping ourselves.'

'She'd mind if we didn't,' I said.

'Maybe we can sit somewhere else,' Amelia said. 'It's a little stuffy in here.'

I found gin, tonic water and glasses, even a lemon, and poured us two enormous drinks. We sat in the kitchen on a bench-seat below the big window overlooking the back garden. Half a dozen blackbirds, male and female, were flitting about on the grass with their characteristic busyness. We toasted Catherine. I said, 'I can't believe she's just taken off like this without saying goodbye.'

'You nearly did the same yourself,' Amelia said.

We sat watching the blackbirds. 'She always enjoyed garden birds,' I said. 'She said there was something optimistic about them. So long as they were singing life couldn't be so dreadful.'

'It's funny, isn't it,' Amelia said. 'You and I, different jobs, but we deal with a lot of the same stuff. And right at the core of what we do sits this nasty old bugger called death. I do my best to send him packing, or at least keep him at bay, and you spend your time preparing people for him, telling them there's nothing to be frightened of, they can walk through death's dark vale and there'll be something good on the other side. Don't you?'

'Depends who I'm talking to,' I said. 'Catherine, for example, wouldn't tolerate any of that. Happy hopeful birds was fine, but she'd have slung me out if I'd started any of the kingdom come routine.'

Amelia said, 'I bet she would have. That's why I'm surprised at you presiding over her funeral. I know you were friends, but it doesn't quite fit with what I imagine her views were. What are you going to say?'

'I'll think of something,' I said.

'I reckon even the most convinced atheist must get a bit nervous when the moment comes,' she said. 'More perhaps than those of us who just don't think about it very much. I mean, if you're an atheist you've really nailed your colours to the mast, haven't you?'

I thought of Pascal's bet, and I thought of David Hume, dying and completely unfazed by the prospect of death. 'Catherine wasn't an atheist,' I said. 'She was very explicit about that. She was an agnostic. She said denying the existence of God was as arrogant and stupid as asserting it. The only sensible way to behave is to believe in what we know to be real.'

'Yes, but that's not how people's minds work. People can't help speculating. That's why your crowd will never go out of business.'

'Who? The Kirk?'

'All churches. People whose job it is to articulate spirituality for other people. You're willing to talk about it. And you're willing to talk about death. Everybody else in the West is running around forming boy bands or girl bands, doing reality TV or being famous for being famous, everybody's in denial about this one inescapable fact, and you guys are the only ones talking about it. Well, apart from us in the medical profession.'

'You can't expect boys in boy bands to spend a lot of time contemplating death. You can't blame anybody for not thinking much about it. Why dwell on something you can't do anything about?'

'I get the sense that we're both playing devil's advocate here,' Amelia said. 'Surely the way you think about death totally determines the way you live your life? If you don't ever think about it can you really be alive in any meaningful way?'

'The unexamined life is not worth living, you mean?'

'The unexamined patient may be harbouring a life-threatening disease,' Amelia said. 'If you find out in time, you can do something about it.'

'Sometimes,' I said. 'Sometimes all you can do is tell them.'

'Or not tell them,' Amelia said. 'Like you said, it depends who you're talking to. Anyway, what about you? What do you think of death after your recent escape from his clutches?'

I thought about the clear white light in the tunnel, I thought about coming back and I thought about my Devil. 'The honest truth?' I said. 'I did come pretty close, Amelia. I know I did, I remember it. The honest truth is, I'm not frightened by death. I don't really want to elaborate on that, but I think there really is something good on the other side. I don't know what, but it's not the end.'

'For Catherine too? Or only if you believe in it?'

'Ah,' I said. 'That's an impossible question to answer.'

'It's where it all falls apart, as far as I'm concerned,' Amelia said.

She finished her gin and said she'd phone when she heard from the undertakers. I reassured her that I would switch off everything and lock up when Catherine had been taken away, and she headed off, closing the front door behind her.

It was coming up to one o'clock. The service would be long over, but Lorna had said she would call in if I wasn't at it. I knew she wouldn't give the manse doorbell one ring and leave it at that. She'd hang around. She'd try to get me in later. I didn't want to deal with Lorna. In spite of the circumstances, I was glad to be where I was. Catherine was giving me a kind of sanctuary.

I went back to the kitchen. It was a very quiet street. The only sounds I could hear were the whirr of the fridge and birdsong in the garden. How strange it was that at that moment nobody in Monimaskit except Amelia and myself knew that Catherine Craigie was dead. She was gone but everybody assumed she was still here. Which, of course, she was. Then I remembered Norah. Word would get around pretty quickly.

I drank up, washed the glasses and went back into the drawing room. She reclined like a statue of herself, or like one of those people overwhelmed by the volcanic fumes and ash at Pompeii. There was a faint, sweet odour in the room, something like warm earth. I went and stood over Catherine and her distinctive old cupboard smell rose around me. The table beside her had a single drawer in it, where she kept her stash of alternative medicine. I opened it and found three unsmoked joints and a wee plug of cannabis, all of which I carefully pocketed. I picked up the whisky glass, swilled it, sniffed it. Strong, pungent: an Islay malt. I put the glass back down and lifted the book, a large paperback: *The Late Medieval Scottish Parliament*.* Like the malt, typical Craigie taste. I hoped she'd been at a gripping part when it happened. But maybe she hadn't been reading at all. Maybe she'd been sleeping, or thinking, or lying, a little stoned, listening to music.

I went over to the stereo, which was still on, opened the CD slide and checked what she'd been playing. Manuel de Falla's *Nights in the Gardens of Spain*. That was Catherine too: classical but a little out of the mainstream. Romantic as well. I could hear her vehemently denying that she was a romantic.

I pushed the slide home again and pressed *play*. The strings of the orchestra began to seep into the atmosphere, slow and dark at first, then gathering pace, and the piano trickling in above them. I sat down in the chair I usually occupied. After a minute I stretched my legs out, leaning back as the music filled the room. I could almost see it. I imagined the notes entering the empty shell lying on the couch, swirling around in her skull, leaving again. She was here but she was away. Like my mother but different. I missed her already. Who would I talk to now?

I closed my eyes and let the music pour over me. Until Amelia phoned to say that the undertakers were on their way, I would be quite safe from disturbance. I liked that. There was a great contentment in it.

* By a strange coincidence, or what William Winnyford might call a 'conjunction', a book of this title has been, written by a Dr Roland Tanner, presumably the same Dr Tanner who 'saw' Gideon Mack several months after his death. – P.W.

XL

I couldn't keep the world away so easily after I returned to the manse. From the Monday I felt obliged to deal with a large number of phone calls, letters, visitors. The press were still interested in me. So were the folk at 121 George Street, who phoned in order to update their own press statement. On the Monday evening about half the Session turned up en masse, to shake my hand and wish me well, to assure me that they would keep parish matters ticking over for a week or two till I was fully recovered and (for they were only human) to see what physical and emotional state I was in. I thanked them for their kind thoughts and said I would indeed greatly appreciate their help while I recuperated. The only business that I could not, and did not wish to, delegate for the time being, I said, was the funeral of Catherine Craigie, who they might have heard had passed away at the weekend. The ways of a small town are wondrous: they had indeed heard, and while some of them were not great admirers of Catherine they all concurred that Monimaskit had lost a prominent citizen, and that it was fitting that I should bury her. I was not surprised that Peter Macmurray was absent from this party. I expected to hear from him in due course.

I had that morning spoken to Catherine's lawyers, a Montrose-based firm. Mr Stewart, the partner whose client she had been, sounded down-to-earth and efficient. He had a copy of her funeral wishes and asked me if I intended to carry them out. When I said yes, he answered – I could almost hear his smile – that he would be sure to attend. Later, after he had talked to Amelia about the cause of death and then to the undertakers, and after I had checked with the council's cemeteries department about the availability of gravediggers, we spoke again and agreed that the burial could take place on the following Monday. He would place the necessary notices in the papers if I handled the special arrangements for the funeral.

I had good reasons, quite apart from Catherine's desire that I conduct the event, for not passing this duty on to anybody else. I went to see the headteacher of the Academy and said that in recognition of Miss Craigie's long service at the school it would be highly appropriate if a class of first- or second-years represented the school at the funeral. The head prevaricated: perhaps, he suggested, older students would be better. Some of the twelve-year-olds were not always well behaved and had short attention spans. I understood that, I said. The more mature pupils would be welcome too, but Miss Craigie had especially wanted younger children to be there. The funeral would be neither long nor sombre, but celebratory. The head was a relatively recent appointment: he had been in post barely a year and knew Catherine only by reputation. After some more humming and hawing he agreed to supply me with twenty-four children.

I went round to Catherine's house by car and collected everything she'd gathered for the funeral from the cupboard under her stairs. I took it all back to the manse and spent a couple of evenings in the dining room – a space I virtually never used – assembling kites, unwrapping streamers and testing different percussion instruments. I ordered a selection of confectionery from Jim Currie, the newsagent, and arranged with the church hall committee to provide tea and sandwiches after the service. I also notified the beadle (the church officer who looks after the building itself) that the funeral would be taking place. It would not be a formal service, I said, and I was happy to organise everything myself if she couldn't be there. There would be no need for the organist.

At six o'clock on the Wednesday evening the doorbell rang. Through the glass I saw the stocky figure of Peter Macmurray hotching from one foot to the other. I opened the door.

I have not written in any detail about Macmurray, but it is necessary to do so now. He is a barrel-shaped, red-faced, aggressive man in his sixties. He has thin, yellow hair plastered across the top of his head in long strands, like unfinished raffia work. He tends, when roused, to stab the air with his podgy fingers, and he seldom smiles – and never did in my company. By day he is an accountant and by night, as Jenny used to say, he adds the saved and subtracts the damned, and always comes out with a minus figure. Certainly in his estimation my wife had been in the latter category, since she never attended church, and I was in there too, for being a wolf in sheep's clothing. I once heard another minister, at the General Assembly, say that in every Session there is an elder given by God to be a thorn in the minister's flesh. I felt that Peter Macmurray had been specially selected to goad me in Monimaskit.

'Peter,' I said. 'What can I do for you?'

'I'd like to come in, please,' he said. Somehow he managed to imply in this brief statement that I was preventing him from doing so and that, since the manse was Church property, this was a breach of his rights.

'Well, you'd better, then,' I said, and led him to the study. I sat at my desk and offered him a seat. He looked me up and down, glanced around the study as if to refresh his mind of its contents, sat down and then fired his opening salvo.

'Mr Mack,' he said, 'I am of course relieved, as is the rest of the Session I'm sure, that you have been safely returned to us after your accident, and I appreciate that you are taking some time to regain your health. Nevertheless there are two matters which it is my duty to raise with you. I fear there is very little that can be done with regard to the first of these but I'm going to raise it nevertheless. The second matter is of some urgency, so I trust you'll allow me to speak my mind.'

'You generally do, Peter,' I said, 'and I'm grateful for your concern. What's bothering you?'

He eyed me suspiciously. 'I'm speaking on my own behalf and from my own conscience,' he said, 'as I have had occasion to do more than once in the years you've been here. The first matter is this exhibition that you got involved in at the museum. I realise that it's too late to do anything now, but I'd heard about your part in it so I went to see for myself. Quite apart from the doubtful merits of the display itself, I see that the artist, I forget his name . . .'

'William Winnyford,' I said.

'Aye, Winnyford. Clearly he's modelled part of his exhibition on this very room, which I don't recall being on the agenda at any recent Session meetings. And clearly you have gone out of your way to help him, reading out bits of fairy tales and encouraging silly ideas about devils in caves, and what I want to say and put on record is, is this really the way for a minister in our Church to behave? It seems to me yet another example of how you have brought the sacred office that you hold and the good name of our Church and faith into disrepute. As for the exhibition itself – '

I held up my hand. 'Peter,' I said, 'if you want to complain about Bill Winnyford's work, go to the museum. If you want to complain about my involvement in it, and put it on record as you say, bring it up at the next Session meeting. I'm not prepared to discuss that any further here.'

He snorted and turned a little pinker. 'That's the response I expected,' he said. 'I'm not surprised that you do not defend the indefensible. I will do as you suggest. The other matter is more serious and immediate. I understand that you intend to officiate at the burial of Catherine Craigie next week.'

'On Monday, yes.'

'You cannot do that.'

I drew myself up in my chair.

'What did you say?'

Macmurray drew himself up too. 'You cannot do it,' he said. 'The woman was an atheist who mocked and derided the Kirk, Christianity and everything to do with religion. She has a family lair in the kirkyard and we cannot prevent her from being buried there, but for you to officiate at her funeral, well, it's just intolerable.'

I felt like getting to my feet and punching him.

'I do not need you to tell me whose funeral I may or may not conduct,' I said. 'She's a parishioner. I surely don't need to remind you that I have an obligation to all the people in this parish, regardless of their faith or lack of it.'

'There are exceptions,' he said coldly.

'No, there are not. We are the national Church. It's in our Articles. She requested my services at her funeral and I cannot, even if I wished to, refuse her.'

'You're doing it because she was your friend, not because she was a parishioner, and certainly not because of the Declaratory

Articles,' Macmurray said, pushing himself forward on his seat. 'Everybody knows how chief you and she were. It was an unfitting relationship for a minister while she was alive, and it is equally unfitting for you to do her a favour like this now she's dead.'

I stood up. 'That's enough,' I said. 'You should be ashamed of yourself. I think you should leave before you say anything more foolish.'

He rose too, but he chose not to hear what I had said. His stubby fingers began to poke at the space between us.

'And I hear that the service you intend to conduct is to be an improper one. God knows what you have in mind. Something sordid that would suit her, no doubt. Some piece of Amazonian voodoo dressed up as scholarship. She was a proud, wicked woman and a fallen one at that.'

'You are an ignorant man,' I said, 'and I don't know what you are talking about, but I ask you again to leave this manse.'

'I'm on my way,' he said. He strode from the room and through the hallway, then stopped at the front door, one hand on the handle, and turned to face me again. 'She told you she went to Mexico, didn't she? She told everybody that. Well, maybe she did and maybe she didn't, but that wasn't why she left. We all know why she left. She was carrying a bairn and she went away to get rid of it. Aye, she did, and if she didn't give it up for adoption she did worse. And when she came back she was a schoolteacher, and you'd think butter wouldn't melt in her mouth.'

'You despicable man,' I said. 'You cowardly piece of shit. How dare you say that of her now, when she's dead. You never breathed a word of it when she was alive. You're making it up.'

'Aye, you would say that, you're cut of the same cloth as her. But we all knew it. You come in here from Edinburgh and you think Monimaskit is a wee, wee place, but let me tell you, Mr Mack, it was a lot wee-er forty years ago. We all knew each other and we all knew what Cathy Craigie was like.'

'Then whose child was she carrying,' I said, raising my voice, 'if you know so much about it?'

'That,' Macmurray said, 'I do not know. I do not know and I do not care.'

'You liar,' I said. 'You do know. I can see it in your eyes.'

'I do not. And I'll tell you something else, I doubt that she did either. She didn't go with just one fellow. She was very free and easy with her favours, that one.'

I said, 'If there was any substance in what you say, she'd have wiped her feet of the place and never set foot in it again.'

He jerked open the door and stepped into the porch.

'Ah,' he said, 'but she was thrawn and she couldn't help but come back. She might have left in shame but she was too proud to stay away. She came back a teacher to lord it over us all and she knew there wasn't a thing we could do about it.'

'Mr Macmurray,' I said – I could no longer bring myself to address him by his first name, and I barely managed the 'mister' – 'I thank God that our children are taught by people like Catherine Craigie and not by narrow-minded hypocrites like you. But you're right about one thing. I'll be burying her on Monday, and there isn't a thing you can do to stop me.'

'No?' he said. 'Maybe not. But I'll be at your *informal* service on Monday, Mr Mack. I'll be there as is my right and I'll be seeing what it is you do. So help me God if you drag my faith any deeper in the gutter I'll have you deposed and turned out of this manse like the false thief that you are.'

I think he was on the point of spitting on the step, but some twisted sense of propriety restrained him. He stalked off down the drive with his shoulders heaving like a bull's. I watched him go. He had angered me, but also he had helped to strengthen my resolve. I didn't believe what he'd said about Catherine but I also knew it might be possible. It didn't matter either way. It told me more about Macmurray's tiny mind than it did about her. I didn't even think it explained her anti-Church opinions. That was too simplistic. But it showed me that the sensible advice of Bill Winnyford, Amelia, Lorna and anybody else who offered it was given to ward off the attacks of people like Peter Macmurray. It was therefore incumbent upon me to ignore that advice. If I was to be stoned and denounced for telling the truth, so be it.

He little knew, when he spoke of 'silly ideas about devils in caves', and when he threatened to appear like a recording angel at Catherine's funeral, what I was shortly to unleash on the world.

XLI

That Sunday, the day before the funeral, I attended kirk for the last time. I knew, deep in myself, that this was what I was doing, but of course I said nothing to anyone about it. I slipped in just before the doors closed, so as not to cause a distraction, and sat at the very back. One or two heads turned, and I received a nod and a smile from those who spotted me. I nodded and smiled back.

Lorna conducted the service in her usual slightly flustered, always hopeful way. She'd brought Jasper in with his own cushion, and after an initial foray round the nearest pews he settled down to sleep at the foot of the pulpit steps. As part of her address, to a reasonable turn-out – 'I'm an optimist,' she declared at the start, 'and I'm delighted to see that the church is not half-empty, but half-full,' – she made reference to Jasper and his recent close shave with death.

'If you didn't know already,' she said, 'you'll know now that I am very fond of my dog. I'm very fond of most animals in fact, and I've often wondered if there are animals in heaven. It's one of these questions that theologians have debated at great length – it's not quite as abstruse as how many angels can you get on the head of a pin, but in the end it's about as useful. For some people, a heaven full of dogs is their worst nightmare. The thing is, we don't really know what it will be like in heaven. Heaven as a place is far beyond our ability to imagine. When Jesus talks about it, he puts it into human terms to help us understand. "In my Father's house are many mansions," he said. "If it were not so, I would have told you." He doesn't mean, of course, that heaven is an estate of executive mansions. He means that there is room for everybody, and that the life we will lead there will be of the highest quality. And when he goes on to say, "I go to prepare a place for you", he means that the needs of each and every one of us will be individually catered for. Now that doesn't mean that people like me are going to be reunited with our pets. I think heaven will be so wonderful, so restful and glorious, that those kinds of desires will be completely subsumed in its loveliness. But, and I've said this to some of you before, from where I am now I find it hard to think of everlasting life without a dog. That's why I sometimes stamp my foot and say I won't go there if there are no dogs. I don't think God minds this. He knows I'm not entirely serious. God has a sense of humour. And he also knows the limitations of the human imagination.'

She paused for a moment and seemed to look straight at me. This was odd because I hadn't thought she could see me. I had been listening to her in a strange, half-awake state, lulled by the cotton-wool cosiness of what she was saying. It all seemed totally pleasant, and totally unimportant. But what she said next jerked me out of my reverie.

'But, you know, this isn't really about Jasper at all. It's about Gideon Mack, your minister, who saved Jasper's life and in doing so endangered his own. That's why I'm here in his place. He's been keeping to himself this last week or so, and I'm sure you can understand why after such an ordeal. People have been saying his survival is a miracle, and I don't think that's too strong a word. God was looking after him, and brought him safely back to us. In fact, he's here with us today, sitting quietly at the back of this kirk, *his* kirk, and joining in our worship. And I have to say how marvellous it is to see him here.'

More heads, whole pews full of them, turned to search me out. More smiles and nods and waves came in my direction. There was even a smattering of applause. I was furious with Lorna, but at the same time I couldn't help but be moved.

'I've been speaking to Gideon since he got home from hospital, and he has told me a little of what he remembers,' Lorna went on. 'The thing that struck me most forcefully was the way he described the moments just before he lost consciousness, as he was being swept down the river. He spoke of being in a tunnel, of an incredibly bright shining light at the end of this tunnel, growing ever brighter, and of a feeling of great contentment and ease. He wasn't frightened any more, he wasn't fighting against death. He was being welcomed by God. That bright light was the light of heaven, and Gideon was heading towards it. There was nothing to be fearful of on the other side of death, there was only the beautiful bright light of God's mercy.

'But Gideon didn't die, as you all know. He's here among us today. Why? Because God sent him back to us. He gave him a glimpse of heaven but Gideon still has work to do here on earth. So God sent him back. He sent him to tell us the good news, that there really is a light at the end of the tunnel, that there really is a life to come, better than anything we might experience on earth, better than anything we can imagine.

'Isn't that the most wonderful example of how close we are to God, how much he cares for each and every one of us? For each and every one of us there is a right moment when God will take us into his arms for ever. Last week wasn't the moment for Gideon, but the moment will come. It will come for all of us, a glorious, happy moment.'

I couldn't stand any more of this. Lorna had betrayed me, exploited what I had told her for her own purposes. I could see what was behind it: she had concocted some bizarre plan that if she could somehow set this ball rolling she could prevent me from telling the truth of what had happened. I stood up and walked from the kirk.

Later, she came round to the manse. I knew it would be her when the bell rang. She started calling to me even before I could get the door open. I let her in, but only as far as the hall.

'Lorna,' I said, 'you had no right to say what you said. You used me. You made up a story based on what I told you that's a travesty of the truth.'

I had never spoken to her like that before. She looked horrified.

'I'm sorry, Gideon, I just . . . I was going to say *something*, I wasn't sure what, and then when I saw you there it seemed so appropriate to follow on from what I'd said about Jasper, and I took a leaf out of your own book.'

'What on earth do you mean?'

'You've talked about speaking off the cuff when you give a sermon, about letting the words take you wherever they're going, about trusting your instincts. You know me, I usually have the prayers jotted down too, and the whole sermon typed up and I tell myself, "Thou shalt not deviate." I'd get so tongue-tied otherwise. But today I felt inspired. I really felt that God was speaking through me, that he wanted me to say what I said.'

'It wasn't inspired, Lorna,' I said. 'It was a downright lie.'

'Gideon!'

'You chose to disregard everything you heard on the tape. You deliberately misrepresented me.'

'But you weren't well when you told me all that other stuff. Surely you don't still believe it? You can't expect *me* to believe it.'

'You have chosen to believe the bits you want to believe, and you broadcast them to my congregation without any problem. But you can't pick and choose what to believe, Lorna, none of us can. I can't anyway, not after what's happened. If I'd been in the pulpit today instead of you, I'd have told the truth.'

'You can't still intend to tell people about . . . what you told me?'

'About meeting the Devil? I do, and I will. I'm burying Catherine Craigie tomorrow. There'll be a big crowd. I'll make a start with them.'

'You can't, Gideon,' she said again. 'You simply mustn't.'

I opened the door for her. 'It's exactly what I must do. Goodbye, Lorna.'

'Gideon . . .'

'Goodbye, Lorna.'

She tried to touch me, but I shrank back. I could see the pain she was in, but she had brought it on herself. I looked away from her, and felt her pass by me into the porch.

'Gideon,' she said, 'I shall pray for you all day and all night if necessary. I'll pray that God makes you come to your senses. If you don't, if you persist in going down this insane path, then there's nothing more I can do for you. I won't even be able to defend you as a friend. You seem to have no regard for our friendship anyway. If you say the things in public that are on that tape, then you'll be on your own. The only possible thing in your defence will be that you are mentally ill. You certainly won't be fit to continue as a minister.'

Once again she was right, but she was right in such a wrong way. I closed the storm-doors against her or any further visitors, closed the inner door and went into my study to think through my plans for the morning.

XLII

The funeral was set for eleven o'clock. I was up early, carrying boxes and bags over to the church by eight. The day was warm, the sky clear except for some high white clouds which didn't seem to threaten rain, and there was a decent breeze blowing, for which I was grateful. The council gravediggers were already at work, opening up the Craigie lair. They use a wee mechanical digger these days, at least for the bulk of the task. It is less gracious, somehow less respectful than men working with spades, but more efficient. A big heap of earth was piling up to one side. There was a roll of fake grass lying ready, and boards and straps for lowering the coffin.

I'd ordered flowers from the best florist in town and they were delivered to the church at nine o'clock. The undertakers came with Catherine at ten-thirty. Some other flowers had been sent to the funeral parlour and were in the hearse. By that time I had laid out the various things I needed for the funeral to go as she'd wanted. All I was waiting for were the mourners, although I didn't think of them as mourners.

I didn't doubt for a second that she would get a good crowd. She was of one Monimaskit generation and had taught another two, and had left her mark on the town in many other ways. People would turn out for her.

At twenty-to-eleven the school party of twelve-year-olds arrived, escorted by several teachers, Gregor Wishaw and John Moffat among them. We shook hands. Gregor asked after my health. John looked awkward, said it was a sad day for Monimaskit. They went on into the church. Elsie appeared too, on her own. She slipped by me without a word while I was speaking to somebody else. Amelia came. So did Alan Straiton from the museum. Most people who had known Catherine appeared. By the time we were ready to start, there must have been nearly 200 in the kirk.

Shortly before eleven a tall, elegant man with silver hair, wearing an elegant black coat over an expensive-looking three-piece suit, approached me with his hand held out and introduced himself as Catherine's solicitor, Finlay Stewart.

'I must say, I'm looking forward to this,' he said. 'Rather typical of Miss Craigie to keep something up her sleeve till the end. You don't have a problem with it?'

'None,' I said. 'We were good friends. We didn't agree on everything, but . . .'

'No, I imagine you wouldn't. But I'm surprised you agreed on this.'

'I'm a very open-minded person, Mr Stewart,' I said. 'As you will find out in the next hour or so.'

'Jolly good,' he said, and passed on into the church.

The last person marching up the red gravel to the kirk door was Peter Macmurray. We did not acknowledge each other as he went in.

I took a last look towards the grave, now open to receive Catherine's remains, raised a hand to the gravediggers, who were having a cup of tea, and limped into the church and up the aisle to the coffin resting on its wheeled carriage. There were sprays of roses and chrysanthemums, her favourite flowers, spread on the coffin. I didn't go into the pulpit. I stood beside the coffin and from there I began my farewell to Catherine, and what would be my farewell to the Church – both this one and the wider one (the 'Church without walls', to use a phrase coined by the modernisers in the Kirk) – to friends and enemies, to the world. I remember precisely what I said that day, and this is it.

'I welcome you all,' I said. 'We are here to remember Catherine Craigie, to celebrate life, not just hers but all life, and to consign her body to the earth. I thank you for coming, even those of you, and there are one or two, who are here with bitterness in your hearts and malice in your minds.

'You will have noticed that you were not handed hymn books as you came in. You will have noticed that I have not begun with any mention of the Christ in whose name we usually gather in this place. You may also be wondering about the collection of objects laid out here at the front of the church. I'll come to them in a while.

'I very nearly didn't wear my dog-collar today. Catherine and I used to have arguments about it. She called me a hypocrite for wearing it. But this morning of all mornings I thought, why stop now? If I'd left it off she would have thought me a hypocrite for that too. She was a difficult person, whether by choice or by nature I'm not sure. She is well summed up by that good old Scots word "thrawn".

'If you knew Catherine you'll know why this is not going to be a religious service. The question you may be asking is, why is it happening here at all? Why did Catherine Craigie, who for the whole of her adult life had no time for the Kirk, no time for organised religion, no time for any kind of religion at all, why did she want her funeral to happen here, conducted by a minister inside a church?

'I can only tell you what she told me. We were friends for about ten years. We had our differences of opinion, but our friendship rose above them. We could argue for a whole evening and still like each other just as much at the end. Like each other more, in fact. And I admired her because she refused to give in to the illness which afflicted her for so long. When we discussed her death and her funeral, she said that she had a very deep feeling of being a part of Monimaskit, the town of her birth and her childhood, the place where she worked for thirty years as a teacher, the place whose history she researched, wrote and spoke about all her life. History was everything to her. It was a solid thing, a real thing, and she felt part of it. She didn't want to disappear from it. History, she believed, would outlive and outlast religion, but religion was also part of history. So, although she rejected the Church, she also understood its significance. Her family are buried here at the Old Kirk. She wanted to stay here too. Which is why we're here today.

'She liked graveyards a lot. She studied archaeology. She was interested in what humans built, and what they left behind – remains of all kinds, from standing stones to old buildings to gravestones. She told me she'd spent a lot of time having conversations with dead people in graveyards, and that she'd learned a lot from them. Don't think this is macabre or spooky. Don't think this is about ghosts. This is about real people like you and me, who lived and loved and died here and whose remains are all around us. Catherine didn't think we should tiptoe around them. She thought we should chat to them, find out who they were and what they did. It's not a bad idea. Next time you've got a spare ten minutes, walk round the outside of the kirk and read the names and dates of the people on the stones. You might be surprised what you find out.

'Catherine once said to me that she didn't want a eulogy. A eulogy, she said, is when one person brushes another's bad points under the carpet and makes out that they were a saint. Catherine wasn't a saint, she didn't believe in sainthood. Somebody who is here in this church told me something about her the other day. I don't know whether it was true or not and I don't care. It was said out of spite because the person who said it didn't like Catherine or her views on religion. The implication was that she was a wicked woman, a terrible sinner. But even if what I was told was true, it would mean only that Catherine was human. As Jesus said when the Pharisees brought an adulterous woman before him, "He that is without sin, let him first cast a stone at her." So if the individual in this church today has anything further to say on this matter, let him speak now.'

I looked around. Not a sound from anyone. I could not see Macmurray in the rows of faces. He did not reveal himself, either by word or by action.

'Well, if that's settled, I'm not going to say much more about Catherine. She wouldn't have wanted it. She was a good friend, a good teacher, and she believed neither in God nor ghosts nor fairies, but in people.

'She went to Mexico when she was a young woman, in the early 1960s. The Mexicans have a day they call *el Dìa de los Muertos*, the Day of the Dead. Again, it's not spooky, it's not morbid. It's a day of celebration. It's a mixture of Indian tradition and the Christianity that the Spanish brought to Mexico. Nowadays it's celebrated on All Saints' Day, the first of November. The Spanish moved it to this date in the Christian calendar to try to get rid of the native elements, but they failed. Maybe, like Catherine, the Indians found it hard to believe in saints, so they kept some of their own traditions going. The same thing happened here in Scotland with Hallowe'en, the end of the old Celtic year, but that's another story.

'What the Mexicans do on this day is honour their dead. They go and say hello to them, make them feel that they are not forgotten. They take them their favourite things – flowers, food, drinks, toys, photographs. They have picnics next to the graves of their loved ones and play music, sing songs, talk to them and talk about them. Sometimes they argue with them. There are sweets made in the shape of skeletons and skulls, and special bread with a toy skeleton baked inside it. If you're the one that bites the skeleton it's considered good luck. The Day of the Dead is not a sad or sorrowful day, it's a happy one. In a way, what the living people are saying is, we're not afraid of death, we accept that death is part of life, we accept that we are part of something much bigger than us.

'You get variations on this tradition throughout Central America. In Guatemala they make huge kites from bamboo and crêpe paper and fly them above the graves. The kites are a kind of line of communication between the living and the dead. Between earth and heaven if you like, or between the present and the past. Catherine was interested in the symbolism of that too.

'Something along those lines is what she wanted to happen today, and that's what we're going to try to make happen. Some of you might feel uncomfortable with this, but we have some young people from the Academy here, who I want to help me to fulfil Catherine's wishes.'

There had been, since my challenge to Macmurray, occasional sounds of disquiet, the shuffling of feet and creaking of pew-backs, a few mutterings and whisperings. I had warned Macmurray off, but I was surprised that nobody else was rising to protest. I had forgotten, of course, the overwhelming weight that bears down on most people who enter a church – the weight of years of learning not to disrupt, not to object, not to speak out against authority. As for Macmurray, I realised that, regardless of my pre-emptive strike, he might have decided to say nothing at all. He was not a popular man, and would not want to be seen as a Pharisee. Nor was he a fool: if he had come to observe, to take notes, to be a witness against me, then the further out of line I stepped without intervention from him, the better as far as he was concerned.

I was past caring about him. I asked the children to come up to the front of the kirk. I explained that in Mexico marigolds were the flowers most commonly used to decorate graves on the Day of the Dead, but Catherine had disliked their smell, which was why I had got her roses and chrysanthemums instead. There were a dozen kites. I handed out eleven and kept one for myself. They were not as big as Guatemalan ones, I said, but they would be fine for Monimaskit. There were also a number of drums, tambourines and rattles, some skeleton masks and some rolled up coloured paper streamers. I distributed all of these and lined the percussionists up behind the coffin.

We were almost ready to go. I said I was going to play some music. They might recognise the tune, but what mattered wasn't the tune but the mood. I told them a little about Mexican *mariachi*, its Spanish, African and Indian influences, its blend of traditional and modern instruments and its comic, often subversive lyrics. Catherine, I said, must have been making a joke when she chose this song, 'La Cucaracha', and this particular version of it, for her funeral. I read out some of the Spanish words, and how they roughly translated: *La cucaracha, la cucaracha, Ya no puede caminar; Porque no tiene, porque le falta, Marijuana que fumar*: the cockroach can no longer walk, because she doesn't have, because she lacks, some marijuana to smoke. *Ya murio la cucaracha, Ya la llevan a enterrar, Entre cuatro zopilotes Y un raton de sacristan*: the cockroach just died, and they carried her off to bury her, among four buzzards and the minister's mouse. And then I asked them to listen.

The kirk has a sound system, operated from a panel behind the pulpit. I'd already set up the CD Catherine had specified, with the volume turned up high. I walked over and hit the *play* button. 'La Cucaracha' is a daft, happy, easy tune. Even if you've never heard it before, you know it in seconds. And the *mariachi* sound – the trumpets and violins along with the five-stringed *vihuela* and the driving bass rhythm of the *guitarrón*, the wild shouts, laughs and whoops of the musicians – is such an outburst of life that you would have to have a very hard heart not to be uplifted by its mood. It sounded totally exotic in the Old Kirk, and totally joyous.

After a couple of verses I paused the machine. I would play it again, I said, and to the sound of the cockroach's song Catherine would be taken from the church down to the grave, and the rest of us would follow. And from the waiting percussionists I wanted as much drumming and rattling and tambourine-bashing as possible. They were not to be embarrassed, but to take their cue from the song. I wanted laughter and chatter. Catherine would have loathed a staid, sombre funeral. When we were outside, I would tell those who were holding kites what they were to do.

I restarted the crazy happiness of 'La Cucaracha'. The men from the undertakers in their black suits and white shirts didn't even blink. In their trade they must learn early not to baulk at the unconventional, whether in a church or anywhere else. They wheeled the coffin to the door, loaded it into the back of the hearse, and the car slowly drove the fifty or so yards down the red-gravelled lane to the grave. Behind came my troop of celebrants. The children didn't need much encouragement to make a noise. The song infected them, and soon there was a competition going to see who could make the most racket. A couple of lads wearing masks began to dance in time to the ragged beat being put out by their companions. There were a few shrill imitations of the Mexican cries on the recording. With the yellow and red kites being held like gaudy birds waiting for release, the procession did begin to sound and look, if not Mexican, certainly not Scottish. We were losing our reserve. Even some of the adults were smiling, pointing, swaying, taking jaunty wee half-steps. Others, on the other hand, looked on stonily, like Edinburgh ratepayers forced to attend some avant-garde Fringe performance involving naked flesh. But even these followed the coffin. In the lobby, I stopped to pick up the last box of items for distribution at the grave.

We formed a large circle all around the open lair. Nobody, as far as I could see, had stalked off in disgust. Like those worthy Edinburgh bodies, they doubtless didn't want to miss anything that might affront them still further. Yet nothing had been particularly outrageous or offensive. It just wasn't what was expected.

The coffin was moved on to struts placed across the grave, and straps were passed under it. Usually there are cords attached to the coffin for relatives or friends to hold as the coffin is lowered, but all the weight is really taken by the straps. The undertakers and gravediggers would handle these. When the funeral director had asked me about cord-holders, I'd said, 'There's to be only one. If you can supply one strong cord attached to the coffin, that will be sufficient.'

From the open door of the kirk came further *mariachi* tunes as the CD played on. Meanwhile, I organised the children. 'Percussionists,' I said, 'keep percussing. Kite-flyers, come with me. Can we have some adults too, please, to help get these kites into the air?'

A wave of unease went round the crowd. I could see some folk wanting to join in, others holding them back with their disapproval. I led the eleven children with kites away from the crowd. Elsie was a foot away from me. 'You're making a fool of yourself, Gideon,' I heard her say. I ignored her. 'Come on,' I said to the people around her. 'If you don't want to do it for me, or for Catherine, do it for the kids. Help them to get their kites flying.'

A couple of younger men that I didn't know broke away, and they were followed by another. They teamed up with different children, and soon we had two, three, four, half a dozen kites sailing in the breeze, their long tails stretching and snaking. I glanced at the crowd. A kite is a wonderful thing: if there is a kite in the air people can't help looking at it, and if they look at it they can't help willing it to stay up. All eyes were on us as we hoisted another, and another, and another. The children unwound the strings and spread themselves out so that the kites wouldn't get tangled up. Some of them began to make them dive and leap in the air. I heard laughter and even a cheer from the crowd by the grave. As each kite went up the drums and tambourines and rattles banged and shook in a welcoming fanfare. I hadn't planned that: the children had intuitively entered into the spirit of the occasion. In another minute we had all the kites, including mine, flying high above the graves of the Old Kirk.

I asked the children to come back in among the crowd and to pass the strings of the kites to anybody who wanted a shot. Then I walked back to the head of the grave and, with the help of one of the gravediggers, tied the handle of my kite to the cord attached to Catherine's coffin. I let it go, the cord went taut, held. Catherine, the one and only cord-holder, was now also the twelfth kite-flyer.

I said, 'We're ready now to let Catherine down into the ground.'

The men stepped forward. Four of them took the strain on the straps while a fifth slid the struts away. Then, with the kite-string rubbing lightly against the edge of the grave, but with the kite still bravely dancing above us, the coffin was lowered.

I had a sheet of Blu-tack with me, and I handed it to the children with streamers and asked them to stick them to the great family stone and two smaller ones that bore upon them the names of three previous generations of Craigies. At ground level the breeze wasn't strong enough to make the streamers really stream, but they rustled and flapped a little. I put the flowers around the stones too, and I took from my box the selection of sweets that I'd bought from Jim Currie and spread them out on the nearest flat stone. There were toffees, wine gums and other sweets, but the main item was a whole box of Skull Crushers, strawberry and cream flavoured chocolates shaped like skulls, bad for the teeth and stomach no doubt, but perfect for my present purpose. I invited the children, and then everybody else, to help themselves. I ate a skull myself. The children didn't need much persuading, but most of the adults in the crowd stayed where they were.

Then I was aware of a movement among them, of people parting to let through a silver-haired man in a three-piece suit. He approached the flat gravestone, and the kids gathered round it felt his presence and stood back. With a sly smile on his face Finlay Stewart reached out his long white fingers, delicately extracted a skull from the box and popped it in his mouth. He gave me a look of intense boyish satisfaction and slipped back into the crowd again.

I had the last two items in my pocket: a miniature of Islay malt whisky and the plug of cannabis I'd taken from Catherine's house. I held them up for all to see. 'Catherine,' I said, 'enjoyed a dram. It was one of the things that kept her going. She appreciated a good malt, but she also hated waste, which is why she's only getting a miniature just now.' I dropped the bottle into the grave. 'And she also enjoyed a smoke. It was illegal but it gave her relief from the pain she suffered. Wherever she's gone, she won't be in pain any more, and there won't be any laws against marijuana, so she can take this with her too.' I dropped it in. 'For the rest of you, there will be tea and coffee and sandwiches in the church hall, and there is also some whisky for those who would like to raise a glass to Catherine. You kite-flyers and musicians will have to go back to school fairly soon. Your teachers will no doubt tell you when it's time to go. Meanwhile, you're welcome to join us in the hall, or to stay out here. Please take the kites and instruments and masks away with you. They're yours to keep and share with your friends. Use them again. And remember, whenever you're near this place, what went on here today. Have you enjoyed yourselves?'

A thin chorus of assent went up. They still weren't sure if this was allowed.

'That's what Catherine Craigie wanted,' I said. 'You were never taught by her, most of you probably never met her, but I hope you'll always remember her name. Maybe, even today, she was trying to teach us something.

'Friends, there is no benediction, no blessing that I can give you. That is not what this is about. I said I would bury Catherine and I have buried her. And now there is something else I must do. I never got to speak to her about the astonishing things that have happened to me in the last couple of weeks. She wouldn't have believed me if I had. But the time has come for me to speak of these things. If you wish to hear, come with me to the church hall and I will tell you what happened to me in those days when you thought I was drowned in the river.

'I said back there in the church that Catherine didn't believe in ghosts or fairies or God. Neither did I until two weeks ago. No, I did not believe in God. I did not believe that there was any life but this life, any world but this world. But in this I was wrong. I believe now that there is another world beyond ours, a world beyond death, the strangeness and wonderfulness of which we can only guess at. How do I know this? I know it because for those three days I was missing, I had a glimpse of that world. I walked and talked with somebody from that world. I walked and talked with the Devil, and if you come with me to the hall I will tell you about him.'

And as I was speaking, and as I raised my voice to tell them this, and as I raised my eyes above their looks of puzzlement and incredulity, I saw him again: my Devil, walking among the gravestones in his black trousers and black polo-shirt. I saw him standing over by the far wall, watching our proceedings. He moved so smoothly along the wall he might have been gliding. I strained to see if that was indeed the case, and I saw his feet, and they were wearing my old boots. And I saw him smile at me and half-raise a hand in a wave. I waved back, but a second later he was gone, and I saw him no more. And then I myself was moving, not gliding but hurrying as fast as my limp would allow me, towards the church hall on the other side of the kirk, with the press and din of the crowd at my heels, and one voice rising above that commotion, the voice of Peter Macmurray, calling me a blasphemer and a false shepherd, an atheist and a hypocrite, denouncing me to my flock and crying down on my head the vengeance of the Lord, and I knew that like Lorna he was right, but right in such a wrong way, and I limped on to the hall so that I could get ahead of him and of them all, so that I could get on to the platform at the far end, where I could tell them what had happened to me and why I could no longer be their minister.

XLIII

I do not need to write here what I said. I have already written it. I told them everything that I have recorded here. I mean everything. I told them about the Stone, how it had appeared to me back at the start of the year, and how I had known it was a sign but had had no idea what it meant. I told them that I had never, since the day I first came to Monimaskit in the hope of being chosen as the new minister – from long before that, in fact, before even I was a student of Divinity at Edinburgh – I had never believed in the existence of God. I was sorry to confess this to them now, but I had to tell the truth. The hall was thick with silence. Tea, coffee, whisky, sandwiches, cakes, nothing was touched. I looked out on a sea of gazing, uncomprehending faces. Now that the moment had arrived, I felt liberated and full of hope, and yet also, before those faces, strangely powerless.

I told them next what had happened when I fell into the Black Jaws, about being rescued by the man in the cave, how he had tended and fed me, and how I had come to know that he was none other than the person sometimes called Satan. The Devil. I described what he looked like. I said I had just seen him in the graveyard, but he had disappeared. I told how my leg had been broken, and how he had mended it with his finger of fire. There was laughter, snorts of disgust. Somebody said, 'You're drunk, man.' Another voice said, 'Aye, or he's been smoking that stuff he put in her grave.' No, I told them, I was completely sober. My head had never been clearer. I had seen the Devil's power but I had ended up neither fearing nor hating him, but pitying and loving him. Were we not told to love the sinner but hate the sin? Who could be a greater sinner than that fallen angel? None of us was without sin. I, their minister, was a sinner. I used to say, as a joke, that being a minister didn't make you a bad person. Being a sinner didn't make you a bad person either. We had all sinned. 'What have you done then?' a voice called. 'Apart from lying and cheating, what sins have you committed?' I took a deep breath and answered. It was all over now anyway. I had coveted my neighbour's wife, I said. Worse than that, I had made love to her. My best friend's wife. Even while I was mourning my own dead wife, whom I had not loved enough, I had had sex with Elsie Moffat in my own bedroom in the manse, in the very bed where my wife and I had slept. I saw Elsie below me turn white, shake her head, put her fists to her temples, I heard her shouting, 'No, no, no.' I saw John beside her, yelling, swearing at me, calling me a liar, sick, insane. He started towards me, but Elsie held him back. She began to drag him from the hall. He saw some of the children from the school, I saw them, their gaping mouths, he could not attack me, and now it was John that was leading Elsie from the hall. I shouted after them that I was sorry, but I had to tell the truth. The crowd swelled and ebbed below me. Disbelief, mockery. I saw Amelia coming to the front, shouting at me to stop, to get down off the platform and leave with her. 'You're ill,' she said. She turned to the crowd. 'Can't you see he's ill?' I denied it. I'm not ill, I said, I'm not insane. Everything I was telling them was the absolute truth. I told how I had walked for hours down the tunnel, how I had come upon the hatch beyond which was the boiling hell of the earth's core. I told of the conversations I'd had with the Devil. It was he who had put the Stone in Keldo Woods. He watched us from the windows of the other world, he knew everything we did, and God watched too. But where was God? The Devil hadn't seen him. God had gone missing. The Devil was tired, he was sick of what he was supposed to do, he was like you and me, a being without purpose, without hope. Everything had gone wrong with the grand design, the plan. There was no plan any more. That was what I had learned in my three days with the Devil. There was no plan. There was no redemption, no salvation, no system of debts and payments. But there *was* another life. There was more to come. That was why I could no longer remain as minister of Monimaskit. I had to find out more about what was to come and to do that I had to go away. I had to go and meet with the Devil again.

I saw the faces, angry and pitying and confused. They were listening but they weren't hearing at all. Some people were leaving, others were laughing, jeering or shouting abuse, and the rest had turned their backs and were talking amongst themselves, and eating and drinking as if that were the best way to restore normality. Finlay Stewart, the lawyer, came up to me; I bent down from the platform, and he said, 'I was with you outside by the grave, Mr Mack, but you're out on a limb now,' he was smiling but there was a mournfulness about the smile as if he were telling a client that his case was hopeless. 'You know where I am,' he said. Then he was gone and others were pressing in upon me. The atmosphere was heavy and dense with noise, I was suffocating with it. I looked to the other end of the hall, searching for space, for fresh air, and I saw him again, he had come in and was standing, smiling, waiting, in his black clothes and my boots, and I shouted, 'Look, there he is. There at the back!' But by then nobody was paying me any attention. I jumped down into them and crashed through the bodies towards him, I saw him slipping out of the door and called on him to wait, but he did not wait. Nobody stopped me. Outside I saw him again, he was striding or gliding across the grass, threading a way through the upright stones, and there was Catherine's kite still flying, the workmen had untied it before they filled in the grave, they had used an iron staple to pin the end of the string to the ground and the kite was flying up there, communicating or not communicating with the dead, and there he went, down the red gravel path to the road, heading for the manse, and I was pitching after him, going as fast as I could but not able to catch up. He was teasing me, I knew this wasn't the time, that I still had much to endure, but he had got me away from that crowd. I made for the manse, my place of refuge, my shelter from the storm, and I got in and I was alone. He had vanished. I closed the doors, and when the doorbell rang and the phone rang and the knocks came at the door and at the windows I did not hear them, I was safe in the heart of this house, in my study, safe from the world, I had told the truth and now all I wanted was to move on, and to see my Devil again.

XLIV

There is not much more to be said. It is January now. I have spent the days and nights of this winter writing everything down in as much detail as I can recall. It was obvious to me, as it must have been to others, that there was no going back after what I had said and done on the day of Catherine's funeral. My mistake, if it was a mistake, was that I did not write this testament first, before I spoke. Had I done so, if people could have read this full and honest account rather than heard me announce it amid the din and confusion of that day, then perhaps they might have reacted with more open minds. As it was, it was too easy for them to dismiss me as a madman. It is for this reason that I have laboured over this manuscript. A prophet, Christ said, is not without honour save in his own country. If this story of mine reaches further afield, perhaps others will recognise the truth of it.

There were those who did try to honour me, even in Monimaskit. Having admitted to being on speaking terms with the Devil, perhaps I should not have been surprised at how many others came out of the woodwork to tell me of their own dealings with him. A number of men – they were all men – came to the door of the manse wishing to swap experiences. Some of them were dangerous-looking, wild and unkempt, some neat, clean and unsmiling, but all looked as though they were no longer, if they ever had been, at ease in the company of others. That much I was able to empathise with: nonetheless, politely but firmly, I turned them all away. They were, without exception, mentally disturbed, religiously deluded or wilfully deceitful. A few minutes' conversation with these men was always sufficient to demonstrate to me, who really had met the Devil, that they had no real conception of who or what he was. They were merely playing a game. The saddest thing was that most of them did not know it.

I had letters too, scrawled semi-legibly on scraps of paper, daubed with the supposed symbols of Satan – geometric designs, the number 666 and so forth. These I burned without answering (often there was no return address anyway). After the initial flurry of interest had died away, I was no longer troubled by these visitors and missives.

I was besieged by others, though, representatives of that good old Scottish institution, the school of common sense. With impressive speed, Peter Macmurray had written a report of my behaviour at Catherine's funeral and formally submitted it to Presbytery. My Kirk Session, which was party to this action, let me know that they could not allow me to conduct any more services or indeed any other business on behalf of the Church until I was 'well again'. John Gless and a group of elders called to tell me this. My response was that I was not ill, but I agreed it would be wrong for me to continue in my duties knowing I did not have the confidence of the Session. In fact I no longer had any desire for those duties. I received notification from Presbytery before the week was out that, in my interests as well those of the Kirk, I was suspended until the substance of the allegations made against me could be properly assessed. If it was decided that I had committed censurable offences, then a trial by libel would follow.

All this wearied me. So, too, did the correspondence and phone calls that began to pour in from 121 George Street. A minister who had settled down at Carnoustie to play golf until summoned to God's great clubhouse was brought out of retirement to conduct services in the Old Kirk, while the Session managed the dispensation of pastoral care as best it could. I was sorry for the difficulties I caused them, but it was made clear that I could not be involved with the workings of the parish. The Kirk, usually a cumbersome beast, can show remarkable agility when it is threatened, and I was perceived to be a threat.

I was not, however, forced to leave the manse, and this meant that they knew where to find me. By 'they' I mean the would-be good Samaritans who imagined I had fallen among thieves and lay half dead by the roadside. Among those who tried to assist me was a woman who came from Edinburgh offering 'manse support'. There was also an attempt to subject me to counselling. I refused these approaches, just as I refused the attentions of Amelia Wishaw, who tried to persuade me to defer to her medical wisdom. I was neither physically nor mentally ill. It would have made life a lot easier for everybody if I had been.

So I stayed in Monimaskit and learned to live the life of an outcast. I had little or no communication with erstwhile friends. It would be wrong to say that this was because my friends cut me off: I was guilty of far more cutting than they. To begin with, indeed, they would not leave me alone. Apart from Amelia, who repeatedly asserted that I had suffered a nervous breakdown. I was also bothered by Lorna Sprott, who came offering spiritual balm. Considering the terms on which we had last parted, it was generous of her to come at all. I let her in out of pity. She had heard about Catherine's funeral, of course. She lamented what I had done. If, she said, it was true that she had used me in her address in church – 'I'm willing to concede that, Gideon. I shouldn't have said those things without checking with you first' – then I had used those children at the funeral; exploited them with toys and sweets; made them a shield with which to protect myself as I played out my irresponsible bit of theatre. But in spite of all that, Lorna said, in spite of the crisis I had brought upon myself, she would stand by me if I would only acknowledge my mistakes, my failings, my betrayal of Christ. I heard her out, but I said I had betrayed nobody, and Christ least of all, since he was never involved. She looked horrified, yet again. She wanted us to pray together. I was beyond prayer, I said. She began to pray on her own, as if to drive demons from me, and at that point I made her leave. I have not seen her since. For all I know, she is praying for me still.

I received a letter from Finlay Stewart a week after the funeral. He trusted – interesting lawyerish word, clearly he did no such thing – that I was recovered from the fascinating events he had witnessed. He had arranged with a stonemason to have Catherine's name and dates added to the family stone. It might interest me to know, he wrote, that she had left about half of her estate, which was substantial, to several different charities, and the rest to establish a trust bearing her name that would provide funds for the protection and upkeep of ancient monuments and historic buildings in the parish of Monimaskit. He concluded by stating that he was at my service if there was anything he could do for me. Unlike most of the correspondence I was receiving, I kept this letter.

I made the occasional visit to my mother, but now I was tolerated rather than welcomed at the care home. Mrs Hodge never seemed to be around when I went. Betty no longer offered me tea. Only my mother's attitude to me was completely unaltered. For this I was grateful, but it underlined the uselessness of continuing to see her. It was one more charade scarcely worth keeping up. I have not gone there for weeks.

I went out less and less often. I drove to Dundee one day to buy a pair of boots to replace the ones the Devil had taken from me, and that was my longest excursion in three months. In Monimaskit I would go down to the High Street to buy a few things for the house, but even to eat seemed a tedious inconvenience. I have found that I can exist well enough on three bowls of porridge every day, supplemented with the odd piece of fruit, an egg, and a few whiskies at night. When I was out I could feel people looking at me, I knew they were shaking their heads in the way they would shake them at sight of somebody with a terrible disability. Sometimes children shouted at me before capering away up the street, squawking and gibbering as they imagined a lunatic would. I took to going for walks at night, but even then I would come across groups of teenagers drinking and smoking in the street, sometimes in the graveyard. The girls shrank back from me, or ran giggling and shrieking: 'Look out, it's Mystic Mack!' The boys watched me with surly cold eyes, or abused me with foul language. These night-time encounters only added to my already ragged reputation.

I tried to maintain my appearance, washing and ironing my own clothes as I have done since Jenny died, but the more I remained in the house the less reason there was for doing this. One afternoon, not long before Christmas, I ventured out to get my hair cut. The barber's shop was empty when I went in. Henry, the barber, directed me straight to the chair before he realised who I was. He was normally a talkative soul, but during the next ten minutes he spoke not a word, except to check with me if the cut was good enough and, when he'd finished, to ask me for five pounds. The silence lay between us like a sheet of glass. I handed over the money and went for my coat.

'Thank you,' I said. 'Goodbye.'

But as I went to the door suddenly words burst from him: 'I'm sorry about your troubles, Mr Mack. It's a terrible place, a wee toun like this, when folk think ye hae ideas above your station.'

'Is that what they think of me, Henry?' I asked.

'Aye,' he said. 'The ones that ken ye are right eager to knock ye doon, and the rest have forgotten ye exist.'

'And what do you think yourself?' I said. 'Have I got ideas above my station?'

'I dinna ken,' he said. 'Ye aye seemed a decent man to me. They say ye claim to hae seen the Devil and so forth, and I'm no a religious man so I couldna comment, but it seems to me if onybody can see the Devil then it's a minister.'

'Thank you, Henry,' I said. 'That's a very sensible view.'

'Aye, maybe,' he said, but I could see him beginning to worry about it already, on account of my having approved it. So I went out of the door, and that was the last time I had my hair cut.

My friend was certainly present in the town during this period, but for how long at any one time I do not know. I assume that he came and went in that nervous, restless way of his, but what he was doing remains a mystery to me, for he never approached me, nor did he allow me to get close to him. I saw him almost every time I was out. He was always at a distance. After I left Henry's that day, I spotted him entering Boots. I hobbled in to catch him, but he must have slipped away down one aisle while I was going up another. I saw him standing outside Jim Currie's one morning, reading a newspaper, but by the time I had crossed the road and reached the shop he had vanished. Once I thought I saw his face peering from the window of a bus as it drove out of town. And once, from an upstairs window of the manse, I saw him in the kirkyard, admiring the newly carved lettering on the Craigie stone. I rushed down the stairs to join him, but when I got there he was gone.

Another day I felt the need for some fresh air and went for a walk by the harbour, and I fancied I saw him going into the Luggie. There is only one door to this pub, not counting the fire escape at the back, so I followed him in. It was approaching three in the afternoon, and the bar was closed. I had never been in it before, but experienced a sense of *déjà-vu* when I entered, and then realised that I was remembering the installation from Bill Winnyford's exhibition. The barman was there, wiping down surfaces, and one customer was finishing off his drink, but it wasn't my friend, it was Chae Middleton.

'Sorry, we're closed,' the barman said.

'Did somebody just come in here?' I said.

Chae looked up at me, half-cut. 'Aye,' he said. 'You did.'

'Before me,' I said.

'Naebody afore and naebody since,' said the barman. 'Come on, Chae, time to go.'

'I'm going, I'm going,' Chae said. 'It's no enough that ye pull ministers frae the drink, but they have to come and dae the same to you.'

The barman frowned at me. 'Is that who you are?' he said. I acknowledged that it was. 'But I didn't come to get Chae,' I said. 'I thought I saw someone come in. A friend.'

The barman made a dumb-show of looking round the place. 'There's just the three of us here,' he said.

He was right, of course, but I had to go and check in the men's toilet before I was convinced.

'This friend,' the barman said when I returned, 'what does he look like?'

'Tall,' I said. 'Thin. Black hair. Black clothes.'

'Aye, he's been here,' the man said. 'No the day, like. When was he in, Chae?'

'Last week,' Chae said. 'Or the week afore. The young fellow.'

'He wasna young,' the barman said. 'Sixty if he was a day.'

'Och, away,' Chae said. 'Nae mair than thirty.'

'Ye should get glesses,' the barman said. 'He was fit-looking, but when ye seen him close up, definitely older.'

A thrill went through me. 'Did you speak to him?' I asked.

'Aye, that's how I ken it's the same guy. He was asking efter ye.'

'After me?'

'Aye. "How's your minister?" he says. I says you were nae minister of mine. Never came in here and nothing to do wi me. He wanted to ken if you were recovered and all that. I put him on to Chae. It was Chae he wanted.'

'He bought me a drink,' Chae said. 'He wanted to see the man that saved the minister and he bought me a drink.'

'What did you talk about?' I asked.

'Oh, he didna stay. He just bought me the drink and then he left. I didna like him.'

'He was polite enough,' the barman said. 'But there was something no canny aboot him.'

'In what way?'

'Here, what's wi aw these questions?' Chae said. 'I'm awa hame.' He stood up. 'I'm no fond of ministers in pubs. They're like ministers in boats. Unlucky.' He started towards the door.

'Chae,' I asked. 'Did you ever see him before? Up the river, for example.'

'Up the river?' he said angrily. 'Up the river? That's where I found you. I never see nothing when I go up the river.'

He staggered out. I was going to follow, but the barman called me back.

'I'd leave it alane if I were you,' he said. 'He's well fou. He was aye a good drinker but he taks a lot mair since that business wi you. He's in here all the time these days. Going to ruin fast. What can ye do, eh?'

'You could try not serving him,' I said.

'Aye, you look efter your affairs and I'll mind mine,' the barman said. 'By all accounts mine are in a lot better shape. It's because of you Chae's in the state he's in. Now I'll thank you to leave the premises, it's well past closing.'

I went back out on to the street. There was no sign of Chae, nor of my friend. I didn't understand why he would go to the Luggie and speak with Chae, but not come to the manse and speak with me. I began to be suspicious of him. Why was he hanging around, yet why was he staying away? He was toying with me. I didn't like that. Was it not he himself who had said 'no more games'?

His presence, or his absence, haunted me day and night. Even if I hadn't seen him in these fleeting glimpses, he was constantly in my thoughts as I wrote these pages, and as I write them now. Furthermore, I could not take a step without being conscious of him. Every lurch that I took reminded me of the 'operation' he had performed on my leg. I began to dwell on that too. What if he had done more than he said? What if in some fateful way he had taken something of me and kept it for himself? Would that explain the bond that I felt with him, the desire to be with him again? This has troubled me greatly in the last weeks.

There is one other thing, which might or might not be connected. Since my plunge from the cliff, I have hardly been affected by any tremors or twitches in my left arm. That niggling physical rumour of devastation, that thing that I long thought of as God's ticking time-bomb, is – almost – completely gone.

In December I had notice from Presbytery and from 121 George Street that the allegations against me had been assessed and found to be of substance, and that a trial by libel would therefore follow. I wrote back, saying that I would not contest any such trial, but that I could not retract the things I had said nor in any way recant, since I had told nothing but the truth. If I was tried I would say the same again. I was willing to demit my status as a minister if that would help, but I would neither change my story nor keep silent about it. The response from Presbytery was swift: it was not acceptable for me simply to demit and walk away from the situation I had created. The integrity of the Kirk itself was undermined by such serious errors as I had admitted. Awkward and embarrassing though it was for all concerned, the trial would have to proceed. A date would be set as soon as was feasible in the New Year.

Christmas Eve came. I heard the ringing of the kirk bell and opened the study window. Soon the carols from the watchnight service drifted through the dark to me. I closed the window and shut them out. I spent Christmas Day writing, sleeping, writing. Nobody came near me, and I did not venture forth. I waited in a kind of vague anticipation for the doorbell to ring. I was hoping for him, of course. But he did not come.

The old year rolled over and died and became the new one. No tall dark stranger first-footed me. Nobody came at all. I remembered that first run through Keldo Woods, seeing the Stone, the start of everything. A whole year gone by. It was months since I had been out there, since before my fall into the Black Jaws. On the fourth day of January, a Sunday, I resolved to go again.

I went to the garage and got into the car, which I'd not used for weeks. The tyres looked half-deflated, and when I turned the key in the ignition nothing happened for a second. Then something caught, and the engine coughed into a kind of life. The battery was clearly run down. When I took my foot off the accelerator the engine threatened to die. I set off cautiously, playing the accelerator against the clutch until the car sounded a little healthier, and headed down the coast road. It was a grey, miserable afternoon. A smirr of rain hung like a veil: a two o'clock gloom that would soon slide into darkness. The road was empty of traffic.

The Moffats' house was on the road a short distance before the Keldo Woods car park, and when I reached that point something made me turn in. I felt bad about John and Elsie. I felt bad about the girls. I couldn't make amends but maybe I could say I was sorry and wish them well.

It was John who came to the back door. He had a bottle of beer in his hand. The smile on his face froze when he saw me, then vanished. I thought he might take a swing at me. He stood with his free fist clenching and unclenching.

'You've got a fucking nerve,' he said.

'I came to apologise,' I said. 'And to wish you a happy New Year.'

'You can fuck off is what you can do,' he said. He slammed the door shut. I heard the key turn in the lock.

I stood there in the drizzle, which was coming on heavier by the minute. I could neither stay nor go away. What had I expected? Then I heard raised voices inside: John and Elsie arguing. She would have asked him who was at the door. He would have told her.

I went back to the car, got in, sat for a minute. Nobody came out. I started the engine, swung the car round ready to leave. Then the back door of the house opened and John was standing roaring at me. 'FUCK OFF! OR I'LL GET THE FUCKING POLICE!'

I drove on the few hundred yards to the entrance to the woods, parked and started to walk.

It was darker among the trees, and the ground was soggy. I had put on my new boots, and they were stiff and unyielding, and my limp slowed me down still further. Getting to where the Stone was seemed to take far longer than I remembered. But it was still there. I saw it in the half-light, with its rounded top like a shoulder hunched against the rain. I was about to step off the path and make my way across the grassy tummocks when I saw a movement, a figure beside the Stone.

I called out, 'Hello!' The figure stepped away, retreating into the trees beyond. It was him, I knew it was him. I shouted on him to wait. My feet slipped on the grass and sank into water-logged divots as I went after him. I reached the Stone. Nobody. I screamed at him, 'Why won't you wait? Speak to me. What is it you want from me?' I pushed on a few more yards, but I would never catch him, and in his black clothes he was almost invisible. I turned back to the Stone, thought I caught a flash of something or somebody back on the path, then nothing. He was teasing me again. I clung to the Stone and suddenly all my unspoken pain and anger and misery came pouring out of me. I went down on my knees. I didn't care about the soaking ground. I howled and howled and howled. I beat my fists against the Stone until they were raw. There was no sympathy out there in the woods, no give, no mercy, no redemption. That was all I wanted, but there was none. Everything I had ever done had failed, had been a total waste. I'd had enough.

I don't know how long I was there, but it was quite dark when I got to my feet and found my way back to the path. I was drenched, and very cold. I tripped and stumbled back to the car park, falling several times. When I finally reached the car I was shivering so much I could hardly get the key in the ignition. Thankfully the battery had been charged enough earlier, and the engine started. I drove home and changed out of my wet things. I lit the fire in the study and stretched out on the carpet in front of it. I fell asleep.

I woke to the sound of something tapping on glass. I thought it was the rain getting heavier, or a branch knocking against the window. But it persisted with a regularity that made me sit up and come fully awake. I went to the window. His face was pressed against the glass.

I unlocked the window and pushed it up, but it would not open enough to admit him. 'Go round to the back door,' I said, and closed the window again. I feared that this was more of his teasing, that he wouldn't be there. But he was, soaked to the skin, as wet and shivery as I had been earlier. I brought him into the kitchen, hugged him. I made him strip off his clothes and fetched him a towel so he could dry himself. His skin was white, and apart from his legs he was almost hairless. His feet were ordinary human feet. His body looked thin and weak as he towelled it but I knew it was immensely strong. I stuffed his wet boots – my old boots – with newspaper and placed them in front of the boiler next to mine, and I hung his clothes on the pulley. I found him a set of my own clothes – black, because I thought he would prefer them black – and he put them on. I made him a mug of tea, and he sat at the table and drank it. I was anxious for him, but also I was happy that at last he had come, and that I could do these things for him.

I said, 'Why did you run from me in the woods? Why didn't you wait at the Stone for me?'

'Someone was coming,' he said. 'It wasn't safe.'

'Is that why you've stayed away?' I said. 'Because of other people?'

'Yes,' he said. 'They've been watching you. But we're safe now.'

I didn't say anything else. There was no need, there was nothing to say.

Later, we drank whisky in front of the fire in the study. He looked over my books, plucking one from the shelves now and then, replacing it. He took down *The Secret Commonwealth* by Robert Kirk.

'I remember this,' he said. 'I sent it to your father during the war.'

'*You* sent it to him?' I said.

'Yes,' he said. 'We used to run into each other on walking trips in the thirties.'

'In the Trossachs,' I said. 'Around Aberfoyle.'

'That's it,' he said. 'Did he tell you?'

'You know he did,' I said. 'But he didn't tell me he'd met the Devil.'

'Perhaps he didn't,' he said.

'He said you were foolish,' I said. 'Or at least, he said it was a foolish man who sent him the book.'

He laughed. 'Well, he thought the world was full of fools.'

He opened the front cover. 'Look,' he said, 'I wrote something. Here are my initials.'

I took the book from him. *To remind you of better days and other worlds*, I read. 'Your initials are my initials.'

'Yes. A coincidence, isn't it?'

'Is it?'

He smiled and said nothing.

'What do they stand for in your case?' I said. 'What's your name?'

'I have many names,' he said. 'But in this instance the letters stand for Gil Martin. The "G",' he added, 'as in Gideon, or God.'

'Gil Martin,' I said.*

'In Gaelic it means a fox,' he said.

'Why did you give the book to my father?' I asked.

'For the reason I wrote down. To remind him of better days and

* My informant Dr Hugh Haliburton tells me that this is the very name given by James Hogg to the mysterious, devil-like figure that haunts the anti-hero of his novel *The Memoirs and Confessions of a Justified Sinner*. I have never read this book, nor, it seems, despite his degree in literature, had Gideon Mack. At least, I assume that, had he done so, he would himself have noticed and remarked upon this curious point. – P.W.

other worlds. He was in the middle of a terrible war. We'd had good times in the Trossachs.'

'What about us?' I said. 'When will we go away?'

'Soon,' he said. 'In a few weeks. I have things to attend to.'

I picked up the whisky bottle and made to refill his glass, but he put his hand over it.

'Not for me,' he said, 'I must be going.'

I was shocked. 'You're not staying?'

'I can't. Too much to do.' It sounded horribly familiar, the same excuse, the same phrases, that I used when I wanted to be on my own. He saw my disappointment. 'But I did want to see you. I've looked in before, from the garden, I've watched Menteith and Cathcart and the others, but I wanted to come in and spend some time with you. You've looked pretty lonely, of late, sitting in here on your own.'

'I like this room,' I said. 'I'll be sorry to leave it.'

'It's just a room,' he said. 'One minister's study's much like another, if you ask me. I didn't mean just this room, though. You've been lonely a long time.'

'I had no choice,' I said.

He shook his head. 'You always had choices,' he said.

I asked him to stay, but he refused. 'No,' he said, 'but you must. You have to finish your masterpiece.' He smiled, disarming that last word of the slightly sarcastic tone in which he'd said it. 'When you're done, then we'll meet again. But in the meantime, remember this evening. I am with you in spirit, if not in person. I'll always be with you, Gideon.'

We went back to the kitchen. He took the balls of newspaper from his boots, which were, however, still wet. I would have given him my new ones, but they were just as bad. I told him to keep the clothes he had on. He saw his old trainers by the door and he pointed at them and laughed.

'To remind you of other worlds,' he said. 'And better days to come.'

We hugged again, and before he stepped out into the rain I reminded him of his promise to meet on Ben Alder. 'Yes,' he said, 'we're going to have an adventure, you and I. An awfully big adventure.'

Then he was gone. I went back to the study and put more coal on the fire. There was a fire burning in me too – a dry, smokeless, crackling fire of anticipation and desire. I filled up my glass with whisky. I picked up the Robert Kirk book and sat turning its pages, not really reading them. I was cheered by his visit, saddened at his departure. But I had not much more to write, and then we would be together again.

And now I am almost finished, and the time has come. Better days and other worlds are waiting. I long for them. The fire burns in me still, fiercer and brighter. *Nec tamen consumebatur.* Tomorrow I leave Monimaskit, never to return. All that remains is for me to take these pages with me, read through them and correct them one last time, then leave them for posterity. They contain nothing but the true history of my life, and I am confident that at some future time, by means unknown to me, the truth will make its way to the surface of this troubled world and be recognised for what it is by those who have eyes to see.

There is a deep satisfaction in having reached this point. Nothing matters any more except that I have reached it. I feel young and I feel old. I feel as though I am standing on the edge of eternity.

END OF THE TESTAMENT

Epilogue

What can this work be? Can it be anything other than the ramblings of a mind terminally damaged by a cheerless upbringing, an unfulfilled marriage, unrequited love, religious confusion and the stress and injury of a near-fatal accident? Who would dare, in this day and age, to suggest that Gideon Mack was, as he maintained to the end, telling the truth?

It was in order to find answers to these questions that I, Patrick Walker, asked Harry Caithness to go to Monimaskit in January of this year, 2005. Ostensibly my decision whether or not to proceed to publication would depend on what he discovered. In fact, I was already committed to publish, and only the threat of serious legal action (which I considered remote) would have made me reconsider. But in the interim I wanted Harry to talk to those who had known Gideon Mack, and to find out their opinions of him. Having both read the manuscript, between us we made out a list of the people he should try to interview. We agreed that, although mention of the manuscript's existence had been made in the press, and there had been some speculation as to what it might contain, it would be better not to disclose to the interviewees that we had a copy of it. However, it might be necessary for Harry to refer to things in the manuscript in the course of his investigations. If anybody asked him where he had acquired his facts, he would use the old defence of 'protection of sources' and, as a fallback, say that he'd had access to documents in the police files in Inverness.

Harry spent three days in and around Monimaskit, and the following, which speaks plainly enough for itself and which I therefore reproduce verbatim, is the report, in the form of a letter, that he sent me:

Dear Patrick,
I'm not sure if you're going to think the information I've gathered is worth the cost (an invoice for fee and expenses, with receipts, is on its way) but here it is in any case.

You told me that you have never been to Monimaskit, and neither had I until this week. You should probably go before you publish, if you publish. You should get a sense of the place. Maybe the museum would want to host a launch! You'd be guaranteed a turn-out, though what kind of mood the assembled masses would be in I'm not sure.

Monimaskit is a typical small east coast Scottish town: a wee bit run down, a wee bit on the up, seen better days, seen worse days. It has the usual mix of High Street shops: Woolworths, Boots, Co-op, Oxfam, Cancer Research, newsagent, florist, baker, butcher, fishmonger, hairdressers, off-licence, chip shop, shoe shop, a building society, three estate agents, a couple of banks. There are some nice-looking red sandstone villas, a neat wee council scheme and some bland new-build on the outskirts. The river Keldo flows through the town and gives it a certain grace. I drove in past the Old Kirk, a simple but handsome establishment, and the manse, which looked as though it was unoccupied. I made a mental note to have a look round there later. Then I went and found my hotel, the Keldo Arms, which wasn't difficult, as it's the only one.

The hotel was almost empty, the ambience adequate but boring. The menu wouldn't win any awards but suited my taste (everything with chips). The town itself was very quiet and seemed a bit sorry for itself, as if a majority of its inhabitants had drunk too much at New Year and were keeping their heads down till spring. It was probably a good time for me to be there. Back in October, when Mack's body was found, the media attention was pretty intense, but the pack has long since moved on to other stories in other places. People, in my experience, often clam up when the circus is in town, but they'll open up again to one old freelance like me wandering around, or most of them do. Anyway, I arrived on Thursday at dinner time, checked in, and then I got out the list of names we'd come up with and started knocking on doors and asking questions. Here is a summary of who I spoke to and what they said:

*

Amelia Wishaw: *I was lucky to catch Dr Wishaw at the health centre. She was about to go to Newcastle for a conference and was only in to pick up some paperwork. I persuaded her to give me five minutes before she headed off, but I didn't get much out of her. A hard-boiled professional, she gave the impression that most of the rest of us are a lowlier species than the likes of her, and that she is* never wrong. *She absolutely refused to divulge any information from Gideon Mack's medical records, saying they were confidential even though he was dead. That was fair enough, I said, but as his doctor she must have an opinion about his mental and physical health before his death. Yes, she said, but she still wasn't at liberty to share it with a third party, let alone a journalist.*

I tried again, putting a hypothetical question to her. If somebody fell into the Black Jaws, spent three days trapped in the river and survived, what mental condition would she expect them to be in? Not good, she said. She would expect such a person to be suffering from severe shock and trauma, leaving aside the effects of any head injuries, oxygen deprivation and so on. I had to be careful about revealing what I knew, but asked whether a poor diet would have an adverse effect on the person's mind. She said it wouldn't help if they weren't getting the right mix of protein, carbohydrates, vitamins, minerals, etc. We talked about that in a general kind of way, and then I asked, 'Would you say Gideon Mack experienced a nervous breakdown?' She gave me a very sharp look. 'I've already told you, I can't answer such questions,' she said. Her expression told me plainly that she thought he had. I mentioned all the stuff he'd come out with about the Devil in the cave. 'Would you say he was mad?' She said 'mad' was not a word she would use to describe any patient. It wasn't a useful term. I asked if 'mentally ill' was a more useful term. She said it was. 'Would you describe Gideon Mack as having been mentally ill?' 'No comment,' she said, and then she stood up, saying she was already late and would have to leave at once. End of interview.

Andrew McAllister: *This was the police sergeant who came to see Mack when he returned from hospital. I found him at the station. It turns out we have a couple of mutual acquaintances in the Highlands, so we found some common ground there. He seemed like a reasonable bloke who had* *grown bitter and frustrated, and who carries a chip on his shoulder because he hasn't got further up the ranks. What did he think of Gideon Mack? 'He was a decent man who never recovered from the death of his wife.' I challenged him on this: that was eleven years before everything happened, I said. 'Doesn't matter,' he said. 'I was there the night his wife was killed. In fact it was me that had to go and tell him.' 'Really?' I said. 'Aye,' he said, 'so you see I know what I'm talking about. He poured all his energies into his work after she died, but it wasn't enough. You wouldn't believe what he did for charity, running marathons and all that. If you want my opinion, he exhausted himself, lost the plot and took himself off into the hills to end it all.' I asked if that's what he really thought, that Mack committed suicide. 'No doubt in my mind,' Sergeant McAllister said.*

I asked him about Mack's accident. Did he really think he'd been in the water three days? 'No, he couldn't possibly have been. He'd have drowned, or died of hypothermia.' Well, where did McAllister think he had been, washed up on the river bank? 'No, he still couldn't have survived.' Well, then, did he sit by a big fire with the Devil in a cave, like he'd been telling people? The sergeant looked at me and nodded. 'Not the Devil, though,' he said. 'Chae Middleton. Something went on between them, but Mr Mack either couldn't remember or didn't want to tell. That was why he came away with all that other nonsense. He needed an explanation as to where he'd been.' An alibi? I asked. But meeting the Devil wasn't much of an alibi. It wouldn't stand up in a court of law. What did McAllister think they'd been up to? The sergeant said that Middleton was a right dodgy character, a known poacher and light-fingered in other ways too. He bought and sold contraband booze and fags but had never been caught. He probably dealt drugs as well. McAllister's theory was that Mack somehow survived going through the Black Jaws, came out downstream the first night, after the searchers had had to give up because of the dark, and was picked up by Chae Middleton. Chae and some mates were up the river that night because with all the police and mountain rescue folk combing the area they were nervous about a stash of illicit goods they had hidden somewhere and were moving it out. That sounded a bit boys' own adventure-ish to me – I mean, do people hide smuggled goods in caves and woods these days? –

but I let him run with it. Chae was a bad bugger, McAllister said, but even he couldn't let another human being drown, so when he saw Mack floating by he hauled him out. Mack came to and realised what was going on, and Chae's pals began to get agitated. Chae took him somewhere and kept him there for two days till the contraband was out of the vicinity and well through the distribution chain. Meanwhile he came back and helped in the hunt for the missing minister. They came to an arrangement that, in exchange for Chae saving Mack's life, Mack would say nothing about Chae's activities. Then they went back up the river and staged the rescue, and Mack came out with his story about the Devil. But then later all this got to Mack's conscience and on top of losing his wife it finally sent him over the edge.

Well, it wasn't credible, and I said so. McAllister started telling me that truth was stranger than fiction, I wouldn't believe half the things he'd seen over the years, etc. Fantasy stuff. I said, well, there's an easy way to find out and that's to get Chae Middleton in for questioning. McAllister said he'd already done that back in the autumn, but Chae had either been too drunk or too canny and didn't let anything slip. He interviewed Mack (as we know) but got stonewalled there too. Basically, he said, there was nothing else he could do.

I said I'd go down to the Luggie and see Chae myself. 'No you won't,' McAllister said. 'It's a free country,' I said. 'It may be,' McAllister said, 'and you can go down to the Luggie if you want but you won't find Chae there.' 'Why not?' 'Because he's dead.' Apparently he fell in the harbour last March after a long night in the pub. Pretty ironic, when you think about it. 'Fell, pushed or jumped?' I asked. McAllister said the Procurator Fiscal concluded that he fell, but nobody saw it happen. McAllister obviously wasn't convinced. He hinted darkly that Chae was losing it because of the bevvy, his business associates were worried about him and they might have given him a helping hand. He's quite into conspiracies of one kind or another, McAllister. Anyway, that scratched my proposed interview with Chae Middleton, so I drove off up into the glens to visit the Reverend Lorna Sprott.

Lorna Sprott: *I'd phoned Ms Sprott a few days before and asked if she'd be prepared to talk to me. She was very reluctant at first, especially when* *she knew I was a journalist. She thought she might have to clear it with 121 George Street. I told her I didn't work for any particular paper, I was just interested in finding out more about Gideon. I said I'd met him once (stretching the truth a little), at the Elgin marathon when he'd got a big cheque out of NessTrek. He'd seemed like a really nice guy, I was sorry to hear he'd died in such tragic circumstances. That helped. She agreed to see me, and I went up to her manse at Meldrick that evening. Beautiful spot, but a bit isolated for my liking.*

Ms Sprott manages to get through quite a quantity of white wine of an evening. She offered me a glass as soon as I arrived and she knocked back the rest of the bottle in the hour and a half I was there. A homely, lonely kind of soul. The dog, Jasper, came and lay on my feet and kept wanting me to rub his belly. I think Ms Sprott would have told me anything once she saw that the dog liked me, but she didn't actually have much to say that added to the picture.

'What was Gideon to you?' I asked. 'He was a dear friend who went insane,' she said, 'and not all the prayers and care I could offer could do anything to prevent it.' 'It looks like he lost his faith,' I said, and added, 'if he ever had it.' 'I can't believe that of him,' she said. 'He was an honest, righteous man and I can't believe he entered the ministry under false pretences.' I said, okay, but it did seem that he'd lost his faith towards the end, judging from what he said at Catherine Craigie's funeral. 'I wasn't there,' she said, 'so I don't know. I like to think that he lost his way rather than his faith.' She thought he'd gone off into the hills at the end to try to find it again. Why you'd go looking for your faith in Dalwhinnie escaped me, but Ms Sprott started singing, very badly, a psalm, the one that starts, 'I to the hills will lift mine eyes, from whence doth come mine aid.' I think she was hoping I'd join in. She stopped after one verse when I didn't.

I said, so what about the Devil, had Gideon met him? No, of course he hadn't. So where had he been those days he was missing? Unconscious. How had he survived? God protected him. Not the Devil? Absolutely not. Did she believe in the Devil? Yes, but not as a being the way Gideon described him. As what then? As a power for evil in the world, the antithesis of goodness, the opposite of God. And (I was chancing it here) did she believe in fairies? Of course not, she said. Yet she believed in

God? She said that my line of questioning was mischievous, and insulting too. She was a minister, God was her entire life. I apologised but said it was surely part of a minister's training to confront such questions and come up with some convincing answers. That was true, she said. Had the whole business with Gideon not shaken her own faith? Not a bit, her faith was what carried her through. 'If I hadn't had my faith I wouldn't have been able to cope. And Jasper, of course.' She looked pretty shaky to me. The dog was relaxed, though, coping a lot better than she was!

I had brought with me a photocopy of part of the first page of Gideon's manuscript, the two texts he'd written out from the Bible and the one from Moby Dick. *I showed her this and asked her if it was Gideon's handwriting. She said it was and asked where I had got it. I said the police had required a sample of his writing when they were searching for him. She said it seemed a strange mixture of things to have written down on one sheet of paper. I didn't have the heart to touch on what the rest of the manuscript said about Gideon's relationship, or non-relationship, with Ms Sprott. There didn't seem anything to be gained by it. She was a very sad woman. I left her to her wine and drove back to Monimaskit.*

I had two or three pints in the public bar of the Keldo Arms and tried to engage the half dozen locals there in conversation about their ex-minister, but half of them didn't know him at all and the others only knew what they'd read in the tabloids. A godless kind of establishment. Long before closing-time I called it a night.

John Gless*: On Friday morning I called on John Gless, the Session Clerk. I located his home address from the phone book and went round unannounced, at ten o'clock. He is eighty years old and a tougher customer than many half his age. He wouldn't even let me in. Having established that I was a journalist he told me he had nothing to say on the subject of Gideon Mack. I asked if that meant he disapproved of how he'd behaved. No, it meant that he had nothing to say. I showed him the sample of Gideon's handwriting, and he confirmed that it was his. I asked him if he thought Gideon Mack had betrayed the Church of Scotland. He declined to comment on this and hoped that no other* member of the Session would prolong the parish's anguish by doing so. I said I had driven past the manse, and it seemed to be empty. Gless said that the parish had effectively been without a minister for fifteen months. What was the situation as far as a replacement for Mr Mack was concerned? Obviously, he said, things had been complicated by Mr Mack's suspension and then his disappearance. Legally it had been very difficult to do anything until it was known what had happened to him. Since his body had been formally identified the vacancy procedure could begin, and this had already happened. It was hoped that the successful candidate would be in situ by the spring. I said that I understood that Mr Mack's body had been buried at Inverness. He said that that was what he understood too. Was I mistaken in thinking that Presbytery was normally responsible for the funeral arrangements of a minister? He said that I was not mistaken, but Mr Mack's will had unequivocally stated that in the event of his death he was to be interred without ceremony or service and without the intervention or involvement of the Church of Scotland. How did he know this, I asked. Because Mr Mack's solicitor had informed him as soon as the body was identified. Who was Mr Mack's solicitor? Mr Finlay Stewart of Montrose.

I asked John Gless if a memorial service or anything of that sort was to be held for Gideon at the Old Kirk. He knew of no such proposal. If I had no further questions then he wished me good morning. I had no further questions, and he closed the door in my face.

In spite of Mr Gless's hopes that the rest of the Session would be as guarded as he in speaking to me, I thought I would try my luck with Peter Macmurray anyway. I went to the offices of the accountancy firm of which he is a partner, but he was in a meeting. When might he be available? That afternoon. I left my card and said I'd call back at two.

I went next to the museum, to see if I could interview the director, Alan Straiton. The woman on reception told me he was away in Edinburgh. Was it anything she could help me with? I said that among other things I was trying to track down an address or contact number for William Winnyford. It was a while since his exhibition, but I wanted to talk to him about his work. The woman was very helpful. She went into her files and found me his mobile number. She said she wasn't allowed to *give me his address for security reasons, but a mobile phone number couldn't hurt, could it? I agreed that it couldn't. Five minutes later I was talking to Bill Winnyford, or at least to someone at the number she'd given me who identified himself as such. I mention this only because the man I spoke to was slow and measured in his speech, not at all like the Bill Winnyford Gideon describes in his testament.*

Bill Winnyford: *His impressions of Gideon Mack fitted the pattern that was starting to emerge, viz. that he was a decent man who went out of his mind. I said that a transcript of an interview between them had been found by the police, which was more or less true. Did Mr Winnyford by any chance still have the tape of that interview? No, he didn't even have a transcript. Gideon had promised to send him one but never had. As for the tape, Gideon had kept it. Why, Winnyford asked, did I want it? I said it would have been interesting to hear his voice, and he said I could hear that on the tape at the museum, the one of him reading the legend of the Black Jaws. I said I'd check that out later. (I never did, by the way. By the time I'd finished on the Saturday the museum was closed. You might want to follow that up yourself.)*

'What did you think after you did the second recording with him?' I asked. 'The one in which he described his three days underground?'

Bill Winnyford: 'I didn't know what to think. He was just out of hospital, he'd had a hugely traumatic experience. I don't know what they were playing at, letting him out like that. He was very nervous, excited. When he asked me to go round to the manse I thought he just wanted some company. We'd got along pretty well before. But he said he had some big story that he wanted to get on record while it was clear in his head. So I went round with the equipment and then he started spouting this stuff about meeting the Devil.'

'In that interview he asks you at one point if he strikes you as being a sane human being. And you say yes. Did you really mean that?'

'If I said it, then yes, I meant it.'

'But did you believe what he told you about the Devil?'

'Of course I didn't. I mean, my work explores myths and legends, but that's what they are, myths and legends. Nobody actually meets the Devil in a cave, not unless they're on a bad trip. But Gideon believed he

had, he really did. I did wonder if he was doing drugs or on some kind of medication or something, but it wasn't really like that. He was sane but he was saying insane things, does that make any kind of sense? He was deluded, but he was genuine. He wasn't trying to wind me up. It was like he'd read a lot of stuff or seen a lot of stuff and on top of what he'd been through it all got mixed up in his head. The Devil healing his leg like that, for example, that's straight out of E.T.*'*

I said I'd been informed by other people that it was certainly the case that he didn't have a limp before the accident.

Bill Winnyford: 'True, but he wasn't nuts before the accident either. I know, I'm contradicting myself. He limped because he'd been through the Black Jaws, and to be honest coming out with a limp was the least thing that happened to him in there. Can you imagine what three days in that river must have done to his mind? It fucked it, basically.'

I asked if he really thought Mack could have spent three days in the river and survived. He said no, he probably got out of the water for a while but didn't remember doing so. People were capable of astonishing feats of survival but often they were left permanently scarred. 'Look,' he said, 'I liked the guy. I really liked him. He was a decent man who wanted to help other people. He helped me and he didn't have to. The fact that he went off his head is a tragedy, just a tragedy.'

I thought there was nothing more to be had from Winnyford and was about to end the conversation when he said something else.

'You know, sometimes I think there was a jinx around that whole project. I mean, of the people who helped me, three were dead within six months of the exhibition opening. First Catherine Craigie, then Chae Middleton, then Gideon. It was as if they were being picked off for getting mixed up in it or something.'

'Did you say Catherine Craigie helped you?' I said. 'I understood that she would have nothing to do with you.'

'I don't know where you got that from,' Winnyford said. 'She was incredibly helpful. We didn't agree on everything, but she was very approachable and gave me a huge amount of information about the town. It's true she didn't want our collaboration broadcast – that was one of her conditions, that I didn't acknowledge her assistance – but I couldn't have done it without her. And she put me in touch with some

key people, too. It was Miss Craigie who suggested that I involve both Chae and Gideon.'

'But Gideon Mack didn't know that?'

'No, I was sworn to secrecy as far as he was concerned. It doesn't matter now, of course, but at the time I think it was important to her.'

'Why do you think that was?' I asked.

'Haven't a clue,' he said. 'Local politics of some sort, I expect.'

As you and I know, Gideon was quite unaware that Catherine Craigie had assisted Winnyford in this manner. She went out of her way to rubbish him in fact. This revelation raises some interesting questions about the reliability of other things which, according to Gideon, she told him – questions, however, which are unlikely now ever to be answered.

'What about Chae?' I asked. 'Did he know Miss Craigie had recommended him?'

'I wouldn't say "recommend". He used to do odd jobs for her, gardening and suchlike, so she asked him herself. A bit of a lad, Chae. If Gideon was on anything, any drugs I mean, that's who he could have been getting them from. But I don't think they had anything to do with each other till Chae found him in the river.'

'And then Chae drowned in the harbour,' I said.

'Yes,' Winnyford said. 'I was quite shaken when I heard about it. He drank a lot, apparently. Mind you, so did Gideon.'

'Really?'

'He certainly poured enormous drams whenever I was at the manse,' Winnyford said. 'I'd hardly have started mine and he'd be knocking his back and topping us both up.'

'Do you think he had a problem?'

'I think he had all kinds of problems. An alcohol problem? I'm not going to say that about him now he's dead, no. He was a decent man. I liked him.'

After this phone conversation I dropped in at the library to see if I could identify Elsie Moffat, but was told she wasn't working. Would she be in at the weekend, I asked. No, she had Saturday off. Then I asked if Nancy Croy was still running her reading group. It seems that Nancy Croy successfully applied for a principal teacher of English post in Dumfries and Galloway. She left Monimaskit at Christmas.

At two o'clock I was back at Peter Macmurray's office. Physically, and in terms of his personality, Macmurray is much as Gideon describes him in his manuscript. I explained who I was and that I was interested in the truth about Gideon Mack, and he invited me into his office. He could barely get back in his chair before the bile started to pour out.

Peter Macmurray: *'I ought not to speak ill of the dead,' he said, 'but Gideon Mack was a deceiver and a hypocrite who brought shame on the Kirk and on this community. I always knew there was something not right about him, and events totally justified my suspicions.' I asked what had aroused these suspicions, and he cited the fact that Mack had married one atheist and after her death had 'taken up' with another. I asked if he meant Catherine Craigie. Yes. Was he implying that there had been anything between them other than friendship? 'Well, what do you think?' he said. 'She was an immoral woman and he visited her on a regular weekly basis. One doesn't need to be Einstein to make two and two equal four.' Did he have any particular reason for denigrating Miss Craigie, who was also, after all, dead? They must have been about the same age and had presumably grown up together in Monimaskit. Did he have any personal reason for disliking her? He went slightly pink and said he always tried to put personal issues aside. He simply stood up for the truth and for the Christian faith.*

I showed him the handwriting sample, and he agreed that Mack had written the texts. He read them through and said of the third one that Herman Melville, whoever he was, might speak for himself and Gideon Mack but he, Peter Macmurray, was very far from being cracked about the head. Did he believe Mack's story about meeting the Devil? 'Not in so many words, no of course not.' Then what could Mack have meant by it? 'He was revealing the depths of his dabbling in the black arts.' I asked him if he was serious. 'Absolutely,' he said. 'He made light of his involvement with that exhibition at the museum, but when I confronted him about it he refused to answer me. He was obviously burdened with guilt and eventually it dragged him down. Sin will out, Mr Caithness, and it did so spectacularly in his case.' I asked him if he himself believed in the existence of the Devil. 'Yes,' he said, 'I do. The Devil exists, and I'm sorry to say that Gideon Mack was one of his servants.'

There was a great deal more in this vein and eventually it was I who terminated the interview. I felt quite depressed after my half-hour with Mr Macmurray, and needed some fresh air. I walked round the manse, which was all shut up, and then I walked round the kirkyard, reading the stones. I found Catherine Craigie's family gravestone with her name and dates freshly cut in it. I saw no children flying kites and nobody speaking to the dead.

I decided to go and get a haircut. A couple of inquiries led me to Henry Leask's barber shop.

Henry Leask: *Mr Leask had a customer and told me to take a seat. I looked at the paper for five minutes, then when the other man had gone I took my place in the chair. After the preliminaries about how I wanted my hair cut, the weather and the football, I brought the conversation round to Gideon Mack. I said I was passing through and had remembered reading about him in the papers. Had he known the minister? Yes, he used to cut his hair in the very chair in which I was sitting. I said it must have been a shock to everybody when they heard about his death. Henry Leask: 'I think we all knew it would come to that, when he'd been missing that length of time. He never recovered from falling in the river. I knew he wasn't long for this world.' I asked him what he thought about the stories Mack had told. Did he believe them? Henry Leask: 'I'd believe Gideon Mack a thousand times before I believe a word of some of the people that didn't like him. He was a decent man.' 'Then you believe that he met the Devil?' 'Well, that's a question it's hard to say yes to, isn't it? But then you wouldn't credit some of the nonsense I nod along to when I'm cutting folk's hair. And half of them believe what they're telling me, and half of what they tell me turns out to be true! So I don't know the answer, but I don't think he lied. He might not have been well by that stage, but he wasn't a liar.' 'But he lied about being a Christian, about believing in God.' 'That's different. Everybody lies about that.'*

By now it was late afternoon. There were just three more people I wanted to see, and two of them would have to wait until the next day, Saturday. I went to the Monimaskit Care Home and asked if I could see Mrs Agnes Mack. Who was I, the woman who opened the door wanted to know. I was a friend of her son Gideon, I was in the area and wanted to say hello. I knew that Mrs Mack wouldn't know who I was, but for Gideon's sake I thought I should call on her. 'You'd better come in,' the woman said. 'Did you know Mrs Mack personally?' 'No,' I said. 'Well,' she said, 'she passed away at Christmas, at the age of eighty-six.'

I said I was sorry to hear that, and would she mind if I asked a couple of questions? Ask away, she said. Had Mrs Mack been aware of her son's death? No, the woman said, she very much doubted it. They'd tried to tell her the first time he'd died, but then of course he hadn't died, he'd come back again, and that was too confusing for her, so although they'd explained about him going missing again and then his body being found, as far as Agnes was concerned they could have been talking about Scott of the Antarctic. Gideon had come in a few times before he went missing the second time, but he hadn't looked well and he hadn't stayed long with his mother. She hadn't recognised him for some years, which was always upsetting for relatives.

I asked the woman if her name was Betty. It was. I said, 'Gideon mentioned you once or twice. He knew you looked after his mother well. That was important to him.' She seemed very pleased about that. 'Well, he must have appreciated it,' she said. 'You know he left everything to the home, don't you?' I said I didn't know that. 'Every penny he had,' she said. 'He may have gone strange at the end, but when you think of all the money he raised for charity over the years, and then this, you have to think well of him, don't you?' 'Did he go strange?' I asked. 'Oh, he couldn't help himself,' she said. 'He was religious. It's something I've noticed with the residents since I've been working here. The more religious they are, the more daft they go. I probably shouldn't say such a thing, but there, I've said it. So it wasn't a surprise to me the way Mr Mack went after he'd been three days in the river.'

John and Elsie Moffat: *On Saturday morning, after breakfast, I drove down the coast road to the Moffats' house. It was a bright, sunny day, with snow on the hills inland, but I wasn't looking forward to the encounter. Neither of them, I guessed, would be pleased to have yet another journalist on their doorstep asking questions about their former friend Gideon.*

I found the house without difficulty, drove in through the open gate and parked, went to the back door and knocked. It was Elsie who answered. She looked tired and anxious, but I could see what Gideon had seen in her, she is a very attractive woman. I apologised for calling without notice, but their phone number was ex-directory (I'd checked this before: a lot of teachers keep their names out of the phone-book, with good reason). I'd been thinking for some time about how to persuade the Moffats to talk, and although you and I had agreed that we should keep the existence of Gideon's manuscript confidential, I couldn't see how I was going to engage them without telling them about it. They had undergone a lot of media attention back in the autumn, and one of the tabloids had run a particularly hurtful story portraying Elsie as a kind of Delilah of Monimaskit. I would have to approach them from a friendlier angle. So I said that I worked for a publisher, and that the publisher had come into possession of a document written by Gideon Mack shortly before he died. We were considering what to do with it and, since it mentioned them by name, thought it only right to come and talk to them about it.

Elsie's face turned ashen. 'Oh, Jesus,' she said. She leaned past me as if looking for a phalanx of cameras setting up in the drive. 'You'd better come in.'

She told me to wait in the kitchen and went through a door leading to the rest of the house. I could hear the noise of a television, children playing, a man's voice. A couple of minutes passed, and then Elsie came back with her husband.

John Moffat looked as tired as she did, but a lot angrier. At first I thought, like Gideon the last time he saw him, that he was going to punch me. He said, 'If it had been me that came to the door you'd never have got through it. I have nothing but contempt for you people. But you're in now, so say what you've got to say and then go.'

I said, 'Mr Moffat, I'm sorry that you're angry. Believe me, I don't want to upset you. The fact is, though, as I was saying to your wife, that we have this document. There's no question that it was written by Gideon Mack. Now, I'm a journalist but I don't work for any particular newspaper and this isn't going to be in a newspaper, but it's quite probable that the document may be published in book form. That's what I've come to talk to you about.'

'In book form?' Moffat said. 'How long is it, for fuck's sake?'

'It's about three hundred pages of A4,' I said. 'I'm not sure exactly how many words that is.'

'I do,' he said. 'It's about a hundred thousand words, give or take a few thousand. Jesus, Elsie, how fucking ironic is that? The bastard's written a book. Not content with trying to ruin our lives, he's gone and written a book, and somebody wants to publish it.'

'Take it easy, John,' Elsie said, which wasn't what he wanted to hear. I remember you telling me once, Patrick, that hell hath no fury like a jealous author, especially an unpublished one.

'Take it easy? How am I supposed to take it easy? Every time this thing dies away, and we're trying to get ourselves back to normal, it flares up again. It's like he's haunting us.'

'Gideon?' I said.

'Well, who else are we talking about?' he said. 'Aye, Gideon. Gideon, Gideon, Gideon.'

He couldn't stay still. He kept swaying and stepping towards me and then pulling back. Elsie put a hand on his arm but he shook it off. I was standing in the middle of the floor, trying to look relaxed but not relaxed at all inside, waiting for him to fly at me.

Elsie said, 'What's your name again?'

'Harry Caithness,' I said.

'Why don't you sit at the table, Mr Caithness, and I'll make some coffee.'

'What?' Moffat said. 'Are you insane? I don't want this man sitting in my kitchen drinking my coffee. I don't even want him in the house. I want him to fuck off and leave us alone.'

'John,' she said, 'he's here now. We can send him away and, like you said, this will go away for a while, then it'll come back again. If Gideon's written something that's going to be published, then we need to know what it is. We need to know what he's said about us. Let's at least hear what Mr Caithness has to say.'

Moffat stood there fuming for a bit longer. Elsie filled the kettle. I said, 'She's right, Mr Moffat. I'm sorry, but you're going to have to deal with this sooner or later.'

'Let's see it, then,' he said. 'Gideon's fucking masterpiece.'

I explained that I didn't have a copy of it with me, but that I'd read it. I said that basically it was Gideon's story of his life and his version of the events leading up to his disappearance. I said it accorded largely with what had been reported in the papers, but there was a lot more detail.

'What kind of detail?' John Moffat asked.

'About everything,' I said. 'About how you all met as students, about his wife, about you two, about Monimaskit, about his falling into the Black Jaws . . .'

'About meeting the Devil?'

'Yes, a lot about that.'

'So fundamentally it's the diary of a madman. And you're proposing to publish it?'

'It tells his version of events,' I repeated.

'It tells a pack of lies in other words,' he said. 'What does it say about my wife? Does he tell the same lies he came out with before?'

'He goes into more detail,' I said.

His fist banged off the table. 'Jesus Christ! We'll sue you, you know, if you publish it. If you publish anything that's not true, we'll sue you for every penny you've got.'

'Like you've sued the tabloids,' I said, and before he could flare up again I went on, 'I'm not being flippant, Mr Moffat, but if the book is published, it would be Gideon Mack's story. It would be his word against yours.'

The kettle came to the boil and Elsie made the coffee.

'Well, there you go, then,' Moffat said. 'His word's worth nothing. He confessed he was a charlatan when it came to being a minister. He came out with all that crap about mysterious stones and speaking with the Devil. Obviously what he's written is total fantasy.'

'Then you have nothing to worry about,' I said.

'But a book's a book,' he said. 'It's different from a newspaper. The papers are here today, gone tomorrow. A book lasts for ever.'

Elsie said, 'Why do you think he wrote it?'

Moffat gave her a look that was half wonder, half hatred. 'Because he wanted to hurt us,' he said.

'No,' she said, 'I don't think so. Why did he write it, Mr Caithness?'

'He says,' I said, 'he needed to tell the truth. He had to write it down

because nobody would listen to him. He genuinely does seem to have believed that these things happened.'

'What things?' Moffat said fiercely.

'All of them,' I said.

'But they were lies. Jesus, man, don't you understand what he did to us? He was once my best friend. My best friend. *But he went fucking nuts and then he made a pass at Elsie, and then, when she rejected him, he made up these lies about her. Don't you see how horrible that is? To go to school and have these lies about your wife flying around? To walk down the street together and you know people are remembering what he said and thinking there might be something in it? Can you imagine what that's like?'*

He kept putting his head in his hands and letting out heavy sighs of exasperation. When he did this I glanced at Elsie. She was looking back at me. She shook her head quickly. There was an obvious question that she didn't want me to ask.

'Look,' I said, 'Nothing's settled yet. I'll tell you what I'll do. I'll speak to the publisher and tell him how hard this is for you. Maybe we can send you the manuscript and you can tell us what you think. I'm not promising anything. I'm not saying we'll cut anything, nothing like that. But at least you could see what it is we're talking about before anybody else does. At least you could decide what, if anything, you want to do about it.'

'Great,' Moffat said. 'You're offering to hold a gun to my head and say, "What does that feel like?" What can we do *about it? There's fuck all we can do about it, is there?'*

'Wait till you've seen it,' I said. Elsie went through to check on her children. While she was away Moffat looked at me with what was almost a pleading look.

'We used to take the piss out of miracles and God and all that,' he said. 'Gideon and me. He was great back then. A son of the manse and he rejected the whole fucking business. We used to rely on facts. That was all: nothing that wasn't a fact counted, nothing you couldn't experience. If it wasn't real it was crap. And he was interested in real issues too, politics and stuff. We were grown-ups. But then I kept growing and he started regressing. It was bad enough when he went into

the Church but he promised me he wouldn't change, he didn't believe any of it. But he did change, and he did start believing it. And then all this shite. It was like he was taken over by some fucking, I don't know, some cult or something, but it was just him, he did it all by himself. It was like he wasn't Gideon any more.'

'So what happened that made him change?' I asked.

'How do I know? Is that why you're here? Do you think we can give you some answers about what the fuck was going on in Gideon's head? There are no answers, don't you see? There are no answers. Gideon once understood that.'

Elsie came back in. 'Are they okay?' Moffat asked. 'They're fine,' she said.

'There's something else I wanted to ask you,' I said. 'The place where he says he saw this standing stone, that's somewhere near here, isn't it?'

'It's up in the woods,' Moffat said. 'Fuck. That was two years ago, can you believe that, Elsie? That was the start of it. Two years ago he came here and told us about that stone. And now look where we are.'

'Where in the woods?' I said.

Moffat laughed. 'Well, that's the point, isn't it? Nowhere. Because there never was a stone. He imagined the whole thing. Nobody else ever saw it because it was never there.'

'Where in the woods did he say it was?' I said.

'I don't know,' Moffat said. 'He was always going to show us, but he never did. For obvious reasons.'

'I know where it is,' Elsie said. 'I mean, where he said it was.'

He looked at her suspiciously. 'You? How do you know?'

'Well, there isn't a precise spot, but I know the path he was talking about. There's a clearing. I know where he meant.'

'Can we go there?' I asked.

They looked at each other.

'What's the point?' Moffat said.

'I'd like to see it,' I said.

Elsie said, 'I can show you.'

'No,' Moffat said.

'We could all go,' I said.

'Sorry,' Moffat said, 'but I'm not wandering about in the woods looking for a non-existent stone.'

'Let me go,' Elsie said. 'What are you afraid of?'

'I'm not afraid of anything,' he said. 'Or anyone. I just don't see the point.'

'We need to make this be over, John,' she said. 'Let me close this bit of it. I'll show Mr Caithness where Gideon thought he saw his stone, and that'll be it. Over.'

'Until his fucking book comes out.'

'We'll deal with that later,' she said.

I realised that she was the strong one in the relationship. He was floundering, sinking. She was the one that would get them through it, if they got through it. But also, she wanted to tell me something.

'Okay,' Moffat said. 'I'll stay here with the kids. You show him. And then it's over, right?'

'Right,' she said.

He looked at me. 'I don't want to see that manuscript, typescript, whatever the hell it is,' he said. Elsie interrupted, 'John . . .' but he carried on. 'I can't be arsed with this any more. Send it to Elsie if she wants to look at it. I don't. It can't say anything that isn't already out there. It's all fucking lies anyway.'

'That's up to you,' I said.

'See when you go for your walk in the woods just now,' he said. 'Take your car, and don't come back. You've already ruined my weekend. Just don't come back, all right?'

I drank up my coffee. 'I'll wait outside,' I said. I thought I should give them a chance to talk on their own, but Elsie Moffat followed almost immediately.

The entrance to Keldo Woods is only a few hundred yards from their house. We could have walked, but I took Moffat's advice and drove Elsie along to the parking area. It was dry underfoot. She'd put on trainers, I just had my ordinary shoes. We headed off along the main track. The sun, as they say, was splitting the trees.

We didn't say anything much at first. We just walked. She was a lot fitter than me and gave me a disapproving look when I lit up a cigarette and smoked as we went. I admit, I was peching a bit until I got into my stride. I'd meant to pay attention, get my bearings for future reference, but it wasn't easy, there are that many wee paths criss-crossing through the trees. For a while we seemed to be going in a big circle, then I thought we were doubling back on ourselves. We turned on to another path that went up a slight slope. We climbed for a bit, then things levelled out. I threw away the cigarette-end and stamped it out.

I said, 'It was all lies, was it? What Gideon said about him and you?'

'Of course it was,' she said, in a flash. She'd been waiting for the question all that time. I knew then that Gideon had been telling the truth, at least about her, at least in part.

The path divided in two. We went left, then a little further on we went left again. The trees crowd in very thick at this point. It was pretty oppressive even on a sunny day: I didn't fancy it much on a wet, dark night. And then quite suddenly we hit an open area of thick, coarse grass and mossy tummocks, just the way Gideon describes it. He wasn't making that bit up either.

'This is it,' she said.

I looked around. 'Where?'

She pointed across the clearing. 'Over there.'

'But there's nothing there,' I said.

She said, 'Did you expect there would be?'

We left the path and made our way across the open ground. It was a bit squelchy in places, once I put a foot wrong and the mud oozed up over my shoe. I swore but she didn't seem to hear. After thirty or forty yards she stopped.

'Here,' she said.

'Here?'

'Yes.'

'But how do you know?' I said. 'According to what he wrote down, he was the only one who ever saw it. How do you know it was here?'

'Because I saw it,' she said.

I didn't say anything. What could I say? She looked at me. 'I don't know what's in this for you,' she said. 'I really don't, but I guess at one level it's the story. That's what you journalists are really interested in, isn't it, the story? Meanwhile John and I are trying to get our marriage back together, but you want the story that will make that impossible.

Well, you can publish Gideon's book and maybe that will finish us off and maybe it won't, I don't know. But I need to tell you this, and you can put it in the damned book or you can leave it out, it doesn't matter. The point is, it's the truth.

'I followed Gideon up here one night, just over a year ago. It was after the trouble at the funeral, after he'd been suspended and everything. Gideon was going downhill fast. We hadn't seen anything of him. I couldn't bear it, it was too painful because I really did love him, as a friend I mean, and John just didn't want to have anything to do with him. And then he turned up at the house one afternoon early in the New Year. He wanted to speak to us. He wanted to apologise. He wanted to try to get back to where we'd been. We'd been such close friends, all of us, him, me, John, Jenny. He came to say sorry, and John threw him out. No, he wouldn't even let him in. It was pouring with rain. When John told me who it was at the door and that he'd told him to fuck off we had a huge row, and I stormed out of the house. I just had to get away from him and I walked up the road to the car park and then I saw Gideon's car.'

I said, 'You wanted to let Gideon in after all he'd said and done?'

'We had to start somewhere if we were going to save him. Save ourselves. But John was so angry. And one of the reasons he was so angry was because he knew it was true, what Gideon had said at the funeral, that we'd had an affair. That doesn't surprise you, does it, Mr Caithness? I can see that it doesn't. It wasn't Gideon that was lying, it was me.'

I said, 'It was hardly an affair. He says you only had sex once, when you were helping him to sort out his wife's clothes.'

She shook her head. 'Is that what he's written? I don't understand that.'

'That's what he says.'

'But it didn't just happen once. That was the first time, but we made love all that summer. And for years afterwards I used to go to the manse at different times of the day and we'd make love. So it was an affair all right, it was passionate and intense and secret, it was like stealing fruit from a beautiful garden, but I think right from the start I knew it was doomed, that it would never be anything other than stealing.'

'Why did you think that?' I asked.

'Because Gideon was weak, Mr Caithness. He was a weak man. His upbringing, his character, the whole religion thing – not being able to reject it and not being able to embrace it – it was all weakness. When he first said he was going to be a minister I thought it showed he had strength and courage but I was wrong. He was never going to really love me, whatever he said. I don't think he ever loved Jenny either. He wasn't capable of loving her or me or anybody, including himself. He'd had that terrible upbringing that strangled love at every turn. So our affair dwindled to nothing. Our secret meetings happened less and less and finally, when I was pregnant with Katie, they stopped altogether.'

'Mrs Moffat,' I said. 'Elsie. Is Katie Gideon's daughter?'

She didn't seem surprised by the question. 'I don't know,' she said. 'Maybe. Yes, actually, I think so. But both of the girls look like me so I'll never be certain. But yes, I think Katie is Gideon's.'

'Does your husband know that?'

'He suspects,' she said. 'Why do you think things are so difficult? Long before Gideon said it in public he suspected there'd been something between us. The children came along, and it ended, but something like that never quite ends, does it? It's blighted our marriage. And then, when maybe it had faded away enough for us almost to ignore it, I began to suspect John. I thought he was having an affair with somebody else. But of course I couldn't say anything.'

'Nancy Croy,' I said.

'Oh, Jesus,' she said. 'How do you know that?'

'You told Gideon,' I said. 'He wrote it down.'

She started hitting her forehead with the palm of her hand. I thought she was crying but she was laughing. 'Jesus Christ,' she said. 'What fucking idiots we all are.'

She was silent for a minute. We stood in the clearing, on the site where the stone had supposedly been, and birds were singing somewhere at a distance and it all felt very unreal.

'I don't know if there was anything between John and Nancy,' she said. 'In the scheme of things, what does it matter? It doesn't matter at all, not any more. Anyway. I saw Gideon's car and I followed him into the woods. At first I was trying to catch him up, just to apologise for

what John had done, and he can't have been that far ahead of me because I could hear him, his pace was much slower with the limp. But then I thought, no, wait a minute, he's come here for a reason, so I hung back, just kept him in sight, and followed him. And he came up here. I was getting nervous, it was so wet and there wasn't much light left, but I stayed back and I watched him. He came over here and I saw him at the stone.'

'You saw the stone?' I said.

'He was leaning on it. Shouting and weeping and cursing. I was frightened. But yes, I could see it in the half-light. A bloody great stone, right here where we are.'

'You're sure?'

'Yes, I'm telling you.' Then she shook her head. 'No, not now. I was sure then, I was positive. I could definitely see it. But now, look – nothing. So how could I have?'

I remembered something. 'Did you see anybody else?'

'I might have. It was getting very dark. He'd been shouting as if he was really shouting at *someone – "Wait, speak to me," that kind of thing. Over there in the trees. So I was looking, and I think maybe I did see someone, but I can't swear to it.' She stopped suddenly. 'Why?'*

'Gideon says there was someone. He thinks the Devil was here that night.'

She shook her head. 'Jesus,' she said. 'I don't think there was anyone. I was scared. I was imagining things.'

'What happened then?'

'Gideon started howling and screaming, and I wanted to go and help him but I was too afraid, I really thought he might be dangerous, and I ran back down the track and got to the road and ran all the way home. And when I got in John was giving the girls their tea, and we looked at each other and he knew where I'd been and . . . Well, that's where we are now, really, a year later. It's like John said, it keeps coming back. It won't leave us alone.'

I looked at the ground around our feet. Grass. Moss. Bog. That was it.

'There's nothing here,' I said. 'No stone, nothing.'

'No Gideon either,' she said. 'That's what I think more and more.

There's nothing. No God, no Devil, nothing. No damnation, no redemption. There's just us and what we do. The things we achieve or the mess we make.'

'And yet you say you saw the stone,' I said.

'I think I saw it,' she said. 'That's all I have from that night – a maybe. I might have seen it. That's not enough. It's not real.'

'So what's real?' I said.

'My children,' she said without hesitation. 'John and me. We'll either sort ourselves out or we won't but we both want the best for our children. That's the only reality that counts.'

We went back to the path and began to retrace our steps through the woods. I realised that she'd said everything she wanted to say, but I couldn't help asking one last question.

'Do you think any of what Gideon said was true? About the Devil, I mean?'

She said, 'Well, he didn't lie about us, did he? But then from what you're telling me it turns out that he did. But why would he make up a story like that about the Devil? Why would he lie about that? He had nothing to gain by it.'

I waited for her to answer my question, and she knew I was waiting. She shook her head and carried on walking. After that the only words she said to me were when we got back to the car and I offered her a lift home. 'No thanks,' she said, 'I'll walk. Goodbye, Mr Caithness.'

So ends Harry's report. And so ends this strange narrative. As you can see, I did decide to publish, and I repeat what I said at the beginning, that this is the complete and – almost – unedited testament of Gideon Mack. The only thing that may frustrate the sleuths among you is that, following the advice of my lawyer, I have been obliged to alter some of the names of the people and places involved in these affairs. I regret this, but it was deemed to be not merely prudent but essential. I had received a communication from the Montrose solicitor, Finlay Stewart, acting not only on behalf of the trustees of the Monimaskit Care Home but also as the late Gideon Mack's executor, suggesting that we come to some suitable financial arrangement with regard to the publication of his memoir and that some discretion regarding its contents would also be appropriate. Mr Stewart was the one remaining participant in all this business that I wished Harry had interviewed, but that interview never took place. I myself have spoken by telephone to Mr Stewart on several occasions, but he has always refused to enter into any discussion of Gideon Mack and his affairs that does not pertain directly and exclusively to the contents of his will or the publication of his testament. I regret, therefore, that no further light is to be shed on this story from that quarter, but you may rest assured that every copy sold of *The Testament of Gideon Mack* will in a small but not insignificant way benefit the residents of the Monimaskit Care Home.

I spoke to Harry Caithness on the telephone the day after receiving his report. We talked it over, and then he told me what he had done after parting from Elsie Moffat. He deemed it to be strictly outwith the bounds of his remit, but he wanted to tell me about it anyway. He got in his car and drove the few miles inland to the Black Jaws.

'I thought you'd have wanted me to do it, Patrick,' he said, 'and if you ever go to Monimaskit yourself you'll have to go and look at the place. It's incredible. You wander along this muddy path, and it all seems very unexciting, and then you start to hear this roaring noise. And the closer you get, the louder the roaring gets, until finally there's this wooden walkway and a bridge over the ravine, and you can stand on it and look down.'

'And what can you see?' I asked.

He didn't say anything. I thought for a moment we'd been cut off.

'Harry?' I said. 'What did you see?'

It was almost not Harry's voice at the other end of the phone. It was as if he were talking in his sleep, or as if it were an actor playing the part of Harry. He said, 'There's this permanent mist of water droplets in the air, like an almost invisible veil or a film between you and the bottom of the chasm. And "film" is the right word because the light plays on it, there are these fragments of rainbow everywhere, and through them you see shapes and images shifting among the projecting trees and in the shadows of the cliffs. If you look for a while you become mesmerised, you start to see a whole world of things. God, I saw such a lot of stuff down there. But of all the things I saw the only ones I can remember are these. I saw a dog scrabbling, trying to get to safety, and not knowing what it was escaping from except noise and water and cliff. And then I saw a man falling into that horrible place, and it was like it was me falling out of myself. I'd gone there for a purpose, or he'd gone there for a purpose, but there was no purpose left, and then he'd slipped and fallen. And I watched him fall, and it was as if I'd fallen, I felt like I'd lost a part of myself. I tell you, it was the strangest feeling. It was as if I'd watched myself go to my own death.'